D0276484

MY KINGDOM FOR A GRAVE

My Kingdom
for a Grave

STEPHANIE PLOWMAN

THE BODLEY HEAD
LONDON SYDNEY
TORONTO

FOR J. B.

(that other dark lady)

ISBN 0 370 01217 8
© Stephanie Plowman 1970
Printed and bound in Great Britain for
The Bodley Head Ltd
9 Bow Street, London WC2
by C. Tinling & Co. Ltd, Prescot
Set in Monotype Fournier
First published 1970

CONTENTS

PROLOGUE

This is the continuation, and conclusion, of the story begun by me in *Three Lives for the Czar*, a story commencing in 1894 with the accession of Czar Nicholas II. Through conversations overheard though not always understood at the time, through later study of family letters and diaries, I did my best to describe the increasing uneasiness felt by my parents because of the inability of the Czar to appreciate what was wrong in Russia, together with the Czarina's conviction that she *knew* how the Russian people felt.

My mother soon had good reason to know that Russia was a sick country. In 1905, my father was killed with the Grand Duke Serge in a bomb outrage, and in the following year my eleven-year-old sister, Alix, was playing with the children of the Imperial Minister Peter Stolypin when terrorists tried to blow up his home. Alix eventually died of the injuries received then.

Alix's dearest friend had been the Grand Duchess Olga, eldest of the Czar's four daughters, but from 1905 onwards we had received less frequent invitations to go out to the palace at Czarskoe Selo. Eventually my mother disclosed the truth—the little heir to the throne suffered from an incurable disease of the blood, and his distracted mother believed that only the infamous Siberian peasant, Rasputin, could keep him alive. Alexei's illness was to be kept secret—so visitors were not encouraged at Czarskoe.

In 1914, I was a twenty-year-old Lieutenant in the Chevaliers Gardes, and enough in the confidence of my Uncle Raoul to realise that France was unready for modern warfare—and her ally Russia even more disastrously so. But even if Russia had been magnificently prepared for war, the prospect could only be dreaded by people like us, with our Austrian relatives and friends. A war with Germany meant war with Austria.

In May, 1914, we had talked in Vienna with the Archduke Franz Ferdinand who was about to leave on his inspection of army units in Bosnia. Two months later in

St Petersburg, after the Archduke's assassination at Sarajevo, Uncle Raoul tried desperately to avert Russian mobilisation, knowing that this would be the decisive step towards war. But by the end of the month, Uncle Raoul, wearing civilian clothes, had left Petersburg in an attempt to get home before France was drawn into the conflict, leaving with me a book of poems for Olga. The declaration of war followed almost immediately.

Andrei Alexandrovitch Hamilton

The Family of Andrei Alexandrovitch Hamilton

AUSTRIA   FRANCE   RUSSIA

Eugen von
Hohenems-Landeck
(*d.* 1914)

Elisabeth Francesca *m.* Alain, Duc de
(*d.* 1912)   St Servan-Rézé

Michael Hamilton *m.* Anne Hilarion
(*d.* 1878)   (*d.* 1924)

Raoul   Avoye

Alexander (Alesha)
(*d.* 1905)

m.

Andrei   Alix
(*d.* 1907)

The Imperial Family of Russia

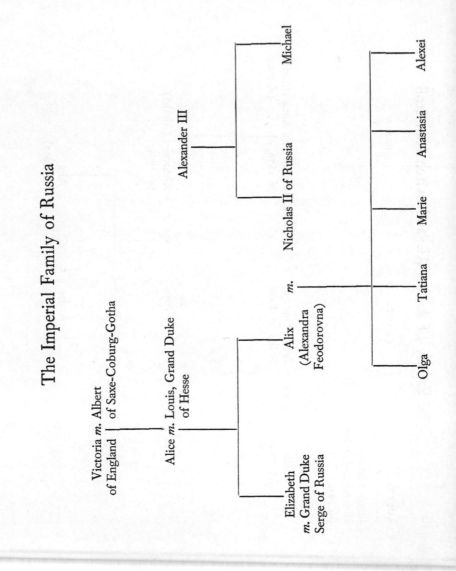

I

Steam-roller à l'Attaque

'A RATHER surprising request,' he said.

Irresistibly he reminded me of one of the more respectable jokes current in the French Army—Why is a staff-officer like a Chinese vase? Because both are highly decorated before they undergo fire.

'Considering the time you've spent attached to the French Army, a staff job, one would think—'

The glitter and heat of the August day had reached their peak. Sunlight blazed in through the window. His braid and decorations were so dazzling that I felt like some lesser Jason confronting the Golden Fleece. Rather, bearing in mind the features of the general, the original Golden Ram.

'However, there *is* a cavalry division attached to the First Army, of course, and a few squadrons of the Chevaliers Gardes—'

Half an hour later I was walking away from the enormous golden arc of the War Ministry, reflecting on the contrast between the splendid façade of the Palace Square side of it and the stinking squalor behind. To get my marching orders I'd had to penetrate to the rear of the almost oppressively impressive building to a network of evil-smelling yards and muddy passages. Typical of Russia? Possibly.

Then my thoughts returned to other matters—Mother, kit, being killed, Mother—

It was difficult to impose any pattern or coherence of thinking in those days of feverish excitement, the first days of war when all Western humanity had seemed to go mad.

I said to Mother, 'Vilna. The day after tomorrow.' Not knowing exactly how to continue after this I contented myself with taking her hand and kissing it. A stupid gesture, I suppose, but as good a way of expressing inarticulate gratitude for many things as I could devise.

After a moment she said that there had been a telephone call from

Peterhof. If I were not leaving directly, the Imperial Family would like to see me that evening.

A few hours later, therefore, I was standing beside Olga on the terrace, looking over towards Kronstadt and a sky out of a Turner painting, a fury of yellow, scarlet and crimson. She had just returned to Mother the book of poems Uncle Raoul had sent her. 'I've copied the one I specially wanted—*Le Vase Brisé*,' she said to me breathlessly.

'But won't you lose a sheet of paper?'

She shook her head. 'Never, I promise you.'

But otherwise we didn't talk much. I remember we watched a great cloud mass, indigo turning to black, so that you might imagine the sky was bruised—it was creeping up to cover the more fiery colours brilliantly reflected in the great jets of the fountains below us. Soon there would be a storm—the air was very still, and voices carried far; perhaps that was why I said nothing.

Behind us I could hear the Czarina declaring triumphantly that after the scenes of enthusiasm attending the declaration of war, no one would ever again dare deny that she had been *right* in maintaining that the people worshipped the Czar.

I looked back for a moment. In the eerie light the red and cream façade of the palace seemed wan, almost spectral; the Czarina looked like a pale marble statue. And then the first spots of rain splashed down.

Driving back with Mother, I said, 'She—the Czarina—has lost that haggard look she had at the time war was declared.'

'There's an even more amazing change in the Czar,' she said. 'You know how broken *he* was when the declaration came.'

'Yes,' I said. 'I couldn't put a name to his mood tonight.'

'I could. Complacency.'

'Complacency! Complacency? About what, in God's name!'

The Czar had told her that on the night after the declaration of war, 'I had my usual glass of tea, and a long talk with the Czarina, and then I decided that a bath before going to bed might help me to sleep. I was just getting into the bath when a footman knocked on the door and said there was an urgent personal telegram from the Kaiser. It was an appeal not to let our troops cross the German frontier. I read the telegram, re-read it, repeated it aloud to myself, and still didn't understand it. A few hours after the German declaration of war, here was this—this supplication, this pretence that it was in my power to avoid fighting. I went to the Czarina, and read her the telegram. "You won't reply to it, will you?" she asked. "No, indeed!" I said. And, after that, though I had never expected it, I slept really soundly!'

After a moment he had added with the gleefulness of a triumphant small boy, '*I* wasn't going to help Wilhelm out of his difficulties!'

Remembering the look on Mother's face when I had said, 'Vilna. The day after tomorrow,' I exclaimed, 'He might have helped more people than Wilhelm out of difficultioo, mightn't he?'

Dinner on my last evening was a wretched affair. That morning a mob had sacked the German Embassy and kicked to death the old servant left as caretaker. Mother, on hearing the news, said, 'Papa once told Raoul and me what it was like in Paris at the time of the declaration of war in 1870. Flushed faces, wild, terrible excitement as if the whole population had fever—' Then she had stood up and said, 'The poor servant! The Czar must act! I'm going to Peterhof, Andrei.'

But all the Czar wanted to talk about was the magnificent co-operation of the railwaymen. 'Loyal through and through!' he kept saying.

The Czarina said with asperity that Mother was becoming hysterical over a 'patriotic demonstration'.

'A drunken, destructive mob, Your Imperial Majesty, murdered a man who tried to do his duty.'

'Oh, come!' said the Czar. 'No Russians could ever behave like that! With respect, my dear Avoye, it's non-Russians who are capable of the most unthinkable actions. Even your own ambassador has suggested we start an intelligence service in the big German socialist cities. We told him, of course, that we would never use Revolution as one of our weapons.'

But even if the Embassy had never been sacked, it would have been impossible to eat much that night at dinner. The servants' emotion, the aching knowledge of the fact that all Germany—enemy territory—sprawled between us and the only two surviving members of our family, the realisation of the fresh calls to be made on Mother's fortitude—all this led me to throw down knife and fork and say, 'Let's go to Uncle Raoul's room. If his things have been packed away, let's get them out again and leave them about as if he'll be back soon.'

We went up; Mother put a uniform jacket over the back of a chair, while I took books from a valise and arranged them on the bedside table.

From across the room, Mother said suddenly, 'Do you remember how every time we'd visited the Tyrol Alix used to say that when she grew up she'd marry dear Franz von Mayrhofen? I think it would have happened—and for that reason these last days have been the only days when I haven't cried out in my heart for her.'

Thoughts of the dead sister, the living friend I might soon be trying to kill, made my hands clumsy, and the book I was holding slipped to the floor. Danzer's *Armée Zeitung* of November, 1909, falling open at a passage underlined by Uncle Raoul. The Russian Army was like a heavyweight, muscle-bound prize fighter, lacking vigour and speed because of his bulk, and therefore at the mercy of any lighter, more wiry and intelligent opponent. . .

The barracks next morning with each officer his own quartermaster, handing out boots, shirts, horse blankets, canvas buckets, emergency rations. 'Your men are to eat these only in cases of extreme hunger.' Extremity of hunger would indeed be necessary—the tins dated back to the war against Japan, ten years before, and had been notorious even then.

But I seemed to be the only person who didn't find this *funny;* I appeared to be the only person lacking both humour and enthusiasm.

Probably because of the emergency rations, I remembered that Goethe had said once that enthusiasm can't be kept bottled like pickled herrings.

Then we were clattering off down the Nevsky for the *Te Deum* to be celebrated in the square before the Kazan Cathedral. We were not in a wholly unrealistic mood—never think that. Each one of us was now aware that soon a real enemy might be taking real aim at us, and real bullets would be flying in our direction. What we were not mentally prepared for was real shells. One cannot be prepared for the effect of real shellfire.

All that I can remember clearly of the *Te Deum* was the hardness of the cobblestones as we knelt for Benediction.

I had said goodbye to Mother—there was no point in her waiting at the station. But she came to the cathedral square, to take a last look at me. She stood very erect at the front of the crowd; she was wearing a cream muslin dress with an amber silk sash, and her parasol had an amber handle. There were some huge yellow butterflies fluttering about

14

her as, with a brilliant smile, she raised her hand in salute and called to us the traditional officer's greeting, 'Zdorova Molodt₂e!'—Good health, my lads! And we all laughed and saluted her.

Then on to the station. We were still bemused with the image of glory. War simply meant cavalry—us—galloping to victory across battlefields that somehow remained bloodless.

The day was oppressively hot; when the sun managed to pierce the clouds the light blazed down, but it never remained for long.

Steady hoofbeats along the Nevsky, and crowds cheering their champions. Of course we were going to win—weren't we going to use the techniques that had always been so successful in peacetime manoeuvres?

'So brave!' cried a pretty blonde girl.

We tried to look brave. On the whole we felt brave. The first clash with the enemy, we told ourselves, would be thrilling—exciting.

The most we admitted to was possible momentary fright. We were unacquainted then with the difference between fright and gut-turning fear.

On down the Nevsky, cheered all the way, a gallant, brilliant, romantic sight—as splendid material as any meat-grinder could wish for.

The station—down to work, getting eight horses, saddles, equipment, hay, aboard each cattletruck. The horses hated the whole business, and so did we, particularly since a group of French and Serbian diplomats had come to see us off; mentally I applied to them Grandfather's description of politicians in general—'singes endimanchés'.

But at last the trumpet sounded, and we were aboard—men, horses, hay, equipment. Little ammunition. But, after all, we were to use human beings as ammunition.

The trumpet sounded again, and we were off to the war—a war in which at the outset we had completely scrapped all our long-planned strategy in answer to frenzied appeals from Paris.

Did Uncle Raoul—wherever he was—know what had happened?

To hearten myself, I began to re-read the letter he had left for me—to be opened only if war broke out.

'Disregard Scripture, and hide your light under a bushel. If you and your squadron cannot control the impulse to act heroically, do it stealthily, because if the news gets around, the gods that rule your destiny will keep sending you to cope with every nasty situation that crops up. In war the shining little cross on the chest will lead inevitably to a bigger wooden one holding you down for good—if only because it makes such a good target for a sniper as it ornaments your tunic.

'You are bound to be afraid. Your men are bound to be afraid. Fear generates itself quite spontaneously, is very infectious, and there is nothing you can do about that.

'But somehow you have to control it. Actually, most people run in a battle; the only difference between a hero and a coward is that they run in different directions. Myself, I hope to be a cunning coward—the kind that survives. . .'

I began to scribble a reply to him.

'The appeal comes from France—"Paris must be saved."

'Russia is to be the great shock absorber. Rather, the magnet. By an insane advance she is to draw German divisions away from the West.

'So our plans go into reverse. The First Army, which was to conduct a holding war, crosses the Prussian frontier; even more crazily, so does the Second, originally intended to wait in reserve at Warsaw. The Second's especially important. It has most of the Gardes à Cheval, Chevaliers Gardes, Red Hussars, Preobrazhensky, Pavlovsky, Tirailleurs de la Garde—I wouldn't take a chance of losing the crack troops of the entire army, I'd cherish them with loving tenderness, all the more so since they've been the mainstay of the Imperial *régime* since the Imperial *régime* started. But then I'm not overawed by our allies, as our politicians seem to be, and I suppose I lack the chivalry and *élan* of our generals. What a mixture! What a war!'

We left the train. The smell of an army still had pleasant familiarity—hay, horses, smoke from wood fires. Later it would be a different smell.

Atrocious roads, clouds of dust, mile upon mile of birch forest, silver trunks and leaves already beginning to turn yellow. The frontier with Germany. Empty houses of Russian and German frontier guards, barriers and poles tossed into the ditch, but the frontier still marked clearly enough, for there before us were the neat German farms and villages. They were nearly all empty, these farms and villages—empty of human inhabitants, I mean, for hens clucked and birds twittered and from some of the farms the flight of humans had been so hurried that not only did we find meals still warm on the tables, but unfortunate cattle still chained to their stalls. And always the sun beat down.

Those will always be my lasting impressions of the first days of the

16

campaign, a sun of molten copper overhead, dust rising in clouds under the horses' tread, the inky shadows in those forsaken villages, and that constant lowing and lamentation of the poor tethered beasts, drowning all other sounds in the neighbourhood. The noise tore at our nerves; when we had time we loosed as many as we could, led them out into the fields, milked them if we were able.

We were half a dozen miles inside German territory, had met no resistance, and so all the talk among officers was that the enemy was evacuating the whole of East Prussia. I said it hardly seemed likely, East Prussia being the heart of Junkerdom. They laughed. 'Look at the smoke ahead—they're burning their own farms and houses!' But those black columns of smoke, when we came up closer, were dumps of straw, and seemed to indicate with fair accuracy our line of march. And always, in the distance, were cyclists, disappearing over the horizon. Boys in their teens. It seemed unlikely that every farm boy in East Prussia possessed sufficient funds to buy himself a bicycle. More likely a gift from a farseeing government—or rather, a payment in advance for services to be rendered. The whole of that deserted countryside seemed watchful to me, listening and waiting.

The early mornings were marvellous, the sky all red and gold, and birds singing everywhere. It had been just after one such flaming dawn when we were still moving up from the rear to a forward position that we had our first view of our general, Rennenkampf. Very trim, with a moustache like a stag's antlers, about sixty. He whirled past in a staff car, he didn't notice us, he seemed to be arguing with his companion, and we saluted and then coughed and spat out the dust that was his legacy to us.

'He hasn't changed much in ten years,' remarked my sergeant.

'You've seen him before?'

'Once,' said the sergeant. 'On the station at Mukden when we were fighting the Japs. When he and General Samsonov came to blows.'

I stared at him. 'What on earth are you talking about?'

'They came to blows, sir; there was talk of a duel, but the Czar forbade it. I thought everybody knew that.' After a moment he added, good fellow, 'Of course—I'm sorry—it was the beginning of your bad time, your family had other things to think of.'

'But General *Samsonov*—'

He misunderstood my appalled incredulity that Samsonov, commanding the Second Army, should be on such terms with the general commanding the First Army, with whom he must work in the closest co-operation. He thought I merely didn't believe in the incident nearly ten years before. He said simply, earnestly, 'I saw it, right enough; I wouldn't make up a thing like that—'

'I know you wouldn't—'

'Especially since my own general was in the wrong, and that dirty German was standing there, sneering—'

He had been in a cavalry division commanded by Rennenkampf. 'We didn't like it because we didn't fancy even then being commanded by a general with a German name.' And then they had all felt very bad because Samsonov's Siberian Cossacks, after a heroic fight, had to give up the Yentai coalmines because Rennenkampf hadn't moved to relieve them despite repeated orders. 'General Samsonov, he's a good man, he *feels* for his men, a kindly, simple soul. Well, he couldn't forget all this, and when he saw Rennenkampf there on the platform of the railway station at Mukden, he went over and said what he thought and knocked him down. And there was a German standing there—'

'What German?'

'A big man. Thick. With a head round like a pumpkin, and shaved nearly bald. He'd eat sausages all night. He talked good Russian, that's what made things worse, because he could understand every word being said—'

'But what was he doing on the platform at Mukden?'

'Oh, we had quite a few foreigners like him. They called themselves observers, and were damned nuisances.'

And any German officer worth his salt would have passed on the details to the High Command.

Who therefore knew of the hostility between the two generals invading East Prussia.

2

'Like haggard tramps'

'We ourselves must not knock at the frontier
like haggard tramps.'
Prince Kutuzov in 1812

SHORTLY AFTERWARDS our first sight of the *débris* and wreckage of war, bodies of men and horses lying in pools of blood in a cobbled street. And a Jew going round with a bag collecting the horseshoes. The Jew collecting the horseshoes made more impression on me than the sprawling bodies. I tried to reason it out. There weren't many dead —not more than half a dozen. And I'd seen violent death before. The snow outside the Spassky Gate in Moscow, the summer dust on Apothecary Island, all had been blotched with blood. I wondered if I would go on being detached. If there were hundreds of dead—

Even then I didn't foresee that one day to speak of the ground being 'carpeted with dead' would be not a poetical way of talking, but the obscene truth.

A cluster of farm buildings, a neat barn, a flurry of crows from a tree, and something singing viciously past me. Even so I didn't think the whistling thing could kill me. The sergeant had more sense. He crossed himself before he crouched low in his saddle. 'Now perhaps,' he said with grim satisfaction, 'these fools will get it into their thick heads that there's more to fighting than guzzling German sausages and swilling German beer.'

And then he was wounded. I dragged him across my saddle and went on galloping forward. We didn't get to grips with the enemy, who brought down two more of my people before they got away. The first was a snubnosed private who had kept telling us that St Nicholas the Miracle Worker would see us through. The bullet spun him round, out of the saddle. For seconds he seemed to feel nothing, but then he began to scream, for a few minutes, and then he was dead.

The other men weren't too much shaken by the casualties. Casualties never make so much impression when you're advancing.

That afternoon, just after I'd seen the sergeant on his way to hospital, I was told to report back to Headquarters, to a staff colonel named Revashov. The name meant nothing to me, and I went in a fury. To be dragged out of action after pestering the War Ministry to relieve me of staff duties—and to be relegated to safety at the precise moment when a noise like a distant roll of drums told me the time of skirmishes and brushes with the enemy was over!

As I dismounted before what had been the mayor's house in a little German town, the sun was setting. I turned to look behind me. The guns were still thundering away, and the sight there in the west was quite extraordinary, flashes of gunfire pale against the red of the sinking sun.

I went into the house in a savage mood, through a parlour all green plush and staring photographs of the mayor's family on the mantle-piece to a back dining-room, so ill-lit that the oil lamps showed little more than an immense dining-table covered with maps and, bending over it, a grey-haired man with a deeply lined face.

'Hamilton, sir. Lieutenant, Chev—'

'Ah, yes, no need to introduce yourself. When I saw you from the car you looked exactly as your father looked when we were commissioned together. I took a chance that his son wouldn't be thick-witted, and sent for you.'

I placed him now. He had been the blurred figure with whom Rennenkampf had been arguing. On the other hand, it seemed incredible that he should be my father's contemporary—and I must have shown incredulity, for he grinned wryly and said, 'A Jap bullet got me in the thigh, played hell with my sciatic nerve. I've been out of action for years; they've let me come on the staff because before I became a cripple I'd come shooting in East Prussia—not that, having brought me back, they make much use of my knowledge.'

He got up and began to limp up and down, the lamps dipping and flickering as he passed. 'I can't get about enough to see things for myself—I should think you'll be an Elder Moltke in comparison with some of the aides they've tried to unload on me.' He beckoned me over to the table. 'And you'll be doubly useful because I can talk like a Jeremiah day in and day out and, if you're your father's son, you'll keep your mouth shut.'

I forgot my rage, was suddenly desperately interested. 'I'll do what I can, sir,' I said.

'Well,' said Colonel Revashov, 'for a start, look at this map. Here we have the North-West Army Group, under General Jilinsky, six hundred and fifty thousand men, thirty infantry, eight cavalry divisions under Generals Pavel Rennenkampf and Alexander Samsonov. Opposed to them the German Eighth Army, under Colonel-General Max von Prittwitz. One cavalry, eleven infantry divisions, one hundred and thirty-five thousand men. We outnumber the enemy therefore by more than four to one, but this is our one lonely advantage—if advantage you can call it.'

He spread his right hand out over the map. He could not spread it far because he had lost the third and fourth fingers, but those fingers that remained could spread far enough. 'Look!' he said. 'Moraine everywhere, and all broken up by forests, lakes, marshes. You appreciate the significance.'

'We'll have to deploy over relatively narrow fronts. That robs us of our only advantage, superior numbers.'

'All the enemy will have to do,' said Colonel Revashov, 'is to wait for us to come through, canalised—'

'Where, sir?'

'Here, behind the north-south line of the Masurian Lakes. A water barrier and behind it an outrageously efficient network of railways so that *they* can concentrate wherever the danger is greatest.'

It was an appallingly hot evening. There seemed to be swarms of stinging insects in the room.

'Advancing, as we are,' said the Colonel, 'one would expect superbly efficient communications, leading to absolute synchronisation of movement on the part of our army commanders. For success it is essential they should arrive in East Prussia, and strike simultaneously, the First to the north, the Second to the south of the Masurian chain—' He stopped abruptly, staring at me. 'And what have you heard?' he demanded.

I said hesitantly, 'My sergeant said the two generals were on bad terms in Manchuria.'

'Oh, true enough; Rennenkampf's not going to bestir himself to pull Samsonov out of a mess. But even if they were David and Jonathan, there couldn't be synchronisation, you know. Blame Rennenkampf and Samsonov for it, if you like, but above all blame the commander of the North-West Group.'

'General Jilinsky?'

'Unless a miracle's happened in the last hour and he's been dismissed, yes,' the Colonel said irritably. He began to limp up and down. 'You know that until recently he was Chief of Staff. He visited Paris more than once. Mobilisation was discussed. The French can mobilise fast, can't they? Jilinsky's as vain as hell. As Chief of Staff, he said, he was going to overhaul Russian mobilisation so that Russian armies could give battle within fifteen days.'

'That's not possible,' I said.

'It is—if your troops stagger along in a daze, half-starved, half-armed, bloody feet bound in rags because they had to start marching before they could be issued with boots, and cavalry and artillery horses starve because the corn's not ripe. Myself, I think it's a high price to pay for one man's vanity.'

There was a knock on the door. An orderly came in with a scribbled message. The Colonel dismissed him, read the message, swore, held the paper to the lamp flame and burned it.

'General Rennenkampf,' he flung over his shoulder, 'reiterates his belief that the enemy's going to evacuate East Prussia. In such a mood of exaltation he ignores my sordid request for railwaymen to be brought up from our rear. They *might* alter the gauge so that we could make use of the German railways—to help our retreat, at any rate! By the way, do *you* think they're clearing out of East Prussia?'

'No. It's their holy soil. They won't retire twenty miles without giving battle.'

'By God, they won't, and d'you know what I see in my mind's eye going on in Berlin at this moment? Fat East German baronesses on their knees to the dull Kaiserin, shrieking, "Majesty, our family land's at the mercy of marauding Cossacks!" and she going off to intercede with the Knight in Shining Armour: a government which has tried too successfully to scare people about us, ending up with terrifying itself. General hysteria. What's the use of gaining Paris if the Cossacks are in Berlin? Do you know what I think they'll do? They'll switch troops back from their Western Front, they'll order up their best generals, who will work together, unlike ours.'

He broke off then, looked across at a lovely little ikon gleaming incongruously in that ugly room and crossed himself. 'One might think at times that God's curse lies heavy over us in Russia,' he said. 'This will be a terrible August, I fear.'

The absent mayor and his family, from the smells that lingered in that dim dining-room, had lived mainly off salt fish and cabbage. We ate a makeshift meal, and the Colonel talked.

'I am sending you to Samsonov. Get a clear mental picture of him. He's a simple, kindly soul, the last man to claim brilliance. He commanded a cavalry division in Manchuria—now he's commanding an army of thirteen divisions with no experience to fit him for a much bigger job in an essentially different theatre under totally dissimilar conditions—against men who've made a lifelong study of war in this very region. He's new to the command, coming straight from sick leave, so he doesn't know his staff or divisional generals. Because of the insistence on haste they slashed four days out of the period of concentration, so God knows what the state of the rear services is like. The forward line's advancing through sand. Rennenkampf had a flying start of half a dozen days—Jilinsky keeps bombarding Samsonov with orders to catch him up. Samsonov lacks the confidence to ignore the orders—although he knows they're disastrous.

'As yet he hasn't reached the frontier—it's then the real danger begins. Oh, and there's one other thing to remember about Samsonov—he's asthmatic.'

The heavy gunfire had stopped as we rode to Rennenkampf's Headquarters. Headquarters itself was jubilant. The enemy had pulled out of the fighting—the terrific outburst of artillery fire was to cover the retreat.

Excited men ran in, ran out. It was difficult to get facts out of the prevailing chaos. At first we could gather only that between three and four in the afternoon, when the enemy had begun to fall back, Rennenkampf had given the order to pursue. Then at four-thirty, in face of the heavy enemy covering fire, he had called off the pursuit. Now he was 'waiting to assess the extent of the damage to the enemy centre' before deciding what to do next.

'The enemy aren't waiting though,' said Colonel Revashov to me. 'They're drawing back to regroup—and then they'll edge southwards, crabwise, against Samsonov. He'll soon be crossing the frontier. They know Rennenkampf won't be inclined to help him.'

'They'll gamble on that?'

'Is it so much of a gamble?'

He went off to urge that the pursuit of the retreating Germans should be resumed. I hardly knew what to do with myself; officially I had no standing here at Headquarters, so I went out for a gloomy tramp about the town. There were signs of looting, household articles considered not worth keeping lay where they had been tossed through smashed windows. I stumbled over half a dozen books tumbled together in the shadow, and on a sudden impulse pocketed one. It might while away the tedium of waiting.

I sat in a corner of the little room allocated to the Colonel, awaiting his return. The book was a medical dictionary. Hardly cheerful reading, but possibly useful. I looked up asthma. Asthma, said the dictionary, frequently arose from emotional reasons. Very often the patient was over-anxious. Occupational strain, any clash between the patient and his colleagues must be eased.

God help Samsonov! At this rate they'd soon be hearing his paroxysms on the other side of the Vistula.

The Colonel came back, looking unbearably tired, limping heavily.

'I've been told to get some sleep,' he said. 'The consideration stems from nothing more than a desire to be rid of me. However, I've been told waggishly I'd better not undress.'

I said, 'I'll call you, sir, the moment—'

'Well,' said the Colonel, 'give me a couple of hours, then rouse me. You'll need some sleep yourself before going off to Samsonov in the morning.'

He lay fully clothed on the camp bed. I went on reading my medical dictionary. In fatigue, said the dictionary, there was a conscious sense of weariness, the power of attention was diminished, thought was difficult. Violent activity continued beyond the stage of fatigue resulted in exhaustion—

Here I myself succumbed to my conscious sense of weariness.

The sound of voices roused me. Frantically I glared at my watch— I'd only dozed for ten minutes, the Colonel had had an hour's rest— Good God, it was Rennenkampf himself talking, Rennenkampf, dapper, grinning as if the Kaiser was knocking at the tradesmen's entrance of the house, asking for peace.

'—the Germans are definitely retiring,' he was saying.

The Colonel was on his feet. 'Then you'll want the orders for pursuit given, sir?'

'What an excitable fellow you are, to be sure. No, I came to tell you that you can take your clothes off now—'

24

The Colonel stared at him wordlessly.

'No need for us to take any action,' chuckled Rennenkampf cosily. 'They're *retiring*.'

'But this is precisely the time when we should be straining every nerve to keep in touch with them—'

'Oh, surely not. Undress, have a good night's sleep. This young fellow here would echo my advice, I know.'

'I entreat you, sir—' began the Colonel.

'What a martyr for duty you are, Serge Mikhailovitch, but I shan't allow it.'

'If we let them get off unhindered, they'll move south against Samsonov.'

'They're retiring westwards.'

He went out, still smiling. I began to stammer apologies for dozing off; the Colonel didn't hear them. He was addressing the wall opposite.

'Ninety-nine years ago another general miscalculated about Prussians. Grouchy thought they were going home then, too, but instead they were cutting across country towards Waterloo—'

I set out at dawn. My mission was simple. Find Samsonov, tell him what the Colonel suspected, beg him in the Colonel's name to take no risks.

This assignment alarmed me. Not so much the prospect of plunging headlong into danger from the enemy—no, being young, I was more terrified at the prospect of an irascible general.

'He's not irascible,' said the Colonel. 'He's the kindliest of men, devoted to his troops.'

'Yes, sir, but even so—'

'You mean he'll hardly listen to what I have to say? I think you'll find he will.'

You saw first a great cloud of moving dust, and then, as you drew closer, you could make out the figures of men—except that with bearded faces and tattered uniforms thick with dust they looked more like animated flour sacks.

I almost despaired of finding Samsonov. It wasn't merely that the ordinary soldier was ignorant—the officers knew nothing. And there were no maps. I don't exaggerate—and God knows I wouldn't wilfully imagine it. *There were no maps.* An occasional compass—but no maps.

Corps commanders couldn't tell me where Samsonov was; if you wonder how I came into contact with corps commanders, the answer is that when they heard a lieutenant from the First Army was loose in their command, they sought me out with an eagerness I found grisly. They wanted to know if I knew what Rennenkampf's objective was, they'd been told nothing. And since they didn't know where their own commander was, or what their own right wing was up to, it was too much to expect to get any information about enemy movements.

The men, even at this point, were apathetic through fatigue. When a halt was called in that broiling heat, they fell rather than sat down in the ditches, lay gasping for breath. Cavalrymen slumped in the saddle, heads resting on their horses' manes.

'When did they last have a decent meal?' I asked one lieutenant.

He screwed up his eyes. 'What's today? One loses track of time. Well, put it like this. Our entire army corps had to advance from Bialystok without bread or oats, and we've been living on reserve rations ever since. Of course, wading for days through this damned sand played hell with everybody.' But then in the next moment he was raging because Rennenkampf had the advantage over Samsonov. 'We'll have to make the devil of an effort if we're to get to Berlin before the First.'

Dear God, it was as much as his starving, exhausted men could do to stumble to the German frontier.

At last as darkness fell I came into the presence of Samsonov. A kindly, patient face, a simplicity of manner, a sudden charming smile when I mentioned the Colonel's name.

'Serge Mikhailovitch! If only I'd known he was back on the active list I'd have insisted on having him here, but I thought the poor devil was done for after he and his Cossacks put up that heroic defence of the Yentai mines—

'—and you say he's with Rennenkampf! That was crass behaviour on the part of the Chief of Staff—and if Rennenkampf had any delicacy—'

But Rennenkampf hadn't, I thought grimly. Certainly there had been no hint of uneasiness in his manner when he'd talked to the man he'd allowed to be captured in Manchuria ten years before, the man whose betrayal Samsonov had so furiously resented he'd struck the betrayer in public.

Yes, Samsonov would listen to what the Colonel had to say, there was liking and respect in his voice every time he spoke of him, but against the Colonel's advice came angry orders from above, from Jilinsky at North-West Headquarters, who'd received from Petersburg the information that the French government 'insisted' on a Russian advance far and fast, beyond sanity and safety, because of the threat to Paris. Even as Samsonov was opening the Colonel's letter, his chief-of-staff, Potovsky, a nervous, *pince-nozed* individual, came hurrying in with such a message. 'Speed up your advance, hasten operations as soon as possible, your slowness is endangering the First Army.'

'They don't realise what it's like, this struggling forward, foot by foot through this hellish sand!' said Potovsky, sounding as if he were about to cry.

'Send in reply that we're advancing according to our timetable,' replied Samsonov. 'They know this is true. Tell them we're not halting, we're covering marches of more than twelve miles in sand, we cannot go more quickly.' He was talking breathlessly now, as if he had been running. 'The men have been on the move for ten or twelve hours a day without halts—' He began to cough. 'Wading through sand, poor devils, wading, lieutenant, I'm not exaggerating—' The fit of coughing prevented him from continuing for a moment, and then he said, gasping, 'But you—you must be exhausted too. We must see you get some kind of meal—yes, I insist—'

I left him coughing, reading the Colonel's letter. I suppose my face must have been eloquent. Potovsky said, 'The attacks are always worse at night—it seems the general case with asthmatics.' He seemed in such a desperate mood he was glad to talk to anybody.

Two rooms away I could still hear Samsonov coughing. I remembered a line from *The Staff-Officer's Field Manual*—'being able to endure the hardships of a campaign.'

This, too, was another mayor's house, this time housing a music-loving mayor—or mayor's wife—or mayor's daughter. There was a piano in the parlour, pushed into the corner to be out of the way. Feeling somewhat in the way myself after supper, I squeezed behind it and sat on the piano stool. I was desperately tired. There had been a day once in Brittany when the tide was out and Alix and I had insisted on walking along the beach for miles, discovering bay after bay—'You're going too far,' Uncle Raoul had said, 'you'll be sorry when you have to wade back through sand.' But we'd laughed at him, and he'd been right, of course, we had gone too far, and when we turned back the wet firm sand had become dry and loose, we'd had to fight our way through it—he'd made us sing *Sambre et Meuse* to keep going.

'Le régiment de Sambre et Meuse marchait toujours au cri de liberté
Cherchant la route glorieuse qui l'a conduit à l'immortalité—'

Unnoticed in my corner, I began to pick out the tune. It sounded awful. The piano was a jangling discordant old wreck.

The light was glinting on Potovsky's *pince-nez*. General Samsonov wanted to see me.

He had, thank God, stopped coughing, but there was a grey shadow of exhaustion over him.

'Do you know what the Colonel has written?' he asked me.

I said I had a fair idea. The Colonel would have been worried in any case because of the way in which both armies were outrunning supplies, but what caused him chief anxiety was the general belief that the enemy would not stop retreating this side of the Vistula. He believed they were retreating in order to regroup, after which they would be launched against one of our exhausted armies when it emerged along a narrow front. He believed they would attack the Second Army because this had had infinitely the harder march.

He heard me out with patient courtesy. 'Good!' he said. 'Evidently he has implicit confidence in you, and that's enough for me. I shall give you a verbal message to take back, partly because I understand he's sent you more or less unofficially, and also because while there's a remote chance you might fall in with the enemy—they're holding out here and there—it would never do for them to capture vital information, would it?'

I said, No, grinning inwardly at such a rhetorical question.

'He wants me to slow down my march until supplies can get through. He also wants me to move crabwise—that's a great phrase with Serge Mikhailovitch, he was always using it in Manchuria, always moving crabwise, we used to pull his leg about it—well, he wants me to move crabwise to the north and keep in close contact with Rennenkampf. Well, you must tell him I can't do that. My supply position's so difficult, in fact, that to ease it I'll have to direct my left in to the Novo Georgievsk—Mlava-Soldau railway.'

'That will pull your right further away from Rennenkampf,' I said automatically.

'It can't be helped. Tell Serge Mikhailovitch he'd better start

28

persuading Rennenkampf to start moving crabwise to the south to link up with *me*.'

I said formally, 'All the talk, sir, was that General Rennenkampf's next move would be west, not south, to mask Konigsberg.'

'Oh, I wasn't sure that he'd move directly west,' said Samsonov's elderly, breathless voice, 'but I was sure the one direction in which he wouldn't move would be to the south. Now, as to the business of calling a halt—well, young man, I said that if Serge Mikhailovitch trusts you, so will I. Look at these messages from Headquarters, memorise them, and tell him I have no choice, I must keep moving.'

I mounted and started out immediately on the return journey.

There was moonlight in a dull glow, seeming unreal, and time passed and I made what haste I could and then on my right hand there was greyness in the skies to the east.

'—Régiment de Samhre et Meuse reçut la mort aux cris de liberté,
Mais son histoire glorieuse lui donne droit à l'immortalité—'

But one didn't want immortality—yet. One wanted just a little more of human life—

Offensive à l'outrance—demanded by big-bellied French Commander-in-Chief Joffre because he'd miscalculated badly and didn't think he could save Paris—passed on to Jilinsky who didn't want it known that he'd been bluffing, bragging when he'd talked of speedy mobilisation, and so an army was being sent wading through sand to destruction after agonies of thirst and weariness.

The Colonel limped out to meet me on my return, gave me brandy. I said I didn't want it, I'd probably throw it up.

This was good cognac, he said, I'd keep it down.

I told him all I could. 'Right,' he said at the end, handing me his flask. 'You've earned another drink. Then get some sleep.'

'What are you doing, sir?'

'Me? I'm going to see Jilinsky,' said the Colonel matter-of-factly.

'Jilinsky! But won't Rennenkampf—'

'General of the Army Rennenkampf will be glad to see the back of me. *He's* not going to move an inch, if he can help it, and I with my face like a coffin-lid keep spoiling his well-earned repose.'

'Sir, may I come with you?'

'My good idiot, do I have to tell you what I'm going to do? After seeing Jilinsky I am joining Samsonov—either with instructions I hope will halt this Gadarene swine-like rush to destruction, or to share whatever dubious fate awaits him.'

'I guessed that, sir, that's why I want to come. I'd rather be with those poor devils than safe here with Rennenkampf.'

'You don't know what you're talking about. Defeat, death, capture —they're just words to you now, they don't really mean anything— how can they? But, my God, I can tell you when they *do* become meaningful there's nothing fine or noble in them.'

'I know how obscene death can be. I saw my father, remember. I can remember him making up his mind to go to Moscow—*this* decision isn't as hard.'

'Well, then,' said the Colonel, 'you can get some sleep in the car.'

A hundred odd miles back to the headquarters of the North-West Army Group at Volkovisk. I slept most of the time, but not enough to relieve the tenseness of nerves, the aching of limbs, the dreadful confusion of fears for the future.

Headquarters at this point consisted of Jilinsky's train, drawn up at a special siding. The Colonel went into the train, I got out to stretch my legs. Sand—a pity one couldn't get away from sand. And forests.

There were lakes, too, ahead of Samsonov's army. Lakes weren't very lucky for Russian armies. There'd been a lake at Austerlitz. The legend of drowning Russians—

One or two people had already given me enquiring glances; if I walked up and down someone would inevitably start a conversation. I got back into the car. There were some crumpled pieces of paper in the Colonel's corner; automatically I picked them up and smoothed them out. They were brief notes, embodying what he had said to me, and I had said to Samsonov. I realised he had set them down to get his arguments in order before facing Jilinsky; unashamedly I began to read.

1. *The enemy is staking everything on one throw; his whole strength will be thrown against the Second Army, gambling on Rennenkampf's continued inactivity to the north.*

2. *The 'retreat' we are assuming is in fact a regrouping of forces for this purpose.*

3. *Two orders must therefore be given:*

    (a) *Rennenkampf must march southwards to link up with Samsonov.*

    (b) *Samsonov must halt his travesty of an advance until he is in contact with Rennenkampf and until his supply position—which at present does not exist—approaches normal.*

4. *The greatest care must be observed in communications. To send messages by telegraph seems barely possible now because of the lack of wire. If we have to revert to the practice of using mounted orderlies the messages must be by word of mouth, written instructions should not be given since we lack sufficient signal officers to transmit these in cipher. The same sanction applies with even greater force to telegraph and wireless messages. If these are to be given en clair* we hand the enemy our own signed death warrants.*

5. *Our poor 'steamroller' has been sent hurtling forward in order to divert enemy troops from the Western Front. Surely we have gone far and fast enough? By this time the effect has been secured, the regiments have been switched. They are now being turned against us; it therefore behoves us to await their coming in as strong a defensive position as possible.*

'Well,' said the Colonel, 'a little *blasé* about the god who's ruling your destiny? He was standing there at the carriage door a moment ago.' He got in slowly, sat beside me.

'I see you've been reading my notes,' he said after a moment. 'Wait until I've given the driver his instructions, and I'll tell you what I couldn't bring myself to put down on paper.'

'Where are we going, sir?'

'To find Samsonov. No, no difficulty at all in the way of our going, we're being useful in fact. Jilinsky sent an officer to Samsonov earlier, pockets stuffed with papers giving the march schedule and the proposed moves of both armies. He hasn't turned up, therefore he's either dead or a prisoner—brood on that happy thought—'

He leaned forward, and spoke to the driver. The car started. 'One hundred and eighty miles approximately,' said the Colonel, sitting back. 'Such a distance enables Jilinsky to surmount heroically such minor irritants as hunger, thirst and fatigue. Now, listen hard. *We're* not carrying written orders, you must memorise what I've been told so that if anything happens to me, you'll know what's happening, God help you. The staff officer, who's probably fallen into enemy hands, dead or alive, carried this information *in writing*. That Rennenkampf's army

* Uncoded.

31

is to pass the Masurian Lakes to the north and advance against the Insterburg-Augerburg line. And Samsonov—well, we know what he's supposed to do, and so, I should think, do the enemy now. So the spider is in his parlour waiting for the fly.

'Now what I didn't put down was this. When you returned from the Second Army you found me on the point of leaving to see Jilinsky, didn't you? I'll tell you why. I'd had an appeal from Samsonov himself half an hour before. Obviously my letter had impressed him more than he would admit at the time, but when you were there he was still unwilling to disobey Jilinsky's directives. After you left, his doubts grew, and finally his advance cavalry patrols brought back information indicating a build-up in enemy strength—as I'd guessed. So he wirelessed me an appeal—the poor devil's among strangers, he can't trust anyone else!—would I in person reinforce his request to Jilinsky. He wanted to veer away, to advance more cautiously, probing as he went. He's had his reply already, but I've also had it from Jilinsky himself just in case it's not sufficiently clear. I'll give it to you in Jilinsky's own words—*I will not allow General Samsonov to play the coward. I insist that he continue the offensive.*'

'So Samsonov's keeping on marching?' I asked after a moment's silence.

'Yes.'

'Rennenkampf?'

'Jilinsky fully accepts *his* argument that if he pushes the enemy too hard they'll fall back to the Vistula too rapidly to be cut off by Samsonov. And he's sent his approval by field wireless *en clair*, just as he's sent his orders to Samsonov *en clair*—God help Russia, three headquarters clacking operation orders and information to each other *en clair*, and the enemy getting every word!'

After a moment he roused himself. 'But at least we've gained something,' he said. 'A real map! You said the Second lacked them, didn't you? Well, let's have a look at it.'

It made sense to us, but might not to others in our armies. Like all the maps issued, it was in Latin characters—not in Russian Cyrillic script. Hard luck on the officers and men who spoke and read only Russian.

3

'The ring . . . was closed yesterday'

'I beg most humbly to report to Your Majesty that the ring round the larger part of the Russian Army was closed yesterday.'
Hindenburg to the Kaiser, August 31, 1914

THEY WERE in much worse physical shape now. Sweat mixed with dust to cake around eyes and mouth, form a filthy mask over gaunt cheeks. They scarcely looked human—until you saw the bloodshot eyes peering from those dirty faces; they were the betraying human element, flickering, vulnerable. An army of so many tens of thousands should carry a murmuring army of sound with it; this weary, dying army stumbled on in silence.

It was August 26 when we found Samsonov. His headquarters were now at Neidenburg; beyond Neidenburg stretched the lakes. On our arrival we were told he was having dinner with General Potovsky and the British Military Attaché.

'Potovsky,' said the Colonel while we waited, 'has an odd nickname —the Mad Mullah. He gained it in this way. He—'

I never learned how Potovsky came by it, for at this moment Samsonov himself came in, to embrace the Colonel and say we must have dinner with him. He looked ghastly. There was the old grey shadow of despair on his face, his eyes had an expression of wretched bewilderment and fatigue as if he spent night after night puzzling over all that had gone wrong.

'You're not well, sir,' said the Colonel.

'I haven't heard from my wife for some time,' said the General. 'It's worrying.'

'I did my best at Volkovisk.'

'I know, no man could do more. You know the reply I got.'

As we had approached the noise of guns had come from the west, heavier than I had ever heard it, but strange in another way, too. It was intermittent, straggling. 'Ragged, isn't it?' the Colonel had said. 'Do you know what that means? A moving battle. God grant it's not moving in our direction.'

Samsonov was explaining now. First there had been an enemy counter-attack at Usdau, then a division of the VIII Corps had sighted the enemy six miles to the north when resuming its march that morning. There had been desperate fighting, the Russians had sent for help to their fellow division which marched back some nineteen miles only to meet another enemy corps. 'With this danger of my right wing being turned, it seems I'll have to be given permission to abandon the idea of enveloping the enemy.'

'My God!' said the Colonel. 'It's no longer a question of enveloping the enemy, it's the problem of saving yourself from being surrounded now—'

Samsonov said nothing. The Colonel said sharply, 'If we can't achieve victory, at least we needn't strive to achieve our own self-destruction.'

There were shouts from the street outside, the sound of horses madly galloping. We all—except Samsonov—ran out of the house— Potovsky came running after us, buckling on his sword, his *pince-nez* dangling. So I saw for the first time men stampeding in the panic of defeat.

Officers fled like men; fine well-fitting tunics might mark a difference even if all uniforms were now soaked through with sweat, but the facial expressions were the same. And then when, through sheer weariness, those at the rear were dropping down at the roadside, an ambulance wagon, clattering up, started them running again, shouting hoarsely, 'Uhlans coming!'

A quartermaster intercepted the Colonel. 'If you're going back to see the General, ask him how in God's name I'm to find accommodation for all these thousands pouring back into the town.'

'No need to be querulous,' said the Colonel. 'If we go on at the rate we're going, at the end of the month a decent-sized barn will accommodate what's left of the Second Army—with room to spare.'

After this it is difficult to write coherently. I cannot subdue the old choking rage and bitterness. If Rennenkampf had marched—

When Ludendorff, who made the battle plan that finished us, came to write his memoirs, he described how Rennenkampf's 'formidable host hung like a threatening thundercloud to the north-east. *He need only have closed with us, and we should have been beaten.*'

But he made no move whatever.

Our left and right flanks had been routed, but next morning Samsonov ordered the centre to resume the attack. There were still tens of thousands of men to move forward. It was a misty day; the sun was an angry shadow behind grey cloud that seemed to intensify the heat. Slowly our columns went forward, moving trance-like through the burning dust. Many men had no shoes; their feet were bound with bloody rags. Their lips were parched and cracked. The Colonel gave a sudden groan, with a gesture motioned me to a halt. He took off his cap. 'Oh, loving Christ,' he said, 'Who also stumbled onward to Calvary on bleeding feet and, dying, knew the agony of thirst, show more mercy today to Your children here than their earthly rulers have done.' He crossed himself, put on his cap again, and said harshly, 'Move on.'

We were in the region traced by the Colonel on the shifting map in the car. Here were the Masurian Lakes, innumerable lakes and pools with belts and clumps of fir and beech woods covering most of the land between one swampy lakeside and the next, though occasionally there was a red-walled village, red because there was plenty of clay for brick-making. What you would not guess unless you had actually been in the area was the sheer treacherousness of the swamps, camouflaged by the reeds and grasses of summer.

Into the forest we were eventually driven, a writhing dismembered army, lopped into a dozen unco-ordinated bits, some thrashing about in a death agony, others mere inert lumps. But it didn't happen all at once, although the beginning of the end came with a tremendous, relentless enemy artillery bombardment that seemed to split both the sky above and the earth here at our feet. I don't think it scared our men —they were too exhausted now to feel even fear—but the sheer noise of it drained them of their last will to resist. Memories are as dismembered as what remained of the Second Army. I can see a red-clay farmhouse disappearing under a hail of shells, a battalion with fixed bayonets advancing into the smoke of the enemy guns, a dozen Riflemen lying, sitting in the dust, all wounded, some trying to stop the flow of blood with their fingers—there were no bandages—but others not caring.

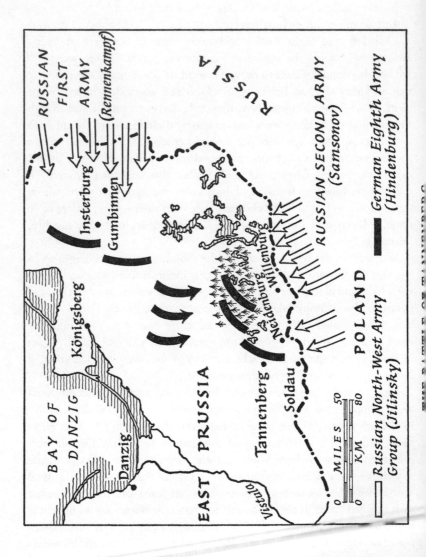

THE BATTLE OF TANNENBERG

I told myself I must get a clear picture of all this, it was my job to take back a factual report of all this to Samsonov. I told myself that I couldn't think clearly because of the continuous roar of the enemy guns, not because of other things, that blood and pain weren't important in themselves, only because they meant fewer men—to send to blood and pain.

The Colonel heard my report. 'What's been done here, sir?'

'Pleading, prayers to Jilinsky and Rennenkampf. No response. Wait here. He may want to hear your report for himself.'

He did more. He stood there in that florid German parlour, that big, kindly man, with the grey shadow of hopelessness darker still on his face now, and after a moment he asked that his horse should be brought round. He said to Potovsky, 'Telegraph General Jilinsky that I'm leaving for the battlefront, and send the baggage and wireless apparatus back to Russia.'

Potovsky stammered, 'Sir, you're cutting yourself off from your base.'

'I know. See to it.'

Potovsky, nearly weeping, hurried out. Samsonov said to the Colonel, 'They always used to say in Manchuria, didn't they, that I shared everything with my men? I must become part of the battle now. No more hearing of it through reports.'

Potovsky rushed back in. 'Hear me only for a moment, sir! It's true the enemy's close, but if you took a car, you could easily—'

'If anyone should escape, it's this boy here. These young officers, they're the irreplaceable material we shouldn't waste, not a—'

Potovsky interrupted, closer to weeping than ever, 'In any case, sir, we haven't sufficient horses, not half a dozen horses—'

'Take them from the Cossacks. Did you send the message to General Jilinsky? Then do it now. I'm going to take personal command under fire—I must see things with my own eyes.'

I went to get the Cossack ponies. When I returned, Potovsky was sending an inept version of Samsonov's message to Headquarters— *The General will feel more at home in the saddle; the conditions will resemble those to which he became accustomed in Manchuria.*

We rode off on the morning of August 28, Samsonov, eight staff officers, the British liaison officer, Knox, a Cossack escort. The sound of the enemy guns was so near and continuous now it seemed almost solid. Everywhere dust and dead and dying, and starving, ragged scarecrows falling back. So Samsonov saw with his own eyes his shattered army.

At mid-morning we halted for a moment. There was a formality of looking at maps spread out on the ground. The horses stood at the road-side munching grass. Then Samsonov stood up and, talking in English, told Major Knox that the situation was critical. 'My own place and duty are with my army; yours is to report to your government. You must therefore return while there is time.'

The Englishman protested. Samsonov mounted, turned in the saddle, said, 'No, you must not follow.' He tried to smile. 'The enemy has luck today, we'll have luck another.'

I can remember riding through a village, across part of a forest, up the slope of a hill through a curtain of smoke, and there a column of Germans—prisoners—incredibly prisoners—was being herded past. It was the last effort of General Martos' corps; the General himself, short, grizzled, was on the hilltop. Samsonov embraced him. 'You alone will save us.' But he knew, Martos knew, we all knew, that nothing could save us now. Some time later Samsonov gave orders for the general retreat of all that was left of the Second Army. It had been a quarter of a million men; 'The thicker the grass,' Attila is supposed to have said, 'the easier we shall mow it down.'

In this wilderness of forests, lakes and swamps, where the roads were causeways and men struggled waist-deep in mud and water, the centre of the Second Army, that section which had fought longest and best, was to be hunted and trapped. They tried to regroup and make a stand—better for them if they hadn't, if they'd broken and run for it days before, when the battle first began to flow against us, even when the riptide set in.

There were still tens of thousands of them, but the enemy enveloped them, and drove them in among the trees and swamps and lakes that completed the separation, the cutting up into ragged segments. Once they'd got us into the forest it was harder still to get a coherent picture of the whole. Some units made their way forward unscathed, for the moment out of contact with the enemy. But at some time or other they would have to try to break out of the swamp, and along the road-causeways the enemy had mounted machine-guns, and there would be dead and wounded and dying. It was useless trying to evaluate the situation. You would come upon little groups of men, no physical casualties among them, but they were so exhausted and bewildered it was impossible to understand the confusion of words passing their dry lips. Potovsky fretted terribly because he couldn't 'assess' the situation, direct a proper defence. 'How can you,' demanded the Colonel, 'when there's no battlefield?'

But if there were no battlefield, there was a very positive enemy. You would hear a crackle of machine-gun fire ahead, and then, crashing back, a stampede of men and neighing horses, trampling through the brushwood, slipping on the treacherous tufts of grass and moss-covered roots. Some of the staff officers shouted to them, but they paid no attention. Samsonov rebuked the officers. 'Do you expect bravery now?' he asked. 'It's irrelevant in these swamps.'

One of the staff officers was cracking under the strain. He kept saying that we shouldn't be pessimistic, what we were seeing struggling through the trees from time to time were mere sections of our splendid army. The trees were deceiving us. But for them, we could see our magnificent Second, stretched out before us and behind us, all the men under the General's command. Samsonov's face twisted with pain, and the Colonel struck the staff officer across the mouth. He fell off his horse and lay on the ground giggling in a silly manner.

Samsonov beckoned to me. 'Tell the Cossacks to shift for themselves,' he said.

The fallen staff officer suddenly began to scream, a shocking sound that made my horse rear, its skin rippling. 'I must find something to hide behind,' shouted the staff officer. 'Something to hide behind.' He crawled away, and then began to scrabble and burrow in the ground with his bare hands. I rubbed my face; his breakdown seemed less important than the fact I hadn't shaved for two days, and the stubble on my chin was hard and thick. I thought I'd make an ugly corpse.

There was another outburst of fire ahead. 'Another attack coming,' said Samsonov calmly enough.

I volunteered to go forward to try to get some information. I came back with news that there were a couple of machine-guns mounted on the causeway ahead, and a bullet in my shoulder. It didn't hurt much at that point—it was rather as if a giant had taken a huge pinch of me between thumb and forefinger. I was so filthy and bespattered by red mud that the little blood on my tunic didn't show.

Potovsky began to argue about something. I sat down on a moss-covered tree stump; my shoulder was giving trouble now and what with hunger and exhaustion my whole body seemed light and heavy at the same time. I wondered what we were going to do when night came on. The machine-guns opened up again.

The Colonel limped across and leaned up against a tree. I wondered how long he could keep up if we had to stop riding. I couldn't help much now that there was the bullet in my shoulder. The Colonel was still bitterly angry because it had been the best men, in the centre, who'd suffered most.

Unwittingly I'd hunched myself up with the growth of pain. He said sharply, 'Are you all right?'

I tried to grin, found my lips too dry and cracked at first, licked them and managed a grimace. 'Tired,' I said, 'and uncomfortable. I don't like reeking of dried sweat.'

'We're all reeking of dried sweat.'

Potovsky came across, stumbling over the roots. I watched apprehensively; if he went down and smashed his *pince-nez*, I didn't know how he'd manage.

'I've talked him out of it,' he whispered. 'He contemplated suicide—did you realise that?'

The Colonel nodded briefly.

'If we keep fairly close to the railway, we should get back to Willenburg by nightfall—that's only seven miles from the frontier.'

'I think,' said the Colonel, 'you'll find the Germans there before us.'

But Potovsky would not have it.

Before we remounted our tired horses the Colonel said to me, 'You understand what we're up against, don't you, Andrei? If we can't get into Willenburg tonight, we're done for. Horses can't move over this swampy ground in the dark, so we'll have to dismount. Triumphant conclusion to the game of *Poddavki*.'

Poddavki is a Russian game of chess in which the object is to lose all your men.

We mounted again. Only the Colonel and I had brought haversacks (his forethought, not mine). By sharing the contents round, we had exhausted all the food and drink.

If my shoulder throbbed, I played a game—round one more clump of trees, and we'd be in Willenburg and safety, cross one more piece of swampy ground, those dark firs—just past them, and we'd see the trees thinning out, and then there would be Willenburg, and a dirty little hotel with perhaps a bottle with a drain of brandy in it. Just one sip of cognac and I could do anything.

Suddenly ahead of us we heard the trampling of hooves, horses snorting, the clink of metal and leather. We heard voices too, too indistinct to make out the language, but the horses pulled in the direction of the sound.

'Hear that!' whispered Potovsky. 'Friends!'

'I'll go ahead, sir,' I whispered.

The Colonel looked grimly disbelieving; there was no expression on Samsonov's pale face.

A few paces forward and I could distinguish words. German. A few more paces and I caught sight of the patrol. Uhlans. I crawled forward and lay behind a great thicket of brambles, straining to hear snatches of conversation. If this were an advance patrol, there was still a chance, we could break out of cover and—

They were laughing, talking of having a celebration in Willenburg (in the dirty little hotel where my drain of brandy was awaiting me?) once the net was drawn tight and the last prisoners were gathered in. If the fellows already in Willenburg, lucky devils, left anything to celebrate with.

Goodbye Willenburg, Utopia, El Dorado of East Prussia.

I squirmed back with my news.

At nightfall we dismounted; the horses in any case were nearly foundering. We continued on foot. We were supposed to be making for the frontier. We had a compass, but the maps had been entrusted to the officer who'd gone insane. We had to keep striking matches to look at the compass, and eventually the matches gave out. For a time we tried to guide ourselves by the stars, but then the sky clouded over. Ludicrously we stumbled on, hand in hand, so that we shouldn't lose each other in the dark. I kept worrying about the Colonel, who was lame. I suppose I should have worried about Samsonov, whose asthma was very bad indeed now, but part of the time, because I couldn't face up to the implications of having a sick man on our hands, I was persuading myself that this tortured, anguished breathing belonged to something else, some heavy kind of animal, perhaps, and for another part of the time I was actually persuading myself that the hoarse paroxysms, growing longer and longer, were useful and beneficial, a guide to us, telling us the General was still there. And for the rest of the time I simply stopped listening.

I think we covered about six miles altogether after darkness had fallen. God knows how we did it, stumbling blindly as we did. I wanted to laugh because earlier on I'd been worried about what would happen if Potovsky smashed his *pince-nez*.

The General was weakening badly. He could no longer walk unaided. Luckily he was on my right side—my right in every sense, because I could give him an arm to help him on. Potovsky was on his other side. When the General wasn't fighting for breath he kept saying, 'The Czar trusted me. How can I face him after such a disaster?'

Potovsky kept making the proper replies. I said savagely, 'You shouldn't be worrying; the people who should be worrying are Jilinsky and Rennenkampf—' But at the mention of Rennenkampf the dreadful choking paroxysms grew worse.

Eventually he and I—I don't know about the others—couldn't struggle on any further. We stopped for a rest. Just as well, for there was a German bivouac ahead of us. As we rested—if you can call it that—they began to sing. The Colonel said it was the *Hymn of the Battle of Leuthen.*

'What is the time?' asked Samsonov.

I said I thought about one o'clock.

He said, 'I'm just going over there.'

We were among trees with slender trunks—larches, I think. To the left was a thicker darkness—pines, I imagined.

He said, 'When they sing again—'

Then in a lower voice, to me, 'I think you've been hit—you can't go on helping me. Help yourself. They'll need all the young officers.'

The Germans started singing again, and again it was the *Hymn of the Battle of Leuthen.* Samsonov struggled to his feet, stumbled past me. I heard him whispering, 'Oh, Christ, let this be easier, simpler than other things have been.'

The Colonel must have heard it, too, as he went past him to the left. Potovsky didn't hear him. When the single shot sounded, not very loudly, half-drowned by the singing, Potovsky said, 'But I thought I'd argued him out of it!'

He wanted to start looking for the General's body, kept on talking until we started stumbling, fumbling about in the darkness, finding nothing, of course. I said, 'He must be dead—if he were alive we'd hear him trying to get his breath.' I thought it good sense; Potovsky thought it bad taste. Eventually he agreed to abandon the search until it grew lighter; I didn't think we'd be able to do much then because obviously with the dawn the Germans would start moving into the forest, but I wasn't going to argue. It wasn't as if we were abandoning Samsonov, he was safe enough now. I lay on the swampy ground, my face covered with mud, and my shoulder even more soaking wet. I wondered if this were mud too, and out of pure academic interest, put my hand to my arm, then licked my fingers in the darkness. A salty taste, so it was blood.

The Colonel touched me. 'We're not waiting for dawn,' he said. 'We'll never find him in the dark—'

'I'm not talking about Samsonov—he's out of it all now, poor devil. I'm talking about ourselves. When it's light, the Germans will find *us*—get up.'

I didn't want to get up. I didn't want to move. I just wanted to sink deeper and deeper into the mud, to become part of it.

'Get up,' said the Colonel. 'I'm getting out of this damned forest, and I can't do it without you.'

If I hadn't been so stupid with fatigue, I think I might have guessed what he had in mind.

We moved forward, just the two of us. Potovsky still intended to stay behind and strike statuesque poses over the dead general—'But he won't when he sees the *pickelhaubes* coming in,' said the Colonel. The Germans had a fire, lucky devils. The smell of wood smoke and food cooking almost made me cry. These were not cavalry. They probably had machine-guns, at least. My field glasses had been smashed hours before; the Colonel still had his, and used them, but said there wasn't time for me to take a look as well. 'You're tired, aren't you, Andrei?' he said. 'Not too tired, though, to run, if need be, just a little run, Andrei—and you're not too tired to get just one idea in your mind, one order—and obey it. Now listen—I'm going to create a diversion. I'm going off to the right there, and I'm going to throw my binoculars at them with a hell of a crash. Nothing wrong with my arms, at least. And the moment you hear the crash, and you see them looking to the right, you'll get past them on the left. Andrei, you hear me, don't you? And you must do it—it's an order.'

Normally, I think I should have guessed what he intended to do but this was not a normal moment. It was possible therefore for me to grasp only one idea—and that an idea implanted in my mind. The moment I heard the crash, and the Germans looked to the right, I started running.

I was past their bivouac when I realised that there was a sudden blaze of unreal light behind me. I swung round—and the moment I stopped running, my legs gave way and I collapsed, but at least I had turned first so that when I fell I fell in the right direction and saw what happened.

He had seen the searchlight, of course, that was why he hadn't let me use his glasses. And he had never thought of escaping himself; the hurling of the binoculars was the first diversion, he himself offered the second.

He came limping out into the dazzling light of the searchlight as it swung and probed. ('Nothing wrong with my arms at least,' but a lame man would only be a hindrance.)

He guessed my first reaction. He shouted as he stumbled forward, 'He bids you live long!'*

The machine-gun opened up. He was hit but he kept coming on.

'He's mad,' said a German officer. He shrugged, did nothing to stop the machine-gun.

'I bid you live long, Andrei!'

Perhaps they didn't think they were pumping bullets into a man, he looked like an emaciated scarecrow. Since Manchuria he'd had a scarecrow's jerky walk.

He was still calling to me when he took the last stumbling pace forward, and pitched face downwards, and they still went on pumping bullets into him.

* The traditional announcement of a death in Russia.

44

4

'We are happy to make such sacrifices'

THERE WAS greyness above the trees. I was lying face downwards amid larches that were ghostly in that wan light. I was cold, but others were colder. Still, lucky devils, they didn't have to wake up and face the tedious business of living, and trying to escape, and having to think.

'*He bids you live long!*'

I set my teeth and began to crawl diligently forward.

When the Cossack patrol found me, they nearly ran me through. I was so caked with blood and mud that the colour and cut of the rags I wore were undetectable.

Just in time I staggered to my feet, hauling myself up by the nearest stirrup.

'Chevalier Garde,' I said.

'Second Army?' they asked disbelievingly. And then, 'Where's General Samsonov?'

'He shot himself in the forest. He couldn't face the Czar. We kept telling him it wasn't his fault—'

I fell down again, and didn't feel them picking me up.

After that, being jolted in a cart. Half a dozen other wounded with me. All ragged, filthy, some half-naked, some streaming with blood. Most clasped a medallion or ikon of St Nicholas; none made any complaint. There was smoke about us, and this scared me, I thought we were in the middle of another battle, but a big Cossack said it was the smoke of villages being burned in the retreat.

When I came to again it was dark—except behind us, where the sky was red with the flames of other villages. In the darkness I put out my sound arm to touch my companions carefully. One—two—three—four—five—six. All cold. All dead. Stiffening now with medallions

45

and ikons still clutched in rigid hands. The cart lurched and one corpse fell across me, its arm pressing across my face. I fought the poor dead thing off as if it were an enemy, dragged myself up at the side of the cart. Thank God the Cossacks were still there. I begged them to let me get out of this death-cart, all corpses; if they had a spare horse I'd stick on somehow. The big Cossack I'd spoken to before leaned over, and took me up before him as if I were a baby.

'Where's Rennenkampf?' I asked. 'He left us to this, he's to blame, not poor Samsonov—they'll have to do something to him, won't they?'

'Nothing will happen to him,' said the Cossack, 'him with his German name and his German cousins living over the frontier. He'll get protection—'

'Who'd protect a swine like that?'

'People high up like him with relatives in Germany. People born themselves in Germany.'

'Are you talking about the Czarina?'

'She's a German. Alyssa Gessenskaya her name is.'

'But she's a good Russian woman now. Were you in Petersburg the day war was declared? You should have seen her praying then—'

'Ah, that's her cleverness. All Germans are clever. And it's not Petersburg any longer, we have to call it Petrograd now. Damned silly, I call that. If it's a city run by Germans, it'll go on just the same, even if they give it a Russian name.'

By the time we reached hospital the bandage on my shoulder was stiff as wood, being saturated with clotted blood, pus, and, eventually, vermin. They had to burn what was left of my uniform, shave my head; it took three baths to get the accumulated filth off me.

A provincial military hospital at first, desperately inadequately equipped, with an inexperienced staff. Long sleepless nights alternating with dreams of blazing searchlights, and machine-gun fire, and of being lost, wandering lost, hand in hand with dead men, in dark forests, swamps, lying in mud in the blackness, waiting for the mud to creep up to drown you, to cover nose and mouth—and eyes, it was worst when it came up to your eyes, because you kept them open, staring into the blackness, and the mud came against your eyeballs, and—

That's when I woke up, and found there was no mud, no darkness, above all, no mud.

Then they carried us on to a well-equipped hospital train running direct to Petersburg—I couldn't call it Petrograd, I still can't—where one evening the nurse gave me sleeping tablets earlier than usual.

'Get a good night's sleep now—before the excitement tomorrow. I'll let you into a secret. We're going to have a Visit.'

It was not heartening, that visit.

By this time I was a walking case. The walking cases were supposed to sit bolt upright in a long row of chairs until the Imperial party entered, to be quite accurate until thirty seconds before the Imperial party entered. Then we were to leap up and gaze straight ahead with loyal if vacant eyes. I couldn't bear the prospect. I knew that the Czarina wouldn't be good at talking to people, and I didn't know whether it would be more embarrassing for us both if, recognising me, she suddenly began to talk naturally, or if she carried on a dreadful stilted conversation. If she met me by chance, as it were, in a corridor, it would be best for all concerned. So once we had all been arranged on our chairs, I arose suddenly and said to the Sister, 'I'm going to be sick.'

'You can't be sick now!' she cried desperately.

'Can I not! If you want proof—'

'Oh, really!' she said, pushing me distractedly from the room. 'Quick! Down the corridor!'

I went down the corridor and stopped abruptly outside the nearest soldiers' ward.

She was there already. It was unutterably depressing—though interesting, I suppose, to a dispassionate observer— to watch the men's faces. She talked with each of them. I knew how deeply she felt for them, how hard she was trying to express that sympathy, but always there was the barrier. She spoke Russian fluently enough now, but it might as well have been a foreign language, the men simply did not seem to understand her. They lay watching her with anxious, frightened eyes, almost like scared animals. If it came to that they were almost as dumb as animals.

It couldn't be that her appearance cowed them, for she was dressed as a nurse. That was a mistake. They were surprised and disappointed —a Czarina should look like a Czarina. But for anyone to hint as much to her would be a sheer waste of time. She could never understand that while there were thousands of women in Russia who could take care of the wounded, only she could play the larger role of Czarina, arousing emotions, stirring loyalties—

'Andrei! We couldn't believe it was you! You're so changed!'

Olga, gazing at me as if she had seen a ghost.

'It's because he's so pale,' said Anastasia. 'When his face was tanned his hair and eyes always looked lighter, and now—'

'Oh, Andrei, when we heard you'd been with the Second Army—' began Marie.

'We mustn't stop talking to him here,' said Tatiana authoritatively. 'We have to go to talk to everyone. I don't think he should be in the corridor, in any case.'

'No, I shouldn't,' I said, retreating hastily. 'I was supposed to be rushing along to be sick.'

'How marvellous!' said Anastasia. '*Keep* rushing along the corridor till we come out again.'

Tatiana marshalled them firmly into the ward.

I stayed in the corridor. I couldn't bear to see a repetition in my own ward. Five minutes more and the Czarina came out. The girls must have told her about me, because she looked quickly about her, and saw me immediately. It was a different woman who came up to me. '*Tis time, descend, be stone no more*, I thought to myself. But why couldn't she have made the sign of the Cross over the others, why had she kept the tears from her eyes at the sight of those in far worse case than I, why hadn't she let them kiss her hand?

After she had gone I did, indeed, feel sick. But then the four girls were surrounding me. 'When will you be coming out? You must come to Czarskoe.' Anastasia.

'Andrei, we didn't know you were with the Second Army. If we had —' Olga.

'I've already said that,' said Marie.

'Did you know we're all training to be nurses?' demanded Anastasia. 'We're all going to qualify as Sisters of Charity. Can you see me as a Sister of Charity, Andrei? We're going to be at operations and everything—'

'Once we've qualified,' said Marie dubiously. 'I hope I shan't cry.'

'Princess Gedroits, a professor of surgery, is instructing us,' said Tatiana.

'And when we've passed our examinations, we'll be Sisters Romanov 1, 2, 3, 4,' said Anastasia. 'The Sisters Romanov—it sounds like a circus turn, doesn't it?'

'Anastasia, you really are impossible!' protested Tatiana. 'Come along, Mamma will wonder where on earth we are.'

48

'She'll know we've been talking to Andrei—'

'You've been talking to Andrei, you mean. No one else has had much of a chance.'

Olga had said scarcely anything.

But as they turned to go, she said quietly, 'You're different, Andrei.'

'I've grown up, I suppose.'

'I'm growing up too,' she said eagerly. 'Now that I'm doing this hospital work, you can't say any longer that I'm cut off from the world.'

'Now a *doctor* is coming to look for us,' wailed Tatiana.

The doctor, in fact, had come to say that the men had prepared a little concert for the visit; Her Imperial Majesty could not stay, but had graciously said that if their Imperial Highnesses wished—

They accepted enthusiastically. 'And mind you come and sit by us, Andrei!' said Anastasia.

'Your Imperial Highness does me too great an honour,' I said formally, to the satisfaction of Tatiana and the doctor. Her Imperial Highness herself went off in a fit of giggles.

It wasn't a particularly good concert as far as artistry was concerned, but the men sang with an enthusiasm I felt they would not have shown if the Czarina had been present. It was mostly choruses. I remember how they sang *The Song of the Volga Boatmen*, and *The Ballad of Stenka Razin*. Marie cried—she always cried when she heard *The Ballad of Stenka Razin*. Anastasia clapped everything vigorously. Tatiana talked graciously to the matron and the doctors. Olga turned back to me. 'I *am* coming out into the world,' she said fiercely.

'I've changed my mind,' I said. 'I don't want you to come out too far now. Reality is vile.'

I was discharged from hospital, given a few weeks' leave. After that, since my arm might give me trouble for months, I was to report to the Stavka* for a month or two. 'You will like serving under the Grand Duke Nicholas,' said Mother, 'and you're not fit for another field appointment yet, are you?'

A telephone call; I was to go out to Czarskoe.

I gave the Czar a bald narrative of what I had seen in East Prussia, but certain things I could and would not leave out. A dead man's

* Stavka was the headquarters of the Russian Commander-in-Chief, the Grand Duke Nicholas, cousin to the Czar.

D   49

despairing, 'The Czar trusted me.' The ruse of another dead man that enabled me to escape. And another matter.

I said bluntly, 'As long as our men haven't been sacrificed for nothing, sir—'

He stroked his moustache. 'No, Andrei, it wasn't for nothing. I ordered my cousin, the Grand Duke Nicholas, to open the way to Berlin at the earliest possible moment at all costs. The French Ambassador begged for an immediate offensive, or the French Army might be overwhelmed. And the switch of German troops saved Paris. When General la Guiche—you know him, of course—expressed his sympathy, the Grand Duke replied, with my approval, "*Nous sommes heureux de faire tels sacrifices pour nos alliées.*" After all, it turned the whole course of the war.'

He meant, of course, that Paris was saved. The French might argue that no price was too great to pay for this; I would say otherwise.

A quarter of a million Russians were slaughtered or captured in those marshes and forests; in a sickening defeat we lost our best men, squandered our scanty munitions; the old Russian Army had been destroyed by the end of August. Not only Russia, but her Allies, would soon feel the effect of this.

I wondered when our allies would show equal joy—and alacrity—to make commensurate sacrifices for us.

I didn't want to go straight home to Mother in such a mood. I went into the Club and stared unseeingly at the papers.

'Hullo!' said a lieutenant I knew slightly. 'Back from Czarskoe? Alexei solved his problem yet?'

I stared. 'The Czarevitch? What problem?'

'Do you mean you haven't heard the joke about the general who went out there and found Alexei bewildered? "When the Russians get beaten, Papa cries. When the Germans are beaten, Mamma cries. When do I cry?"'

'There's a letter from your uncle,' said Mother. 'He gave it to someone going to the Embassy in Sweden to send on from Stockholm.'

Uncle Raoul wrote:

'Well, we advanced in the massed formation of the last century, assembling in full view of the efficient German artillery observers. My cowardly suggestions of surprise or concealment were scorned— hadn't we *élan* in abundance? Flags, regimental bands, officers in nice white gloves and twenty paces forward—on we swept like a stage army from an Offenbach operetta, bugles blowing—full tilt into twentieth-century massed firepower.

'Then, my God, an even better idea sprung into the mind of one of our *"Garde à vous-fixe!"** war lords. We had dismounted cavalry—horses dead or exhausted. Send them charging across the field *armed with long lances.*

'*Tac-tac-tac* from the damned German guns, and they were done for.

'So those of us who were left fell back. By September 2 our heroic government had fled to Bordeaux. The forsaken Parisians began to sing a doleful version of the *Marseillaise:*

> '*Aux gares, citoyens!*
> *Montez dans les wagons!*

'What has saved the situation temporarily is your invasion of East Prussia—which wrung from this Western Front sorely needed regiments—and the characteristic that a month ago it would have been blasphemous to allege the French soldier possessed—tenacity in defence. So—*adieu, élan.* The next stage is inevitable. I have already been summoned by my general—I don't think he'll last much longer, his nerve's gone, but he's trying to do a little to retrieve his reputation. "I remember," he said, "that two years ago you told me that the Balkan Wars had proved the value of trenches." By silent mutual consent we made no reference to the reception given to my ideas *then.*

'*Au revoir,* my dear Andrei. Damn all politicians. As your grandfather has frequently remarked, *au fond* even the best of them are a low lot.'

The leaves had all fallen now; a chill wind from the north blew them gustily about the Petersburg streets. Soon it would be winter; there was uneasiness, nervousness, an air of gloomy tension because against all expectation it seemed as if the war would last until 1915 at least. The enthusiasm of late July and early August gave way, as far as ordinary folk were concerned, to loss of hope and apathy, always with the danger that this might give way to discontent, and discontent in its turn give way to violence. And one became conscious of our isolation from our Allies. Our geography couldn't be altered, and it didn't always fight for us.

* The 'Attention!' command for a general.

5

Five Cartridges per Soldier

IT WAS good to leave Petersburg with the mist creeping in from the sea, seeping into everything.

Stavka was at Baranovitchi at this point, a few trains with huts serving as workshops set up on sandy soil among pine trees, in a dull bleak countryside. The Grand Duke Nicholas suffered more than anyone else from this railway accommodation; being six foot six, he kept cracking his head against the low doorways. Strips of white paper were pasted at all danger spots so eventually the risk of permanent concussion grew less.

Mother had said to me the evening before I caught my train, 'Were there any reactions at Czarskoe to your appointment?'

'It was rather pointedly ignored.'

She nodded thoughtfully. 'The Czarina opposed the Grand Duke's appointment as Commander-in-Chief. It's the old story—any man who's popular or admired is disloyal to the Czar. She doesn't try to conceal her feelings. When he left Petersburg for Stavka, the Czar was supposed to come to the station to take formal leave. The Grand Duke and his staff and their families all waited—the escort too—crowds all about the station—but the Czar didn't turn up, the Czarina wouldn't let him. I've never seen such a subdued gathering; they said goodbye in whispers, boarded the train in silence—'

'That was unpardonable,' I said.

'And, of course,' said Mother, 'the Grand Duke loathes Rasputin, and doesn't mind who knows it.'

He had, I discovered after joining Stavka, received a telegram from Rasputin saying he intended to visit Headquarters. 'Come,' the Grand Duke wired back, 'and I'll hang you.'

The Czarina detested the Grand Duke for his popularity; possibly her detestation was all the greater because even she had to accept that he was a mystic figure to the soldiers—the kind of figure she wished the

Czar to be. They—particularly the men and junior officers—never lost faith in him. To them he was almost a legend. You were always hearing fresh stories about him from them—he'd discovered some treachery, he'd dismissed Major X for laziness, Colonel Y because he ill-treated his men, General Z because he was incapable of leading his troops. The most incredible stories were believed and circulated, and in all of them the Grand Duke invariably appeared as the perfect knight, avenging wrongs, the scourge of Germans and pro-Germans, the protector of ordinary folk.

To my misfortune, I didn't serve under the Grand Duke later when he was Commander-in-Chief in the Caucasus, and took Erzerum, but I suppose he captured my imagination so much that when he went south, part of my mind went with him, I went on identifying myself with his fortunes and so when I was reading *Greenmantle* by the Scottish writer John Buchan, with its description of the capture of Erzerum, there were tears in my eyes. '*For sweeping down the glen came a cloud of grey cavalry on little wiry horses, a cloud which stayed not for the rear of the fugitives, but swept on like a flight of rainbows, with the steel of their lanceheads glittering in the winter sun—*'

One is so damnably, humiliatingly grateful for any word of praise from an ally! One became more or less inured to accusations that 'Russia let us down'—Russia who lost fifteen men to every one German. It is the occasional kindness that is unbearable.

The field army I rejoined, fully cured, with the ill-deserved rank of captain towards the end of 1914 was very different from that of three months before. That—the old Russian Army—above all, the officers—had died in East Prussia. For they had gone, the casualties among them had been frightful, and it is the officers, the platoon leaders, the company and battalion commanders, who make a weapon out of the huge shapeless mass that is a modern army.

I came back to a changed army, and a changed kind of fighting. As in France, as autumn fell, the troops began to dig themselves in— at first nothing more than little rifle-pits, then shallow trenches, eventually deeper ones.* From the air, these trenches looked like mass graves; they were to become precisely this for many.

This pattern of trench warfare was followed on both Western and

* Colonel Knox, the British Military Attaché, reported, 'A call was made for volunteers from cavalry regiments for service in infantry units, but few responded.'

Eastern fronts, with the important difference that the Russian soldier loathed the idea, and evaded trench digging, if possible. Many officers turned a blind eye to it. The principle of entrenchment had been neglected in peacetime; a few unorthodox officers might echo Uncle Raoul's 'See what happened in the Balkan Wars!' but most had an almost pathological hatred of the idea. It was a reaction from the war against Japan; Kuropatkin had dug up most of Manchuria—and then had gone on retreating without using his prepared positions, and there was a tacit understanding after 1905 that this kind of warfare should be avoided at all costs. No decision could have been more popular— the troops detested working at field fortifications. In any case, as a general once remarked to Uncle Raoul, 'We know that Germany plans to snatch victory in a short war, defeating her opponents rapidly—she won't waste time on a war of position, so why should we!'

All the officers in the world, of course, could not have made up for another deficiency—the shortage of munitions, above all, of heavy artillery. Without this no real result was possible. For a successful attack one should assemble enormous masses of artillery of various calibres, precede the actual assault by a violent bombardment, sweeping away barbed-wire entanglements, demolishing enemy trenches and their occupants, and when the infantry attacked support them with a further artillery barrage. If you wish to win the war, you sustain the offensive spirit; an army which can only defend its front is doomed to defeat. And we couldn't even defend our front, because—well, let us take the Carpathian campaign of 1915 as an example.

The German, Mackensen, started it in May, firing three hundred rounds of shrapnel against each one fired by us.

Statistics, however, can't give you the whole picture—of how our guns would fall silent, and our men would have to face the German charge with rifles of the 1878 model *with orders not to fire unnecessarily* and to take ammunition from the killed and wounded. Some new drafts were actually sent forward weaponless—there would be rifles waiting for them at the front, they were told. Well, so there might be—if we were advancing. In that happy state of affairs special detachments were detailed to collect the rifles, Russian or enemy, left on the battlefield. This couldn't be done on a retreat, the rifles of the dead and wounded fell into enemy hands. The further we retreated, the greater became the number of weaponless men—and you can't train men without weapons.

As for the drafts supposed to 'replace' the old Army, generally they knew nothing except how to march. I don't exaggerate. As God is my judge, many couldn't even load their rifles. I suppose this was one way of solving the ammunition shortage—

This poor army I rejoined before the snows melted. I found a few survivors of the old Imperial Army, who through bitter experience had grasped several essential facts.

One; that the only way to gain any ground at all was to prepare the attack with plenty of artillery, vast masses of it, of huge calibre, plus mountains of ammunition to be fired by it.

Two; that, if you were not so ambitious, and merely wanted to defend yourself, you needed bullets for your rifle.

Three; that, in either case, raw courage wasn't enough. It was no match for high explosive or barbed wire.

Above all; that so many men had died, and nothing had been achieved except terrible futility . . .

They—the survivors—were completely discouraged. They had lost all their old enthusiasm, carried out orders mechanically. It was dreadful to see the destruction of morale which had once been so high.

The first enemy offensive came even before the snow had melted. Every senior officer had to admit 'they' were planning something when 'they' began to be fantastically prodigal with their shells. There was a sudden frantic interest in trenches—ours weren't deep enough, we must get to work on them. But we couldn't because the earth was still frozen three to four feet deep. The artillery was now registering all along our front line; HE shells had long since flattened the barbed wire; the noise had gone on so long you didn't think of iron sledgehammers now, you thought heavy Heaven itself was falling on you to crush you, it seemed to assault not only your ears, but all your senses; you huddled numb, blind, deaf in the shallow remains of a trench now nothing more than a rubbish dump of smashed, shattered humanity.

And then the crescendo of noise died away. You found you could feel after all, you could feel sick because you knew why the din had stopped, the attack was coming. Within seconds it started again, but the shells weren't plastering us any longer, the barrage was moving towards our rear to stop reinforcements coming up.

It was odd, that lull. In it the slightest sound seemed to come like a thunderclap. What I found particularly unbearable was the attempt made by the wounded—where it was possible—to check their moans and cries which now carried so horribly in the still, frosty air.

I peered over the shattered parapet, trying to pierce the smoke. 'Any minute now,' I said. 'Be ready—'

A lieutenant, his voice unnaturally loud (or perhaps not so unnaturally, for we were not waiting machines, but men) cried, 'Can't we get the artillery at them?'

'On the field-telephone the shellfire cut days ago?' The men, incredibly, laughed. All the time I was fumbling with a flare, but my fingers were numb, and every second counted. In any case our guns always registered too late, if at all—there was no point in ploughing up No-Man's Land after the attackers had already passed over it.

My fingers were numb, and every second counted. The men stared at me big-eyed. I managed to grin. 'Where's your patriotic pride, Lieutenant? Don't you know the Russian steamroller's such a wonderful machine it can function without any oil to run its works?'

And again, incredibly, they laughed.

I managed to set off the flare. And then:

'Here they come!' I shouted, crossing myself. 'God be with us, lads!' And there they were, grey figures crouching on the parapet, throwing in hand-grenades, then jumping down. Eventually I managed to organise some kind of resistance behind a traverse and beat off the attack. 'It won't be for long,' I warned the dozen or so men with me. 'They can't get at us with the bayonet, but once they get more hand-grenades we're done for. So we're getting out while we can.'

The ground had been too frozen to dig a communication trench. 'We get up and run in the open, Your Honour?' came a whisper. This wretched icy hole seemed at the moment as safe and strong as a fortress.

'Yes, in the open,' I said. 'They can't kill all of us.'

And on with the deadly psychology of retreat, and corpses, corpses, corpses, fewer living men. What looked like trenches were now mass-graves.

If we had ever possessed sufficient artillery support, this would not have been the case—far from it. We could have counter-attacked. The enemy assailants should suddenly have become defenders, enduring what we had endured, scrabbling desperately to throw up a parapet on what had been the back of the captured trench before the inevitable counter-attack, being pulverised as we had been, and then, as we had done, made to listen to the brief silence before the shifting of the barrage, shells crashing into the second wave of their troops coming up in support—

But we didn't have the artillery, so it all remained academic textbook stuff.

When the snow turned to mud, there was a brief respite, which brought little consolation. We knew it was no more than the lull in the bombardment before the fresh assault. Once the mud had dried and became dust—as it did with astounding speed—we could expect something frightful. We could only pray that it would, notwithstanding, prove endurable.

By mid-April we all knew that the biggest offensive of the war was on its way. Colossal numbers of guns and troops were being brought up, sited; there was tremendous digging as forward trenches were advanced. The enemy had probably thought up some new tactics too. I had my hands full with my drafts of new recruits, schooling the poor devils for what was to come; it was at this point that I received an order to report back to base with some half dozen veterans of the winter campaigns, as the Czar was coming on a visit.

To say the least, it was an honour that the overtaxed army could have done without. A formal visit of this kind was always a damnable nuisance, distracting officers and men from essential work and always therefore creating disorganisation, but this particular visit was particularly ill-timed, taking place as it did on the very eve of the big attack the enemy had been preparing for two months.

'Doesn't he *know*?' ventured the lieutenant.

I grimaced and said, 'I should imagine he thinks the visit will hearten the men.'

'It won't, you know, sir,' said the lieutenant suddenly. 'With respect, you know how there's this general belief that the Czar's unlucky —that everything he does will turn out badly.'

I nodded, thinking it better not to add that the Czar himself was of this opinion.

It all proved horribly reminiscent of the Czarina's visit to the hospital; worse, in a way, because, as I heard one disappointed private whisper, they hadn't realised he was such a *little* man. His physical insignificance was needlessly emphasised at the beginning because no arrangement had been made about horses, and the Czar began to walk down the line on foot which meant those in the rear couldn't see him.

Luckily the Commander-in-Chief, accompanying him, ordered up a car, and suggested the Czar should go down the ranks standing up in it.

Well, he gave the men the customary greeting, but after that failed to find the right words to say to them, though he tried hard. It was extraordinary, this inability to talk to troops *en masse*, because in individual conversations he always showed the utmost charm. The whole business was a series of embarrassments; he was nervous, didn't know what to say or do, where to go. The men stood there in the bitter cold, and the lack of enthusiasm was almost suffocating. His bearing didn't impress them, his manner didn't reach their hearts. And yet he was trying hard, we all knew that, he was doing all he could.

My only cause for gratitude was that I was not presented to him.

And when the great enemy offensive began, it was worse even than what we had expected, or endured in the past.

They had evolved a new method of attack all right; because of the unbroken front lines, flank attacks were impossible, so, searching for some variant of the frontal assault, they'd gone in for the 'phalanx' method. They assembled enormous masses of artillery of various calibres, including 12-inch guns, they had brought up seemingly endless reserves of infantry, all concentrated in the particular sector selected for breaking our front. The cleverness of the idea was this—once they'd forced a gap and enlarged it, the Russian sectors on each side of the gap had to retire although not actually under attack themselves.

Not that we hadn't done our part, too. Our fortified areas were below criticism—we'd known the attack was coming, but in too many regiments no real preparations had been made to meet it. And there was no heavy artillery with which to retaliate. There were no munitions at all.

In that same spring of 1915 the French in a single day were firing 276 rounds a gun from their 75s for the whole of their attacking force of twelve divisions; I was staring through the smoke as the bombardment lifted and was reminding my men that they had only five cartridges each. After those were expended, we were expected to meet howitzers with bare hands.

The retreat before that German offensive in the spring of 1915 was the second great martyrdom of the Russian army. We had no shells, no cartridges, but we had marching enough, bloody losses enough, physical and mental weariness enough, fear of the future enough.

Two regiments were wiped out by gunfire alone. At times you wondered why a merciful God kept us living.

And then—just once—some munitions *did* arrive, not really heavy stuff, just for our 6-inch guns, and that night I squatted in our trench and scribbled a letter:

'Uncle Raoul, for three days our 6-inch battery was silent, but then— a miracle! We received no less than fifty shells. Immediately—I don't exaggerate—this wonderful information was conveyed by telephone to every regiment and every company, and we cheered, we cheered, Uncle Raoul, as if the hosts of Heaven themselves had descended to our aid!

'For the rest, they expend metal, and we expend life.'

By the end of the offensive the enemy had occupied nearly a quarter of European Russia, captured two million prisoners, inflicted incalculable casualties.

It wasn't war, it was carnage, yet we had fallen back, we who remained, in good order. There was no trace of panic, or mutiny. And the Grand Duke remained the soldiers' hero.

I was informed that I was to receive the Cross of the Order of St George. Everyone said inevitably, 'Don't forget your number.'

Everyone who gets the decoration gets a number, reckoned from the time of its institution, the idea being that on Judgment Day there will be a last review at which all holders of the George Cross will rise in numbered places under the command of Suvorov. Presumably St George himself will also be present.

At the end of June I was at Czarskoe to be decorated. The Czar talked to me afterwards; I wasn't looking my usual cheerful self, he said.

Wondering if I'd always, then, run round grinning like a dog, I said that I found Petrograd—luckily I remembered in time to give the Russian name—a very depressing place.

'I know how you feel,' he said. 'I find it intensely depressing myself, I can't tell you how much I look forward to my visits to the Front.'

Mother had not come to see me decorated. She sent word that she wanted me to join her in the country as soon as I could. Her reason she did not put in writing.

6

'Gracious lady'

SHE WAS waiting at the top of the wide, shallow steps when I finally reached our country house. 'Forgive me, darling, for not coming to the station to meet you, but I daren't stay away from him too long, he frets so much, gets the horrors again—I'm the only person who can drive the horrors away, but now you'll be able to do it, too—'

'*Maman*, for God's sake, who are you talking about?'

'About—' began Mother, and then, abruptly, she stopped. 'No,' she said slowly, putting her arm through mine, 'I shan't tell you. I want to see if you react as I did.'

Into the hall, up the staircase, along the gallery, into the room looking westward where Grandfather always slept when he was with us, where, now, a grey-haired man older than Grandfather lay on a couch before the fire. He put out shaking hands to me, and said, half-crying, 'I can't get up, forgive me, I'm a cripple now.' His face was a skull covered with taut, papery skin. It seemed no thicker than the blade of an axe. I thought in panic, 'Oh, God, I'm so scared I can't even think what language he's talking.'

And then he said, 'Andreas—'

The Austrian form of my name.

Vienna nearly a year before, in another life, and light-hearted talk of a tour including Sarajevo.

I was kneeling beside him, my arms about him, choking, 'Franz! Franz von Mayrhofen.'

I was sobbing; he was making dreadful dry, racking, retching sounds; Mother said level-voiced, dry-eyed, 'I didn't break it gently to you, my darling, because I wanted you to feel as I felt when I first saw him—and he's much better now.'

We didn't talk much then; Franz was in such a state that the excitement of my coming necessitated sedatives after half an hour. But when he had fallen asleep, clutching Mother's hand like a scared child, she began to tell me what she had pieced together from the broken, halting whispers which were all he could manage yet.

He had been captured in the first weeks of the war; he had been the only survivor of a small rear-guard in Galicia shelled to shreds.

Prisoners-of-war were sent at first to one of three great centres, Petersburg, Moscow or Kiev. Franz was sent to Moscow; he was badly wounded, and so he was put into a so-called hospital where he received nothing which could be described as treatment. For weeks—literally weeks—his bandages were not changed, so blood poisoning set in, and eventually his leg had to be amputated.

Doctors did their best, but the prisoner-of-war hospitals were wretchedly staffed and supplied, and what staff there were seemed paralysed rather than stimulated by difficulties. As for the orderlies, they stole the prisoners' clothes, and those who survived had to face the Russian winter half-dressed and barefoot.

'How long was he there?' I asked, and Mother said until December. 'But things got better then, didn't they? The Czar visited Moscow last December, and went to a prisoner-of-war hospital.'

'Is this the face of a man for whom things improved? He said, *"Our worst day was the day before your Czar visited the hospital. We— the lousy and gangrenous—had to be turned out, sent to barracks outside the city. Men who'd just been operated on, the dying—they were all moved. No one was spared. Your Nicholas' visit cost many lives."*'

A few days after the Czar's visit, Franz was discharged from hospital. His wounds were still open, but he was passed as well enough to be moved from Moscow—as far as Siberia. In hospital, despite the dirt, the vermin and the stench, he had told himself desperately, 'This is abnormal; things are bound to improve.' In Siberia he realised what 'normal' life was to be.

Three men died in their wagon—in transit. The corpses were left there; the correct number of prisoners had to be handed over at the end of the journey.

There was a march of thirty-five miles to the camp. This was the Siberian winter. Hardly any prisoners had overcoats, a quarter had no shoes and had wrapped their feet in straw and rags. Many were suffering from starvation, and among the others the appalling quality of the food provided (after most of the funds for it had been embezzled) caused blindness and scurvy. But when Franz and other officers protested, there were only blows, curses, and the inevitable, '*Pasholl*—Go on!'

61

It was the first Russian word most of those Austrians heard—'Go on!' For many it was also the last.

But some survived and came to a camp where they were treated as criminals, were denied the right to attend Catholic services, were horse-whipped, kicked, starved, died in greater filth than they would have let animals die in on their fathers' farms. The officers were separated from their men, to their mutual bitter grief.

Then in February 1915, a government decree said that peasants and farmers were to be handed over as many prisoners-of-war as they wanted.

'But not Franz, surely!' I interrupted. 'How can anyone look so ill and go on living—'

'In his camp the doctors classified men as really ill if they had only a few days to live. If they had typhus or smallpox they were classified as slightly ill. If they didn't have typhus or smallpox, they were healthy —even if they had TB, gangrene and dysentery—'

But Franz—though classified as healthy—was ignored by most peasants until one came fairly close—and Franz croaked the longest Russian sentence of his life, learned in laborious desperation. 'Take me and let the Hamiltons of Petersburg know. You won't lose by it.'

'But why hadn't he sent word to us before?'

'I asked him that. He said he'd only been one soldier among many— there was to be no preferential treatment. But now—well, he thought he was dying, and he knew his mother had no idea what had become of him. When I first saw him, he kissed my hand and said, "Please give Mother all my love—that's why I tried to get to you—but for God's sake don't let her know the conditions in which I lived and died." '

There was silence for a moment, then:

'That Franz should be brought to this!' I whispered.

'No,' Mother corrected me. 'That *anyone* should be brought to this.'

After a moment she said, 'I'll get Franz out of the country, and I must go to the Czar, mustn't I?'

'*Maman*, you know he has this—this crazy idea of what the ordinary Russian is really like. If you go to him with a story told you by an Austrian—'

'Then,' said Mother, 'I must go to Ekaterinburg to see for myself.'

She went to Ekaterinburg. She managed to see—and hear—enough and returned to Petersburg, asked for an audience, and was received in the Czarina's boudoir. The Czarina lay on her couch, the Czar walked nervously to and fro, tugging his moustache, staring out of the

62

window, lighting cigarette after cigarette. Mother quietly recounted how she had verified all Franz had told her—'Although this was not easy. The camp authorities so contrived it that I arrived after dark, and took me into a hospital—a hospital with no coverings, no pillows, not even straw to lie on!—which was lit only by oil-lamps. Luckily I had foreseen this, and I told my chauffeur to bring up my car and turn the headlights on so as to illumine the place.'

She related what the headlights had shown, ended by quoting what had been said to her before—'They were dying in filth they wouldn't let the animals on their fathers' farms lie in.'

She had said to the Commandant in cold fury, 'I am coming back tomorrow. I want to see things in broad daylight.'

She had returned, to find hundreds of lousy living skeletons of men —adequately clad. Immediately she was suspicious; gratefully she remembered that while it was general knowledge that she was French, the Austrian part of her ancestry was less well known. She didn't think the camp authorities realised she spoke German—however, deciding to take no risks, when she called out to a row of men standing before a hut, she spoke in the most drawling of Viennese accents, '*The Old Gentleman's** *my godfather. Tell me, is it always like this?*'

A tall, haggard man replied, 'Gracious lady, we knew something was up last night—they started giving us palliasses, boots, beds, there were medicines for the doctors—they had us up again at dawn doling out our back pay—oh, we knew something was up!'

'I'll do what I can,' said Mother.

A score of voices shouted desperately, '*Vergisst uns nicht*—Don't forget us.'

I could easily picture how Mother had told all this at Czarskoe. That magnificent, almost unique fusion of the two sides of her ancestry— that flame-like glow of vitality coming from her mother illuminating her face, lighting up her eyes, with the disciplined quality inherited from her father controlling her voice so that she spoke in a steady, almost professional manner—like Uncle Raoul discussing a military problem. Thirdly, the qualities all her own—courtesy, natural grace, mingled with independent judgement. Any of these aspects, I think, should have brought belief, combined, they should have compelled acceptance from Thomas Didymus himself. But there was no acceptance on the part of her hearers.

* The Emperor Franz Josef.

I asked her, 'Did the Czar look angry?'

'No,' she said, 'but then he never does, does he? If you tell him something he doesn't want to hear, he tries to get away from you—remember how he galloped away from your father the last time they really talked together! He couldn't gallop away from me, so he stared out of the window with a—a trapped expression on his face—trapped, unwilling—'

'Irritated?'

'No, but petulant—you can be petulant without being irritated. He was trying to close his mind to all I was saying, but he couldn't manage it altogether, and then, his expression changed again, he looked uneasy, he even said, "Yes, we have heard something about this—there've been defects of organisation—"'

'Sir, it's not merely a question of organisation. Helpless men, soldiers who've honourably done their duty, are treated with the most appalling brutality by peasant guards—'

It was here that the Czarina spoke. Mother had been conscious of the rigidity of her pose ever since the audience began; there was a magnificent bowl of creamy freesias and roses behind her—Mother never forgot the harmony and graciousness of the flowers. But there was nothing gracious in the cold, stiff voice that said angrily, 'We admit there are faults in the way the camps have been set up, but, for the rest—Remember, Avoye, that you're speaking to the Ruler of the Russians about his people!'

'Your Majesty,' said Mother desperately, 'those Austrian prisoners know the Russian peasants better than we ever can—they've lived with them.'

The Czar lit another cigarette and said with nervous affability that he was sure Mother was mistaken. He knew for a fact that *because* Siberia was so remote from the pernicious influence of western culture her peasants retained all the old-fashioned virtues.

Ah, God, thought Mother, with a sense of sudden fatality, Rasputin, of course! She stared at the creamy flowers; if she saw the Czarina's ecstatic face, she would cry out in protest.

The Czarina said intensely, 'A peasant, especially a Siberian peasant, is closer to God, indeed, is *sent* from God—' With sudden, shocking violence she cried, 'Don't look away from me, Avoye! You know of whom I'm speaking!'

So it could be avoided no longer. Mother drew a deep breath. Yes, Your Majesty, I do, and would to God that you knew nothing of

64

Siberian peasants.' She stood up swiftly. 'You're challenging me for my opinion, so I must give it. A Siberian peasant can drink like a beast, indulge in the pastimes of the devil—and could prove the death of the dynasty and Russia!'

She would tell me no more details—except that the Czar had bidden her goodbye in his usual way, then left her for a few moments with the Czarina. And of those last few moments, nothing.

No longer in attendance at Court, she now had more time to ponder on escape routes from Ekaterinburg, to be taken by only the most desperate of men, who feared that if they did not take the most suicidal of chances, there was no prospect of seeing again an elderly parent, an ailing wife. She received despairing appeals by word of mouth, on pathetic scraps of paper, 'Gracious lady—'

Despairing herself, she began to read books acquired by Father before he had gone to Siberia, read and re-read his diaries. Odd little postscripts began to appear in her letters to me. 'I've just been going through your father's papers—how interested he was in the development of a water road from Siberia to the outside world—along the river north of Tobolsk up into the Kara Sea, and beyond. What hope for many in Siberia to have a direct way of communication at last! A prospect of a new kind of life—'

She was working indefatigably; she turned half our Petersburg home into a hospital staffed by a team of doctors Grandfather sent from France. In this way she saved hundreds of Russian lives. But the prisoners haunted her. It was not only a question of Siberia now; in the North, on the Murmansk Railway, prisoners were dying in thousands, 25,000 at least, while three-quarters of the survivors were sick with scurvy and tuberculosis. For those strong enough, desperate enough, here too plans must be made, and dozens managed to reach neutral sanctuary before the line was finished in December, 1916, after which those who remained were taken away—in unheated carriages.

Those who escaped spoke of their own experiences; they carried messages. Through neutral Switzerland and Sweden a message reached Mother; an Old Gentleman was grateful to her. 'My dear child—Incomparable One they call you.'

But if Mother were the Incomparable One to the Austrian Emperor and certain of his subjects, her name was no longer to be mentioned at the Russian Court. Because she had visited a prison in Ekaterinburg and maligned a Siberian peasant.

7

'A great step'

*'We had taken a great step towards Russia's overthrow.
The Grand Duke, with his strong personality, resigned and the
Czar placed himself at the head of his armies.'*
General Erich Ludendorff

MEANWHILE, OUR armies were still falling back.

In the second week of June there were riots in Moscow, and panic was growing in the capital. With the enemy advancing along such a vast front, nobody knew whether the prime objective was Petersburg or Moscow.

Russian troops burned Russian villages, and their ripe, unreaped corn. Despairing peasants formed a vast horde of refugees trailing desolately through the dust clouds.

Warsaw fell—was the chief target Moscow? In Moscow they were feverishly calculating—it would take the enemy at least six weeks to get there, and then the winter would be commencing. In their frantic search for reassurance, they looked up the date when snow had first fallen in 1812. October 12. In Moscow they prayed for an early winter.

The French didn't launch a suicidally chivalrous attack on the Western Front to save Petersburg.

In July of 1915 the Grand Duke Nicholas asked the Czar to proclaim that the men—or at least those showing exceptional courage—should receive allotments of land.

The idea was turned down. It was 'insulting to the Russian soldier'.

It was desire for land that was to bring them crowding back from the Front two years later.

Against my will, I was sent back to Stavka for liaison duties with the foreign military representatives.

Stavka had moved back to Mogilev, for the time being we thought, and hoped, for it was a wretched little place, the provincial town at its dullest, on the western bank of the Dnieper about 450 miles from Petersburg.

The day after my arrival there, the Grand Duke sent me to Petersburg to escort a French military mission on the first stage of its return home.

Four hours, nearly a hundred miles by slow train to Vitebsk. And then the express, and Nevel, Dno, Oredezh, Czarskoe Selo, Petersburg. I saw my charges on their way, had to kill time until my return next morning. Mother was away, and our town house was desolate without her. I went, therefore, to the Astoria, the biggest of Petersburg hotels, in Isaac Square opposite the former German Embassy. It had been built by German capital and managed by Germans (and in 1915 everyone was saying that every waiter had been employed by the German General Staff). Therefore it had been requisitioned at the outbreak of war for the benefit of officers arriving on short leave or for service work.

I managed to get a room, cleaned myself up after the journey, went down to dinner. I hoped to snatch a hurried meal, and then get up to my room unnoticed, but by bad luck when I went into the dining-room there were four or five late diners—elderly officers—just ending a meal, and one of them, a fat old general, knew and hailed me. So I had to go over, and be introduced as Alesha Hamilton's boy, and then, since it was expected of me, I had to give a brief *résumé* of my service career to date, after which, I hoped, I could withdraw gracefully. But they wouldn't let me. The moment I said I was at Stavka, they started exchanging meaning glances, and the old general, who seemed to have been putting away a fair amount of liquor, said, 'Then you're the very man we've been looking for! Sit down, my boy, and tell us what's in the wind there!'

I gazed at him in some bewilderment, and reminded him I was a very junior member of Stavka.

He laughed and said that junior as I was, surely I'd know about the big change about to take place.

Well, it wasn't giving away an army secret to say, as a matter of fact it had already taken place, Stavka was now at Mogilev.

The general roared with laughter again, slapped his thighs. The others, who hadn't taken so much liquor, gazed at me with different expressions.

'The boy really has no idea, you know,' one grizzled colonel observed.

Another colonel, with hair cut *en brosse*, said in some consternation, 'It occurs to me that the Grand Duke himself knows nothing of it.'

67

Light beating down from the chandeliers on bald heads, flushed faces, decorations. A waiter offering me *bortsch*. The colonel who had shown such dismay pouring me a glass of wine and saying, 'Well, let's look on the bright side, and assume the rumour's completely false.'

'What rumour, sir?'

'Why,' he said, 'that the Grand Duke's going to be superseded by the Czar.'

The bright light went on beating down. It showed old, freckled hands, red-veined faces, pouched, lined eyes. There was the smell of my soup and wine, and the smell of their brandy and cigars, but another smell too, that unmistakable smell of fear. I knew the reason for the fear, and tried to avoid it. I chose to concentrate solely on the one rumour—that the Grand Duke was to be relieved of the command.

'They can't remove him—the men love him, trust him!'

'They?' pounced the colonel who wore his hair *en brosse*, but I shook my head miserably, and began to drink my soup, though I felt sick.

One officer had remained silent as yet—a very thin-faced general with a hideously racking cough. He drank some water and said, 'We can't expect the boy to commit himself, but in any case, his avoidance of the most startling part of the rumour is eloquent in itself—'

'Precisely,' said the fat old general who'd known my father. 'Do you know how it's all been worked? *She's* jealous of the Grand Duke's popularity. She knows how *he* likes playing at being a soldier, and she takes advantage of it, especially since fat Vyroubova's* told her the Grand Duke's involved in a plot to arrest her and send her to a convent, that he's spoken of himself as Nicholas III—she collects any spicy, spiteful rumour going, that one!'

'For God's sake keep your voice low!'

'Your Excellency, this is unbelievable. The Grand Duke would never—'

'I know, my boy, I know, but it's the kind of rubbish a neurotic woman would believe!'

'In any case,' said the grizzled colonel, 'she thinks overshadowing her husband's the same as high treason.'

'Also, God help us,' said the thin-faced general, coughing, 'she really believes it will give the troops confidence.'

---

* Anna (Anya) Vyroubova was the Czarina's closest friend, and the essential link between the Imperial Family and Rasputin. Her stupidity was equalled only by the disastrous nature of her influence.

The grizzled colonel said, 'Let's have this boy's reaction. *Will* it give the Army confidence?'

I said, 'They think he's unlucky. He came to review us in Galicia in the spring when we were expecting the enemy offensive. All the men were convinced we'd be driven back after that.'

The thin-faced general said, 'Surely it can be—er—conveyed to them that he'll be only a nominal C-in-C, and that his Chief of Staff, who's bound to be an experienced man, will really be in command?'

'No, sir, that would make no difference. They'd know nothing of the work of the Chief of Staff; they *do* know that the Czar is unlucky.'

'Look,' said the grizzled colonel to me, 'you're breaking the waiter's heart, not eating anything. I suggest we go up to my room where I've a bottle of brandy, and they'll bring up oyster patties or something of the sort for you.'

It was very hot in his room, though the window was wide open, and there was the outline of the Cathedral and behind it the pearly sky, a Petersburg White Night.

'Of course,' said the old general, 'everybody'll say he's taking over because Rasputin wants it. Everyone knows that filth hates the Grand Duke.'

'We're seeing the end of the reign of Nicholas II, the beginning of the reign of Alexandra and Rasputin,' said the grizzled colonel. 'Once *he's* at Stavka, that vermin gets a clear field—'

The fat old general said, 'He can pay daily visits to Czarskoe. Through *her* he'll govern Russia.'

I said hesitantly, 'But surely there's a glimmer of hope—*if* the Czar goes to Stavka—'

'Out with it,' said the thin-faced general.

'Well, sir, hysteria in letters or over the telephone shouldn't have the same effect as hysteria in the same room.'

'True enough, but—my God, think of the reverse side of the medal. The Czar is at Stavka, Commander-in-Chief. We all know he keeps nothing from her. She'll be told all the important decisions being taken, *and she'll blurt 'em out to Rasputin to get his blessing on 'em!* And either deliberately, or because he's drunk—and he's drunk almost every night—he'll babble about it to those shady swine about him, they call themselves Swedes, but they're German spies all right. And whether it's done drunkenly or soberly, accidentally or intentionally, the result as far as the men at the Front—or Russia—are concerned will be the same.'

'As for *him* as Commander-in-Chief,' said the old general. 'He couldn't run a village post office!'

It might all have seemed better in the months that followed if we had not stayed at Mogilev. We had never dreamed that this mean, dirty little place would remain Supreme Headquarters for the rest of the war.
Many small shops, all of which stank differently, all filthy.
Gloomy streets, paved with noisy cobbles. One of the Allied officers said one day those cobbles 'would almost echo the steps of a cat upon them.'
When the snow came we had some respite from the noise of Mogilev, but there was no respite from the smells.
I was billeted in the travesty of a hotel where the wretched Allied officers were also accommodated. It was by the Catholic Cathedral endowed by Catherine the Great, and called itself the Hotel Bristol. It was like no other Hotel Bristol in Europe, for there was nothing remotely opulent about it. We all slept on uncomfortable little camp cots in the corners of rooms screened off by fusty and hideous old curtains. Immense white stoves gave off fumes, but little heat. To get to HQ we had to drive along the Moscow road, through the lower town, and over the Dneiper Bridge. You then came to the Governor's House, now the centre of both the civil and military governments of Russia.
It was an unattractive house, white, two-storeyed, the usual kind of provincial building. There was a muddy path between the gate and the front door—I can remember every inch of that muddy path. Inside the rooms were cramped, mean and uncomfortable. Four in particular remain in my memory—the bare little place with scarcely a stick of furniture in it where we met before meals—I remember this particularly because when the Czarina was visiting Mogilev we would stand here in chilly embarrassment as she made the circle of the guests. When this ordeal was over, we went off into the bare, oblong dining-room with the long, narrow table that could take twenty to thirty guests. The Czar's sitting-room was dominated by a large, bloated, bulbous writing table finished with German ornateness. They'd also managed to cram in a little sofa and two or three chairs, no more. The walls were quite bare. And in his bedroom were two camp beds, one for himself and one for Alexei, a cupboard and a quite hideous stove.
It may well be asked why I set down these details, when at the front

men were living and dying like rats. I did not often forget what had been endured, what was being endured, in dust, or mud, or frozen earth, or snow; as soon as I could, I would go back to that life, where the idea of a night on a camp cot in the Hotel Bristol at Mogilev would at times seem like a dream of paradise. But the point is that this mean house in that squalid town beside the Dneiper meant paradise to the Czar of All the Russias. I can remember talking one day to the British Military Representative at Stavka; we had become friendly enough for frankness, and he commented, 'A most unattractive house—crazily inconvenient for business, always overflowing with people.' And then he turned to me with honest bewilderment in his blue eyes. 'Yet the Czar adores it here!' he exclaimed. 'He loathes going away, doesn't he?'

I said grimly that he wasn't the only member of the Imperial Family to find Mogilev delightful.

'I know,' said Sir John Hanbury-Williams shrewdly. 'The children can't come here often enough, can they? God help us—I look at those pretty young girls and I wonder how their parents can't guess how deadly dull they must find the monotony of Czarskoe If they're so excited at the thought of a few days in this dreary little place!'

'Yes,' Olga had said when they had visited Stavka a week before, 'we love these visits—if only they weren't so short! It's so free here, and so exciting—things are always happening!'

One of these so exciting visits—what did it amount to? They lived in a train in a siding at a drab station, they joined their father at lunch, chatting gaily to the Staff until their mother appeared, after which the usual glacial constraint chilled everything, and then they would visit the peasants of the neighbourhood and the families of railway workers. Olga, who adored children, was always accompanied by a mob of urchins whom she stuffed with sweets. 'The girls enjoy their visits so much,' their parents would say smilingly, never realising that if *this* were excitement and gaiety what monotonous austerity there must be in their lives at home.

It was at about this time that the *Russkie Vedomosti* published a 'fable' written by Vassily Maklakov, a reasonable, moderate Liberal leader. The fable was headed *A Tragic Situation*. Conceive, said Maklakov, that you are being driven with those who are dearest to you along a road so steep and narrow that one wrong turn of the steering wheel would bring disaster. And suddenly you realise that your chauffeur can't control the car. Either he can't drive in difficult circumstances or he's overtired, and doesn't know what he's doing. If he continues at the wheel, you're all lost.

There are among the passengers people who can drive. They should take over the wheel as soon as possible, but it is difficult and dangerous to take over from the driver while the car is moving at speed along a hazardous road. One false move, and it's the abyss for everyone.

Still, the attempt must be made, and you nerve yourself for it. But the chauffeur refuses to give way, he clings to the wheel, won't surrender it—and you can't make him. It could be done in an oxcart travelling slowly over level ground, but on this dangerous road, at high speed, it can't be done, and he knows it, knows you daren't touch him.

So what can you do? You can only offer advice, warning, assistance.

But how do you feel when you realise that even with your help the chauffeur can't cope, and your own people in the car, becoming aware of the danger, beg you to act, and, misunderstanding your inaction, accuse you of cowardice and indifference?

8

King Log and Queen Stork

MOTHER WROTE, 'Vyroubova's telling everyone that the Czarina knows the Czar feels nervous before meeting the generals— she's therefore sent him a comb blessed by "Our Friend", telling him to comb his hair with it before any awkward conference, and he will receive divine help. *This I have checked, and it's the truth.* Meanwhile, the newspapers and magazines contain attack after attack on Rasputin and his influence; what is *said* passes all belief. Can no one open the Czar's eyes to the danger?'

Yes, people had tried, the most loyal servants, and they had been sent away. There had once been officers with whom the Czar had been intimate—Prince Orlov, Colonel Drenteln, and my father. They had all been dismissed because they were honest men who had told the truth—and in those weeks at Stavka I suddenly realised how completely isolated the Czar had become. He had not a friend left now, only time-servers who told him the comfortable untruths they thought he wanted to hear—or, rather, which the Czarina wanted him to hear. It was she who had isolated him. You didn't notice the loneliness at Czarskoe, where he was absorbed in his wife and family, but they were all he had now.

He would say betraying things sometimes. 'Hurry up and get through that work, Andrei, and then come walking with me this afternoon. This is where I miss Drenteln—he always kept up with me, and no one else can do it.'

Truer than he knew. He was, as it were, receding from us.

He was quite out of touch with people, and quite out of touch with reality. Sometimes in those autumn afternoons of 1915 when I was his companion for his daily outing, we'd spend some time sitting on fallen logs or treestumps, talking. At least, he would talk. He would talk for hours, sometimes until darkness was falling. I used to have nightmares after that—nightmares of a drowning Czar trying to get out of the

Sargasso Sea of love and solicitude and dominance in which his wife had suffocated and submerged him. Yet there was never any desperation in that low, slightly husky voice, it was, if anything, complacent. It was as if he didn't know the real meaning of words—he had to talk because of a deep inner distress, but the words all came out wrongly.

'Of course,' he said one day, 'ministers, poor fellows, living in town, know terribly little of what's happening in the country as a whole. Here at Stavka I can judge correctly the real mood among the various classes of people.'

(By reading rose-coloured reports? By reviewing troops on occasion?)

'My coming here to Stavka was, of course, the only logical step to take. Now both civil and military governments are identical; I can give any order I like, and it's carried out.'

But on another occasion he spoke in a different vein. He was glad to be rid of the business of government. 'I never was a business man, I simply can't understand all these questions of supplying and provisioning.'

'It's good to be a soldier, Andrei!'

And he said something quite incredible about being 'on active service'.

Still, his assumption of the command was less disastrous to the Army than to the civil government; at Stavka he was passive enough, but, God help us, the Czarina was too active in the rear.

King Log and Queen Stork.

What had she said once to Mother? That she considered herself 'the medicine of muddled minds after the microbes from town.'

From all accounts, the unaccustomed physical exertion of nursing and her assumption of an informal regency had intensified her mystical hysteria. In her morbid religious ecstasy she was now convinced that she had a special mission, to save Russia—under the guidance of that stinking travesty of Joan of Arc, Rasputin.

Beside me the Czar was silent. He was smoking a cigarette. Such silence was a relief. Otherwise I might have imagined that sitting next to me was not the Czar of All the Russias but a ventriloquist's dummy.

There was only one consoling feature during those weeks at Stavka—Alexei. Whenever he could, he joined his father at Mogilev—

74

on one occasion he more or less stowed away on the Imperial train, clutching his dog in one arm, his balalaika in the other.

If the Czar's love for Stavka was that of a small boy playing soldiers, Alexei's was that of a small boy at last being allowed to be a boy.

I remember how the Allied representatives had awaited his coming apprehensively; so few people had ever seen him, there were so many rumours about him that they expected a creature with so little life in him that death would have small horror or significance. Instead they met a child, certainly delicate but, when he was well, with twice the spirit and gaiety of any ordinary boy, and, above all, he wanted to live—my God, he wanted to live!

There had always been the danger that he would be thoroughly spoiled by an adoring mother, guilt-stricken because of the illness he had inherited from her, unable to deny him anything. Certainly at Czarskoe he had at times become unmanageable. He was quite different at Stavka.

I shall always remember his first appearance there, his initial shyness as he followed his father round the circle of Allied representatives, shaking hands with each, and then, as he sat beside the Czar at lunch, a sudden happy grin of pure delight, brilliant blue eyes shining with joy—'I'm going to like it here!'

That afternoon the Czar wanted to see the Chief of Staff, Alexeiev; 'Andrei, will you take me out for a walk?' pleaded Alexei. 'Joy, too, of course.'

Joy, the little liver-coloured spaniel, danced on his short hind legs in anticipation. 'Don't you think he looks more intelligent than me?' said Alexei.

He chattered endlessly as we walked along the path beside the river. About Olga and Marie and Anastasia, about M. Gilliard, who 'Made a long face about my coming here, because he says I shan't keep up my lessons—I do a *tremendous* number of subjects, Andrei—Russian, French, English, arithmetic, history, geography, some people say I should learn German, but I *never* want to learn German, silly old Wilhelm, did you ever see the stupid letter he wrote Papa when I was born, Andrei, and the mug he sent, to drink his beastly health in his beastly German beer, I suppose. Andrei, you will find out for me a shop where I can buy rubber balls for Vanka, my donkey, won't you, you know he likes putting his nose in your pocket and finding them, but only before I go, Andrei, not before, and I wish I never, never had to go!'

Oddly enough, he didn't mention his mother.

Within a day or two he was chatting as cheerfully and confidently to the Allied representatives, who adored him. He liked checking that all the buttons were fastened on the tunic of General Hanbury-Williams; the General always carefully left one unfastened so that Alexei, with a sigh of 'Untidy again!' could chidingly button him up.

Before lunch, while the rest of the representatives were eating *hors d'oeuvres*, he would invite his special friends into a little alcove room leading out of the dining-room, and there we would play football with anything that came handy. The jolly old fat Belgian, General de Ricquel, always played a leading part—Alexei was extremely fond of him.

For what it is worth, he was never ill when he was at Stavka.

He had a toy gun he loved very much—shouts of laughter after dinner one evening, so we hurried upstairs and found he had fixed the toy bayonet and had cornered two orderlies with it.

The Czar said to me once, 'He's always well when he's here, isn't he?'

'Yes, sir.'

'He enjoys it so much. If only it were not for the war, Andrei, he could be travelling widely, seeing other countries, gaining from his experience of them knowledge which would be useful in ruling Russia.'

One couldn't say, 'His mother would never permit it.'

'Knowing Russia alone isn't enough,' said the Czar.

To learn about the outside world when he wasn't allowed to know anything of his own country, when his family lived at Czarskoe aloof from the very capital!

On another occasion I took Alexei boating. He said, 'I *do* like it here, Andrei, I wish I didn't have to go back tomorrow.'

'Because of the lessons?'

'No, because of living with *women!* Always women, women, women—unless they bring in Derevenko's* two boys, and they're a lot younger than me and rather stupid. Andrei, it's funny, isn't it, there are masses of cousins, but they're never invited to come and play with me, even on my birthday? I don't know what I'd do if it weren't for Olga, who's good at games, and Joy and Vanka—

'I get so bored at Czarskoe,' Alexei continued after a moment, 'and—and people fuss so. I wouldn't be allowed to play football there. All women and stuffiness, and I get ill, too, and people tell lies, saying I've

---

* His sailor attendant.

a cold or sprained my ankle.* I'm never ill here, am I? If I could stay here for good, I'd never be ill, I'd live for ages, I—I'd outlive Papa! Is that a—wicked thing to say, Andrei, that I'd outlive Papa?'

'I don't think so. It's what His Majesty wants, isn't it?'

'Andrei, will you tell me something?'

'If I can.'

'Lower your voice. Andrei, you were here before Papa came, weren't you, you knew Uncle Nicholasha?'

'Yes,' I said with no idea of what was coming.

Alexei leaned forward. 'Is it true that when Gregory wanted to come here, Uncle Nicholasha wired, "Come, and I'll hang you!"? *Did* he, Andrei? You promised you'd tell me!'

'Yes,' I said. 'He did.'

'Oh!' said Alexei ecstatically. '*Marvellous* Uncle Nicholasha!'

I stared at him in stupefaction. 'You don't think he acted wrongly?'

'That's what—what *they* said he did, not so much wrong as wicked. But he did only one thing wrong—he didn't actually hang him!'

He used to come to me on later visits, on one pretext or another, and stammer out how he despised and detested Rasputin. 'Only one other person knows—Olga. I told her because that's the way she feels about him, too.' One afternoon he dragged me off to the bedroom he shared with his father. 'Look around and see one of the chief reasons I like it here so much, Andrei!' I stared round, said, 'I'm sorry, I can't see anything.' He laughed delightedly. 'That's just it—it's something you *can't* see. Do you know whose picture I must have by my bed at Czarskoe? *His*. It's always put out for me to bring here, but I always "forget" it—M. Gilliard knows all about it, of course! When I'm at Czarskoe I always keep pushing things against it, so that it falls on the floor, that's where it ought to be, on the floor, all the time, with people trampling up and down on it.'

He never mentioned his mother; I did not realise how he had turned against her until a week after he'd gone back to Czarskoe. I was being sent to the capital on a flying visit and the Czar asked me to go to Czarskoe with the latest batch of photographs he had taken—they were, of course, nearly all of Alexei.

So I was admitted to the mauve boudoir where nothing ever seemed to change. The Czarina, as always, lay on the lace-cushioned *chaise*

* The true reason was of course never given if illness kept him from public functions.

longue, the shawl of lace lined with mauve muslin covering her legs, the glass screen behind her to shield her from draughts. She and Tatiana and Marie were knitting for the Army, Olga and Anastasia sewed. She was exclaiming delightedly over the photographs when Alexei came in, carrying his pet kitten, Zoubrovka. He came in slowly, quite unlike the boy who raced about Stavka, his face set, pale, sullen. Then he saw me, and rushed forward. 'Andrei! Andrei! Has Papa sent you to take me back with you? When can we go—tonight?'

He had put the kitten down; Zoubrovka began to walk along the tables containing the Czarina's innumerable photographs, knocking most of them to the ground. Then he noticed Tatiana's bulldog, Artipo, as usual snoring dreadfully at his mistress' feet. Zoubrovka flew spitting to attack him. Fondly the Czarina begged Alexei to take his little cat away. 'No, I won't!' he suddenly shouted with extraordinary violence. 'He's a *good* cat—'

'My darling, he's a dear little cat, but—'

'—and he never gives any trouble at Stavka because he's not bothered with women who get on his nerves!'

She didn't hear him properly, because by this time the barking and spitting was deafening, but I, standing beside him, heard him clearly enough. So did Olga, who gazed at me despairingly.

'Alexei,' I said rapidly, 'that's just how the German Emperor used to talk to his mother. You don't want to be like him, do you?'

He said, '*Aren't* you taking me back to Stavka?'

'No, but don't talk like that and don't look like that. What do you think General Hanbury-Williams would say if he knew?'

I grabbed the furious kitten by the scruff of his neck and handed him to Alexei. Marie said, 'My Siamese cat never makes a nuisance of himself like that!'

'I haven't a pet at all!' lamented Anastasia.

'Never mind,' said Marie, 'Anya* says she'll buy you a little dog, if you'll make up your mind what breed you want.'

'A King Charles spaniel,' said Anastasia, 'or a pekingese—'

Alexei's face had become extraordinarily rigid at the mention of Vyroubova. He whispered to me with a gasp, '*Can't* you get me back?'

'Soon,' I murmured. 'Soon.'

We sat down and looked at the photographs. He kept himself under control though once he whispered, 'I'm glad you came to cheer up

* Vyroubova.

78

Olga—she's been in trouble again, *they* say she's been "grumpy". I wish she and I and you could be at Stavka for ever, Andrei!'

If he had ever become Czar, I think he could have been the ideal ruler of a new Russia. He had endured so much pain himself he showed extraordinary compassion for any kind of suffering. He was intelligent, and already showed an insistence on learning the truth. I think he could have united Russia, as that first Alexei Romanov had done.

I have said he was the only compensation for life at Mogilev, but because knowing him at Stavka gave one some idea of the man he would have become had he lived—well, I wish to God he'd never come there.

9

'La neige est rouge'

IN MARCH 1916 we started an offensive in the North. I escorted a party of Allied observers. We saw our infantry slaughtered in liquid mud, and at night the mud froze, and the men who still lived would have to be literally hacked from ice.

If we had waited for a month, the mud would have become dust, it dries so quickly, but we could not wait a month, because the German attack on Verdun began on February 21, and we must attack, regardless of the cost to ourselves, in order to save the French. The old story all over again. We Russians were so noble and self-sacrificing we attacked the moment France shrieked for help, no matter how our own position was affected.

And once again, of course, we had to fight technique and steel with flesh and blood.

It was in Petersburg early in 1916 that I heard a Russian journalist had coined a new word; it was 'defeatism'.

In our offensive, the Smolensk Regiment, to which we had been attached for observation purposes, lost twenty-eight out of its thirty-five officers. For days it lay and fought and died in freezing mud, but every night, it being Easter, the men sang the refrain from the Easter midnight procession, *Christ is risen from the dead, death by death down doth he tread*—But *we* couldn't conquer death, here or elsewhere. I had frozen tears on my cheeks those nights, because of what I had seen daily, because of what I had not seen, too. Uncle Raoul was missing at Verdun.

There is a memorial to him and his regiment in the little Breton church overlooking the Atlantic. *Qui ante diem periit, sed milites, sed pro patria.** Not very Christian, acknowledged his father, but what Christianity was there in the obscene mud about Verdun?

* 'Who died before their day, but as soldiers, and for their country.'

The best of France was butchered there, and the rats grew fat, because the German General Falkenhayn had spent the Christmas holiday in working out a method of bleeding France white. Presumably in parts of Germany there were still carollers singing of peace on earth when on Christmas Eve the decision was taken to launch Operation *Gericht*. *Gericht* means place of execution. Verdun was to be Golgotha.

Some of Falkenhayn's officers misinterpreted the plan, thought he wanted an offensive to capture Verdun. He soon corrected them. He didn't want to capture Verdun; if the fortress fell quickly, the fury of the fighting would die away—and there wouldn't be so much bloodshed. They got the idea then. Not the fortress—human lives.

What was Verdun? A dilapidated ring of fortresses denuded of guns since the beginning of the war, when the French General Staff had the idea that a ring fort was a deathtrap. Having made this decision, they removed most of the cannon—only to allow Verdun to become the biggest deathtrap of the lot eighteen months later.

The Germans had no idea of this, thought Verdun was for the French a bastion worth fighting for. It wasn't. It was dead ground, dead glory. The grandsons of Charlemagne had signed a treaty there dividing Europe between them, Vauban had practised his skill there. It was decay and dilapidation, fallen-in trenches, rusted, broken barbed wire, mud. To have lost it would have meant a useful shortening of the line. Its loss wouldn't threaten Paris. But when the attack came, the French General Staff poured in living men to defend a dead fort—because of sentiment. Beyond this, they had no reason at all.

It is as if these French generals, this privileged class of 1916, took belated revenge on the Revolution. In 1793 the *canaille* had dragged the men of privilege from their luxurious *châteaux* to the guillotine; now from their luxurious *châteaux* these new men of privilege sent the *canaille* in their tens of thousands to death. And if the guillotine made pitiful wreckage out of human bodies, high explosive and jagged lumps of steel could produce effects that cannot be set down in words.

Uncle Raoul's regiment had been posted to the Verdun area just before Christmas. The sheer defencelessness of the fort disturbed him so much that he had appealed for more men, or at least more barbed wire. Nothing could shake the complacency of pot-bellied Commander-in-Chief Joffre (here at least was one indestructible element in the

F   81

French Army) so in desperation Uncle had written to one of his few political friends, begging him to draw the attention of the War Minister to the state of affairs at Verdun. The War Minister had taken note, Joffre raged, and so Uncle Raoul was expecting trouble—possibly a court martial.

His reputation, at least, was saved by Operation *Gericht*.

Uncle Raoul believed there was going to be an enemy attack; deserters, chiefly Alsatians, kept coming over, and this was usually the surest of signs. They talked of immense troop build-ups, the cancellation of leave. Uncle Raoul went to the Staff at Verdun; had there been any reconnaissance flights, and if so where were the photographs? Yes, there had been a few flights. And the photographs? A shrug. 'The point is, my dear fellow, we've no one on the Staff who can analyse air photographs.' 'I can,' said Uncle Raoul. A few hours later he was reporting to his officers, 'A frightful build-up on a narrow front, too narrow for a breakthrough. Whatever they're planning is irrational, we can't grasp it, but God help us, something atrocious is about to happen.'

I am glad that he, because of his *sane* intelligence, could not guess what went on in the darkened mind of Falkenhayn.

So, believing themselves doomed, he and his men waited. Every day from the beginning of February they expected the assault, but there were snowstorms and blinding mist, and, when the wind dropped, silence. The snow stopped falling, thawed, and then there were gales of rain, and the slush became mud and the mud froze at night. One couldn't dig trenches.

'So we exist—still exist a little,' Uncle Raoul wrote to Grandfather. 'We live like lousy rats in stinking slime; the difference between us and the rats is that *they* are better fed. Outside the freezing sleet is falling; soon we'll be knee-deep in icy water, but we don't mind that; as long as the weather's vile the answer to the perpetual question, *"When?"* is *"Not yet"*——

February 17, 1916.

'The answer now is *"Not much longer,"* for the sun has appeared, the mud is drying out. It is a night reminding me of the first line of *Le Coeur de Hialmar*.* The snow will be red soon enough.

'The cold is numbing, but the moon is magnificent. The men ask if they may leave the trenches, and I agree. They stand behind me,

* *Une nuit claire, un vent glacé. La neige est rouge.*

82

bearded, in tattered uniforms—no one would think us in our filth to be men of the twentieth century. For the sake of warmth many of us wear sheepskin jackets. Attila and his Huns must have looked like us as they assembled for the burning of an earlier Verdun.

'I will send this off tonight. What news from Russia? How remote from all this those last days in Petersburg appear now—the heat, and the yellow evening sky paling to the luminous pearl of a White Night, and the Neva golden glass and the Peter and Paul bells ringing—'

It was his last letter. One more day of quiet, and then came the morning when the bombardment started, two days of it, till the gun crews stopped from exhaustion. Phase One of Operation *Gericht* was to create a 'zone of death'—the official phrase. On a narrow front of six miles they rained down two million shells at the rate of 100,000 an hour. And there was poison gas, and a new weapon, a flame-thrower that burned men alive.

As dusk fell the German shock troops went in to take over the slaughter house. But among the corpses there were smoke-blackened scarecrows of men who obstinately endured, crawling from splintered trees and obliterated trenches to fire rifles and pistols and yell defiance, survivors of Uncle Raoul's regiment. Uncle Raoul fell back with a handful of men, dug a fresh trench from the ruins of one that had collapsed, sent back word that there was no ammunition, the boxes of cartridges had been buried under the *débris*, so had the hand-grenades. But there were still the bayonets.

Next day at dawn the bombardment began again, with even greater ferocity. There were no further messages from Colonel de St Servan-Rézé.

Many months later they found the trench. It was completely filled in, but the rusted tips of bayonets protruded at regular intervals. When they had time and curiosity enough, they dug. A corpse was beneath each bayonet. Throughout the night before that final bombardment they had stood with their bayonets fixed ready to drive back the assault, and when the great guns had opened up they had been buried alive rather than quit their position.

At the end of my mission I went to report to Petrograd. There were a few hours I was still able to spend with Mother. She said to me, 'Don't worry about your grandfather—he's not invulnerable, but he's invincible. He'll take an even more active part in war-work now—imagine, they've restored his old army rank to him!'

There are different ways of paying blood money.

An officer at the War Ministry had told me, 'You're going off to Novgorod until next spring—training work. Chevaliers Gardes.'

'Isn't there any hope of front-line divisions being sent behind the lines to have a rest?'

'There was some discussion a few days ago about sending a division or two (who'd deserved it) back here for a spell, but the commander reported he has too many troops already—he can't take any more.'

'*Troops!*' I said. 'But you've seen them, sir? Untrained, slovenly recruits—'

'I quite agree,' he said, 'but my dear fellow, there's nothing to be gained by losing your temper over what might have been—'

What might have been, indeed. Two crack divisions, officered by capable men, could have controlled Petersburg in the following spring.

10

'Ubili!'

THE BEST thing about Novgorod was the sight of a familiar face the day after my arrival, the sergeant of my squadron as we rode into East Prussia in the grotesque confusion of the first days of the war. The chest wound he had got then had nearly done for him, but after months in hospital he'd been allowed to rejoin what remained of the regiment.

I was glad of his company. Now, as never before, living away from the Front, one became oppressed by the hatred felt for the Czarina, the contempt felt for the Czar.

It is still possible to see copies of a deadly little caricature by Ivanov, *Russia's Ruling House*. A gigantic Rasputin has perched on each knee, like two ventriloquist's dummies, a little Czar and Czarina, he, eyes closed, smiling vacuously in his sleep, and she, angular and scrawny, simpering up adoringly at her master. But this is preferable to the scribbles and drawings that were beginning to appear on the walls of buildings throughout the Empire—on the walls of the Winter Palace itself, I heard.

At the beginning of December, there was a hurried note from Mother. 'A letter has just been forwarded—Olga writes that the Czarina and the girls will soon be visiting Novgorod. She hopes to see you.'

The splendid Imperial train drew into the station. There was the Governor-General with other dignitaries on the platform, swept clear of snow. The Czarina, the four Grand Duchesses. The three elder girls looked serious; the irrepressible Anastasia, recognising me, winked.

It was a grey, iron day. There were few people along the Imperial route—Novgorod was a land of milk and honey compared with Petersburg, but still you couldn't live without queuing and you weren't going to give up your chance of bread or fuel in order to applaud the woman you blamed for all that had gone wrong in Russia.

85

There were a few scattered cheers, sounding thinly on the cold air. It would have been better if there had been none at all, for they served only to underline the general silence, apathy, sullenness.

The Czarina seemed to notice nothing.

Hospitals, the Cathedral, back to the Imperial train for lunch. A courtier I didn't know—but, of course, nearly all the people I'd really known at Czarskoe had spoken out against Rasputin and had been dismissed—told me to be in attendance. The Czarina gave me her hand to kiss. 'How lucky you are to be here in Novgorod, Andrei—I've always wanted to visit it because of the beautiful old churches, but because of the war I can only visit hospitals.'

But she had managed to get hold of half a dozen ikons, nevertheless, and was signing one on the back as she spoke. 'No, girls, you can't gossip with Andrei now, I want you to sign these ikons at once. Perhaps you'll have the chance to talk to him at tea—will you be at the City Hall, Andrei? No? Then you must come to the train to say good-bye before we leave.'

After lunch they went to the Zemstvo Hospital, and then to a tea-party given by the Novgorod nobility at the City Hall. I could have gone easily enough, but had evaded the invitation through sheer cowardice. I'd known the excitement and anticipation that had gone into the planning of it all—girls in agonies over the choice of dress, frantically practising curtseys—'Prince, will this be *good* enough?' And I knew how it would all turn out. Flat. Chilly. Lifeless. As it did.

The last visit was to a convent which possessed relics of St Barbara. It was also the home of a much revered, very old recluse.

I stood at attention alongside the train when they returned. The Czarina had her exalted look; the others looked depressed and apprehensive—not to be wondered at after the cold, ominous reception they had received.

'How *chilled* he looks!' said Anastasia. 'Mamma, can we all have tea? Hot tea would *revive* Andrei—'

I said, laughing, I wasn't dead yet. Then I stopped laughing. Olga had been hanging back at the rear of the little group, and it was only now that I saw her clearly. She looked ghastly.

So we drank tea from glasses in golden holders, and then the Czarina, accompanied by Tatiana, withdrew to make notes on the hospitals she had seen. The girls could talk to me for twenty minutes, she said—after this the train would be leaving.

86

So I stood for the last time in the warm drawing-room coach with the grey and mauve hangings.

'The engine's warming up,' said Anastasia, 'but there's plenty of time for you to see him.'

'Him?'

'My puppy. Jimmy. Anya gave him to me.'

Jimmy was a very small, very fat, snuffling King Charles spaniel.

'His legs are so short he can't get up stairs, and he has to be carried about a lot, but he's very affectionate. He loves Mamma, and curls up beside her on the *chaise longue*.'

Jimmy made unmistakable signs of distress. 'Oh, my angel!' cried Anastasia, swooping down on him. 'Quick—out on to the platform! Isn't he clever!' she flung over her shoulder at me. 'He heard the engine warming up and knew it was his last chance! Marie, you'll have to come too in case he starts running off—'

Olga sat in one of the leather armchairs. I stood looking at her. Eventually she raised her eyes and looked at me. I can still see that expression. It was more than mute appeal. It was more than pathos. It was realisation of a deadly situation.

'Andrei,' she said, 'why has the feeling in the country changed against my father?'

I said, 'Novgorod hasn't been very welcoming, I know—'

'It's not that. It's not simply this visit to Novgorod that worries me—although,' she amended hurriedly, 'that's not altogether correct. But I was worried before we came to Novgorod—you're not the first person I've asked, Andrei.'

'What did the other persons tell you?'

'Oh, I had an embarrassed sort of lecture on the unfortunate counter-manding of the progressive plans of Alexander II. You won't fob me off with that, will you?'

I tried to meet the steady eyes. 'No,' I said.

She looked away from me then.

'You know how I go into Petersburg—*Petrograd*, I mean—every week to accept donations for my soldiers' families? At the Winter Palace? I used to look forward to it all, if only because—because—'

I said gently, 'Because it was a change. Go on, I understand.'

'Well, in the last months, the feel of it all has altered. I noticed that people were beginning to avoid my eyes, smile only with an effort, break off conversations abruptly when I came in—at first I thought this was embarrassment because I'd said or done something stupid or wrong—Oh, Andrei, don't let's pretend, I know perfectly well that because the only young people we mix with much are Derevenko the sailor's children or—or *his* daughter, because Mamma says only "plain" people can be trusted, when we go out in society we're lost, bewildered, we say or do *gauche* things—have you forgotten how you came to my rescue in the year before the war when I started to go to dances?'

'Believe me,' I said, 'I shall always, God willing, come to your rescue.'

She was looking at me again now. 'I know. Do you remember the time when we were out at the farm? I wandered away and got lost, and you came looking for me shouting, "Olga! Olga! Don't be afraid! Andrei's coming!" It all came back to me the other night in a dream. I was back in that hayfield and Mamma was with me, sitting down, playing with me, and a snake came out of the long grass. I was frightened, but Mamma said I mustn't be frightened, it wouldn't hurt me, and she put out her hand as if to stroke it, but—but it stung her, Andrei, and I screamed, and I could hear you, far away, calling that you were coming.'

'Did I come?'

Olga said after a moment, 'I knew you *were* coming, but the nightmare ended first.'

'Just like that?'

Another pause. 'No. There were some men, close to us. I called out to them to help Mamma, but one of them was just concentrating on killing the snake. And the other one said, "What's the use of killing the snake? The damage has been done." Neither paid any attention to Mamma at all.'

I said, 'Marie and Anastasia will be back soon—we haven't much more time. From the way you looked when you came back to the train, something unpleasant happened in Novgorod. What was it? Something at the City Hall?'

'No, there wasn't a *happy* feeling but it passed off quietly enough. It was afterwards.'

'Where?' I asked incredulously. 'At the convent?'

She nodded. 'We went to see the relics of St Barbara, and then Mother wanted to visit the old woman, Marla Mikhailovna. She was lying in bed in a little dark room—they had to bring a candle for her to see us and us to see her. Suddenly I felt happy. She's supposed to be a hundred and seven, you know, but she looked so *normal*—young, smiling eyes, and such a sweet smile. She kissed us and blessed us, said the war would be over soon. And then—?

She got up abruptly, walked over to the window, drew back the silk curtains and peered out. On the lamplit platform Marie and Anastasia were chasing fat little Jimmy. They waved cheerfully.

'I've time to tell you,' said Olga, letting the curtain fall.

'She wanted to give Mamma a present—all that she had was a little withered winter apple, but Mamma was terribly pleased, comforted, too, because the old woman said, "Don't fear the heavy cross." But then—' Again she hesitated.

I looked out of the window. 'You must tell me. You'll have to be quick, too—they've caught Jimmy.'

'You must have an ikon,' said Olga. 'We'll sign it on the back.'

'It doesn't matter about the ikon—'

'It does, it does!' she said with surprising passion.

'Tell me what the old woman said.'

'I will, but you must let me give you an ikon. If only you knew the people we have to give them to—'

'I think I do,' I said with sudden grimness. 'Give me an ikon, then.'

She wrote on the back with a kind of desperate energy, 'From Olga. Novgorod. December, 1916.' As she wrote she said in a low voice, 'It was a little room, and everyone was fidgeting around us, and I was tired, so what with this and all the people moving about I probably imagined it all. Mamma went on looking happy, didn't hear it—'

I said gently, 'You've come so far. You must tell me now.'

Olga raised her eyes to mine. 'I thought she called Mamma, "the martyred Czarina Alexandra Feodorovna".'

'Got him!' said Anastasia breathlessly. 'What have you been doing, Olga? Giving Andrei an ikon? What a good idea! Is there time for me to give him one?'

'I think not,' I said, hurriedly kissing their hands. 'I'll have to jump for it or I'll be on my way to Czarskoe with you.'

Marie leaned out of the window. 'We wish you could! Can you come in the Spring?'

Anastasia raised Jimmy's paw to acknowledge my salute. The puppy licked her face enthusiastically. Olga was standing a little to the rear, quite motionless. Her face was suddenly calm and untroubled.

And then within a few days there came a telephone call from a friend in Petersburg. At least, I thought I could identify the voice, for he gave no name. He merely said, 'Andrei? They've got him at last,' and put down the receiver.

No need to ask to whom he referred.

By mid-day, the news had spread through Novgorod. There were incredible scenes in the street. Complete strangers embraced each other in the streets, as they would at Easter. Amid all the sounds of rejoicing there was one word you heard repeated again and again with indescribable exultation—'*Ubili!*'—'They have killed!'

Rasputin's body had been found beneath the ice of the frozen Neva. There was no certain information as to how he had got there, but there was a certain pattern in the rumours which reached Novgorod—a nobleman, a Grand Duke, a member of the Duma, poisoned food and wine, poison enough to kill a dozen men, but to no effect. And then revolver shots in the basement of a great house, and a macabre scene in a courtyard at midnight.

I heard that hysterical messages from the Czarina had summoned the Czar back from Stavka, where he still played at soldiering. A few days later I recalled with a pang the nightmare evening when I had heard he was taking over the command. In a crowded street, someone called my name. At first I didn't recognise the gaunt-faced officer; then an appalling fit of coughing made me recollect a hot hotel room in Petersburg.

General Milyutin smilingly dismissed my stammered apologies. 'I should have gone months ago, and so it's not surprising I look like a walking skeleton.'

His home was near Novgorod; I was free that afternoon, so I drove out to his estate with him.

He, too, had heard the story of the poison which had proved ineffective. 'Not a miracle,' he said. 'I discussed it with my doctor—the swine drank so much, he said, that he probably had acute alcoholic gastritis. Did you know this often thickens the stomach lining?'

As we drove he told me that Rasputin had been buried in the park at Czarskoe. The Czar was present, so were the Czarina and the Grand Duchesses. Before the coffin was nailed down they had put inside an ikon the Czarina had brought back from Novgorod.

('If only you knew the people we have to give them to!')

II

'He's still ruling here'

A WEEK after Christmas, Mother decided that she must contrive to go
out to Czarskoe. The grotesque quality of the menacing situation in
St Petersburg spurred her on, the craziness which had increased with
particular speed since the death of Rasputin, with polite society talking
loudly of Karsavina dancing in *Swan Lake* at the Mariinsky, the race
meetings at the Semenovsky parade ground, and then, under its breath,
switching to incredible talk of plots and palace revolutions such as you
might have heard a dozen times in the eighteenth century. The only
hard reality in it all was hatred of the Czarina—nothing fantastic there.
After Rasputin's murder, if anything, it increased. He had gone, but
nothing was changed, for the Czarina remained. She was the sole
obsession now, *she* must go—to a nunnery, a sanatorium, a lunatic
asylum. She must be kidnapped, sent to England. Or she should be
given the Rasputin treatment. The Czar, who had not returned to
Stavka, was rarely mentioned.

Society was involved, the knaves or fools among the Grand Dukes
were involved, but the hatred expressed for the Czarina in the great
palaces didn't scare Mother as much as the hatred muttered in the food
queues standing—so rarely shuffling forward—on the bleak, icy
pavements.

No one could recall so bitter a winter. Everywhere the engines of the
trains bringing food supplies broke down because of burst frozen
pipes. In Petersburg you had to start queueing overnight, stand for
long hours in the freezing darkness if you hoped to get a little bread
next day, the bread that cost four times what it had done two years
before. By this time, most people took the food queues for granted.
They'd been a feature of life so long now that the patience of those
docile figures was unquestioned. But Mother questioned it. She could
never see those huddled lines without feeling equal compassion and
fear. They had been patient for so long—*how much longer could they go
on?* The real danger was there, not in the German armies.

The ghost of an idea came to her. She had been invited to go to Geneva in the Spring because of her work for the Austrian prisoners-of-war, and on her way through France she would see what could be done to remedy the great shortage in Russia of surgical appliances for war cripples— Within five minutes she was trying to contact me by telephone.

'What?' I repeated incredulously. 'Leaving for France within days— in *January*?'

'I'm not mad, though I think I'd go mad if I stayed here, and did nothing. Don't you see, my dear, it's my only way of getting received? I'll be ordering supplies for the Czarina's own hospitals—she can't deny *this* request!'

'It's a hideously dangerous journey at any time,' I argued frantically, 'and in January—'

But she was not to be dissuaded. She started preparations at once, requested an audience of the Czarina, and was eventually instructed over the telephone to take a certain train to Czarskoe where an Imperial car would be waiting for her. But the time of her audience was earlier than that normally given to the Czarina's few callers; despite herself she expressed amazement. The discreet voice at the other end coughed, then said guardedly: 'You are to have the honour of first being received by His Imperial Majesty.'

'The Czar! Why?'

The discreet voice merely repeated the time of the train she was to take. At the French Embassy, when she went to make final arrangements for her journey, an attaché was more helpful. 'May it not be because your father's a member of the Mission?'

'What Mission?'

'Well, thank God for a little secrecy at last; we feared it was being blabbed all over the Palace! A special Allied Mission is coming in February. Since the Duke was a friend of the Czar's father, people thought that what he'd have to say—'

'Father coming! At his age!' Mother was aghast.

'Madame, he volunteered—no, *compelled* his services.' The attaché's eyes were grave. 'The fate of those dearest to him is part of the fate of Russia, after all.' But when she continued to protest in a low, furious voice, he could not help laughing. 'Only ten minutes ago,' he said, 'discussing your journey, you dismissed it as the easiest thing in the world!'

But she did not think her father's coming was the reason the Czar wished to see her. We have often pondered over it. I myself think he had a number of reasons, each, such was the state of his mind at the time, vague, ill-defined, blurring one into the other. He wished to salute her courage and spirit—yes, that I believe—and he wanted, as best he could, to convey to her that the old liking was not dead. Each, after all, knew very well that this might be the last time they might meet though, God help us, even then everyone thought the danger was all hers. And perhaps there was a muddled idea that she might carry reassurance to France, and persuade her father that little was really wrong, causing him to pre-judge the issue before he ever set foot in Russia.

As if, after that audience, there could ever be reassurance again!

The shock was all the greater because the preliminaries were so normal, so unchanged. The snow-covered park was the same and the Cossacks riding round in an endless ring, and the long white palace; she knew the doorman, who welcomed her with a smile; the same courier led her to the reception room, the same pictures and portraits were on the walls, there was still courtly, elderly Count Benckendorff to talk to while she waited, and Dr Botkin, with his kind, clever face. And there were the photograph albums. 'Dear God,' she thought, 'will nothing stop them taking photographs of each other?'

And then she was ushered into the Czar's presence, and she thought her heart would stop beating, for here was change of the most dreadful kind. Physically he was almost unrecognisable. His face was thin, hollow, covered with the network of tiny wrinkles normally seen only in very old men. The colour of his eyes, once so brilliant, had faded; the retinas seemed grey, colourless, lifeless. Throughout the audience he rarely looked at Mother; instead his gaze wandered aimlessly, troubledly, from object to object over her shoulder. There was a fixed, mirthless smile that appalled her, a slight tic in his upper lip. He must have been aware of it, because he kept pressing his finger to it, helplessly. And then, feeling Mother's eyes on him, he dropped his hand like a guilty child. There was something so inexpressibly lost, desolate, about him that, regardless of etiquette, once she had risen from her curtsey, she said chokingly: 'Your Imperial Majesty is not well, I fear!'

An interval of silence, and then, as if recalling his wandering thoughts from a great distance, the Czar said carefully: 'I beg your pardon, I did not catch—'

Mother clasped icy hands as she repeated her remark. Another long silence, then: 'No, I am perfectly well, though perhaps I'm not taking enough exercise. Please be seated.'

He sat in a kind of bleak isolation behind his gold-encrusted desk; she sank on to one of the familiar green leather chairs and, dreading another silence, began to describe her mission to France and Switzerland, going into dozens of details with which he must be perfectly well acquainted, anything to avoid another silent pause. But eventually her voice died away; she could not bear much more of the atmosphere in this oppressive mahogany-panelled room. Formally she ended with: 'If Your Imperial Majesty has any further instructions for me—'

To her consternation, as if she had not given a word of explanation, he asked her to remind him exactly what she was going to do. She never knew whether she sobbed or cried out at this, but she has always believed that for a moment the Czar looked at her and really knew her and that, knowing her, he gazed at her as if begging for help. He called her by her name. 'Avoye,' he said. 'It's these headaches—'

'What headaches, sir?'

But then he had slipped away again. She repeated her question. 'Headaches?' he said, with that dreadful, vacant, helpless smile fixed on his face again. 'Oh, yes, headaches. I never used to have them, did I? Headaches? They say—the Czarina says—I had a head wound in Japan years ago.'

Mother said, 'Do you want me to go over everything again, sir?'

He looked past her in silence. His eyes were vague, but not wholly unseeing. 'It's beginning to snow,' he said.

'It's been snowing all day, sir.'

He got up and walked stiffly across to draw the heavy curtains; it seemed to Mother, fantastically, that his face mirrored the twilit, snowbound world he was trying to shut out. 'Oh, yes, I recall what's slipped my memory, but I haven't collected my ideas,' he said, and repeated this two or three times. She realised with dismay that this was a formula repeated parrot-like a dozen times a day.

She said, with a break in her voice, 'Since it may be that I shall never have the honour of an audience with Your Majesty again, may I thank you for all the great kindness you have shown me, especially when my—little girl—died.'

She was crying openly. He turned and looked at her with that rigid rictus smile. 'When do you leave?' he asked. 'Tomorrow? I'll write

94

to you—when I've collected my ideas.' He lit the inevitable cigarette; his face was the colour of the smoke.

She left him in that dreadful, impenetrable loneliness, no longer crying, but shaking uncontrollably from head to foot. Botkin was in the reception room. He took one look at her: 'Sit down, madame!' he said. 'You're about to faint.'

She said, her teeth chattering in all that tropical heat: '*I* don't need your attention, but God knows someone else does. He's on the verge of a mental breakdown. He's—he's an automaton.'

She was too dazed to recall exactly what Botkin replied, but either he saw nothing strange in the Czar's appearance or he refused to discuss it. He said something about His Majesty being tired—that was all.

Count Benckendorff came in. Her Imperial Majesty was ready to receive the Princess. Mother gazed at him, distraught; the shock of the Czar's appearance had driven all thoughts of the audience with the Czarina clean from her mind. Never had she felt less prepared for a difficult interview. She rose up, biting her lip. At least, she thought, this time I'll be prepared for change, if there is any.

But here all seemed the same. Familiar chamberlains, ladies-in-waiting in ante-rooms, and then the big room all mauve and green, the portrait of Marie Antoinette and her children on the wall, the Nesterov Annunciation, the insipid water colours, more endless photographs, the pots of azaleas and lilies, mimosa and iris and violets, and lilac, lilac everywhere. The Czarina, in nurse's uniform, lay on a *chaise longue*, with fat little Jimmy curled up at her feet. And the Czarina was furious. Her face was hard and set; the ominous unbecoming red patches covered her cheeks. There had been a letter from Princess Vasiltchikov, telling the Czarina in the name of the women of Russia to leave Petersburg, informing her that all classes were against her, and daring her to meddle further in national affairs. The grotesque touch to the whole affair was that the Czarina's fury seemed chiefly provoked not by the contents, but because the letter itself had been written on paper torn from a letter pad. The dreadful statement that she was universally detested did not seem to affect her so much as the atrocious breach of etiquette of writing to the Sovereign *on a letter pad*.

'Writing such things, Your Majesty,' said Mother.

'Oh, I pay no attention to what she says! I know the smart set in Petersburg hate me, because I know them for what they are, but the

95

Army and people are unswervingly loyal, and that's all that matters! Do you know, every day telegrams come to me from peasants from all over Russia, assuring me of their devotion to us, and calling me the deliverer and hope of the country.'

Her face was transfigured now. With shining eyes, she pressed sheaves of telegrams into Mother's hands. 'Every day!' she said. 'Look —the deliverer of Russia. They love us—they adore Alexei. Look, here's one from a village on one of your estates.' Numbly, Mother read the flowery phrases, signed by a name she did not know. She thought: They're all fakes, like this one.

Mother nerved herself, then said in a low voice, 'Your Majesty, for the sake of the husband and child I've lost for Russia, I beg that you'll listen to me—and to the truth.'

She was heard for no more than five minutes. Then there was angry incoherence: 'You dare to tell *me* what the people of Russia think— but then I've known for a long time that you, too, have turned against me—your wicked ideas against *him*—it's no wonder the poor Czar says I'm the only person he can trust. You are to go at once, and I hope never to see you again!'

A last impression of sound, of shallow, rasping breathing, a last backward glance at a face terrifying in the lamplight, distended nostrils, fixed expression under reddened, half-closed lids, pallor which had reached even the tightly compressed lips.

Outside Olga was waiting. 'I heard you'd come,' she said, with a nervous, darting smile utterly unlike her usual frank approach. 'We saw Andrei at Novgorod before Christmas—but I expect he'll have told you that. *Oh, what's wrong?*'

Mother said, 'I think you had better not talk to me—Her Majesty might be angry. I *had* to try to—to tell her—'

'That the feeling in the country is turning against us?' For a moment she was silent, then slowly, as if she had assumed a burden she was too weary to bear, she resumed: 'You could never persuade her we're unpopular. She won't even see things there before her, even when the men in the hospital—behave badly. Oh, I wish she wouldn't go, but when I ask her to stay away she gets angry. I—I seem unable to do anything right, but then that's been so for a long time now. I hated *him*, you see, the way he looked at us and talked to us. He'd say horrible things if we seemed to like talking to—to any young Guards officer.'

'Oh, my dear!' whispered Mother.

'I hoped things would get better after he'd gone, but they haven't. He's still—ruling here.'

'But things *have* changed,' said Mother. 'His Majesty's unwell.'

'I can't understand it; I didn't think *his* death would affect Papa except in a good way, because Papa didn't really like him. But now there are these dreadful headaches—'

There was a clearing of the throat. Count Benckendorff stood there, his kind old face wretchedly embarrassed. 'The car, Madame,' he said. 'The car Her Majesty ordered to take you to the station.'

Olga kissed Mother suddenly; Mother, on an inexplicable impulse, made the sign of the cross over her. 'But you need the blessing!' said Olga. 'You're going into danger. I know you will be busy in France and elsewhere, but you must tell Andrei to let me have all news of you.'

Mother whispered, 'Would your mother allow him to write to you?'

Count Benckendorff was ostentatiously looking out of the window. Olga said, 'I'm over twenty-one. If I were a man I should be old enough to fight for Russia—'

Mother sat shivering in the car taking her to the station. Through the driving snow she could see a policeman ineffectually trying to put up a government proclamation; it was so cold that the glue froze before the paper could be secured. Already half-a-dozen were being blown about by the wind or trampled in the snow.

Such was her last view of Czarskoe. Within a few days she had said farewell to Russia.

12

'You are, in effect, questioning my judgement?'

I WAITED in a kind of suspended animation for Grandfather's arrival. Summoned from Novgorod to be attached to the Mission for liaison purposes, I stood shivering at the ungodly hour of three in the morning in the flaking grey and pink of the Finland Station, that squalid poor relation of all Petersburg stations.

I can remember how all the muscles of my stomach seemed to contract when we heard the thunder of the wheels, and then the hiss of steam as the brakes were applied. And then there was Grandfather, still topping most people by a head, looking a little strange only because for the first time I was seeing him in uniform; otherwise his back and head were unbowed, and his face was still all cool intelligence and good sense and resolution.

'Well,' he asked, once we had got home, 'this large menagerie of British, French and Italian generals, politicians, technical experts of the kind who would argue with a midwife—is it likely to produce any effect whatsoever?'

'A shipload of munitions would have been far more welcome,' I owned. 'No one in Russia really wanted you to come, but everyone was too polite to say as much. Didn't people in France sense the lack of enthusiasm?'

'Oh, yes, but the effort had to be made,' said Grandfather. 'Things here couldn't be allowed to jolt on from bad to worse—for purely selfish reasons. After all, if Russia dropped out of the war, the whole German effort would be switched to the Western Front.'

'Russia won't drop out of the war,' I said. 'This new offensive planned for the Spring—everyone's hopeful about it.'

'Even when, from what your mother said, your government may be waging two wars—one against the Germans, the other against its own people? But let me have some sleep before we talk of *that!*'

The days that followed seem quite unreal to me now. Sometimes it is almost possible to believe that I imagined it all, the shadow lifting before it closed down for good.

We had precisely one month of the old life left to us.

'This visit's doing no good,' Grandfather concluded soon enough. 'We irritate, we alienate, we don't stimulate.'

Then he, too, went out to Czarskoe, was received in the room overlooking the snowy park.

What he had heard from Mother and me put him in a rather desperate mood. The composed bearing of the Czar on the semi-public occasions at which they had met in the past few days had little significance; Royalty could almost automatically assume a mask at these times. But at this private interview, with someone known to him for over twenty years, on whose words he had hung pathetically in the past because of the friendship with his confident father—how would he appear? Platitudes whirled through Grandfather's mind as he entered the palace. The captain of a foundering ship with a mutinous crew, a man tottering on the brink of a precipice, a fugitive sinking into a swamp. Instead he found himself ludicrously in the presence of a little boy gleefully explaining how he was able to slip away from boring lessons to play soldiers.

At Stavka, said the Czar confidentially, he could find peace and quiet. Of course, there was military work to be done, but only at certain hours, unlike things here at Czarskoe where he could not call his time his own from nine o'clock onwards. And all the politics, and the question of railways bringing food to Petersburg, people in general expecting instant solutions to the most complicated problems, and ambassadors and members of the Imperial Family and politicians always expecting to see one— It was so restful at Stavka. Occasionally there were people one must have for lunch, but mostly life was peaceful and planned, with the same routine every day. He had plenty of time now to read and write, and when he went back in a few days' time he meant to take up dominoes.

God have pity on us all, thought Grandfather, aghast. He looked away from the Czar who, babbling on happily, did not notice—and gazed distractedly round the study in search of inspiration. And then he noticed something odd. Almost directly before him, a curtain was hanging—not over a window, possibly over a door. There was suddenly a little tremor of the curtain. A draught? He did not think so.

Incredible! he told himself. This isn't a low farce.

And, No, he answered himself: it's low tragedy as opposed to high. He saw the curtain twitch again. Of course she would be there. The other audiences had been formalities. The other members of the Mission were strangers, and in any case, couldn't speak with the energy of one personally involved in the fate of Russia.

The Czar was still talking about the delights of life at Stavka. Every afternoon you could go for a long walk. Sometimes you lost your way, but that only . . .

Well, he'd lost his way, sure enough, thought Grandfather, squaring his shoulders. Aloud he said: 'And what about the position further back behind the lines, sir?' He could not tell whether the Czar could be brought to listen, but he was addressing an audience of more than one. 'Sir, let me talk of one aspect of the situation that causes me particular anxiety. It has always been the policy of the military authorities here to have in hand as large a number of reserves as possible.'

The Czar's expression had changed completely, was a mere mask of formal politeness. 'We like to have them to fill the gaps in the fighting line,' he explained painstakingly. Grandfather would have preferred irritation, impatience, more normal reactions than this total lack of real interest in what he was saying, this obvious waiting for him to finish. But he persevered: 'Yes, sir, I understand that, but the truth is that you're calling up far more men than are strictly necessary, so that now you have literally millions of reservists and recruits accumulating in camps and barracks all over the country, doing nothing, receiving no training.'

The Czar explained carefully that there were not sufficient arms to keep the front supplied, so it was quite impossible to train the reserves, and—

'By your leave, sir! In addition to all this, your army lacks good officers. More. There are defects of quantity as well as of quality. There simply aren't enough of them. Yesterday I visited a camp of forty thousand men. In it there were only eighteen officers, and of those only two had ever seen actual fighting. And the supply of good, experienced NCOs—the backbone of any army—is even worse.'

The Czar asked puzzledly, 'You are saying the Spring offensive is endangered?'

'I don't mean that, sir, I mean the war on the other front, the front of whose existence perhaps you're unaware. Consider. You have millions of men, inactive, untrained, undisciplined, left to their own devices, open to all suggestions by agitators, of whom there are legion. In your capital you have a garrison of a hundred thousand reservists, badly trained, badly officered, idle and worked upon openly by agitators—I've seen it for myself, sir!'

The Czar said, like a child repeating lines learned by heart: 'You are forgetting the traditional attachment of the Russian peasant and the Russian soldier to his Czar. Of course, not being Russian . . .'

'No, sir, I am not Russian, but I think you know I am devoted to the country my only surviving child has made her own. I do not think I can be classed with those foreign visitors who, after a stay of no more than four-and-twenty hours, can give an accurate description of all the ills of the country, the description, in most cases, leaving one with the impression that they've spent their entire stay fishing in the gutters and sewers of Petersburg.'

The Czar said after a moment, 'You mean that you have heard criticisms of me?'

Grandfather said strongly: 'Criticisms, sir? What is being said of you—and *yours*—is as unjust as it is untrue, and as malicious as it is unjust. I know—as every rightly-informed person knows—that Your Imperial Majesty is bent heart and soul on bringing this war against Germany to a speedy and victorious conclusion, and, by God, Germany knows it, too! The pity is that your allies *and people* aren't as well-informed as your enemies are. One cannot doubt, sir, that Germany knows the easiest way of beating Russia is not to defeat her armies in the field, but to stir up discontent *behind* the front line. This German mischief must be dealt with before the German Army can be beaten, and there is one sure way of doing this. Tell your people that Your Imperial Majesty trusts them, that you will consider any advice they can give you, that you will employ ministers who enjoy their confidence!'

'Surely,' said the Czar, with the faint, meaningless smile Mother had seen, 'the first essential is that the ministers should enjoy *my* confidence? You are, in effect, doubting my judgement?'

God forgive me for telling a lie, said Grandfather mentally, before plunging on aloud. 'No, sir, but I have grave fears as to the effect of so much—so much enormous lonely responsibility on your health. Has not the moment now come for you to appeal to your people to assist you in a task far too heavy to rest on one pair of shoulders alone?'

The Czar gazed at him in surprise. 'But how can you forget—you who know my family so well! I don't bear the responsibility alone, I share it with Her Majesty, who is ready to assume all the duties of a Catherine the Great, I assure you.'

'Sir, I know you believe Her Majesty is as extraordinary a woman as Catherine, I know Catherine gave Russia strong government, but, sir, *these are not the days of Catherine!*'

Silence from the Czar, who turned away to light a cigarette, the old familiar action when he was at a loss. From behind the curtain a sudden movement; could one hear the hurried breathing of an hysterical, angry woman? Grandfather continued gravely: 'As I was coming to this audience, sir, and turned over in my mind what I had to say, I knew that I laid myself open to the rebuke that this was none of my business, that, indeed, I might be sent packing from Russia at the end of it, but I have been impelled to speak as I have done in the consciousness of two devotions—the first, Your Majesty's devotion to your Allies, the other my own devotion to the country claiming the loyalty of all who are left to me now. The country needs to be trusted, and it needs to be led! No appeal is ever made to the people's reason or their imagination; in fact, the Government seems to think of Russia as a—a gigantic hen, hypnotised into immobility by a chalk line drawn before her beak!'

The Czar stared away from him, out of the window. After a moment, he began to reply in French, and then suddenly switched to English. Significant enough again, thought Grandfather, that's what he talks to his wife. 'Will you wait a moment outside? Possibly Her Majesty would like to see you.'

Excellent as the Imperial command of English might be, reflected Grandfather, on this occasion the choice of words might be criticised—like?

It was dark when Grandfather returned finally from Czarskoe. When I met him in the front hall, he said, 'I won't talk to you yet; I want to set everything down while it's still fresh in my memory. Come to me in an hour's time.'

I gave him ninety minutes. When I went in, he was bending over the great porcelain stove. He was burning some sheets of closely written paper.

'How did it go?' I asked ineptly.

He jerked his head towards the writing table. 'See for yourself. All that I wish to record is set down there.'

So, standing, I read what had passed between him and the Czar; Grandfather sat in a low chair, shading his eyes from the light.

I finished reading. 'And the Czarina?'

He pointed to the stove. After a moment he said slowly, 'You know that in the Paris Commune I was held prisoner for a time.'

'They condemned you to death, sir.'

'Yes, and there were others with me. I had four days of it—it seemed much longer, of course. One thing I shall never forget; the different ways in which men reacted to a sentence of death; most at the end walked steadily enough, side by side with their executioners, but before that—ah, there were great differences then. In some the fear was so great, so saturating, that it left them numb—does that sound absurd, that fear can grow to such an immensity, you can feel such an excess of it that it seems to leave you? And there were the others—those bursts of hysterical terror, that inability still to realise—above all to *accept* the situation, those frantic attempts to hold the thoughts on a steady course, those cries of hopeless, helpless anger—God, even now there are nights I wake sweating at the memory of them. I've seen these two reactions today, André, and while I can describe the first, to recall the second sickens the spirit, and good clean fire's the only remedy. I could not let what she said stand on record.'

I muttered, 'Some people say she is a little mad.'

'Say rather it's still a case of diabolical possession. I'll tell you one thing only. She had beside her in her boudoir a little piece of wood. "From his dear tomb," she said, fingering it as if it were the relic of a saint. "When I am there, I feel the peace of God. He—Our Friend— died to save us." I said: "Madame, that verges on blasphemy." But, of course, she doesn't really believe that Rasputin's death has saved them; she's convinced that now he's dead they're done for.'

We said little when we parted a few days later; what was there to say?

'I could ask you to come to France,' said Grandfather, as we parted on the last evening. 'One could arrange it easily enough. But when I asked your mother to leave Russia twelve years ago, she refused for reasons which I suppose still hold good.'

'Yes, sir, but will you keep her in France as long as possible?'

'Yes,' he said, considering. 'I'll do that.' In a lower voice he added, 'I don't think matters *can* go on in this way much longer.'

They took their official leave of the Czar. There was the same strange half-smile, the lonely, haunted look, the impression that only a small part of him was here in the present, facing reality. He had as yet not made up his mind when to leave for Headquarters.

If he had not gone so soon . . .

If the Mission had stayed a little longer . . .

Farewells at the Finland Station, the rest of the day to be endured somehow, thinking of the erect old figure journeying into danger, then tomorrow, Novgorod.

Plenty of invitations to dine out, but I preferred my own company. Then one invitation came that I could not refuse. A 'phone call from Czarskoe. Her Imperial Majesty, as always on Thursday, was having a musical evening. My presence was requested. 'Commanded, surely!' I said. 'No, *requested.*'

I went out to Czarskoe in a mood to be imagined. The two people I cared for most had been driven away like dogs; I was in no mood for *soirées musicales.* I turned up late, and didn't care. I wanted the sparks to fly. I went into the salon where Goulesco's Roumanian orchestra played, and there they were, all the usual faces—Count Benckendorff, officers from the Imperial Yacht, Madame Voiekov, wife of the Palace Commandant, the inescapable Vyroubova, and, huddled before a huge fire, the Czarina. She beckoned to me to sit close to her. She looked like an old woman.

My anger left me. I saluted. 'Your Majesty,' I said. 'I'm sorry I'm late.'

'I couldn't be sure that you'd come. I want to talk to you later, Andrei. Sit by me—is that chair comfortable?'

It was, I suppose, but I sat rigid, trying not to stare too obviously at her haggard face. The Grand Duchesses were there, across the room. The three youngest were gay, smiling; Olga looked worn, fine-drawn, exhausted. She was doing the worrying for the four of them; she was the only one who'd grown up.

And then the Czarina rose hurriedly. We all sprang to our feet but she gestured to everyone except me to sit down; to me, she said in a hoarse voice that I was to follow her, and went, half-stumbling, to her boudoir. Vyroubova came rushing after us, bleating inanities about it being a mistake to have such sad music—so depressing. I shut the door firmly in her face.

'It's not the music,' said the Czarina in English, not turning. 'I can't stand anything these days. The strain—Gregory is dead; why can't people leave me alone?'

From the door I stammered something about her doing too much, couldn't she cut down her visits to the hospital, her work in general? She disregarded the question, went across to her sofa, sat down and said, 'But I didn't send for you to talk of my own troubles, Andrei—I wanted to see you because you're leaving for Novgorod tomorrow, aren't you? God go with you, and . . .'

There was a scrabbling on the door, and there was Vyroubova, saying childishly, 'We all seem so much out of sorts, let me tell the servants to bring champagne, dear madame!'

'No!' said the Czarina. 'Go away, Anya! You know the Czar can't bear women drinking wine!'

For the second time that evening, with great satisfaction I firmly closed the door in Vyroubova's face, and turned back to the Czarina in time to catch the despairing whisper: 'And all the talk is that he's a drunkard himself—and that I deliberately made him so!'

And then she continued, 'You've just come back from saying good-bye to your grandfather, haven't you, Andrei? I want you to know that we are all praying for his safety, as we prayed for the safety of your mother. And when you write to them—for I do not think they will want to hear from me direct—I want you to tell them that I am sorry I was so ungracious at our last meetings. Tell them that the person who spoke then was someone saturated with veronal; it's the only thing which keeps me on my feet.'

Again I said something incoherent about not doing too much; I'd prepared speeches enough, but all calculation was thrown out of gear by the sight of that lined, exhausted face, the glazed weariness of the eyes. Yet changed, terribly changed as she was physically, in her manner she was far more like the Czarina I had known as a child, nearly twenty years before. And I found myself talking soothingly to her almost as I would to Mother; I put my arm about her and helped her to her *chaise longue*, put shawls over her feet, about her shoulders, said I would get the doctor.

'No,' she said. 'No. Just leave me to myself. Tell people not to come to me.'

'Indeed I will!'

'You're a good boy, Andrei. Take my blessing, kiss my hand, and go. I know you won't talk.'

I kissed her hand, and she blessed me. The light caught the great pearl on the one familiar ring, the swastika on the other. As I turned to salute her at the door, her eyes were closed. I thought for a moment that she had fallen asleep, beneath the familiar portrait of the Czar by Serov, the sketch below of Alexei. But then I saw her lips moving soundlessly, and I left her, praying, and hoped that her thoughts might remain for a time in that impenetrable withdrawnness.

The unapproachability of the Czar was different. It was merely that he had lost whatever meagre capacity he had ever possessed for expressing interest in anything outside his immediate environment. He might be physically exhausted, but there was no mental rack for him.

Outside the door I encountered the inevitable Vyroubova. I blocked her path. 'Her Majesty doesn't want to be disturbed,' I said.

She tried ineffectually to dodge round me, saying archly, 'But you know that doesn't apply to me, Andrei Alexandrovitch!'

'It does, indeed, madame, my own private opinion being it applies to you more than to anyone else. And in that conviction I'm prepared to stand here with my back to the door all night to keep you out.'

'Oh,' she panted. 'How dare you! You're going too far!'

'So long as you don't on this occasion, madame.'

'Ah, you're as intolerable as your grandfather!' she said, retreating.

The musical evening, I supposed, was breaking up in some confusion. I wondered if it might be possible to present my respects to the Czar, and began to walk uncertainly along the corridor.

But the Czar, Count Benckendorff told me when I re-entered the salon, was leaving for Mogilev next day, and could see no one. (This might mean anything or nothing; even the prospective delights of dominoes could not induce him to shake off his inertia. But each day he would say, 'I've been here long enough; I must go.') The Count was quite alone in the salon. He said Madame Vyroubova had come in and informed them that the Czarina had retired, so they must all go away. The Grand Duchesses had asked about me, and Vyroubova had told them I'd gone.

'She . . .' I began.

'Careful, my boy!'

'I wasn't going to say anything obscene,' I said. 'I was just about to remark that she's a ludicrous figure to be the gravedigger of a great monarchy.'

There was a light step, and a sudden exclamation. 'I thought I had left a book here,' said Olga, the tide of colour rising in her face.

'Which book was it, Your Imperial Highness? French verse in a blue binding? I believe I saw it in one of the other rooms.' The Count, always the accomplished courtier.

Olga looked after him, made an odd, helpless little gesture. 'He thinks it was a lie. It wasn't. I *was* looking for the book—all the more so because I believed you'd gone.'

'Never mind, I'm so glad you came, otherwise it would have been such a messy, badly contrived goodbye to Czarskoe.'

Olga said, 'That would be in keeping with the rest of things, wouldn't it?'

'Messy, badly contrived? Yes.'

'You also said *goodbye*. Do you think it's come to that? Don't avoid frank speaking—rather let me go on talking frankly to you, because no one but you and your mother will listen to me, for long at least. Here, they think I'm being awkward and difficult if I try to tell them the things I told you and your mother, and then I get impatient. In the end I just have to wait until Tatiana is asleep, and the light is out in our room; darkness is the only way of escape now, to clear thinking, I mean, and reality.'

'It's not pleasant, this reality,' I said in a whisper.

'Oh, no. Sometimes I think, in the dark, that I must have fallen asleep, and what I'm thinking or remembering is a nightmare. And do you know what I do then, Andrei? I put my hands up and I touch my forehead, and bring my fingers down over my cheeks, and then I know this is myself, my face, my flesh, and I'm awake, and not in a dream.'

As, half-unconsciously, she was doing now, drawing her fingers across the wideboned face, broadest across the clear eyes the colour of harebells, eyes that were always so perfectly candid, had always been so tranquil, were now so desperately unquiet. An hour before I'd mentally called her the only one of the family that had grown up, but now, in her uncertainty and loneliness, she was like a solitary child.

13

No Glue at the Winter Palace

My ENGLISH tutor once handed me *The Golden Treasury*, and told me to learn the poem I liked best in it. I chose Cowper's poem on the loss of the *Royal George*—why, I can't remember—and recited it with great relish. He heard me out, then said thoughtfully after a moment, 'It wasn't really like that, you know. The ship was so rotten that the bottom simply dropped out.' Which is what happened in Russia in the spring of 1917.

Helped by the weather, of course. General February had a habit of turning traitor to the Romanovs.

The Sunday after my return to Novgorod I went to visit General Milyutin. He was desperately ill now, but insisted on seeing me. His bedroom had curving windows overlooking lawns, a lake, trees. In spring and summer the view must have been enchanting, but in the grey half-light, and with the lake a sheet of ice and the trees leafless, it was bleak to the point of being sinister.

The General wanted to know had I heard of the audience granted to the President of the Duma, during which Rodzianko had begged desperately, 'Your Majesty, do not compel the people to choose between you and the good of the country!' And the Czar, pressing his head between his hands, had exclaimed, like a lost child, 'Is it possible that for twenty-two years it has all been a mistake?'

I said I could believe it, and spoke briefly of Grandfather's impressions.

'By the way,' said the General suddenly, 'did you know that the Czarevitch and the Grand Duchess Olga have gone down with measles? A Petersburg specialist came to have a look at me this morning and told me.'

For all my feelings for Alexei and Olga, my first reaction was, 'So that will obsess the Czarina who always insists on nursing her children, and she'll have no thought for anything else. Thank God the Czar's still at Czarskoe!'

'But, my dear fellow, he's not! He went back to Stavka on Thursday*, the day before the children went down with measles—otherwise, of course, being a fond father, he would never have left.'

'At Stavka he might as well be on another planet,' I said.

'Planet? You're over-pretentious there. It's more the case of a schoolboy going on holiday. He actually told a cousin of mine his brain can rest there—no ministers, no awkward questions demanding thought or immediate action.'

'He's going to take up dominoes, he told Grandfather,' I said with a groan.

The short winter's day was drawing to a close; a servant brought in lamps.

'I must go,' I said. 'I've been here far too long.'

'No,' he said, 'stay as long as you can. I've so little time left—let me *think* while I can.'

His face on the pillows was ghastly. He had never been so plainly a dying man—and yet, with his persistent grappling with problems, his sheer strength of will, there was infinitely more life in him than there was in the Czar of All the Russias.

Snow fell against the dark windowpanes. The General, as if he could read my thoughts, said, 'I give myself three to four days more. Could you get in touch with my cousin when it happens? Here's his Petersburg address—the Kirotchnaia—'

He had over-estimated his strength—typical enough, I suppose; we were all over-estimating the durability of dying organisms. When I returned to my quarters the next night there was a message waiting for me—General Milyutin had died at four o'clock. Next morning I telephoned his cousin.

I got through as easily as we ever did in Russia. A voice answered within seconds. Yes, His Excellency himself was speaking. He sounded breathless, as if he had been running.

I identified myself, then said that General Milyutin was dead.

A brief silence. Then:

'I don't know whether to pity or envy him.'

* February 22, according to the Russian (Julian) calendar; March 7 in the Western (Gregorian) style.

The detached, philosophic reaction nettled me a little. I raised my voice. 'The funeral, Your Excellency, will be on—'

'My dear young man, you're not expecting me to get to Novgorod, are you? It's not safe to put one's nose outside the door.'

I started to make some remark about the weather—another blizzard was brewing here, too. He interrupted, 'Because of the firing in the streets.'

I forgot politeness. '*Where?* Not near your house, surely, sir!'

'Wait,' he said, 'I'll carry this instrument closer to the window. Now—can you hear?'

Faint but unmistakable, the sound like a coffee-mill. I blurted out the first thing that came into my head. 'But they wouldn't be using machine-guns near your house! Opposite the Preobrazhensky barracks!'

'That's where the firing's coming from.'

'The *Preobrazhensky* is mutinying—'

'They're not the first. The Pavlovsky and the Volhynsky started it. Good God, don't say this is all news to you! Are you at Novgorod or on another planet?'

I thought of someone else who seemed to live on another planet.

'What's the Czar doing?'

'The Czar!' There was gasping laughter at the other end. I found that unconsciously I had seized a pencil and paper and was writing down everything—possibly to convince myself that this was all real. The laughter stopped. 'He knows. He was warned when the demonstrations and window-breaking started at the week-end. He sent a telegram ordering all disturbances to cease. They were *inadmissible* at this difficult time, he said, and must cease next day. Well, the crowds weren't out the next day, but if there was no trouble in the street, there was trouble enough in the barracks. The Volhynsky killed one of their officers and trouble really started.'

'But the authorities—'

'The authorities!' Again that gasping laughter. 'The *authorities*! Listen—they decided that a state of siege must be proclaimed—they'd had the notices printed for months because of the growing unrest. *But they'd forgotten to provide glue.* No glue at HQ, no glue at the Winter Palace. So they ordered the few troops still loyal to *scatter the notices in the streets*—where a blizzard was blowing.'

I said, 'I must let people here know; I'll try to telephone you again, sir.'

'Why did you telephone me originally? I've forgotten.'

'To tell you that General Milyutin is dead.'

'I don't know whether to pity or envy him,' he said in precisely the same tone he had used at the beginning.

I was an alarmist. If there were riots in Petersburg, what were the Cossacks doing?

I said I'd try to find out.

And, in any case, if there were trouble, why was the telephone service still functioning?

Students making a noise, as usual.

As for the absurd story of the Preobrazhensky mutinying—the *Preobrazhensky*—

Yes, the Preobrazhensky, pride of the monarchy—'*The Turks know, the Swedes know, the whole world knows about us*'—the Czar's own regiment. But the Preobrazhensky, like the Pavlovsky, had died in the first weeks of the war, these half-trained men in Petersburg weren't the Preobrazhensky—*cucullus non facit monachum*—and merely wearing a uniform didn't make a man a soldier.

Although perhaps there was a ghastly logic in it. The real Preobrazhensky had been butchered by the idiocy of the High Command, and now their substitutes were butchering the generals.

The first person who accepted immediately what I said was my sergeant.

'Oh, it's true, I've no doubt,' he said. 'You know the old proverb, Your Honour—the big lie has short legs and doesn't go far.'

I went back to the telephone. The voice at the other end still sounded breathless.

I said, 'Nobody believes me. They say that if there were such trouble, the telephones wouldn't be functioning.'

'That is one of the comic features of the situation. The chaos is such that neither side has so far thought of occupying the telephone exchange, which is working normally and neutrally. But not for much longer, I think; the employees will simply stop working, as everyone else seems to have done, and then we'll all be cut off.'

'Do you mean that even though the government didn't think of it, the revolutionary leaders had no idea of taking over the exchange?'

'But there are no revolutionary leaders. The whole thing has just *happened*. The government hasn't been overthrown—it's simply collapsed, and looks like burying us all in its ruin. All's ignorance and chaos here. No newspapers because of the general strike, so there are no inflammatory articles urging on the revolution. The bread shortage was the last straw—and that's all there is to it.'

'But haven't they used the Cossacks?'

'Ah, the Cossacks! But this is 1917, and we've liberal western allies we mustn't offend. What would be the Allied reaction to corpses on the snow?'

The victims of Bloody Sunday, it seemed, were also taking a belated revenge.

'Troops were given orders to fire only in the last resort, in self-defence. As for the Cossacks—well, if the trouble became anything more than naughty boys and girls out on the spree, they were to use their *nagaykas**. But most of them hadn't got their *nagaykas* with them —they'd believed they were only in the capital *en route* to the Front, so they hadn't brought that particular article of equipment with them. After all, even our government hadn't proposed to counter trench mortars with whips. When this was eventually discovered, the authorities thought of issuing money to the Cossacks—each to buy his own whip. But by this time it was too late.

'For the rest, *troops not given any orders to fire can't keep crowds at a distance.* When the people realise they're not going to be shot down, they'll approach, talk. After this, if the order *is* given, the troops won't obey. Whether they ever would have done is a moot point. Most of them were reservists from the local factories. A week ago I asked one of the Olympians at the War Office why the devil these fellows were allowed to hang about Petersburg for weeks on end—when were they going to be sent to the Front? Oh, he said, that would be too dangerous —these men were notoriously seditious. They'd give far less trouble in Petersburg. I wonder if he's remembering that now—ten to one he's dead already. They stormed the Astoria between nine and ten this morning, killed all the officers they could lay hands on. It was a shambles.'

'And Czarskoe. What's happened at Czarskoe?'

'Until yesterday they were as ill-advised about the real state of things as ever. You may know that my neighbour is Senator Neidhardt, brother-in-law to Madame Sazonov, who's staying with him. Yesterday she had a telephone call from a lady-in-waiting—the Czarina invited

* Long leather whips with a short stock.

her to lunch. Madame Sazonov said she didn't think she could get to the station, and at first they couldn't understand why. I swear that's the first inkling they got of the true state of affairs, and even then they couldn't or wouldn't understand the way things are going. "Oh, it's the food shortage! Well, fresh supplies have been ordered up and that will be the end of the affair!" '

His voice grew brisker. 'Well, the telephones still function, but not much longer, I should say, so I advise you to contact other people while you can. Keep away from this damned city—there's a curse on it. If you're fool enough to return, let me pass on a piece of possibly useful information. They say the most comfortable cells in Peter and Paul Fortress are those between 30 and 36. Good night.'

I telephoned my home. After an interval, Vassily, our old butler, answered, but the delay might mean anything—he loathed using the telephone and always waited for five minutes before answering—with luck the caller might lose patience and hang up.

'Vassily, it's me—Andrei. What has been happening?'

'Master, for God's sake stay away. They're killing all the officers here.'

'But you're safe, everybody in the house is safe?'

'Now, yes, but God knows how long we'll stay safe. There's hardly a policeman left alive in the city now—there's no law and order left, they're looting and murdering, the soldiers and the crowds, drunk, just as they please. Thank God the mistress is in France!'

'Amen!' I said.

I telephoned the French Embassy. By good luck, though to my surprise, I managed to get hold of one of the few attachés for whom I had much respect, a new arrival in the past year, a gunnery expert who had known Uncle Raoul well.

I said, 'But I thought you'd be at Stavka!'

'I was supposed to be joining the Czar yesterday, but since nobody knows where he is—'

'But he's at Mogilev!'

'No, he's left it, but where he is now, God knows. He sent a telegram yesterday saying he was leaving at the head of a large force to restore order, everyone's been expecting him to turn up ever since, terrible as an army with banners, but he seems to have vanished into a kind of limbo. The latest reports say he's at Pskov.'

'But it's only a night's journey! If he left yesterday, he should have been in Petersburg this morning! Why in the devil is he going in for this ritual ramble round the countryside?' A sharp pain suddenly made me conscious of the fact that I had been beating my hand against the wall like a frenzied child. 'Why in God's name did *he* leave Stavka? The moment he got on that damned ghost train he lost all contact with both the Army and Petersburg!'

The Colonel said expressionlessly, 'His motive was anxiety for his family. Let us face it—there are no Swiss Guards at Czarskoe.'

'Not that this excuses *him*. The best way to safeguard his family was to act like a Czar—for once! In any case, he's not likely to reach Petersburg.'

'Why do you say that?'

'Because the railway workers have been disaffected for months now. Far more sensible to stick to horses.'

'What do you mean by that last remark?' the colonel demanded sharply.

'Why,' I said, 'one must do what one can. I must bring my squadron up—'

'You damned young idiot, stay where you are! What in the devil do you think you can do? Hold Peter and Paul? Too late—the garrison's mutinied. Throw a cordon around the government? *That's* disappeared —the electricity failed at their last meeting, so they broke up and never reassembled.'

'I'm not going to sit passively here in Novgorod while everything's being settled in Petersburg,' I said obstinately.

'But how can you be sure—' he began, and after this there was only silence. So the telephone workers had at last decided to give up.

I4

'Do you think it might have been avoided?'

EASY ENOUGH, of course, to finish the uncompleted sentence. 'How can you be sure of your men?'

I thought I could.

Later I went to look for my sergeant, told him all the fresh information I had gathered, ended by saying that at dawn I would begin the long ride to Czarskoe. If necessary I should ride alone.

'No, Your Honour.'

'I've tried to get other squadrons to ride with us. No other officers agree.'

'They're scared of the stories they've heard. They can only think of their own necks. They don't know their men well enough—or their men know *them* too well. We're better off without them.'

'At dawn, then.'

It was snowing again when we left Novgorod. When day came, the blizzard ceased, but the sky remained the colour of lead. We saw only one sign of life—if one could call it that—during the morning. A funeral. I tried to remember the day that had been fixed for General Milyutin's funeral. *To be pitied or envied?*

Darkness fell, and after some hours the clouds broke up and then it was sustained riding across that flat, endless country stretching away from us in the light of a bright wintry moon. And then a halt snatched at an inn—I would never have thought that I could sleep, but hadn't foreseen the mere physical effect of coming into sudden smothering heat after hours of bitter cold in the saddle. The cold had got into my brain, and now the heat invaded and thawed it out too quickly. Perhaps it wasn't so much sleep as half-consciousness.

It was fine next morning, though the snow lay deeper on the roads, but with the afternoon the weather worsened and a great black promontory of storm clouds built up, with battered edges of crimson. And then there was the brilliant rim of the setting sun itself, shining directly into our eyes, blinding us.

'If it snows again,' I said to the sergeant, 'we'll never reach Czarskoe tonight.'

Before darkness fell the flakes were driving in our faces again. The last snowfall of the year, probably. This knowledge didn't help.

Another night of snatched, begrudged sleep. Snow still fell at dawn, but less heavily. It was in the half-way stage between snow and sleet when we rode into Czarskoe. The wind drove what was falling into our faces; one could see only dimly. And then, through the murk, appeared the great palace gates, closed, with troops before them, some infantry and, to the right, and seeming to hold aloof, a handful of Cossacks. Behind, the white and green palace. All appeared quiet enough.

I was suddenly aware of what a spectacle we were, bedraggled, horses hanging exhausted heads. Never could a squadron of Chevaliers Gardes have had a less military bearing. Half-unconsciously I was slowing to a halt—and the same thought must have occurred to the men with me, for they too were squaring shoulders, sitting determinedly upright in the saddle. And perhaps the falling sleet and snow would hide how desperately weary our poor little scarecrow squadron had become.

'Now, lads,' said the sergeant, 'remember you're at Czarskoe, and the whole Imperial Family may be watching you.'

We moved forward slowly, and one of the younger troopers, a Caucasian with amazingly keen eyesight, said agitatedly, 'With permission, Your Honour—is *that* the Imperial Escort?'

'What else, from the way they're strutting about?' grunted the sergeant.

'But they're wearing red ribbons in their coats!'

The sergeant pushed his tired horse forward. 'For God's sake, be careful, Your Honour! Lads, close up! My God, no need for us to worry about how *we* look—see this lot!'

Unshaven, unkempt, but armed. One must remember that. There were more lounging in the great courtyard—one could see them now.

'Be careful, Your Honour!' from the sergeant again.

(Of course. Don't antagonise them—you must find out what's happening in the palace).

There was one man standing a little ahead of the rest, obviously a self-elected spokesman, but I addressed the cluster of men as a whole.

'Who set you on guard here? Where's the Czar?'

'Well!' said the thrustful man, smirking. 'Here's one officer at least who's heard of Order Number One—none of this traditional "thou"* business, though he's not as polite as he should be.'

'He hasn't heard everything though, has he?' another man said, grinning. 'Shall we tell him?'

'Wait! Let's ask him where he's sprung from, since he's so ignorant.'

'We've come from the Mouraviev Barracks, Novgorod,' growled the sergeant. 'All right, what's so funny?'

'And when did you leave Novgorod?'

'Two days ago.'

'What—rode through all the snowdrifts for nothing? There's Chevaliers Gardes for you!'

'What do you mean—for nothing?'

'Well, you came looking for the Czar, you said. Go on looking for him—you'll never find him.'

'Dead?' I said after a moment.

They all burst out laughing, slapping each other on the back. 'Dead? You mean he put up a fight? Not on your life! He abdicated—just like that! Sat in his train at Pskov and abdicated. Showed a bit more energy, too, in abdicating than he'd ever done in governing. Russia got a bargain from him. He abdicated for the boy as well.'

'When?' (My sergeant.)

'Two days ago.'

They began yelling with laughter again. 'Just when you were beginning the long ride through all the snowdrifts!'

The Caucasian said bewilderedly, 'Then who's Czar now? There's bound to be a Czar!'

'Nicholasha said he abdicated in favour of his brother. Just like his nerve. Never showed much life as Czar, but now he's been pushed out of the job, he's trying to make himself felt. His mistake! In any case, Michael—I can hardly say it for laughing!—says he'll only take the crown if—it's killing me!—if it's offered to him by the Russian people!'

'Are you telling me,' said the sergeant incredulously, 'that there's no Czar at all now?'

The Cossacks had been listening without taking part in the

* The familiar form of address used by officers to men.

117

conversation. Now they rode slowly forward. One of them said, 'Come to your senses now?'

'Meaning?'

'Not much point in fighting for a man who won't fight for himself.'

'I've seen you before,' I said suddenly.

'Yes,' he said. 'After Tannenberg. We were the patrol who picked you up—remember?' In a voice so low that only I could hear, he went on roughly, 'I saved your life then—well, it would be a waste of a good turn if you got a bullet through your head now, so I'm telling you to get off damned quick. You can't reason with this lot; they looted the wineshops days ago and you never find them sober now. Lucky for you they're in a good mood this morning—you've given them a laugh.'

Other soldiers had come lounging up to join the first group. It is difficult to describe their bearing. As the sergeant had said, they strutted—yet at the same time they slouched. As for their faces, some were grinning, others were sullen, but most of them showed only excitement—excitement without reason. They were so excited they kept twitching. And there were others you could scarcely call faces at all, they were mere masks, masks cleverly made of flesh, but still masks—because the eyes shining through the holes in the flesh showed no expression whatsoever.

My gaze shifted past them. I remembered that Olga could see the gate and street from her window, but couldn't remember the details. Could she see us?

The Cossack said in a fierce whisper, as if he could read my thoughts, 'Will it help them if they see you shot down? Get off, and look hang-dog as you go!'

No need to ape dejection. I sat there, shoulders sagging, gazing ahead almost vacantly. It was as if my brain refused to accept the messages sent by my eyes. The courtyard beyond the three great curved iron gates all greasy mud and dirty water—there had been no one to sweep away the snow. I was half glad of the drenching sleet—sunshine would have shown up the squalor more clearly.

There was a brief lull of absolute silence. The only sound seemed to be the panting of our exhausted horses. I sat slumped in the saddle, my own head drooping, and stared down at my poor beast's bulging eyes, flaring nostrils, veins pulsing under the sagging skin. I patted his neck automatically. I had no idea what to do next. Our ride had been quite pointless—as pointless as most things in the reign that had just ended.

'Tell us,' said my sergeant to the Cossack, 'what's this Order Number One that bit of floating scum was talking about.'

'You'll find out soon enough. It means the end of the Russian Army. *Start moving!*'

I said, 'We'll go to my home. It's big enough to take us all.'

And so we rode from Czarskoe along the tree-lined roads, light in the sky above us, sleet turning into drizzle, dripping heavily from the leafless trees.

Most of the fourteen miles we covered in silence. We were, I suppose, in a state of shock; in any case, what energy we had at first we used in encouraging our poor horses to make this last effort. Heavy clouds came rolling in from the Gulf of Finland. And then, quite suddenly, the sergeant shouted violently, 'I don't believe it! A Czar doesn't abdicate because there's a shortage of bread and women rioting!'

I pulled up. We halted there in a little group, furious, fully alive now.

'If they told him the Petersburg garrison was mutinying—' hazarded a trooper.

The sergeant spat. 'Garrison! Untrained recruits! He knew that, didn't he? He had an army of fifteen million men, and he was afraid to tackle reservists!'

I said, 'He felt he'd done wrong by making any move to sharing power in 1905—the power wasn't his to share, because it had been entrusted to him by God. And to give it all up—*I still can't believe it.*'

'If he'd abdicated in 1905—' said one of the troopers, 'everything would have been different, wouldn't it?'

The sergeant said fiercely, 'Were they lying to us, then, Your Honour?'

'The Cossack wouldn't lie,' I said.

No, they all agreed, the Cossack wouldn't lie. Yet how could one believe that the Czar would give up so easily—

'Perhaps,' said a trooper, 'the poor gentleman didn't realise what he was doing.'

'But he gave up his boy's rights, too,' said the sergeant. 'Are we to believe that? That's what *she* used to keep on about, wasn't it—keep the monarchy strong for the boy to inherit?'

'It's not legal, in any case!' I said in sudden rage. 'He couldn't surrender Alexei's rights for him.'

'Surrender's the word,' said the sergeant in a low, furious voice. 'He had troops, generals—and he gives in because strikers are making trouble here, and a garrison of lazy wasters and cowards join in because they don't want to go to the Front!'

'Come,' I said roughly. 'Let's get into the city.'

In the city there were dirty red flags everywhere—above the Winter Palace, the Admiralty, Peter and Paul. The Imperial eagles on the gates of the Palace covered with a red cloth—at other places hacked away. And everywhere soldiers, dishevelled, slouching, strolled or stood idly. Armed workmen in groups, carrying rifles, pistols, officers' swords. No policemen. No ordinary citizens. No trams or cabs. Shuttered shops. One couldn't note everything, however, because for days no one had been sweeping away the slush or sanding the roads which were terrible. Our poor tired horses found it difficult to keep their footing on the icy surfaces. I could hear the sergeant swearing steadily behind me. 'Damn them,' he kept saying to his horse. 'To hell with them. May the ravens pick their bones if you fall because of their damned revolution.'

At last the most familiar street in the world. There was a great bare patch in the snow just outside the house.

The door was barred. I banged on it, calling to Vassily. From the other side I could hear men's voices raised in argument, a woman crying, finally Vassily's voice, in furious scorn. 'It's he! It's he! Tell me I don't know that voice!' and the noise of bolts being drawn back, and Vassily thanking God and kissing my shoulder.* Behind Vassily, the servants huddled together, some of the women weeping hysterically. 'In! In! for God's sake!' said Vassily. 'Dmitri and Ivan, see to the horses—'

The door slammed shut behind us. I stared round at the familiar faces. The women looked ghastly. 'In God's name, what's happened?' I whispered.

'That patch of melted snow outside,' said Vassily, grimacing. 'They burned a policeman alive there. Yesterday. Drunken soldiers. They tied him up and dragged him face downwards over the snow, and put an end to him—here.'

The women began to sob again. 'Give them something to do,' I said. 'The ballroom which was being prepared to take wounded after the Spring fighting—the men will sleep there. And food. Get some brandy up from the cellar. And, Vassily—*has* the Czar abdicated?'

He shook his head blindly. 'I don't know! I don't know, master! They say he has, but it can't be so.'

* The old traditional form of homage.

120

Actually he could tell us little as we ate like famished wolves. The yellow and black Imperial flag had been pulled down everywhere, to be replaced by the red flag. 'Dirty bits of rag,' said Vassily, 'and poor dye and material too. The colour'll run and go streaky—you see!' He kept repeating this, as if the revolution would be washed out with the dye. But again and again he reverted to the murdered policeman. 'The police weren't all that wicked,' he said. 'Good and bad—as everywhere else, Master, do you remember that good fellow who came to your father the night before Bloody Sunday and was shot down next day? You can't tell me he was the only one with a bit of decency in him!'

'I don't know about decency,' said the sergeant, who had been listening with great intentness, 'but, by God, they're the only fellows who've shown guts and fought for a government that didn't help them! Where are the ministers? Gone into hiding, I'll be bound! But the poor devils they told to stick to their posts did what they could.'

Vassily said, 'You are right, my friend. It looks as if only the police and you from Novgorod were ready to fight for the Czar.'

'Who won't fight for himself,' said the sergeant.

'Wait,' I said. 'We must get at the truth first. Vassily, is the telephone working again?'

It was and I telephoned the French Embassy.

'Where are you? *Where?* You rode from Novgorod after all—my poor boy!'

The last three words told me all that was necessary. 'It's true then—he's abdicated?'

'You're at home? I'll come round to tell you all I know. At once.'

In the interval of waiting, I tried to telephone General Milyutin's cousin. There was no answer, although I tried three times.

The men were snatching a few hours' sleep while their clothes were being dried. The sergeant went out to have a look at the horses. A car drove up outside and Vassily unbarred the door. The colonel came in, embraced me.

'Thank God your mother's out of all this,' he said. 'Shall I send her a telegram on your behalf saying you're safe and well? I won't stay long—you look as if you haven't slept for days—and I'll get on with the wretched story at once.'

Only one question. 'He abdicated at Pskov? He never reached Petrograd?'

'Yes, at Pskov. The railwaymen wouldn't let his train through.'

'But if he'd come direct—I know that damned line from Stavka, every inch of it, and if he'd come direct to Czarskoe—When in the devil did he start?'

'At five on Tuesday morning. He didn't come by the direct line because he didn't want to interfere with regular troop traffic, so he made a long detour through Smolensk—'

'With everything depending on *speed*—'

'Also,' said the colonel, 'this was an Imperial train. For security reasons the speed had to be strictly regulated.'

'Security!'

'—and, of course, as it entered a fresh province there was a halt at the capital, so that the governor could present his report—'

'And were there routine inspections of guards of honour?'

'Until they reached Pskov, yes.'

I was walking up and down, waving my arms. 'When he grasped how bad the trouble was here, he should have made concessions, which he refused to do. That's right, isn't it?'

'His own ministers begged him to do this. He ordered them to do nothing until he appeared.'

'After which he left Stavka from which he might have controlled the situation—or which at least might have provided a refuge—and disappeared into limbo, taking great care not to interfere with normal train services. If he'd made straight for Czarskoe—'

'At least he might have safeguarded his family,' said the colonel in a low voice. 'The Imperial train there was actually under steam, the Czarina had asked Dr Botkin what risks the children ran, and he said he was less afraid of measles than he was of revolutionaries. But she decided she must wait for the Czar.'

A sudden thought struck me. 'Where is he now?'

'You should ask the Duma emissaries, Shulgin and Guchkov, who saw him at Pskov. I only know he's not at Czarskoe.'

'I know Shulgin, we've had him to dinner often enough. Is he at the Duma now?'

He seized my arm, aghast. 'You young fool, when I said you should ask them, I was only talking metaphorically. My God, André, *keep off those streets!* Are you mad, talking in this way?'

'No,' I said. 'Merely demanding my rights. What happened at Pskov has ruined my country and possibly my life—I have a right to hear a first-hand account of what actually occurred.'

After much argument, he said, 'Then let me drive you there in the Embassy car,' but the sergeant coming back to report, had another suggestion. 'We all wish to know what happened—why we were made fools of, coming all this way. So we will all go with His Honour—'

Twice in the lampless dusk we heard shooting—a lorry full of soldiers and workmen lurched past us and at the far end of the street gave a burst of machine-gun fire. There was no target. They were simply showing who were the masters.

The Duma was like a madhouse. Glaringly lit in the headlights of the lorries and armoured cars jamming the approaches. Inside, pandemonium. The white Catherine Hall reeking with tobacco smoke and the smell of unwashed bodies, packed with dishevelled soldiers, their greatcoats steaming, hysterical students of both sexes, shouting workmen, bawling, swearing, brandishing guns, spitting on the floor, waving their arms, being sick—or slumped down asleep against the wall. One private was contentedly eating herrings and jam.

'The street's come into the building,' said the sergeant.

We were given different answers when we asked for Shulgin. The noise was indescribable. Soldiers and workmen kept making speeches. There was constant bawling of the *Marseillaise*.

'You go off and find him, Your Honour,' said the sergeant. 'We'll be waiting here for you.' I left them standing in orderly formation and fought my way towards the White Hall, where the Duma had its sessions. It was a cross between the Black Hole of Calcutta and a country railway waiting-room; wedged bodies, with sweat pouring from them, and sleeping soldiers, stacks of arms, sacks of meal, dirt, disorder, noise, smells, a few scared deputies at the far end—and above the President's chair, where the big shining blue and white Repin portrait of the Czar had hung, an empty frame with untidy shreds of canvas—hacked by bayonets?—protruding from it.

I found Shulgin at last in the rooms in the Right Wing being used by the Duma Committee—or, as it was now calling itself, the Provisional Government, two small rooms facing the Duma library. I suppose I should have taken a good look at the titular new masters of the country as they sat apprehensively round a table covered with green velvet, but I merely pushed the double doors open and said to Shulgin, 'Vassily Vitalevitch, I want you to explain to me and my men what has happened.'

Someone groaned, 'Oh, my God, not another speech!'

'No,' said Shulgin, rising, 'no more speechmaking with appeals at the end for hurrahs for Mother Russia—thank God! Here's someone at last who wants the facts.'

'You're a Chevalier Garde,' said a professional type with eyeglasses. 'You're safe—in no danger?' When I stared at him uncomprehendingly, he explained fussily, 'We've had a succession of officers coming to us begging for protection.'

I laughed. 'My men are with me—they rode with me from Novgorod and they're waiting for me now in the Catherine Hall.'

'Why did you ride from Novgorod?'

'Because we thought the Czar would need us,' I said. This reply so astounded them that there was absolute silence as I turned to Shulgin and continued, 'And because we were told that you would be able to explain to us why we have no Czar now, sir, we have come to you.'

He came away with me; they watched us go like men in a dream.

My people stood exactly where I had left them, drawn up in a compact little group. 'We can't talk here,' said Shulgin, who looked like a man at the end of his tether.

'Will you come to my house, sir? We are all there.'

'Your private army, eh?' he said, trying to smile.

'Well,' said a trooper, 'that's what it amounts to—who do we take orders from except from His Honour now that the Czar's gone?'

'This stupid scum here!' said the sergeant. 'They've never seen active service, but, by God, according to them, if they haven't killed any Germans they've killed enough Russian officers to get a dozen Iron Crosses apiece.'

'They're not all bad, though,' said the Caucasian. 'There was that poor fellow who came up to us—we thought he was trying to cadge a cigarette.'

A soldier from the Preobrazhensky had come up to them when I left them and whispered, 'Have you got any more to spare?'

'More what?'

'Officers.'

'What kind of officers?'

'Any kind—it doesn't matter. We've got rid of the lot we had because they were a bad lot, but I know it won't do to be altogether without 'em, we can't get along without 'em, but they must be the right kind.'

'Still,' said the sergeant with ferocious good humour when we were outside, 'what does it matter if there aren't enough officers, when we have Napoleonchik?'

As I stared at him, wondering whom he nicknamed 'little Napoleon', the rest of the squadron with one exception rocked with happy laughter. 'Yes, little Napoleon!' The one exception was the Caucasian trooper, who explained, 'Your Honour, he didn't *say* he was Napoleon—he told us he wasn't going to be somebody else.'

I thought they were talking about some drunken soldier. Shulgin, however, grinned wryly. 'Kerensky's up to his tricks again, then. Did he stand with his hand inside his coat—like this—'

'Yes, that's right, like Napoleon in the pictures! And we asked him where the Czar was, and he said *he* wasn't going to be a Marat. Excellency, what is a Marat?'

'He was stabbed in his bath by a girl,' I said, staring.

'Good God! Good God!' said the Caucasian, deeply shocked. 'No wonder he doesn't want to be like that.'

'No one would have a chance to kill *this* one,' said the sergeant. 'He'd talk the hindlegs off a donkey.'

The Caucasian informed me, 'He has bristly hair and sharp little eyes, Your Honour.'

'A sharp little nose, too, like a bird's beak,' chimed in someone else.

'He talks like a bird, in a harsh scream!'

'He is as good as a play, very dramatic, and making gestures all the time.'

Democracy had obviously come to Russia with a harlequin leap.

Shulgin drove to my home; we followed close behind. It was difficult to imagine we were in Petersburg; with the rattle of machine-guns sounding from time to time and the blaze of burning buildings in the distance, it was more like being in a town close to the front line.

When I offered refreshment, Shulgin stared at me blankly for a moment, and then said, 'Do you know, I don't know when I ate last! It's been a long nightmare, no beginning, no ending, everything jumbled, the only punctuation the singing of the *Marseillaise* which tears at one's nerves, or Kerensky making another speech, or the eternal belching out of *Svoboda!** My God, I was glad when you gave me the chance to escape for a moment!'

'When did you sleep last?'

'Sleep? In bed? Six days ago. Since then it's been armchairs of a

* Freedom.

125

spindly kind in the Duma—or in the train, but we couldn't sleep then—'

'You must eat and drink now,' I said, and, touched with sudden compunction, for he looked ghastly, I added, 'If you don't want to talk—'

'Oh, yes,' he said with a wretched laugh, 'I want to talk. We have much in common, after all, two nightmare journeys to save the monarchy—to find the monarchy bent on suicide.'

What the Cossack had said. No use fighting for a man who wouldn't fight for himself—

By four o'clock on the morning of Thursday the Provisional Committee set up by the Duma as the emergency had developed had been forced to take more positive action. The Petersburg Soviet— Council—of Workmen had already taken over rooms in the Duma itself and had invited the mutinous soldiers to send representatives to join it. On the Wednesday the Soviet had issued what Shulgin called the infamous Order Number One—soldiers everywhere were to form committees, elect delegates to the Soviet, and obey only orders issued by the Soviet. Officers were to be polite to their men, and not use the traditional form of addressing them.

The Duma member Guchkov was a Liberal, but the prospect of an end to all discipline appalled him. Order must be restored. The situation grew worse hourly. Russia must be given a new Czar— Alexei—around whom the country could rally, and it must be done quickly. He was ready to seek out the Czar, and Shulgin, the devoted monarchist, agreed to go with him.

They had gone down to the station at dawn, secured a train of one engine, one coach, and begun the long search for the Czar. It was ten o'clock that night that, sleepless, hungry, and dishevelled, they arrived at Pskov. They stumbled across badly-lit snow-covered tracks to the Imperial train, and the drawing-room coach with the green silk hangings. The Czar, wearing a grey Cossack tunic, shook hands with them in a friendly manner. They sat round a small, square table. Guchkov had spoken—very well. He said they had come to report on the situation in the capital and to discuss what measures might save the situation, all the more menacing because the disturbances were un- planned and spontaneous, and thus anarchy threatened. The govern- ment had ceased to exist. The revolutionary spirit in the army was contagious, might spread to the Front. Only the Czar's abdication in

126

favour of his son, with his brother Michael as regent, could save Russia and the dynasty. He begged for a decision within twenty-four hours.

It was now that the Czar, who had listened impassively, dropped his bombshell.

'He said in a calm and matter-of-fact manner that he had made up his mind before we arrived. "I have decided to abdicate. Until three this afternoon I thought I would abdicate in favour of my son Alexei, but then I changed my mind, and shall abdicate in favour of my brother Michael."

'I don't know what I said, but I remember thinking, the atmosphere of the Duma has followed us here. This is a madhouse, too. The only hope of saving the monarchy depended on the accession of Alexei—the country wouldn't accept Michael, he'd be just another Romanov Czar. Guchkov told me afterwards that I'd actually asked for time for a brief consultation, and the Czar agreed.'

So the two men, already lightheaded because of lack of food and sleep, held a nightmare discussion in appalled whispers.

'I hope you will appreciate this decision of a father,' the Czar had said.

Shulgin had blurted out that, with respect, he could not. The Czar had replied he could not bear to be parted with the boy, particularly because of Alexei's ill-health.

Shulgin had said to Guchkov, 'It's illegal—he can't do this. The boy's a minor—he's not even here! One can't pass over a minor's rights!'

Guchkov replied, 'We must argue along these lines—that we understand the feelings of a loving father, but *this* is a betrayal of the dynasty. Surely he'll comprehend that—after all, for years he's been obsessed by the thought of his son's succession!'

Shulgin, who always suffered from migraine, found that tiredness and tension had brought about a headache that almost blinded him. Dimly, he was aware of a general arguing, 'This is impossible! A man can't relinquish a throne just as if he were handing over the command of a cavalry squadron to another officer!'

Beside him, Guchkov, always more realistic, not so emotionally involved because he had no affection for the Czar, said harshly, 'His own abdication doesn't signify much—he's been abdicating throughout his reign, no more than a fond father of a family at Czarskoe, no more than a caricature of a Commander-in-Chief at Stavka—but this abdication for his son is the cruellest blow he has ever dealt Russia.'

The Czar returned. 'You cannot persuade me to change my mind,' he said, and produced a typewritten sheet. 'I had my abdication typed out before you came—here is my signature, in pencil—'

The sergeant brought his fist down with a crash. 'By God, no!' he shouted. 'Czardom ending because in a railway coach in a siding a good family man hands over a bit of paper with typewriting on it and a signature in pencil!'

There was one more piece of business to transact; since the government had ceased to exist, new ministers must be appointed by means of a message to the Senate, the highest legal authority in the country. The Czar agreed to every name suggested by the Duma. It was too much for Shulgin, who burst out, 'Oh, Your Majesty, if you had done this earlier, even as late as the last summoning of the Duma, perhaps all that—' He was too distressed to finish.

And the Czar 'looked at me in a curiously simple way—like a child—and asked, "Do you think it might have been avoided?" '

It was too much for the sergeant, who could only sit cursing, head in hands. The Caucasian trooper said suddenly, 'That devil Rasputin was right, wasn't he?'

That at any rate stopped the sergeant swearing. We all stared. The Caucasian spooned some jam into his tea, then gazed in surprise at our questioning faces. 'He was on a river steamboat once,' he said. 'Very drunk. My uncle heard him shouting out terrible things about the Family. And he kept saying about the Czar, "He is a child", and "Him—he has no insides!" And he was right!'

'Where is the Czar now?' asked the sergeant.

'He wanted to go back to Stavka to say goodbye to people there.'

This led to another sensation. 'Gone back to Stavka! But he was worried about his wife and children, that's why he'd *left* Stavka to go to Czarskoe!'

But I had even more bitter thoughts. Here, in a way, was the most scathing of all condemnations—he had been allowed to return in perfect freedom to Stavka surrounded by his retinue and bodyguard, unaccompanied by a single representative of the new government, a single guard, back to the heart and brain of the Army. It *should* have been forbidden as hideously dangerous to the point of lunacy—what was to prevent him from putting himself at the head of an army corps and marching on a capital from which the revolutionary movement had not yet started to spread? The reservists, recruits and workmen who were looting houses, lynching solitary officers, terrorising the civilian population, could offer no defence of the revolution against experienced troops. But, exhausted as they were, Guchkov and Shulgin were still able to assess the Czar's character accurately enough. He represented no threat. He could be safely left to play soldiers a little longer. And there would be no one at Stavka, where he had been Commander-in-Chief, to urge him to make a fight for it—to put into his head the idea of resistance, to pledge loyalty. It was the most merciless indictment of his unfitness to rule.

Shulgin was ashen-faced; I escorted him away, telling the men to settle down and get some sleep. It had been an incredibly long day and, to say the least, a strain on the nerves.

I said to Shulgin as we walked along the corridor, 'Can I write a letter to Czarskoe?'

'I think you could get permission.'

'And if I wanted to go to Stavka—'

'Guchkov's the War Minister now. Ask him.'

'Are you going home now?'

'I think so—I may sleep tonight. Do you realise it's only a week since it all started? I heard this muffled noise and said, "The trams are being extraordinarily noisy going over the bridge today," and my companion said, "It's machine-guns in the distance." '

15

'As a dead man out of mind'

'I am forgotten as a dead man out of mind'
The Book of Job

NEXT DAY was Sunday. The men asked me where they could go to church, and I suggested the Preobrazhensky Church. They conferred, then agreed to this, but first they carefully escorted me to the French Embassy. They would come for me on the way back.

I attended Mass at the Embassy Chapel, sent a second would-be reassuring telegram to Mother.

My squadron rejoined me in a state of disgust.

'The sword of the Czar Liberator is still there in its glass case, Your Honour, but they've covered the eagle at the back of the Czar's seat with a red cloth—'

'And the priest left out the names of the Imperial Family!'

'The clergy's ratted,' growled the sergeant. 'He told me he'd done it on the orders of his superiors.'

It was still snowing hard, with a high wind. We went to the house of General Milyutin's cousin, the man I had never met, who had given the first news of revolution. The reason why the telephone calls had gone unanswered was plain enough; the house was an empty shell, looted, wrecked to such an extent that it was almost impossible to believe that men had done this, and not beasts irrationally, insensately smashing, fouling everything. There were three photographs of the Imperial Family. Obscenities had been scrawled and drawn across them. There was a trail of blood across the floor of what had been a study. *Who would have thought the old man had so much blood in him?*

I never found out exactly what happened.

We rode out to Czarskoe.

The snow had stopped falling. The trees sparkled in the brilliant sunshine. There was a child on skis, playing. It seemed like a normal Sunday at Czarskoe until we came in sight of the palace itself.

The forecourt was full of people, a dirty, noisy mob, soldiers, workmen, sporting red rosettes, mostly unshaven, some drunk, singing the eternal *Marseillaise*, shouting obscenities.

We drew rein. The Caucasian said after a moment, 'These—and the gentry in the Duma—'

'Well?' asked the sergeant.

'They haven't got much in common, have they?'

Even without the crowd, the forecourt would not have been a pleasing spectacle. It was fast becoming an untidy rubbish dump, with broken bottles predominating.

A deep voice said, 'Do you believe it now, then?'

It was the Cossack to whom we had spoken the previous day. He was sitting on his horse as only a Cossack can, staring with contempt through the railings.

'Yes,' I said. 'There have been changes.'

He looked at me with a sudden gleam in his eye. 'Meaning that you've been here before and it looks different now—'

'Meaning that there are changes all round,' said the sergeant hastily.

'Let His Honour speak for himself.'

'Aren't you forgetting Order Number One?'

'Order Number One issued by the representatives of *that!*' He gestured derisively. 'Well, what's it going to be—Your Honour or Andrei Alexandrovitch Hamilton?'

I tugged at the sergeant's reins. 'Keep back—we can trust him. Why do you think that's my name? But I was forgetting—when you picked me up in East Prussia, I had identification papers on me.'

'Maybe, but they were black with blood—no one could read them. No, I'll tell you a story. They've still got footmen in the private wing, you know. Yesterday when I was patrolling the grounds, there was a young fool cutting across to the hothouse—he was risking being shot to get some lilac—"to give them pleasure". I told him I thought he was a damned fool, but I let him take a branch back. Just before dark he comes creeping out again. "Here!" I shouted. "Do you *want* to be caught?" "Yes," he said. "Caught by you, that is. I told—people—what had happened—and that you'd let me go. She—*they*—made me describe you. You'd been seen talking to a cavalry squadron at the front gates. They'd come from Novgorod, hadn't they?" "Suppose they had?" I asked. "It is thought the officer may come again. If he does will you give him this letter? There is nothing—nothing threatening

131

the Revolution in it." It was the devil's own job getting the name of the officer who was to have the letter, but after he'd seen it was necessary, he told me. Andrei Alexandrovitch Hamilton.'

I took the letter. 'If you see the footman again, tell him I am trying to go to Stavka.'

'It was you, wasn't it? I told Mamma, "Andrei came to the gates; he must have ridden from Novgorod in all the snow!" She says she will try to find out, but I *know* it was you.

'You must not worry about us. We have all been ill, but are getting better. Anya had measles too; Mamma had her brought here, too, so that she could nurse her with us. It is, of course, a miracle that Mamma didn't get it because we are always with her, night and day; whenever Papa was away at Stavka, one of us always slept in her room. At the same time, it is a dreadful thing that she alone remained well all the time—that is, knowing what was going on, with no one to be of any real help. I can remember only vague, disconnected things—the time when the electricity was cut off, and the way people's feet echoed so uncannily in the darkness as they moved about, but mostly my memories are of Mamma, bending over me to smooth my pillows, give me a drink—talking to the doctor, then saying, "And now we must go to see the other children and Madame Vyroubova," and she would stumble a little as she went out, because her sciatica is so bad, but also because she was so desperately tired. Anya said that sometimes as she sat at her bedside, she would fall asleep in the chair.

'I have been a hindrance, worse than a hindrance. The measles left me deaf for a time, Andrei, so when Mamma told me about Papa, she had to write it down. I think this made it far worse for her. She has been wonderfully brave; Anya has been crying a great deal, but Mamma says we must be strong, and think only of Papa. "He was all alone when he abdicated—what he must have gone through!" '

As she, too, had been alone at Czarskoe. Her children—and Vyroubova, inevitably!—ill. The isolation had been complete.

I went back to the sweating madhouse of the Duma, and eventually found Guchkov. I said I wanted permission to go to Stavka, where I would ask to be sent to the front line as soon as possible. He agreed in a voice slurring with fatigue.

I left that night. It was early morning when I reached Mogilev but the faint light was bright enough to show huge red flags hanging from the windows of the town hall opposite Stavka itself, and most of the people I saw in the streets now wore large red armbands. I decided to go across the town to the Hotel Bristol, where I should find the Allied representatives. From them I should get a more factual account of the situation than I could expect from the Czar's own entourage.

Old General Hanbury-Williams was having breakfast when I arrived. He sprang up and came towards me—what was I doing here? Hadn't I been sent to Novgorod?

I told him why I had left Novgorod, why I had come back to Mogilev.

'Sit down and have breakfast with me,' he said. 'Do you want my summing up of the situation? Anarchy in the town, and as for Stavka—' he hesitated.

'Please be frank,' I said.

'The atmosphere is appalling,' he said, getting red in the face. 'Of course, it was bound to be a fantastically unreal situation, because of the Czar's *placidity*. He's taken up the threads again as if nothing's happened—Alexeiev's trying to nerve himself to hint he'd better not present the reports still expected of him! A motor trip after lunch, then tea—afterwards cards or dominoes, finally bed! The only real change is that he doesn't get ministerial reports any longer, but I don't suppose he minds that, he always hated them, didn't he? It is all so dreadfully wrong, isn't it? When he returned, I plucked up my courage to go and pay my respects. I didn't know quite what to expect—a man completely broken, or at least a man who was *uneasy*, uncertain. This, surely, would be the normal reaction, a—a most careful treading of this treacherous soft ground between two worlds. But instead—something fantastically like complacency. I asked him if he'd slept well. "Oh, yes, very well," he said, "and I did quite a lot of reading about Julius Caesar."

'But I was telling you about the atmosphere at the Governor's House. It's vile. The old etiquette is maintained—but the hollowness of it! They bow, they talk respectfully, but the words mean nothing, and the eyes—ah, the eyes, my dear boy, they look sideways all the time! How they used to strut about with their gold shoulder-knots, the Imperial initials on their epaulettes—and how quickly those insignia have been removed. I challenged one yesterday. "Hullo!" I said. "There's a subtle difference in your uniform—what is it?" "Merely something done for the sake of convenience," he replied.

After a moment, I said, 'There was another Imperial train at the station—I was told his mother's come from Kiev. Perhaps she'll make him face facts.'

'*She's* under no illusions—she was sobbing after their first conversation, whatever it was about.'

'And he?'

'He was sitting quite silent, smoking a cigarette.'

'He's never been made for high drama. At every crisis he's sat silently smoking a cigarette.'

'You will pay your respects to him, of course. I know, my dear boy, how difficult it will be—all that I could say was, "I am so sorry!" I don't think I've ever felt so terribly broken-up in all my life—even when I received the news that my son had died.'

The valiant, warm-hearted old man was silent for a moment. Then he resumed, 'God help us, when I went to that ugly Governor's House to take official leave of him, I found that every part of the building was haunted for me—the stairs along which the boy used to run, the anteroom where I had spoken to the Czarina on her last visit. I remembered how she had stood there by the piano—and I'd looked at those pretty daughters, like the girls you meet at an English tennis party, and I worried again about what would happen to them, and suddenly I made up my mind I *must* give some warning. And I went across and had just begun to speak when the Czar interrupted us, and the chance was lost—'

The ex-Czar, I was told, would be with his mother most of the day, but would be very pleased to receive me the following evening. I made my request for a return to the Front; yes, they said, they would send me to Kornilov's Eighth Army.

I spent the rest of the day walking around Mogilev. Here, too, the police had disappeared, and disorder was growing, but perhaps the oddest aspect of the situation was the feeling—or rather, the lack of feeling—towards the Czar. Troops and civilians alike showed absolute indifference. He was so completely erased, deleted from their consciousness, he might never have reigned. In a way the hostility of Petersburg was more complimentary.

And then evening. The streets tonight were brightly lit, crowded. I went slowly to that small ugly house certain courtiers and Stavka staff had insisted, with ludicrous pomposity, on calling 'the Palace'. The muddy path. The terrible imitation oak grained wallpapers, the ghastly curtains.

The good old English general had been right; it was a place of ghosts.

It was time for me to go to the Czar. I walked slowly along the dingy corridor, ill-lit as ever. People had always been walking down corridors towards him—down long corridors after they had been graciously granted audiences they had come clicking or marching towards doors softly opened, softly latched.

The doors would be flung open more roughly now.

Did he realise this?

Surely, despite what the English general had said, he must see that he was nothing more than a cipher, and completely defenceless? Was fear sprouting in this ugly, badly-lit house, like a hideous fungus?

I stood in the anteroom—in the spot where General Hanbury-Williams, wondering what would happen to the pretty daughters, had stood talking to the Czarina. There was just one bracket light, and when the Czar came in, he stood under it. I saw then that, for all his torpor, lethargy, his face was covered with innumerable wrinkles, and his hair was quite grey at the temples. He looked like an old man.

'Why, Andrei,' he said simply. 'I am very glad you have come. I've been very lonely here.'

I told him that I had received a letter from Olga, that all the children were beginning to recover, though they had been very ill, and that the Czarina had been wonderfully calm and courageous.

'How did you manage to get a letter? I've heard nothing from them for days.'

Neither of us knew then that the Czarina had been sending telegram after telegram to him at Mogilev, and that they had been returned with a blue pencilled scrawl across them, 'Addressee unknown'.

I told him that I had gone to Czarskoe from Novgorod, and had been seen at the gates talking to a friendly Cossack.

'How long will you be here at Mogilev?'

I said that my first purpose in coming—to give him news of the children—had been accomplished; my second was to get sent back to the Front.

'Ah, yes, for the great offensive!' He talked quite animatedly about recent French operations in Champagne. Then he said, 'I shall be going to Czarskoe the day after tomorrow—why not come on my train?'

'My grateful thanks to Your Majesty.'

'After dinner tomorrow we'll play a game of *bézique*, and I'll tell you my plans.'

Still he didn't realise that it was not for him to make plans now—the plans were being made for him. And he wasn't 'going' to Czarskoe—a week before he had been—to crush the riots in Petersburg. Now he was being taken. When I got back to the Hotel Bristol, I was sick.

I was invited to attend the ceremony in which, to quote the official phraseology, 'The retiring Supreme Commander takes official leave of the Staff.' The mean hall of the house was full of officers, packed in a tight little circle, standing in nervous silence. I kept saying to myself, 'Here he is, at Stavka, with not a single guard or representative from the new government—all these officials are monarchists—good God, he still has his ADCs, his court, his bodyguard.'

I could hear myself arguing—how many days ago?—that it was insane of the Czar to leave Stavka *where he was in a position of strength.* Well, he was back at Stavka now.

It was true that he had resigned the throne—but to his brother, and his brother had refused it.

The door opened. He came in, followed by the Marshal of the Court and the Palace Commandant. The Palace Commandant looked furious —scarlet face, hot eyes—but entirely on his own behalf. He'd backed the wrong horse; all his sympathy was for himself, there was none to spare for the wretched creature who'd let him down.

There was a string of ADCs. Several without gold knots and insignia'd epaulettes.

The Czar walked lightly, rising a little on his toes, as usual. He bowed. 'Gentlemen,' he said, 'the welfare of the country, the necessity for putting an end to revolution, of preventing the horrors of civil war, and of diverting all the efforts of the State to the continuation of the struggle with the foe at the Front made me decide to abdicate in favour of my brother—'

One or two people were sobbing. A big old general next to me was groaning as if in anguish, tears poured down his withered cheeks, he seemed on the point of fainting. But no one protested, 'And he hasn't accepted the throne! There's a vacuum of power at the top, it's hideously dangerous—for God's sake reconsider your decision! We are all Czar's men here, we'll stand behind you, here you are at the heart of your Army!' No, no one cried out in protest. They sobbed—but people can sob at funerals and, in an obscure way, enjoy themselves.

Guchkov had taken no risk when he had let the Czar come back unsupervised to Mogilev. There was no danger of a restoration; the chief obstacle to this was the Czar himself.

'—I wish you all good luck.'

He embraced Alexeiev, who wished him all happiness in his new life, then came around the circle, speaking to each of us. More tears. One or two people collapsed. But people collapse, too, at a funeral and have no ideas about applying artificial respiration to the corpse.

These people did not feel personally involved. They hadn't been in Petersburg. They hadn't heard the whimpering noises made by crawling officers—and those the lucky ones—beaten half-senseless by the rifle butts of soldiers.

At dinner in the Dowager Empress's train there was the usual etiquette and punctilio, more talk about French successes in Champagne. The Dowager Empress was red-eyed, but calm. After dinner, the Czar talked about his hopes for the future. He wanted to take his family to the Crimea, but it seemed more likely they would go abroad, to England. He spoke quietly so we couldn't always hear him—there was singing and shouting outside. Mogilev, if we could say such a thing about Mogilev, was *en fête*.

We played *bézique*.

We drove back to the Governor's House through brilliantly lit, crowded streets. The Czar paid no heed to this; the crowds paid no heed to him. It was as if we were in a cinema when the lights have gone up too soon and faint ghostly figures are still flickering on the screen.

'I still drink my glass of tea last thing at night; you must have one with me, Andrei.'

The telephone rang. 'Shall I take it, sir? It's General Alexeiev— good news.'

The Provisional Government was quite agreeable to the idea of the Imperial Family going abroad. There would be, quite soon, a safe conduct to Murmansk, where, they hoped, a British warship would be waiting.

As I took my leave, he said, 'Have you any recent Petersburg newspapers, Andrei? I might read them in the train tomorrow—it will be something to pass the time.'

Over breakfast, I consulted General Hanbury-Williams. I had brought a bundle of newspapers with me, but they were anything but pleasant reading—'Suicide of the monarchy'—'Kronstadt sailors

137

condemn officers to death'—'All power in the hands of the Provisional Government,' said the *Vestnik*.

'Take them to him,' said General Hanbury-Williams. 'He *must* realise what he's going to. And, for charity's sake, be there with him when this morning's ceremony is taking place.'

That morning the General Staff and the Mogilev garrison were to take the oath of allegiance to the Provisional Government. The little parade ground was in front of the residence, under the Czar's study window.

There they were—a familiar picture, clergy with the altar inside a hollow square of troops, Alexeiev, generals, ADCs. There were prayers. I thought, If I'd been there, for the first time in my life I should be hearing prayers in Russia where the Czar's name wasn't mentioned. And then the whole parade lifted right hands and loudly repeated after the priest the new oath of allegiance. Despite myself I looked at the Czar; not a muscle moved in his face.

He lunched at one in the dining-car of his mother's train; his own train, which would take him to Czarskoe that afternoon, was getting up steam in another siding. It was a fine, cold day. There was a crowd at the station, but they were quite silent. A detachment of the Third Baltic Regiment separated the onlookers from the Imperial trains.

At three o'clock the Czar was still at the luncheon table. Suddenly there was a burst of cheering from the crowd. An express had just steamed in from Petersburg, bringing four representatives from the Provisional Government, who were to accompany the Czar. They made speeches, there were more cheers. Then silence.

'What has happened?' asked the Czar.

'I imagine they've gone to call on General Alexeiev, sir.'

He nodded. There was no reaction to the fact that he was so completely disregarded that, for the first time for over twenty years, there was cheering in his presence, but not for him. He seemed to have no apprehension as to *why* the newcomers should have gone to see Alexeiev. He probably thought that this incredible state of unsupervised freedom would continue indefinitely. He sat there in his leather armchair and smiled across at his mother. 'The railwaymen here are being overworked today!' he said. His was still the face of a man used to deference. To call it mildly arrogant would be to give it too positive an emotion. It was—how can I put it?—oddly complacent for all the new lines about the eyes.

At four o'clock the men from the Provisional Government came back to the station. Alexeiev was with them. The Czar, taking leave of his mother, broke down for the first time. Then, moving at his usual deliberate pace, and his face quite expressionless again, he walked across the platform to his own train. His mother stood motionless at the window of her compartment, watching him. When he in his turn came to the window, she made the sign of the Cross.

It was a long train—ten carriages. The Provisional Government representatives occupied the last coach. For the first time a guard was set over the Czar—ten men of the Railwaymen's Battalion. He had forty-seven members of his suite with him. Even now, therefore, the situation was fantastically unreal; the warm train was, in a way, his last refuge from reality. Once he reached Czarskoe he would encounter the situations his wife and children had been meeting for days.

Doors closed—they were never slammed on an Imperial train. A whistle blew. The blue coaches with the golden crest began, very slowly, to move. On the platform, Alexeiev and the Staff saluted the Czar. I stood staring back and saw something more. As the last coach, the coach containing the Duma representatives, passed him, Alexeiev took off his cap and bowed deeply.

'This time,' said the Czar, 'we go direct.'

Perhaps, but it was an unbearably slow journey. The train crawled through the flat snowbound countryside, because the Provisional Government had insisted on tremendous security precautions at all stations. Most of the time the Czar dozed.

Late in the evening the four delegates wished to see him. After a short interval he joined them in his sitting-room. There, nervously, they told him what Alexeiev had known before the train left Mogilev—that the new government had ordered the arrest of the deposed Czar and his wife.

It was fitting that he, once more, should have been kept in ignorance of a fact known by everyone else.

It was after eleven on the following morning when the train reached Czarskoe. It was a fine, cold day. A colonel, the station-master, and two lesser officials stood on the dirty platform. There were dingy red flags everywhere. The Duma representatives got out of the train first. 'Have you had instructions to take charge of the former Czar?' The colonel replied, 'I am Kobylinski, Military Commandant of Czarskoe-Selo. Full instructions have been received from the Provisional

Government through the Commandant of the St Petersburg Military Division.'

'Then our mission is at an end; we can go.'

Not only they. The Czar, wearing the uniform of a Cossack colonel, left the train, saluted, walked very rapidly, glancing at no one, speaking to no one, across the platform to the waiting car. But even before the train had stopped another less ceremonial debarkation had taken place. It had been full, that train, with forty-seven official members of the Imperial suite. Even before the train had stopped, the vast majority of these had leaped out on the wrong side and scuttled over the railway tracks, pushing each other in their haste, looking furtively over their shoulders to see if they had been observed, trying frantically to escape detection in the worst crime of all—to be seen in the Czar's company.

There were still food queues, but they were no longer quiet. Women screamed shrilly, fighting like animals for a place at the head of the line.

'It all started because there wasn't enough bread,' said the sergeant. 'Well, the Czar's gone, but the bread hasn't come yet.'

They had been waiting at the station for some time, had been amazed to see me coming out almost alone after the Czar, standing absolutely alone at the salute as he drove off.

'Before we came to the station we rode past the palace. That Cossack was there. He had another letter for you,' said the sergeant.

'We all bless you because you are going to Mogilev. Mamma, who has been so brave, cried when I told her.

'The Little One knows now about the abdication; Mamma could not bear to tell him herself, so she asked M. Gilliard. He said, "Your father will be coming back from Mogilev tomorrow morning, and will never be going back there."

' "Why?"

' "Your father doesn't want to be Commander-in-Chief any more."

' "*What? Why?*" He was astonished, and stared up at M. Gilliard as if he might read in his face what had happened.

' "He's very tired, and he's had a lot of trouble lately."

' "Oh, yes, Mamma told me they stopped his train when he wanted to come here. But won't Papa be Czar again afterwards?"

' "No, he gave up his throne to your Uncle Michael, but he doesn't want to be Czar either."

' "But who's going to be Czar, then?"'

' "I don't know. Perhaps nobody now—"'

'The Little One said nothing of his own rights, but after a moment he asked agitatedly, "But if there isn't a Czar, who's going to govern Russia?"'

'After Mamma had been put under arrest yesterday, people were told that anyone still here at four would be confined to the palace. Dr Botkin, who was visiting Marie, said immediately that he would stay; others did not.'

Still, whatever reason for bitterness the present might hold, the future was assured—safety in England. So I reassured myself as I rejoined the Army.

16

'Fit partner for a League of Honour'

'A fit partner for a League of Honour'
President Wilson

I HAD a friend who eventually died of cancer. We were close enough to talk absolutely frankly, and one day I said I had been amazed at the way in which he had tried to carry on for so long as if nothing were wrong. He said, 'There was nothing heroic in it, rather the reverse. I was too scared to admit the truth to myself, it was a bad dream, it couldn't happen to me. If I ignored it, it would pass as a nightmare passes.'

Mutiny is like that. Officers dare not admit to themselves what is happening, and because they are afraid to show any awareness they will take no action which will give the game away. It has always been so—that is why my Scottish grandmother's family was massacred in India.

Soon the average officer was a man whose lips trembled, whose face was waxen, who groped or stumbled like one condemned. He was nothing more than a terrified animal in the power—never at the mercy—of cruel, stupid children.

I remember one incident very vividly. We rode into a town which housed a headquarters staff, rode with difficulty because lorries were roaring along the narrow, muddy streets, lorries crammed with soldiers waving red flags and screaming, 'Down with the war!'

Outside headquarters itself a lorry was parked to act as a platform for an NCO who yelled that instead of killing Germans, the Russian soldiers should be killing the officers and gentry 'like cockroaches'.

At last I tracked down the officer to whom I was to report. When I went in he was huddled like a baited animal, crouching in a corner, staring about him with desperate, short-sighted eyes, shrinking back, pressing his body against the wall. At first he only mouthed sounds, dreadful gulping noises. Then, as I went across, he gave a kind of whispered shriek, 'Don't!' and tried frantically to creep even further into the angle of the wall. At last I managed to get him to accept me for what I was. Then he began to sob convulsively.

'I'm sorry!' he said. 'I've broken my *pince-nez*, you see; I couldn't see who was entering, but I'd heard you coming—'

But he would not come away with us, or let us protect him in any way.

'I have my squadron with me, sir,' I said formally. 'If you have any orders for us—'

'I've forgotten how to give orders,' he said flatly.

'My men would obey them.'

'There are too many for you to handle.'

'We'd take the chance. Are you *accepting* mutiny?'

'As long as there have been armies, there have been mutinies,' he said, almost complacently. 'In fact, it's surprising there haven't been more, when you realise what discipline is—the most artificial of inventions which has to be *accepted* by the men subject to it. When they don't, they become an armed murderous gang, but what can one do? Such a flimsy convention—I didn't realise how flimsy until I saw that the trouble was coming our way.'

He sat there with his face all blubbered with tears, academically discussing the nature of mutiny—in a voice high with barely suppressed hysteria.

I said, 'As long as there have been armies, there have been mutinies, as you said, sir. But the majority of these mutinies have been suppressed.'

He said, dabbing at his lips with his handkerchief, 'By brute force—that's the traditional way, isn't it? You surround the mutineers with loyal troops; here there aren't enough loyal troops.' He began to laugh. 'I could find enough officers for a court martial, but I couldn't find a dozen men for even one shooting party. You know, I vomit every morning before I leave my quarters; if I had any sense I'd blow my brains out.'

'If you won't come with us, if you won't let us protect you in any way, a quick suicide's preferable to what others may do to you.'

'I know,' he said, 'but I keep thinking it's a bad dream, that I'll wake up soon—'

Like the man suffering from cancer.

He said, giggling, as I left, 'We couldn't have firing parties, in any case. The death penalty's been abolished—for them.'

There was a screaming uniformed mob at the far end of the street. The Caucasian said, straightfaced, 'Wouldn't a talk by Napoleonchik make them good boys?'

They all laughed. I suppose I should be grateful to Kerensky for one thing at least—he made my squadron laugh.

By early summer he was Minister of War. Guchkov had given up in despair when the Army went to the devil within weeks, but Kerensky thought oratory would cure everything. He had come to harangue our sector of the Front. He wore a soldier's tunic and—to the men's incredulous delight—he even thrust his hand, Corsican-wise, in his jacket. He acted the democrat—started his speech by telling the soldiers they weren't to call him His Excellency the Minister of War, but 'Comrade'. And on in this strain. But when at the end of the oration, the Caucasian asked him if it were true that all orders issued by the Provisional Government had first to be submitted to the Soviet, he shouted, 'Hold your tongue when the Minister of War is speaking to you!'

'Alexander IV, I'd say,' muttered the Caucasian morosely, now, in our bivouac.

'What's wrong with Alexander the Great?'

'He'll be having Petersburg called Alexandria next! That would fool the Germans, at least!'

'Well, it's more likely to beat 'em than this scheme he's thought up—'

For Kerensky, with a mutinous army, was going to launch a great offensive over a forty-mile front along the Dniester and the foothills of the Carpathians. Forty-five Russian divisions against far less formidable enemy forces. On paper.

One heard the lunatic arguments. There must be an offensive. Cavalry and artillery could still be trusted to play their part, but most of the infantry was doubtful. So from the infantry form shock battalions of volunteers. In other words, exterminate the last stabilising force left to you, your last hope of restoring law and order, take from the disintegrating regiments the better elements, the officers and NCOs deserving their rank, the men with a sense of duty. Pass sentence of death on them, for few assault troops ever returned.

Perhaps you told yourself later that at any rate you saved the poor fellows from violence at the hands of their own comrades.

I am not altogether ironical. I wish my squadron had gone that way, by Austrian bullets.

People are still talking—rightly—of the horrors of the German destruction of Louvain. Nobody here in the West seems to have heard what happened to the inhabitants of the Polish town of Kalusz at the hands of the army boasting it was now the freest in the world—'Here is a fit partner for a League of Honour!' trumpeted the American President Wilson.

Kornilov's Eighth Army broke through the enemy front because of the heroic self-sacrifice of the shock battalions. Towns were taken, including Kalusz. The storm battalions operating here were composed entirely of officers. They—what was left of them—moved on, and two regiments were brought up from the rear to 'consolidate' the position.

It should be remembered that this was a Polish, and not a German or Austrian town. There was not even that wretched excuse.

The two 'consolidating' regiments found wine. There followed a wild orgy, drunkenness, then bestiality, the most brutal of all Great War atrocities.

We had been sent back with a convoy of prisoners. We found the town at the mercy of four thousand drunken savages.

Our first inkling of what was happening was the sight of the flames, street after street of flames. It was a windless day, and the flames went up into the cloudless summer sky as straight as lances. Flames produced by distant enemy gunfire are not like that. And then we heard the screaming, women screaming. Their screams—I do not exaggerate —drowned the noise of the bombardment by the retiring enemy.

I said to the sergeant, 'Someone must go to get help from the cavalry —the Caucasian Native Division will be best, their religion won't let them drink.'

He showed his teeth like a sick dog. 'What will they think, the Caucasians? *These* are the sons of the men who conquered them.' He was shaking as if he had ague.

I told our own Caucasian he must go. He seized my hand, begged me not to send him away—he knew what we were going to do.

'Are you another mutinous dog, then?' growled the sergeant, and, weeping, the boy galloped off.

I addressed the rest, told them we were forty, the odds were a hundred to one, and they—I called them *the enemy*, I think—were armed with machine-guns.

'Yes, yes, Your Honour,' said the sergeant impatiently, 'but while we argue—Mother of God, that scream!'

But he—and those others who were close—wasted seconds in snatching my hand and kissing it as we got into formation.

There were women—and children—still alive in the main square. Our aim was to strike down as many men as we could, get as many survivors as possible away.

Scream after scream, the most awful in the world, to pierce your eardrums; my arm rising and falling until not a single khaki figure stood upright and there was a fair-haired girl huddling herself like a thin little animal. As I bent over her the childish arms made feeble efforts to cover her head. 'Don't!' she said. 'Please, don't!'

We lost eight men in that first charge. When we had taken our pitiful cargo to the edge of the town, and told them—there were two or three not dazed or crazed—to hide in the woods, we rode in again. I forget how many times we returned.

Eventually two Caucasian squadrons came up; not enough to restore order in Hell, but enough to shepherd the women and children to safety.

I was lying by the roadside, with blood streaming from my head. The two squadrons went into the town with my own trooper to try to pick up any of my people who were wounded. They were all dead.

They tried to bandage me up, but I refused any help. Otherwise I lay dumb, and quite apathetic.

'Do you want to die *here*, Your Honour?' cried my Caucasian. 'In this horrible place?'

True, Kalusz wasn't the kind of place one would choose to die in, charred, smouldering, dead women and children everywhere, drunken soldiers lying in the gutters, blood from broken bodies and wine from broken bottles flowing everywhere, mingling.

The Caucasian leader said something to my trooper who seized me and dumped me in the saddle.

It was a boiling hot day, as hot as in the advance into East Prussia three years before.

And that is how I came to leave the Russian Army.

17

His Majesty's Government
no longer insists

*'Le gouvernement anglais n'insistait plus sur le départ de la
Famille Impériale pour l'Angleterre.'*

Statement of Paul Milyukov, Foreign Minister in the
Provisional Government, to Nicholas Sokolov, Official
Investigator into the murder of the Imperial Family.

AT THE beginning of August I came back to Petersburg in a train
crammed to the roof with deserters.* I sat—slumped, rather—with my
bandaged head against my Caucasian's shoulder. He guarded me
zealously, growling in his throat like a watchdog if ever he felt I was
threatened in any way. In actual fact, I suppose, I was safe enough,
except from suffocation. Men were deserting in hordes now—and the
only idea in their minds was to get home as soon as possible. They
would kill anyone who tried to prevent them, but I wasn't in physical
or mental state to hinder a child, so they left me alone. One even gave
the Caucasian what he grandly called a 'requisitioned bandage' when a
new dressing was needed for my head.

The Caucasian carried me into one of the few cabs at the station, and
we began to drive across the city. More than ever it looked like a town
in the front line under enemy occupation—filthy streets, shuttered shops,
empty buildings, gutted, burned-out ruins, dilapidation everywhere.

Indistinctly I heard snatches of conversation between the Caucasian
and the driver. 'It didn't look as bad as this two months ago when we
left!'

'Well, there's been more fighting—two days of it in July. The
Bolsheviks—Lenin—brought back from Switzerland by the Germans

---

* An English newspaper printed a photograph of such a train with the caption, 'Russian
soldiers hastening to the front.'

—taking German pay all the time—*they* started a rising, too.'

'When we were trying to keep up the big offensive,' said the Caucasian simply.

'What does this scum know about the Front?' demanded the cab driver. 'They've never done honest fighting, damn them—God, how I hate them. My lad died in Galicia two years ago, and there are these swine swaggering about the streets while all these damned fools in the government keep praising them to the skies—"deepening and saving the Revolution", that's what one of the government said they were doing!'

'They're scared,' said the Caucasian. 'Scared of this rabble.'

'No need to tell me that. They lick their boots every day. You've heard of a general called Krymov? He went to that Prince Lvov who heads the government and said he'd clear the city in two days with one good division. "Oh, but there would be such a commotion!" said Lvov.'

'My God! How's he lasted so long?'

'Oh, he's not Prime Minister now—hadn't you heard? Kerensky's pushed him out.'

'Kerensky!' The Caucasian roared with laughter. 'Napoleonchik? He came to give us a talk, told us we were all comrades, but when I asked a question he bit my head off. Still, I'll forgive him all that if he's shot the Bolsheviks.'

'*Shot* 'em? He let 'em all get away. That dirty spy Lenin hopped off to Finland, just waiting there he is, the Judas, for more German money, and then he'll be back.'

'But if Kerensky let the leaders go,' said the Caucasian slowly, 'the Bolsheviks will try again—'

'No need to tell me that—and they'll have better luck next time, I say, because—Does your gentleman mind plain speaking?'

'He likes honesty.'

'Even about *officers?*' There was a pause. Then the cab driver said, 'To my mind, then, many of the officers hate Kerensky and his government more than they hate Lenin and the Bolsheviks.'

'In God's name, why?'

'Because they say a Bolshevik government couldn't last. Give it just a couple of weeks, and it'll get so unpopular, the people will rise up against it and bring back the monarchy.'

'Nobody could be as mad as that!'

'I tell you, there's a song they're singing in the cabarets these days—very popular it is, too, all the audience roars it out:

148

> *'First came the Mensheviks*
> *Then came the Bolsheviks,*
> *Then came the Anarchists,*
> *And then will come the Monarchists!*

If you want my opinion, a lot of people are *hoping* that the Bolsheviks will finish off Kerensky—to make way for the monarchy after them.'

'And I still say only a crazy man could think like that,' said the Caucasian firmly. 'What's the point of talking about bringing back the monarchy when the Heir with the rest of the Family's gone off to England?'

We stopped outside my house. The driver stared at the Caucasian. 'You've been a long way away, lad. Didn't you know? They're still here—at Czarskoe. The English wouldn't have 'em.'

In the past weeks, when the Army became a rabble of mad dogs, there had been little thought to spare from the effort to remain alive another day. Yet there had been moments when a sight, a sound, even the smell of lilac in a deserted garden was enough to make me think, 'They're in England now.' I had thought that Mother would, of course, go to them and I'd pictured the Czarina holding both hands out to her, the last dreadful interview forgotten.

I'd never doubted that they would go to England. Kerensky had made a speech saying he'd personally escort them to Murmansk if necessary; before the Czar had even left Mogilev, the new Foreign Minister, Milyukov, was saying, 'He should lose no time in getting away,' was anxiously asking the English Ambassador to telegraph London asking for political asylum to secure the lives of 'those poor unfortunates'. The English King was the first cousin to the Czar, and the Czarina was not only George V's first cousin, but the granddaughter of Queen Victoria. It was true there was little warmth in the feelings she and the English Queen Mary had for each other, but the Czar and the King had been exceptionally close.

But no British cruiser ever came to Murmansk.

As to why, guilt blurs memories, blots some out completely. There are half-truths, silences—more cowardly than lies.

Kerensky has given one explanation of why the Imperial Family found no refuge in England; the Kaiser himself, he says, agreed to give safe conduct to the warship carrying his cousins, but no warship was sent—the British government, obeying God knows what promptings, withdrew its offer of sanctuary.

I believe Kerensky; he couldn't resist any chance of being theatrical, but there was sincerity beneath the play-acting. He did his best—even if he has ever since been reviled as a murderer by such ardent monarchists as those who had scurried out of the Czar's train and scuttled over the railway lines.

In this matter Kerensky has nothing on his conscience; there are—and should be—those in England who might well flinch when, say, they read or hear the terrible words of Cassandra, *Children weeping for their own bloodshed.* Yet the self-deceptions practised by the human mind are infinite; in any case, I do not think it likely that those I believe instrumental in withdrawing the offer are any more likely to read or attend the plays of Aeschylus than was the Czar himself.

So a letter awaited me at home.

'You know the Little One's gun, don't you—the one he is so fond of? He was playing with it on the little island on the lake and an officer came up quickly to tell us that the soldiers had seen this toy, and were shouting, "They're armed! They're armed!" They were coming to get the gun. The Little One put it down and went to Mamma, who was sitting on the grass a few yards away. A moment later the soldiers appeared and demanded the "weapon". His tutor said, "It's only a toy, can hurt no one!" Alexei began to cry. Mamma begged M. Gilliard to get it back, but it was useless.

'Later, when it had been broken into pieces, the officer retrieved it, brought it back to us, hidden under his coat. Alexei has been told that he can only play with it in his room, and with the door shut.

'It was horrible. He looked dazed. And afterwards—'

I put the letter down abruptly. As far back as he could remember, Alexei had been assured—and had trustingly accepted—that all Russia adored him and his family. Now he was learning the brutal truth.

It wasn't his tears over the incident of the toy gun that could wrench at the heart, it was the look before the tears, when he was still struggling to be brave, the trembling lower lip going down, the dumb reproach that followed the first startled expression in the blue eyes. And his mother, sitting there, impotent. 'We must do as I say so that Baby inherits a strengthened autocracy.' And so the heir to an army of millions couldn't even have a toy gun to play with.

With an effort, I picked up the letter again, went on reading, came to the hurried postscript:

'Kerensky has just told Papa that the Provisional Government has decided we must leave Czarskoe. It is for our own sakes, he says. I think the Bolshevik rising scared him. Even before it happened, he said to Papa one day, "They're after me, and then they'll be after you." He said it would be much better if we were in some remote part, far from Petersburg. Papa said we should like to go to Livadia. Kerensky said this might be possible, but he was also considering other places.'

There were no longer any wounded to be tended at Mother's hospital, but the senior French doctor was still there, and insisted on looking after me.

On August 12, he went out to Czarskoe, to find out when the Family was likely to leave—anything, he grumbled, to keep me quiet. The Caucasian went with him, to see if the Cossack were still there.

When they found him, he looked at the Caucasian, spat, and said, 'I thought you'd gone off to the Eighth Army. So you ratted like the rest.'

The Caucasian, suddenly unable to speak, could only shake his head blindly. The doctor explained in his halting Russian what had happened. The Cossack's face relaxed a little. 'I know how he feels. I'm the only one left out of my squadron—we buried the rest in Alexander Nevsky cemetery after the Bolshevik rising.' Quite suddenly he beat his hand against the park railings. 'They were killed—and this damned government let the Bolshevik scum get away! No Cossack will risk his neck for *this* government again! I'm getting out. Tell your captain to do the same while the going's good, because when the rats come creeping back and start gnawing away again, the Cossacks won't be here to stop them!'

And just before he turned away, he said in an even lower voice, 'It's said *they're* leaving tomorrow. Midnight.'

The evening sky had been glorious, but there was little colour left when I took up my position beside one of the trees lining the road between the park and the station. It was that sickly colour that always seems curiously artificial to anyone unaccustomed to Russian summer nights, neither light nor dark, a pallor, as if the day had been drained of colour.

They were hours late in coming.

'This is madness,' said the doctor suddenly. 'The Cossack was mistaken—or the plan's been changed.'

A motor horn hooted, and a great car swept by. In the wan light we could just discern who sat in it.

'That's Kerensky in the Czar's Rolls-Royce,' I said. 'Delay perhaps —but the plan's unaltered.'

I wondered how they were enduring this delay. Was the Czarina weeping at the thought of leaving her home for so many years? Was the Czar—as usual—lighting cigarette after cigarette?

And I thought of Olga in her room, turning slowly from side to side, taking in every detail her eyes could absorb, her last look at the old life, the final, half-desperate attempt to record in her memory the only world she had ever known.

It was half past five when at last they came. A Cossack escort before and behind them. That, at least, was familiar. They would hardly recognise the station, though—more like a fortress with the armed men and machine-guns and dirt everywhere.

The first rays of the sun were appearing as the cars passed. In the first Kerensky, in the second the Czar, the Czarina—her profile was quite clear—Alexei, his face buried against Joy's neck as if he had been crying.

In the third car, looking straight ahead and showing no emotion, the four girls.

'What is it?' demanded the doctor.

'I'd forgotten,' I said, 'that their hair was cut so short during their illness.'

They were wearing white dresses, too.

I was very tired, and some of the drugs he'd given me were still at work—he kept saying this in a low voice. And the wan light helped to give a fanciful impression.

Shorn hair and white dresses—sacrificial victims.

The victims of another revolution had had their hair cut, too.

I wished they had covered their hair.

'They're on the train now. Here are the Cossacks coming back.'

A whisper from a sergeant I knew who rode very close to us as they returned. 'Tobolsk.'

That meant Siberia.

18

'Don't behave like cads!'

AGAIN I believe Kerensky when he says there was no malice in his choice. Refuge, and not revenge was what he had in mind when he chose Tobolsk. Tobolsk itself was a backwater. It was two hundred miles from the railway, it had no factories, its population was one of well-to-do peasants, with no incentive to revolutionary feelings. When snow fell in autumn, Tobolsk was effectively cut off from the rest of Russia for months on end. And by the spring thaw Kerensky felt he would have solved every problem. After this, he assured old Count Benckendorff before witnesses, the Czar would be free to go anywhere he chose—he might return to Czarskoe itself if he wanted to. Or if he chose to leave the country via Japan, he would be admirably placed for this.

Wildly optimistic, perhaps, but not insincere. The last thing Kerensky anticipated in August was that by November he, too, would be a hunted fugitive. The new rulers would not tell guards, 'Don't behave like cads, no kicking a man when he's down!' as Kerensky did the evening before the Imperial Family left Czarskoe.

Gradually details filtered through of the departure. Kerensky working frenziedly to get the Family away, addressing the soldiers, grappling with the situation at the station when the train did not appear—the suspicious railway workers refused to couple the coaches together. This was the reason for the interminable delay.

But there was one aspect of the journey which would be familiar enough to the Czarina, although on this occasion she did not issue the order. When the train stopped at stations all blinds were to be drawn. So she had always wanted it.

The hospitals everywhere were closing. There was no more fighting, so no more wounded. 'Therefore,' said our own French doctor, 'one takes one's talents where they are needed.' He estimated that by

November his usefulness in Russia would be over; in the meantime he ruled me with a rod of iron. One didn't play with head injuries. He also wrote frequently to Mother. No, she was not to return. Russia was going to get out of the war—that was clear enough—and when I was well enough I was going to Tobolsk. There was nothing for her to return to in Petersburg.

He came in to me laughing one day. He had met two British workmen's delegates, Will Thorne and James O'Grady, who had come to bring fraternal greetings to the young Russian democracy, and were returning disgusted by the so-called 'workers' in the Soviet. 'One look at their hands is enough—the lazy devils haven't done an honest day's work in their lives!'

In September came the failure of Kornilov's *coup d'état*.

The Bolsheviks, having been handled too tenderly by Kerensky, were raising their heads again. Petersburg was full of deserters who kept up a reign of terror. Kornilov, the Cossack general, wanted a sharp fierce cleansing of the pesthouse before all Russia was infected.

I was in a feverish state at the time, and had no clear idea of what was happening. I can remember the Caucasian hurrying in, grinning widely. 'Your Honour, those damned deserters, who've kept decent people off the streets for months—they've panicked and run! Not one to be seen!'

Tens of thousands of people waited one long September day and night for the first sounds of the Cossacks coming.

But they never came. The attempt failed.

Better if it had never been made. Kerensky, to meet the threatened attack, turned to the Soviet, armed sixty thousand workmen, allowed them to keep their weapons after the danger was over. Now the capital was completely in their power; and the deserters crept out of their holes back into the light, and a fresh wave of atrocities took place.

A few mornings later there were shouts from the street, and the sound of shooting, coming closer. My Caucasian was with me, staring at the door, as if expecting something to happen. The doctor came in suddenly, and nodded briefly. 'Now!' he said. Before I could say a word, the Caucasian had rolled up my pyjama sleeve and there was the familiar prick of the hypodermic needle. I didn't lose consciousness entirely; I was aware of the extraordinary fact that Anna the housemaid had come in with arms full of dust sheets, was stripping my bed, that I was being bundled along to the room that had always been Uncle

Raoul's, was being put into bed there. Whatever the doctor had pumped into me was powerful enough; I couldn't move my head, can remember thinking, 'I can't speak a word even to save my life.' It was probably because I couldn't speak a word that my life was saved.

Anna came flying in. 'Dear God, he's in a fever! He'll die of cold! Not enough on the bed!' She pulled over me a rather dreadful travelling rug in Royal Stuart tartan that was a relic of my Scottish grandmother's travels in her native land   Anna had always admired it and it had been given to her years before, but she always brought it out if one of the family were ill.

And then, standing in the doorway, half a dozen soldiers, dirty, unshaven, the deserters who had run, and reappeared now that Kornilov wasn't coming. They had rifles and bayonets.

As in a dream, I could hear clearly but could say nothing. I could hardly keep my heavy eyes open.

'Be quiet!' said the doctor imperiously. 'A high-ranking officer of the French Republic —seriously ill with a fever—how dare you disturb him?'

'French officer?' they said owlishly.

'Yes, I'm French—a doctor in the hospital here—and as for this officer—'

Dramatically he pointed to Uncle Raoul's uniform, still on the hanger where we had put it when he had left Russia for the last time.

They went and gazed at it. Yes, they agreed, this wasn't a Russian uniform. But to prove the man in the bed was French—what was that book there on the table?

A version of the Bible, in French.

'Open it then, and read!'

He opened it at random, began reading in a steady voice, 'And I looked, and behold a pale horse, and his name that sat on him was Death, and Hell followed him.'

'Enough!' said one, interrupting. 'It sounds foreign enough. And this man in bed must be the right kind to choose that colour for his coverlet!'

They stood round admiring the amount of red in the travelling rug. I thought confusedly I should be giving effusive thanks to the late Victoria and Albert for their rather dreadful taste when they had concocted the Royal Stuart tartan.

At this the drug completely overcame me, and I was blind and deaf.

The evening was closing in when I regained my senses. A wind had risen, and was dashing rain against the window.

'Not long before the really cold weather sets in,' said the doctor, rattling the curtains across. 'I myself don't propose to see another winter here, and if you've any sense you'll come to France with me. The luck can't continue. That little episode this morning was only a foretaste of what's to come. Kerensky can't last now that he's antagonised the Cossacks. The next time the Bolsheviks revolt, they'll win. Then God help Russia.'

He gave me something to drink. 'Sorry I was drastic with the hypodermic, but I couldn't trust you to keep your mouth shut. I'll be leaving in three weeks—you should be fit to travel then.'

'As far as Tobolsk?' I asked.

'Tobolsk! I haven't patched you up so that you can run out and commit suicide. What use is there in dancing attendance at Tobolsk?'

'I shouldn't dance attendance—in fact I shouldn't approach them directly at all. But they must start considering plans for escape. If the Bolsheviks take over—'

'But it's all too late now!' he said in a fury of exasperation. 'The Siberian winter's started. It lasts for six months. Any rescue attempt should have been made weeks ago!'

The rain fell without ceasing. The bitter winds howled in from the Gulf of Finland. If there was neither wind nor rain there was icy fog.

Under the drizzle Petersburg seemed to contract to a maze of muddy lanes, a squalid town, endlessly dreary, of shuttered houses, dismal empty courtyards, gutted ruins. The fact that the theatres and cinemas and gambling clubs remained open only made the rest seem more like a town in the front line.

A town in the front line expecting the enemy to strike again, and as capable of resisting the enemy as a hypnotised rabbit is of resisting a stoat.

It was a nightmare town of fear and suspicion, where no one could trust his neighbour. There were never many ordinary people in the street; the few you passed gave you a furtive, sideways glance. One of the strongest recollections I have of Petersburg in that late autumn of

1917 is the deep mud underfoot and scared white faces at the few un-shuttered windows.

The doctor had made me promise never to go out alone—my head injury was still unpredictable, and there were moments of acute pain or giddiness. I did not quarrel over this; I had at last found in an old trunk a notebook three-quarters filled with Father's distinctive handwriting. The heading was vaguely reminiscent of an epic to be related in the nursery—*The Voyage of Captain Joseph Wiggins*.

Wiggins, despite his unheroic name, was a considerable fellow who had caused a sensation by appearing in the north of Siberia in the 1870s.

And then, to my amazement, scribbled notes in Mother's graceful handwriting.

'Alesha spoke once of a Vostrotin who spent his honeymoon journeying with Captain Wiggins in 1894. I recalled a Duma deputy for Siberia of the same name. It must be the same man—or a relative—'

'It is the same man. More, he made the trip a second time with Nansen only a year before the outbreak of war! I must try to get in touch with him. Alesha's name is still a passport for all those interested in the development of Siberia—'

'I have seen him—it was not safe to put my questions in writing. He did not seem surprised by what I asked—I suppose any man with an obsession thinks everyone shares his feelings. For seven years out of eight the route is open for about six weeks in the summer. Ships might come to the mouth of the Ob with machinery, and take back furs. All the time I was calculating furiously—a chartered *Norwegian* schooner could wait there—leave Russia via the Arctic Ocean—Norwegian schooners come to Obdorsk every Spring now; one more won't be noticeable—and it is the most difficult place in the world for a pursuit—'

I took a deep breath. I could have kissed what she had written so hurriedly. Wonderful Mother—working out plan after plan to help the escape of the Austrian prisoners from Ekaterinburg—and making the way clear for me now.

I drifted off to sleep, dreamed of the sweetest kind of revenge. Obdorsk behind us, the silvery morning light all about us as we stood on the deck of the specially chartered Norwegian schooner. The Czarina—'Andrei, how has this been possible?' Myself—'Your Imperial Majesty, because my mother took that reprehensible interest in Austrian prisoners of war!' Yes, there I strutted—Perseus—St George—Ivan Susanin combined.

And then, from outside, a spattering noise. Machine-guns.

The crack of rifles.

And a sudden boom. Cannon.

The end of the dream.

I lay there in my sick world of fantasy while in the Winter Palace in a gold and malachite room hung with crimson brocade, the Provisional Government of Russia, defended only by a women's regiment and military cadets, sat in paralysed indecision waiting for the Bolsheviks to make sure this time.

It was the dull shock of the guns from the cruiser *Aurora* and the Peter and Paul Fortress rather than actual damage done to the Palace—the shooting was abominably bad—that more than anything finished them.

There was no storming of the Winter Palace as the Tuileries had been stormed. It was more infiltration than anything else. Both defenders and attackers became hopelessly lost from time to time in the ornate rabbit-warren; most of the soldiers made the wine-cellars their chief objective. Many of those who got there first were unable to get out because of the hundreds pressing furiously behind them. Casks were broken open, wine flooded the floor, men, drunk or trampled down by those behind them, drowned in it. The first sounds of the Bolshevik triumph were shouts, shrieks, groans, obscenities coming up from the cellars; the first signs broken bottles, crimson on the snow that was wine, not blood.

'Well, you can get about now,' said the French doctor. 'There's still time for you to change your mind and come with us, you know. No? Then at least I'll make other restorations—less animate restorations—to your mother.'

He, the Caucasian and Vassily had carefully cut all the best pictures from their frames, and canvases painted by Clouet and Canaletto, Fragonard and Claude were used as wrappings for medical instruments. Mother's pearls and emeralds went into large brown and dark blue medicine bottles. The Sèvres, the Venetian glass, the tapestries were crated as 'medical sundries'. I managed to find space for the pieces of Fabergé Father had given her.

The servants were sent off with a year's wages. They cried as I embraced them. Vassily I managed to persuade to go with the French medical team to Mother in France. I said, 'If, when all these things are being unpacked, some clumsy fellow lets fall—'

'Enough!' cried Vassily, blenching. 'Enough! I'll go, then, but as soon as they're safely unpacked, I'll come back. This madness here must be over within a year.'

Only the Caucasian remained with me. He said stubbornly he would come with me to Tyumen—after that he would make for the south and join Kornilov's army of resistance to the Reds.

Red mobs were roaming about the city, looting and destroying. One night we shuttered all the windows and stuck a glaring notice over the gate and door—'Requisitioned by the Soviet.' After this we could finish our preparations in peace. Such as, by a series of secret interviews, discovering when contact might be made with the more practical members of the suite in attendance at Tobolsk.

The journey to Tyumen took four days, we were told. We amassed a certain amount of other information about travelling conditions. Better to travel by night—one couldn't leave Petersburg without a permit, and the chances of deception were better in a poor light. Besides, the Trans-Siberian *de luxe* ran at night; this was the last month of its existence.

It hardly lived up to its reputation. Every window was broken, every seat covering ripped off. 'The gorillas have been loose,' the doctor commented.

He had come to see me off—to give additional authenticity to my French uniform. His parting gift was a phial of tablets. 'Cyanide,' he said briefly. 'You may need the quick way out.'

The train was crowded, and—fortunately—quite without lights. So the Bolshevik official who came to examine all papers had only the light of a candle to see them by; in any case, the French uniform acted like a charm. His idea was that every Frenchman was a socialist revolutionary and an atheist; therefore no difficulties were to be placed in the way of such a one travelling with an interpreter across Siberia to Vladivostok. He congratulated me on the glories of 1793—which, however, would soon be surpassed in Russia.

Next morning we stopped at Vologda, the junction with the Moscow line, and the train was stormed with deserters from the Front. After this all inspection of passes and permits was impossible, for the deserters blocked every corridor. Soon they were sitting on the outside steps, the buffers, even the roofs. They were equally weighed down by loot—

mostly crammed into pillow-cases—and weapons of every kind—rifles, revolvers, even hand-grenades.

So, with the crowds our safeguard, we crossed the Urals.

Forest unending of pine and birch. An occasional fox walking daintily alone in the snow. A deer now and then. Once a wolf.

When we reached Tyumen, no official on earth could have checked papers with that tidal wave of a crowd flooding off the train.

I said to the Caucasian, 'Here we split up, I go northwards, you to the south. That was the understanding.'

'Ah, but keeping a promise is a thing only the *bourgoui* do, and the glorious Order Number One said officers weren't to be obeyed any longer, so as a loyal son of the Revolution, I go on sticking to you, *comrade.*'

His only reaction when I tried to show him the desperate nature of my mission was to say, 'Well, you'd better hand over half those pills to me, hadn't you?'

Eventually we managed to get hold of a *voȝok*—a kind of dog-kennel on runners. No seats or windows except for a tiny opening in the front.

The endless noise of hooves drumming over the frozen ground, the crunch and scrape of the runners lurching over ruts and hummocks. Changing the ponies, exhausted for all their wiriness, at post station after post station. Poor little beasts, they did us good service, pulling weakly towards the end of a stage, heads hanging low, ears flapping dejectedly, staggering and skidding on the icy travesties of roads. It was hideously cold. The long hair on their heaving flanks was frozen in patches where sweat had turned to ice, and their laboured breathing shot jets of vapour which formed into tiny icicles in their nostrils.

Dawn comes late to Siberia in winter. It was still dark when we drove into Tobolsk.

19

'Good Russian men'

THERE WAS little movement in the streets that dark morning, not because of war and revolution, but because few people cared to venture out in cold intense enough at times to break iron. The first signs of life came in the centre of the town where the daily market was held. There were Ostyaks, Tartars, fishermen in furs and huge waders haggling over old clothes—anything from a baby's layette to a general's full-dress uniform—and food. The food fascinated the Caucasian—it was all frozen. 'By God,' he said. 'They're chopping the milk with a hatchet and buying it by the pound!'

We paid off our driver, wandered round. I remember there were six-foot sturgeon, frozen stiff, propped like petrified guardsmen against the stalls.

Eventually in a bored manner I asked my way to the Tobolsk Museum, stood staring at the armour of Yermak, the Cossack conqueror of Siberia. A voice said, 'It must have been stripped from his dead body, of course. He was drowned trying to swim the river here.'

A grey-bearded man, tall, spare, eagle-nosed, frostily sparkling blue eyes. He, like me, was bundled in furs, but his bearing and voice was that of a cavalry officer of the old school. General Tatischev. Old Count Benckendorff had been unable to accompany the Czar from Petersburg because of his wife's illness, and the Czar had asked Tatischev to take his place. Although this involved leaving behind his ninety-year-old mother, who had since died, Tatischev had immediately packed a small suitcase and gone out to Czarskoe.

He said now, 'You must let me point out to you the more interesting exhibits—*It is, so far, better here than it was at Czarskoe. More peaceful, for a start.* This relic of Peter's reign is interesting—*I can't stay for long; as a "voluntary" prisoner I'm allowed to move about freely, but one's always conscious of being spied upon—Botkin's allowed to have a surgery, that's really the best way of communication—*By tradition Yermak's armour was a gift from the Czar—*Have you letters?*—Antonius was Archbishop here in the 1740s—*We're quite alone now. You know they're in the Governor's House?*'

'Where Vyroubova stayed last year when she came with Rasputin,' I said under my breath.

'Still we can't escape the swine—We passed his village as we came up the river—the Czarina insisted on spending the whole evening on deck, gazed at the wretched village as if it were a vision of Paradise. *He'd* always said they'd come to his home. For God's sake let's forget it! They're here—at the corner of the street that's Nobility Street on the map, but the name's changed now to Liberty Street.' He smiled briefly. 'That's practically the only revolutionary change in Tobolsk so far!'

'Where are you staying?'

'We're all in the house just across the road from the Governor's, the Kornilov House. There's a merchant's widow living in the next house, rather a bore because she visited Paris once and can't forget it. I'm sure she'd let a room or two to a French colonel.'

He wrote down her name. 'Don't go to Botkin's surgery too soon—instead visit the Cathedral—tomorrow about noon. Someone will be there.'

'You'll let *them* know I've come?'

'Yes.'

'What's their mood? Has the Bolshevik *coup* alarmed them?'

Tatischev said, 'Only Olga sees the implications.'

'Only Olga has seen the implications for months. What about her father?'

'Angry—he says Lenin's an unsavoury blackguard in German pay. He regrets his abdication now. He realises it didn't help Russia.'

'The Czarina?'

'Oh, my God, she still hopes for a restoration—for Alexei at least! She still talks of *the good Russians*. The other day when one of her ladies talked about the bad behaviour of some of the soldiers she flew into a violent rage. "The soldiers and peasants are all good—they've merely been led astray. Soon they'll come to their senses, and everything will be all right again. The whole Revolution is the fault of the officers—if only they'd been more energetic!" '

The question was wrung out of me, before I left him. 'How could you come, foreseeing what would happen, leaving your mother?'

162

General Tatischev stared at some uninteresting mineral specimens in a dirty glass case. 'It will get worse,' he said. 'Much worse. God knows what the end will be.' He turned away. I thought—and hoped now—he had not heard my unforgivably impertinent question. But then he said, 'Expiation, I suppose. I have always been haunted by the part I played three years ago. Do you know what I started then—by one thoughtless sentence?'

In the biting cold of a Siberian winter I remembered the intense heat of the summer days before the declaration of war. 'You said to the Czar that it—the decision about full mobilisation—was a difficult one to make, nothing more.'

'But I *knew* him!' The blue eyes were desperate. 'I knew his weakness, knew how he always anticipated sneers at that weakness, and how he would react. I could have shot myself the moment the words left my mouth.' He crossed himself suddenly. 'And all this may be part of expiation.'

Two hours later I walked along Liberty Street, the main street of Tobolsk. I was looking for the house adjoining the Kornilov House, but it was natural enough for any stranger to notice the moderately-sized white house on the opposite side of the street. In itself it was unremarkable; what riveted the attention was a high, rawly-new wooden fence cutting it off from the street and patrolled by sentries about ten paces apart.

Someone was staring out from an upper window. I saw a white blouse, the flicker of a hand raised as if to wave. My blank stare stilled the movement. I moved slowly on before the sentries became suspicious; she disappeared to tell the others.

The fur merchant's widow who had visited France years before was delighted to let two rooms to someone who had been in Paris as recently as the summer of 1914. She would have willingly given me the entire upper floor instead of a mere two rooms overlooking the street. 'I find the passers-by so interesting, you understand, Madame—'

'But won't the noise distract you?'

'No noise with your admirable double windows!'

I spent the rest of the day conversing with her and trying to eat the immense meals prepared for me.

The Caucasian went out to buy extra felt boots. 'Get good ones,' I said loudly. 'Don't just buy the first ones you see.'

So he took his time.

Later that evening we talked low-voiced upstairs.

He had come back demanding, 'Who's Soloviev?'

I stared. 'Soloviev? I don't know. Should I?'

'I was coming past the Cathedral and there walking towards me was an officer I'd served under months ago—before I came to you at Novgorod for training. I tell you, we were glad to get away from *him* —brave as a bear he was, but stupid as a donkey. He hasn't changed much. I was going straight past him, eyes front, when damned if he didn't stop me. "I know you!" he said. "You served under me at—" I tried to shut him up, put on what I hoped was the local way of talk. "Perm is the furthest point *I* ever got to!" I said, and went on past him. But he followed me, came abreast of me and said, but lower this time, thank God, "Have you been sent by Soloviev? I'm living in the Upper Town," and he told me his address. Your Honour, I think I'd better go to see him—just in case—to find out who Soloviev may be.'

Inside the Cathedral next day it was icy; I was glad of my felt boots and my thick coat. It was fairly dark still; one could just distinguish a tall man in a violet mantle—the abbot?—taking leave of another man who came towards me, a man in uniform without insignia, youngish still, fair, with an impassive face. Prince Dolgoroukov, who had been the Czar's playfellow and my father's.

He embraced me. 'They'll be in the garden this afternoon—have you taken the rooms Tatischev told you about, and can you see the house from there?'

'Yes.'

'Good—I'll tell them when I join them for lunch. What I call the garden was, of course, never more than a cabbage patch—at the best. It was a quagmire a month ago—the snow's made things a little better. I tell myself things are better here than at Czarskoe. No Red Guards, no factories, no agitators—and then I think of the children, four young girls and a small boy, *not* State prisoners, never State prisoners, shut up, never allowed a walk outside, even under guard. All they can do is walk round that damned cabbage patch or tramp round the wretched enclosure inside that hideous new fence. This afternoon they'll be shovelling snow—God help us, how they look forward to it!' After a moment he added, 'I think you'll see changes.'

Outside the Caucasian was waiting. 'Much to tell you, Your Honour,' he said in an undertone, 'but I don't like any of it.'

'Not a word before we get indoors,' I said.

I was lucky to get indoors at all. As we passed the ugly wooden paling a gate opened and, suddenly, careering across the snowy road towards me, stopping to chase his tail in delight, skidding to a halt before me and rearing up on his hind legs ecstatically, came a deliriously excited spaniel Joy. I think I felt more panic at that moment than I had felt since leaving for Siberia. 'You'll have to beat him off,' said the Caucasian. 'Aim a kick at him—it's all you can do. The guards are laughing now, but any minute they'll—'

A better idea occurred to me. I said in a low voice, in English, 'Find Alexei!' Memories of summoning Alexei in this way when General Hanbury-Williams was waiting at Stavka—

Joy looked at me intelligently, licked my hand, then went racing back into the house.

'It's all right,' said the Caucasian. 'He went off again so quick they think he made a mistake. He's the Heir's dog, isn't he? I want a drink, don't you?'

We entered our lodgings, told the landlady we would eat in half an hour, ran upstairs and drank brandy. Then I said, 'Well, who's Soloviev?'

'He's the man who's going to be the saviour of the Imperial Family,' said the Caucasian. 'Ivan Susanin'll* soon be forgotten.'

'Who says so?'

'Well,' he said slowly, 'so far as I can make out, the Czarina says so.' And as I gazed at him in astonishment, he added, 'Not so surprising— he's Rasputin's son-in-law.'

'Rasputin didn't have a son-in-law.'

'No, Soloviev married his daughter only a couple of weeks ago.'

'There was a Soloviev—a lieutenant—who led his men to the Duma in the first days of the Revolution; *that* couldn't be the man?'

'Was his father Treasurer of the Holy Synod?'

'Yes— Are you trying to tell me that dirty little rat is the man who's going to *save* them? And that they trust him?'

'He's married to Rasputin's daughter, and he brought letters from fat Vyroubova. *She*—the Czarina—thinks he's an angel from heaven.'

Soloviev had first appeared in Siberia in August, at much the same

* The peasant who saved the life of the first Romanov Czar.

time as the Imperial Family. He had then returned to Petersburg where he had married Rasputin's daughter, encouraged by Vyroubova in the all-too-solid flesh, and by Rasputin in the spirit in a series of *séances*. He had then returned to Siberia. From Tobolsk he got in touch with the Czarina—his newly-acquired family connection, ecstatically written recommendations by Vyroubova, all made her accept him and all his promises as she had accepted the persons and promises of other would-be miracle-workers in the past.

By this time I had my head in my hands. The same dreadful pattern —a fool's paradise that was really the road to self-destruction.

'I won't come up,' the Caucasian said after our mid-day meal.

'Don't be a fool; you've earned the right to see them—'

'There'll be other chances for me. You have this one to yourself.'

I almost said, 'Is it so obvious?' Clearly he saw that I was scared— though I don't suppose he guessed what precisely scared me so much. Quite simply, the prospect of seeing that familiar expression on the Czar's face—vacant fatalism.

That's what I was dreading. But it was the expression on another face that left me white-faced and shaking. I should have listened carefully to what Dolgoroukov had said—*You'll see changes.*

It is still as if my heart turns to ice-water when I recall my first sight of Olga after so many weeks.

Easier to remember the cold stuffiness of the little room and the starched white muslin curtains, the strong smell of polish rising from the bare boards that were so hideously slippery. The landlady had a fat canary; I remember how, at the moment they came out, the sky was suddenly radiant with the glittering Siberian winter sun and beneath me, in that lower window overlooking Liberty Street, the bird broke into song. At the same time the door opposite opened, and birdsong and sunburst seemed to me so auspicious—

They came out. Dolgoroukov had said, 'They'll see you dimly—an outline.' The Czar, coming first, could see that I was rigid at the salute; slowly he raised his hand to his cap in acknowledgement even though, for fear he should be observed, he swiftly altered the gesture so that it appeared he was merely adjusting the peak to keep the sun from his eyes.

And behind him, closest to him as always, came Olga Olga with a lagging step, walking slowly, eyes on the ground. The other girls—

Anastasia carried fat little Jimmy—raised smiling faces, seeming to scan their surroundings with casual interest. Alexei caught Olga's arm, whispered urgently to her, and then she too raised her eyes pathetically, beseechingly, managed a valiant smile as if to say, 'I am not very pretty now, but I hope you are not showing shock—or pity.'

There had never been any vanity in her, God knows, and I had been her friend from babyhood, but she was aware—so I was told afterwards how sorrow and anxiety had changed her, at twenty-two, into a faded, sad woman, unbearably worn, middle-aged, and she knew how harshly and mercilessly the transformation appeared in the bright sunshine.

It had been such a youthful, radiant face. Now it seemed as if the round young flesh had been eroded from the bones.

I could do nothing. I couldn't fling open the double windows and shout, 'There's no need for you to fear *my* reaction!' I simply stood there stiffly, like a log of wood, and while the sun poured down and the canary went on singing, the Czar of All the Russias and his children shovelled snow, and one of them, at twenty-two, looked like a saddened woman of forty, and knew it.

I looked so drawn next morning that my landlady noticed it. I said, truthfully, that I hadn't slept because of a blinding headache.

'It's the sun on the snow, I've no doubt,' she said. 'It often affects people. You should see a doctor. And the best doctor in all Russia is here in Tobolsk.'

Botkin's waiting-room; my turn at last. The doctor shook hands with me without flickering an eyelid. Headaches? Possibly eye trouble —we'd try eye-tests. So the room was plunged into darkness and I reeled off letters from a chart loudly while a quiet voice talked beside me.

'It takes more than a revolution to cure certain ills. A tendency to hysteria, that implicit trust in those, alive or dead, who contrived to bring the throne down in ruins. Physically she's changed, she's an old, grey-haired woman, but mentally and emotionally she's still the same.'

'I'll be at the Cathedral again at three. I must talk about Soloviev.'

'Yes.' And then, in a loud voice, 'Well, there seems nothing organically wrong. We'll try this treatment for a week—'

'Doctor, are you hopeful?'

He put on the light, and shook his head. 'I was never very hopeful. I pretended to be—for other people's sakes. I pretended to believe we were going to England—I babbled like an idiot about taking tennis clothes. One learns as a doctor to make a reasonably false façade of one's face.'

'And yet you volunteered to stay.'

'I'd seen that offal Derevenko, Alexei's attendant for ten years, the recipient of untold kindnesses, sprawling in a chair and bawling orders at the dazed child—and I didn't want to ape that behaviour.'

There was a rising wind that afternoon. Beneath it, the snow seemed to seethe.

The dull Cathedral. A few people inside, staring at the relics of John of Tobolsk. Tatischev knelt in a dark corner; eventually I went over and knelt beside him.

'You don't seem to have much faith in Soloviev,' he said.

'Have *you*?'

'In Rasputin's son-in-law? But if I dare say anything, she flares up. Of course he hasn't arranged anything yet, but who else has? My God, she tells us that Soloviev's built up this escape organisation of three hundred officers, waiting in the neighbourhood for the signal—she's even given a name to these "good Russian men"—the Brotherhood of St John of Tobolsk!'

'Doesn't he tell her anything about his plans?'

'Oh, yes. He's going to seize Tobolsk, destroy the telegraph, put the Family on sleighs and get them away. Sometimes it's to Turkestan, at other times it's up to Archangel. It hasn't happened so far because it will take a good deal of money. So the Czarina smuggles out appeals for large sums of money—to be sent or taken to Soloviev in Tyumen—and people aren't sending enough—'

'As long as she believes in him—'

'There's only one way to put a stop to it. I'll get a list of the people who've been asked to help. I'll also get copies of Soloviev's heartbroken little notes—So-and-so's sent only half the amount required, Such-and-such hasn't answered at all. And you must go to these people and find out the truth.'

'I can't go away so quickly—how will they feel?'

'Is that so important? Won't you be doing more for their safety by exposing Soloviev? Go to Botkin tomorrow; he'll have the information. And here's a letter.'

'I have seen you twice now. Once you were passing in the street and

Anastasia saw you. I didn't join her in the window, but I saw you very clearly. And the other time you were a blur at the window of your lodgings, but I think I would have known it was you even if we hadn't been warned. Tobolsk has become real to me now. It wasn't before. There is never much light in the rooms these days—when you look in a mirror behind you it's mostly shadows. Sometimes I have told myself that if I stare hard enough the shadows will disappear and I'll see the sun on the willows lining the canal bank at Peterhof.'

Botkin gave me closely written lists. 'Go quickly,' he said. 'We've managed so far to prevent her from writing ecstatically to Soloviev about your coming, but sooner or later he'll be told of your arrival. She thinks at present you must have come from him; she said to me rather nervously, "I hope Andrei took to Boris—he's a dear good boy, but he makes hasty judgments." '

20

'Doctors demand immediate departure'

Moscow, TOO, looked like an enemy-occupied city. The Reds had encountered much tougher opposition here than in Petersburg; in the Tverskaya shop windows were shattered, there were shell-holes in the walls, torn-up paving stones.

Odd how some memories remain almost luridly vivid. Our stay in Moscow was brief; we had been told over the telephone to go to a vegetarian restaurant reassuringly called 'I eat no one', and there we had been given lists of money sent to Tobolsk, and told of the fighting in Moscow, and the rumours from Petersburg and the Ukraine, and then, almost casually—'Oh, yes, the animals have started peace negotiations with Germany. At Brest-Litovsk. They sent a Red Commissar with orders for a cease-fire. Dukhonin, the new commander at Mogilev, opposed this, and his own men lynched him.'

We were sitting opposite a rather dreadful picture of Tolstoy, looking as mad as Lear. In the wretched candle-light he seemed to be winking at us.

Poor Samsonov, I'd thought over three years ago. But at least he hadn't been lynched by his own troops.

Petersburg and familiar faces seen in unfamiliar settings.

'Letters were smuggled out from the Czarina. All money to go to Soloviev. No escape plans to be made without consulting Soloviev—'

And I talked about Obdorsk. Foreign schooners came to Obdorsk in great numbers every year in the early Spring—

Not that we should wait for the Spring before leaving Tobolsk; winter was, in fact, the great equaliser where numbers were concerned. Tobolsk wasn't Red—yet. If we were given sufficient time to escape northwards with a guard of about thirty, there wouldn't be that number of Reds in Tobolsk, they'd have to get them up from Tyumen. Furthermore, they would be virtually unarmed—it being practically impossible to use firearms in regions so icy that machine-guns froze. And we should have had time to dig ourselves in.

'It's a desperate plan, this escape over snow with women and a child. Why not wait until Spring, when they can use the river?'

'I intended that once—before I heard of Soloviev. Now I think we can't afford to wait.'

There had been incredulity when I first voiced my suspicions of Soloviev—'But *she* sent explicit orders that we should work only through him.' But a brief glance at the lists supplied by Dr Botkin had soon put a stop to that. '*Thirty-five* thousand roubles—I sent a hundred and seventy-five!'

I don't wish, however, to give the impression that there were many such meetings. There were few people in Petersburg ready to risk their necks for the Imperial Family, but this, I suppose, was not to be wondered at. For years the Family had been metaphorically as cut off from most Russians as now they were isolated by the Urals and the snows. Of a hundred and fifty million Russians, only a very few were prepared to give a life for the Czar.

Perhaps the strangest sight of all in Petersburg was the number of Germans swaggering about. A German admiral had arrived with his staff for the peace talks, had an entire hotel assigned to him. So it was quite alien now, a dead city belonging to a dead world. Even night didn't make it familiar again—Petersburg had never been this city of darkness, sickness, starvation, fear, with vast frozen squares, absolutely empty, of huge shadowy deserted buildings. The only illumination was the sullen glow of the Red Guard watch-fires.

As it must have been when the barbarians camped in the deserted streets of Roman cities.

We lived like ghosts in a graveyard, slipping in and out after dark through a side window of what had been my home. I wore felt boots, a dirty sheepskin and fur hat. It was easier to travel in Siberia than it was to cross Petersburg; snow fell day after day, and as there were no street cleaners it pitched in huge masses everywhere. A sky by day grey and hard as iron, a freezing wind, a mockery of a bread ration scarcely eatable, darkness, no fuel—dead horses lay with swollen bellies in streets that had not been swept for months. Soon cholera and typhus would be added to starvation.

The Caucasian began to cough and spit blood; I felt as if the end of the world had come. There were literally no medical supplies in Petersburg. As for warmth, nourishing food, these things existed on another planet. He would cough himself to death here in the freezing darkness of the empty house.

If he were to survive, he had to be rushed to the south.

I was returning one night after a vain search for something to ease his cough. I passed the hotel where the German Admiral Kaiserling was staying; there was great activity outside—someone was shouting that sledges must be found by the morning to take to the station the party that had come up from Kiev.

'Lucky swine,' came a comment in the accents of a Potsdam barrack square. 'Some are going even further south. To the Black Sea.'

I hung on in the shadows, desperately interested. The belongings of the Kiev contingent were being assembled in the foyer of the hotel under the eyes of a typical German sergeant—sandy-haired, square-headed; a Brandenburger by the look of him. Well, even Brandenburgers had been known to serve Kaiser and Mammon. I shuffled forward and asked in broken German if he needed any help.

He laughed, '*Me* need help? It's you Russians who need the help!'

No one showed any interest in me, beggars came almost as thick as snowflakes. I said in a low voice—and in noticeably better German—'True enough. But some of us are prepared to pay.'

His eyes narrowed. 'What are you ready to pay for—and how much?'

'A sick man taken south—no, it's not infectious. You'll have a special train, won't you?'

'Well,' he said, 'what would you pay me in? Russian money's no good. It would have to be gold.' And he named a huge sum.

'You can get money from Austria, can't you? I'll write you a draft—'

'How can you promise Austrian money?'

I stood there in my stinking sheepskin and said, 'My great-grandfather was Prince Hohenems-Landeck. You may have heard of him. He was the Old Emperor's personal ADC.'

'Yes, I saw him once at a review.'

'He died just before the war. He left everything jointly to my uncle and me.'

'Your uncle's Austrian?'

'French. Dead at Verdun. I suppose it's all mine now.'

'They'll have confiscated it. Enemy property.'

'No. The Old Gentleman—I'm sorry—the late Emperor—sent a message telling us it wouldn't be. He was my mother's godfather.'

He hesitated. 'I'm not taking a chance. For hard cash I'll take your friend south—you, too, if you like. Not otherwise.'

I moved away, my shoulders sagging. He strode off. And a little corporal came up to me and said in a Rhineland accent, 'Sorry he wouldn't help. I was listening all the time—wish I could do something. Can your friend talk German?'

I shook my head.

'Wait,' he said suddenly. 'If I gave you one of our greatcoats and a cap, we might be able to smuggle him on board. You'll have to put it on—chuck that sheepskin coat away—'

It was the slenderest of chances. I didn't even know how I was to get the Caucasian across Petersburg. But I wrung the little Rhinelander's hand, said huskily, 'I'll write a letter to the steward in Vienna—'

He said with sudden dignity, 'I don't want money. When this filthy business is over I want to be a priest. *Until* it's over, can't I be a Christian—at least?'

So I set off in Prussian field grey. The unexpected kindness, the need for furious thought as to how I was to get the Caucasian accepted, made me blind and deaf to my surroundings.

The hoarse challenge, when it came, took me completely by surprise. Three Red Guards, rifles pointed at me, grinning. A German in a good thick greatcoat—that should bring in some money! Should they kill me? No, better not. The Germans would take Petersburg apart if one of them was murdered, but if a fool wandered too far out of his way—and returned unhurt—that was his own damned fault.

One, a huge bearded fellow in a sheepskin coat, who reeked of drink, pointed a rifle with a bit of red rag tied round it at me. I was in such a murderous rage I almost sprang at him, rifle and all. The greatcoat was the Caucasian's last slender chance of going south. But for all my fury of despair, I didn't lose my wits entirely. If he didn't finish me off, the others would, with bullets, rifle butt, boot. My carcass tossed into a canal wouldn't help the Caucasian. He'd die alone in the icy darkness. So I set my teeth and I took off the greatcoat—they were either too drunk to notice I wasn't wearing German uniform underneath or they thought that even a German stopped being dressy in a winter night in Petersburg—but there was still enough fury in me to make me say (although I had sufficient sense to keep the Russian broken), 'Well, are

you going to leave me to freeze to death? Come on, *comrade*—you're
so keen on fraternising—let's have your jacket!'

It tickled the others. 'Come on—let him have it.' And within minutes
they had gone off, roaring with laughter, leaving me with an incredibly
filthy sheepskin jacket on the snow at my feet.

Choking with rage, I picked it up and pulled it on, hurried home as
best as I could. It stank of sweat and spilled spirits, it was as heavy as
Hell, it weighed me down, it was the obscene reminder of the last faint
chance left to my friend.

I think that by the time I dragged myself into the courtyard I was
sobbing with rage. Getting through the window was difficult, the vile
coat was so enormously heavy and bulky. I fumbled my way across the
hall. At the foot of the staircase was a treasured stump of a candle. I
lit it with shaking fingers, then threw off the disgusting jacket; the
Caucasian would immediately want to know why the change had been
made, and I was so exhausted by futile rage I was incapable of any
invention.

The coat fell on to the marble floor with a thud.

It hadn't thumped when its previous owner had tossed it to me—no,
the snow would have deadened any noise.

Something in the pockets—weighing it down?

Not a bottle. It would have smashed.

A heavy revolver, perhaps.

I lifted up the coat and shook it.

I felt they couldn't be real, the necklace and bracelet with the cold
glitter when the light fell on them. I sat on the floor, staring. These
glittering things, plundered from some luckless wretch by a brute too
drunk to remember, were to take the Caucasian to the south.

I didn't tell him, of course. He would have refused to go. So first I
wrote a letter and then searched the kitchen quarters and found an old
sledge on which firewood had been delivered, and then I went upstairs
and hit him on the jaw and tied him onto the sledge and dragged him
across Petersburg. The sledge slithered and jolted up and down the
hummocks of snow that made any journey along a Petersburg street a
miniature trip on a switchback, but he didn't wake. I had a dreadful
feeling I might have killed him by exposing him to these Polar conditions.

The Brandenburger took the necklace—to my amazement, saluted.

He would see the sick man got down to the Black Sea. To the corporal, who suddenly appeared, I said, 'When he's conscious, give him this letter and the bracelet. And see he doesn't escape. He'll try to get back!'

I had had to word the letter carefully; he had joined the Army too late to learn to read and write easily. 'You must go to the south to get well again. Whatever you do, God go with you, my friend, my last friend. I have given the German corporal a bracelet; sell it for a house or a field or, if things go badly, to get abroad. Go to this address in France, where my mother will welcome you.'

He has never come to France. I do not know if he is alive or dead. Because he may be still alive in Russia, I have never named my last friend.

A new organisation—the Cheka—had been set up 'to combat counter-revolution'. It would have branches in all cities.

'Even in Tobolsk?'

'You can be sure the Reds haven't forgotten *them*. When the time comes, they'll act.'

'Is Soloviev, then, a Cheka agent?'

For the rest, my last stay in Petersburg was a series of vigils in mean houses, in flickering lamplight (if one was lucky), waiting for frightened people to come furtively for brief, whispered conferences.

One of the changes the Revolution had brought was the altered sound of footsteps. Snow, of course, had always brought obvious differences—a muffled softness, an indistinctness, but footfalls a year before had never been secret and wary like this.

It took nearly a month to get back to Tyumen. I had been told in Petersburg to go to a house in a back street; here I was given an attic room and a meal. I had two questions to ask. What news had been received from the Family, and how could I manage to see Soloviev alone?

Both replies filled me with apprehension—Alexei was ill again, and Soloviev was in prison.

'But he—the Heir—has been so well!' I argued foolishly.

Yes, very well, I was told, so well he'd enjoyed more vigorous exercise in the wretched confines of the yard than he'd ever been able to take at Czarskoe. In January a little toboggan-run, a snow-mountain, had been made for him and Marie and Anastasia, and they'd careered down, shrieking with laughter. But then the Czar and Czarina had used

175

the hill as a vantage point for looking over the stockade into the street —they wanted to wave goodbye to a contingent of soldiers who'd behaved decently. Immediately the rest of the soldiers had ordered that the 'snow-mountain' should be demolished. Alexei had tried to have toboggan runs down the stairs, nobody was able to check him, and he fell—inevitably—and the bleeding started.

'One of the worst attacks ever. Extraordinary pain. And, God help *her*, no Rasputin to give the illusion of hope.'

In between screams, Alexei was gasping, 'I want to die. I'm not afraid to die, but I'm so afraid of what they'll do to us.'

So all the planning and contriving in Petersburg would be wasted. Any amount of Norwegian schooners might be waiting in the north; Alexei's illness made any idea of movement impossible.

There was not even the consolation of dealing with Soloviev, scotching one snake at least. He had been arrested ten days before.

My informant and I sat silent for a few minutes, so silent that one became very much aware of small incidental sounds, from outside the house the thud of melting snow falling from the roof, inside the noise of the fire roaring in the stove, for in Siberia there would never be a shortage of wood, at least.

Then I said harshly, 'I must go to Tobolsk at once, something's being planned.'

'How do you know?'

'*Because Soloviev's got himself arrested.* He'll want to safeguard himself, won't he? If anything happens, even his dupes will ask, "Why didn't you stop it? Where were the 'Good Russians', the Order of St John of Tobolsk, the huge organisation you built up with the millions of roubles entrusted to you?" And he'll say, "Ah, God, I was in prison!" '

During Alexei's illnesses pain had been relieved a little by keeping his legs warm with a Fohn apparatus. A replacement had been ordered, and had actually arrived at Tyumen. I would take it up to Tobolsk, it was a new, improved model, and I was a French technician sent to explain how the best results might be obtained. From my dilapidated luggage I hurriedly took Uncle Raoul's uniform, asked my host to keep it for me.

A last-minute attempt to get definite confirmation of the rumours whispered in Petersburg—yes, Eastern Siberia *had* declared its opposition to the Reds, yes, the Czechs who'd enlisted in the Russian army had turned against the Reds, too, and were fighting to control the railway—and I was on my way to Tobolsk once more. The only transport I could get was a Siberian cart. This is a kind of wicker basket hung between two long parallel poles. The passenger squats or lies at the bottom. The horses gallop at sickening speed while the 'carriage' bounces and flings itself from side to side.

The last stages of the journey, through a countryside blotched brown and white with the approaching thaw, was hideously uncomfortable. The horses' hooves churned up flying snow and mud. I was just trying to take comfort from the fact that with its mask of mire my face was quite unrecognisable, when with a grunt the driver pulled the horses in to the side of the road. 'Riders behind us,' he said. 'Many of them.'

As they went past in fresh flurries of mud, I calculated there must have been about a hundred and fifty of them, Red Guards, heavily armed.

'Have you any idea where they come from?' I asked.

'Not from Tobolsk—they're all strangers to me,' the driver said, in his halting Russian. 'From Ufa, perhaps—do you know it, south of Ekaterinburg?' He shook his reins. 'Let's hope we can get across the Irtysh. The ice will be starting to melt—*that* lot will make it unsafe for people following behind.'

The ice was thin and melting, but we managed to cross it. And, later that night, Tobolsk. Most of the town was dark, but lights enough shone in the Governor's and the Kornilov Houses.

I sent in the driver with the information that the man with the new Fohn equipment from Petrograd had come, and busied myself with various packages.

Tatischev's tall figure appeared in the lighted doorway. 'Bring it in —you'd better stay here tonight, then take it across tomorrow.'

We bent over the apparatus. 'What in God's name is happening?'

'It's been like a nightmare. We had two sets of Red Guards, one from Omsk, the other from Ekaterinburg, each trying to take control. Then this evening the biggest party of all turned up—'

'They passed us. My driver said they might be from Ufa.'

'The Guards are from Ufa, but the man in charge has come from Moscow.'

'You're sure?'

'He even has a telegraphist to keep him in direct touch with Sverdlov.'*

* Chairman of the VZIK (the Soviet Central Executive Committee). Later Ekaterinburg was to be renamed Sverdlovsk in his honour.

'Have you met him? What's he like?'

'An educated man, well-travelled, I'd say. A cool customer—but, by God, his jaw dropped when he heard how sick Alexei is.'

I was wet and cold, tired and stupid. 'Why?' I asked dully.

'There's only one possible reason—he planned to take them away.'

The newcomer's name was Yakovlev. His consternation on learning of Alexei's illness had almost been comic, he had gone time and again to the boy's room, almost as if he expected Alexei were shamming, and hoped to catch him out. Next morning he was bringing an army doctor for an exhaustive examination.

'Will Alexei live?'

'I think so, but I don't believe the boy will ever walk again, his leg is flexed too badly after the bleeding.'

'Hasn't Yakovlev explained why he's come?'

'He spoke to the Czar—politely. I had the feeling there was a great deal he wanted to say, but not before witnesses. The Czar thinks they want to bring him to Moscow to ratify the peace with Germany. *She* believes it, too. She became hysterical—all we could get from her at first were denunciations of the Duma representatives a year ago.'

'But that's insane—what have they to do with Yakovlev's arrival?'

'She thinks the Reds in Moscow are taking a leaf out of their book. All very well for the Czar to say he'd cut off his right hand before signing any peace treaty, but if they got him alone—"It'll be like the abdication," she said, sobbing. "If they get him alone, they'll force him to do the wrong thing."'

After a moment he added, 'And then, within seconds, she's swung to the other extreme. Do you know, when the Red Guards came in from Omsk, *she thought they were rescuers*—'

'Good Russian men,' I said with a groan.

'She went out on to her balcony and waved to them, called to the Grand Duchesses to come and see them. "What good faces!" she said. The Czar said to me, "They're mostly officers enlisted in the ranks."'

Heavy feet began to come up the stairs. 'I must go,' said Tatischev. 'That's the Red Commissar. I'll try to see you in the morning. Who do *you* think is employing Yakovlev?'

'The Germans perhaps. A puppet Czar with the Germans pulling the strings would be useful. Goodnight.'

The inevitable frost was on the windowpane next morning, but behind it one could see a pale sun.

178

No one took any notice of me. There were so many strangers in Tobolsk that one more face didn't seem important.

An army doctor examined Alexei, informed Yakovlev that the boy was, indeed, seriously ill. Yakovlev saw the Czar again, addressed him as 'Your Majesty', but still did not explain his mission except to reiterate that he had been sent direct from Moscow.

'He's come to take the Czar to Moscow,' I said. 'Either to stand trial or to be handed over to the Germans.'

Tatischev asked which theory I believed.

'The second. Lenin and the Reds think that trials are relics of *bourgeois* stupidity. We'll have to find out if the monarchists know why Yakovlev was sent here; I'll send a telegram.'

I was allowed to go to the Post Office to wire my employers that the apparatus had arrived safely. Not knowing how much longer I should be allowed to stay in the Kornilov House, I sent the telegram in Tatischev's name—'Doctors demand immediate departure to health resort. Much perturbed by this demand, and consider journey undesirable. Please send advice. Extremely difficult position.'

Next I went in search of the officer known to the Caucasian. A frightened woman said he had been arrested after Christmas and taken to Tyumen. There he had been shot, two of his friends with him.

I went back to the Kornilov House to tell Tatischev of this. As we spoke, a dark clean-shaven man came into the room. He was dressed as an ordinary sailor, but neither speech nor manner accorded with this.

Tatischev said, 'This is the Frenchman who brought the Fohn apparatus yesterday.'

Yakovlev smiled, put out a clean, well-kept hand. '*Bonjour monsieur.* It was a bad journey, wasn't it?'

He smiled again, and went on past us. I asked in a low voice, 'What's the Czar doing?'

'Reading. He's read a great deal this winter—Dumas and Sherlock Holmes and now a book Olga recommended to him—she'd cried over the end—*Greenmantle.*'

If that day had been spent in waiting, action followed action on the next. Yakovlev went off with his telegraph operator; I followed at a discreet distance and saw them go into the telegraph exchange. They were not there long; soon Yakovlev was hurrying back to the

Governor's House, forehead furrowed, lips compressed. I followed at a distance, so much so that he was inside the house, and I was halfway along the street when a band of horsemen rode past at a great rate, splashing everyone with mud and slush.

An old woman, wiping her face clean, muttered, 'Yes, get back to Ekaterinburg as soon as you can, you heathen; it's the only place fit for you!'

I tried to brush some mud from her coat. 'Do you know them?'

'Only what I've been told, but when they came the other day someone told me they were Red Guards from Ekaterinburg, and the ugly fellow at their head called himself a Commissar.'

I went back into the Kornilov House. Within minutes Tatischev came hurrying across. 'He's come out into the open. He was sent to take the entire Family from Tobolsk. He had to change his plans because of Alexei's illness, but now he's had fresh instructions—to take the Czar alone.'

'He's *told* the Czar this?'

'No—he asked to see the Czar as soon as possible, and the Czar said he'd see him at two.'

'At *two*?'

'Yes.' Tatischev's face was expressionless. 'The Czarina never gets up before lunch, and she insists on being there.'

I groaned. 'God help us, don't they realise they *must* get Yakovlev to talk—and he'll only talk to the Czar? I may be insane, but I think he means them well.'

'So do I.'

'I want to speak to him.'

'They won't let you into the house.'

'Then ask him to come here. There's something he should know.'

'If you think it important. You're still the Frenchman, are you?'

Yakovlev came rapidly across the street. 'Whatever the purpose of this mysterious communication, it had better be worth while,' he said firmly—and in very good French.

I said, 'The Ekaterinburg Commissar and his men have gone back in a hurry. If you're trying to make for Moscow, you'll have to go through Ekaterinburg, won't you?'

'When did they go?'

'Half an hour ago.'

He bit his lip, then said, 'Why have you told me this?'

'I think you intend no harm to the Czar.'

'I will answer for his safety with my head,' he said slowly, and then, with a sudden burst of irritation, 'But this mad refusal to speak with me before two o'clock!'

I went back to the telegraph office and hung around for the reply to my telegram. At last it came: 'Hesitate to give opinion—Advise postpone journey if possible.'

Meanwhile the Reds from Ekaterinburg had hours to get back with their news to the town which was not only the most revolutionary town in all the Urals, but also *a railway centre that had to be passed on the way to Moscow.* I felt sure that Moscow was the first planned destination, if not the ultimate. A German ambassador was coming to Moscow; the Czar could be handed over to him there. Or—to be more hopeful— was Moscow the first stage in a journey that would bring him eventually through neutral Sweden to his mother's country, Denmark?

But the dreadful point was, one couldn't be optimistic about the Czar. He was unlucky. He himself said he was unlucky. He was particularly unlucky on railways. Bad luck on railways had led to the Abdication. And if he liked people, he transferred his bad luck to them. The moment he trusted Kerensky, Kerensky was finished. If he approved of Yakovlev —

Ridiculous stuff, I know, but tension, tiredness, doubts and fears alternately battled and allied with each other.

After darkness fell, Tatischev came over to the Kornilov House and asked me to send another telegram.

'Had to submit to doctors' decision.'

He said the Czarina believed a miracle would happen. 'She's on her knees praying for a thaw, a melting of the ice. She's told them, "I know the river will overflow tonight, so that we can't go." And if the river doesn't overflow, she'll still be staring into the faces of the Red Guard escorts, believing that here are the "Good Russians" escorting them to safety.'

'Them?' I echoed, thunderstruck. 'Is *she* going with him?'

'Yes.'

'Leaving Alexei—*ill?*'

'Yes. But go and send the telegram—I'll tell you everything when you come back.'

Yakovlev had said with great courtesy that he wanted to speak to the Czar alone.

'I won't go,' said the Czarina. 'What next, indeed? Why shouldn't I remain?'

For a moment Yakovlev seemed nonplussed; then he said, as if to himself, 'There is no time to waste in arguments,' and did not insist on her leaving them. However, he spoke only to the Czar, explaining that his original orders had been to take the entire Family from Tobolsk, but, since Alexei was ill, the Czar must go alone.

The Czar said, 'I shall not go, and that's that!'

Yakovlev showed remarkable patience. 'Please don't adopt that attitude—I have my orders, and if you won't come freely, I shall have the choice of using force or giving up my mission, in which case someone far less considerate may take my place. You need have no fears for your safety; I answer for your life with my head. There is, of course, no need for you to come literally alone, you may bring anyone you choose. But we must leave at four o'clock tomorrow morning.'

He bowed and left.

The Czar said, 'They want me to sign the Treaty of Brest-Litovsk. I won't do it.' He went out into the garden and started pacing up and down. The Czarina was distracted; her first action was to send an ikon to Soloviev. Then she began to repeat, over and over again, that the journey could not take place, would not be allowed to take place, the ice was melting, and the rivers would overflow. Then she said, 'I must go with him. He mustn't be alone, as he was before. He's necessary to them—they realise that he alone represents Russia. I must be beside him, to strengthen him—' And finally she began weeping. 'But Alexei's ill—there may be complications—I can't leave him. What shall I do, oh, what shall I do?' She raised tear-reddened eyes and said despairingly, 'I've always felt inspired whenever I've had to take a decision, but now I can't think! But God won't allow him to go! It can't happen!'

One of the girls ventured, 'Father has to go whatever we say,' but the only reply was, 'God will not, cannot allow it!'

The Czar, who seemed the least concerned of all the household, came in from the garden. The Czarina went across to him. 'I am coming with you.' He replied, 'Very well, if you wish it.' Tatiana said, 'One of us must come with you—it had better be Marie, Anastasia's too young, and Olga and I will be needed to look after Alexei and run the household here.'

Just before five the Czarina went up to tell Alexei what had happened. The rest of the Family joined them; the other members of the household had been told to join them at ten-thirty, the intervening hours would be spent at Alexei's bedside. As Tatischev had come away, he had heard the Czarina's voice repeating, 'I *know* the river will overflow tonight. If a miracle is necessary, I am sure it will take place.'

It did not.

Sometimes, when I have been unable to check my thoughts in time, I have wondered when she had to accept that it was not going to happen.

I kept wondering that night. Would she lose her faith in God because He had failed them?

Dolgoroukov was to go with them, and Botkin. A maid, Demidova, and a footman.

From two o'clock onwards there was a rattling of wheels in the road outside. The party would leave in vehicles no better than the one which had brought me from Tyumen, no seats, no springs, though I was glad to see that one at least had a wretched hood. Somebody put a mattress for the Czarina to lie on; someone else, I heard later, went to the yard where a servant kept some pigs, to get straw.

It was very different from the carriages lined with white satin.

The little courtyard was alive with the dark figures of soldiers and servants dragging cases and packages, and stowing them away. Light streamed out from the door, and then, at about half past three, the Czar and Czarina stood silhouetted against it. Yakovlev, I noted, saluted as they came down the steps. There was a short argument—the Czarina was protesting about something. Easy enough to guess from Yakovlev's gestures what the commotion was about; she wanted to be with the Czar, but Yakovlev was polite but firm; she would ride with Marie, *he* would ride with the Czar.

Soldiers with rifles took their places in the first two sleighs, then came the Czar and Yakovlev, and behind them the Czarina and Marie. I could see the Czar's face quite clearly, as he was seated on the right; he was smiling as he talked to his companion. I could not see the Czarina because of the hood on her conveyance.

A lurching start, but in a moment it seemed that the carriages were moving at almost breakneck speed. They swerved left around the corner into the main street, and disappeared.

It was bitterly cold—Yakovlev had told the Czarina that one fur coat would not be enough—but three figures in simple grey dresses stood motionless on the steps of the Governor's House, staring down the road long after it was empty and silent once more.

At last they turned and went slowly back into the house, and the door slammed behind them.

Now, no doubt, they were going with lagging steps up to Alexei's room.

Beside me Tatischev said, 'I must go across to them. If I don't see you again—'

'Oh, you will. I'll be here tomorrow.'

'Aren't you planning to follow the Czar?'

I shook my head. 'No. *She* completely misunderstands the situation. *These* are the people who matter to Russia.'

It was amazing how the last day had made everything quite clear. The Czar did not matter now because he offered Russia nothing for the future. But Alexei was different. Intelligent, quick to learn, with a strength of character formed by illness and the events of the past year. A boy of great sympathy and delicacy of thought. Legally the Czar had had no shadow of right to abdicate for him.

With Alexei lay the future.

21

The House of Special Purpose

THE MIRACLE, of course, didn't happen. On Sunday, April 28, a telegram came saying the travellers had arrived safely at Tyumen at 9.30 on Saturday evening. Later on the same day came another telegram, sent after the party had left Tyumen—'Travelling in comfort. How is the boy? God be with you.' After this—silence. I calculated that they should reach Moscow by Tuesday, but there was no news of them until Friday. Then came a telegram saying the party had been detained at Ekaterinburg.

I have related the facts baldly. It is impossible to relive the anxieties, uncertainties and frustrations of that waiting period.

The day after the party left Tobolsk, the thaw began. There was the unmistakable sound of ice beginning to break up—like the creaking noise of old timbers in a ship. Then, not gradually, but as in a paroxysm, you saw the ice cracking into huge blocks that went whirling madly past. The snow in the town melted, the level of the river rose, the boards that made the pavements disappeared under a filthy stinking mess of mud and slush. One waded through this to get to the telegraph office and all the while thoughts churned in the mind—when would Alexei be able to travel, when would the river be navigable, might the Czechs arrive first?

The Sunday (April 28) when the first telegram was received, Archbishop Hermogen of Tobolsk ordered that services of intercession for Russia in her troubles should be held before all the churches in Tobolsk. It was Palm Sunday, fine, sunny, very warm for the time of year. It was the last big religious procession I saw in Russia, the air seemed to throb with singing. The Archbishop, deprived of his See of Saratov because of his opposition to Rasputin, but a true Christian towards the Family from the moment they arrived in Tobolsk, stood in his glittering vestments, his beard white as lamb's wool.

Red Guards and soldiers were posted at some street corners, but there were no incidents during the actual procession. The moment the Archbishop returned to his palace, however, a bunch of soldiers rushed in and arrested him—because he had held an unauthorised public meeting. They took him away to their barracks—he was still in his vestments. The news created a furious agitation in the town—hundreds of townsfolk petitioned on his behalf, merchants offered bail. After two days he was released—but not for long. A second order for his arrest was issued—for being party to a 'plot'.

They searched his palace, but no compromising papers were found. The Cathedral and his private chapel were ransacked. Peasant women ran sobbing into the street—'Mother of God, the shameful things the infidel are doing with the Blessed Sacrament!'

The Archbishop was away at the time; on hearing of the fresh warrant for his arrest, he immediately returned to give himself up, knowing he could prove his innocence. The same night he was taken to Ekaterinburg under heavy escort. They shaved off his beard and long hair* and made him wear ordinary clothes so that he would not be recognised. Tobolsk erupted with indignation, demanded his return, Tobolsk was in a dangerous mood. The Czechs and Cossacks continued to advance, the great blocks of ice were beginning to melt in the river, but Alexei improved only slowly. The complete lack of knowledge concerning his parents kept him feverish.

I had hoped to be allowed inside the Governor's House, but permission was not granted. There was a Red Guard in charge now— Rodionov, undersized, cruel, repulsive. When the girls begged to be allowed a service in the house, he agreed, but had the nuns who came to take part searched so indecently that Olga, weeping, said they must never ask again for anything.

I was allowed to stay on in case Alexei had a relapse. Rodionov interviewed me in the Kornilov House in the room Yakovlev had used; I remember there was on the table a huge map of the province of Tobolsk with lines marked in red pencil—possible routes by which he hoped to get the Family away, I suppose. Rodionov flew into a violent rage at the sight of it. 'Still here!' he bellowed, snatching it up and trying to tear it into shreds. 'Filthy traitor!' He threw it into a corner, sat down on one of the two chairs in the room. 'Now!' he said. 'Show me your papers!' I showed him Uncle Raoul's rather battered relics. He couldn't read them, but, again as had happened with so many Reds,

* Obligatory among Russian Orthodox clergy.

he thought that if you were French, you were bound to be a revolutionary. 'Yes, you can stay,' he said. 'For a bit at least. I can't make up my mind whether the brat's shamming or not. I keep going into his room—sudden—to see if I can catch him.'

I said, 'If this is how he seems—' and described the symptoms, 'he's not shamming.'

'You can't trust any of 'em. You can't tell what the girls are up to. I told them to leave their doors unlocked at night—I might want to inspect the place at any minute.'

On the Wednesday in Easter week, the officers and men who had gone with Yakovlev returned from Ekaterinburg, where they had been imprisoned for two days after the train had been surrounded by Red Guards. 'Romanov' and his party had been taken to a house in the town. Yakovlev? He had gone back to Moscow, after an angry scene with Red Guards demanding his arrest.*

One of the men was in pain; his horse had slipped in the slush and thrown him and his side was badly bruised. They put him in one of the empty rooms in the Kornilov House, and forgot him. I heard the poor wretch groaning and calling for a drink, and did what I could. Before I came away, I said casually, 'Haven't you any idea where the ex-Czar was taken?' I grinned suddenly. 'I want to know the address because I'll be sending in my bill.'

He began to laugh—and ended with a yell of pain. 'There was one man,' he recalled, after some thought, 'who was laughing because "Old Ipatiev"—whoever he might be—was being chucked out of his house —maybe because they were being taken there.'

I turned away from him and picked up the cup. 'Oh, yes?' I said.

Five years ago, and the tercentenary of the dynasty, the pilgrimage to the monastery near Kostroma where the *Zemskie Sobory*† had offered the crown to the first Romanov—the Ipatiev Monastery.

The soldier composed himself for sleep. 'But that address won't reach 'em. The place was getting a new name, one of the Red Guards said. You'll have to send your bill to the House of Special Purpose.'

The long farce of Tatischev's 'voluntary attendance' was over, and he, having been formally arrested, was confined to the Governor's House. But the tutor, Gilliard, because he was Swiss, I suppose, was

---

* Later he joined the White Armies. *Whom* he was working for has never been satisfactorily established.

† The most widely representative of the old Russian assemblies.

still living in the Kornilov House and as soon as he returned that evening, I told him what I had learned.

He stared across at me with a frozen look; 'This—the changing of the name of the house—is horrible, horrible!' he said in a low voice. 'It's a—a nightmare expression, and, God help us, just as in any—any icy dream, one is helpless.'

'Not altogether,' I said. 'Surely one thing is glaringly obvious? *The children mustn't go from Tobolsk.*'

'It's all they talk of—rejoining their parents. Besides, what choice have we? The moment the boy is well enough to travel—'

'Then the boy mustn't become well enough to travel. He's intelligent enough to fake a very slow recovery.'

'Rodionov—'

'Was suspicious, I know, but now I think he's reluctantly convinced. If they can stay on here until the end of May, anything can happen! The Czechs may arrive, the townsfolk, because of the Archbishop's arrest, are on the verge of revolt. I think the second alternative's the likelier.'

'Would one of their aims be the release of the children?'

'Even if it were not, a rising—a riot, even—would give the necessary diversion. The moment Alexei can travel, get down to the river, go north—Yakovlev's mistake was to choose modern transport. A train is appallingly vulnerable, but the river, or horses—that's what should be used.'

'Very well—I'll talk to them. Olga first, I think. She's the person Alexei listens to.'

'For God's sake don't tell her how the name of the house has been changed. What *do* they know about conditions in Ekaterinburg?'

'Very little. One letter has come from the Czarina, but it's mostly about something that happened on the journey.'

'From Tyumen?'

'No, getting to Tyumen. The last place at which they changed horses was the village of Pokrovskoe—'

'Rasputin's village!'

'They changed horses outside his very house. His wife and two daughters stood in an upper window and made the sign of the Cross.'

'I wonder,' I said, 'if Soloviev was a member of this charming family group—somewhere suitably in the background, of course.'

Next day Gilliard returned pale-faced and grim. 'It's no use,' he said.

'I talked to General Tatischev first and he immediately agreed—the departure must be delayed. Then we spoke to Olga. But she refused. They must join their parents as soon as the boy is fit to travel.' He gave a wretched laugh. 'Be assured, we did all we could to persuade her—but she was inflexible. Yes, she said, she knew it would be unpleasant and dangerous—only this morning there had been a hidden warning in the brief message her mother had been allowed to send—but to do anything but join their parents at the earliest opportunity was absolutely unthinkable. And if the girls won't co-operate, we can do nothing.'

All I could say was, 'What message did the Czarina send?'

'That they were to dispose of the medicines as had been agreed. By medicines she meant jewels. She left in such a hurry nothing could be done about hiding them, but she told Tatiana that if she sent back a message about medicines the girls were to conceal the jewels in their clothing—they're covering diamonds with scraps of material, for example, and using them as costume buttons.'

Rodionov drove the Tobolsk Guards very hard; with newly-imposed security measures inside and outside the house, there was little time left them for leisure. I learned all about it from the Guard who'd received the bad bruising when escorting Yakovlev and who was surprisingly grateful for the scant attentions I'd given him.

May 15 was a day of grey drizzle. The Guard—who, like Rodionov, thought I had a great fund of medical knowledge—brought my heart into my mouth by coming up suddenly behind me, gripping my arm, and saying hoarsely, 'I want you!' However, there was nothing sinister behind the wish—he only wanted me to see his ribs. We retired into the Kornilov House. Yes, I said, they were still discoloured. 'There you are!' he said furiously. 'I'm in no fit state to be on sentry duty at night in this rain. Particularly,' he added plaintively, 'when tonight there's a celebration at my brother's house because his wife's had their first son.' He began to drag on his various garments. 'It wasn't even,' he said in a muffled voice, 'that I wanted all the evening off. Just half an hour, I said, for me to look in, have a drink—drinks. But no, there I've got to be in the rain and mud underneath the damned balcony. Think of it, all the candles and the singing and drinking at my brother's, and me in the wet and dark—'

It was easy enough to persuade him—indeed, within a few minutes he believed it was his own idea. All I had to do was to stand under the balcony. It was quite dark there—the other sentry would see only an outline, he wouldn't know who it was, and Rodionov usually didn't make the outside rounds in the evening. Just half an hour, and he'd be back—

Gilliard would take the message . . .

'But of course we must go. We owe it to them. If we hadn't been ill when the Revolution started, Mamma could have got away—the train was waiting—and Papa could have gone straight to the frontier. When we were still at Czarskoe, *we* were told we could go to our grandmother in the Crimea, but we didn't— Yes, I know what kind of men are in control now—isn't Rodionov enough? But I don't hate him. He's—'

'For God's sake don't say he's a misguided child!'

'No, he's a sick child, as all Russia is sick. He believes in visiting the sins of the fathers upon the children, I suppose, or that we're the scapegoats, to expiate all the wrongs done so easily, so thoughtlessly, by our ancestors.'

The rain splashed down remorselessly. I couldn't see her—she couldn't come out on to the balcony, because the other guards would have seen her; she stood just within the room and we talked in low voices.

'But that's irrelevant,' she continued. 'Even if the people in Ekaterinburg are as wicked as they say, don't you see we must go? That it's our duty?'

I forgot what I'd said to Gilliard. 'Do you know what the Reds are calling the place to which they mean to take you? *The House of Special Purpose.*'

'You mustn't talk like this—as if *I* alone matter—my future—my inclinations—' I could hear her sobbing.

I set my teeth. 'I think of you especially,' I said with dogged calm, 'because you and Alix were so close, and after Alix died—'

'Yes.'

'—but of course I am also thinking of your sisters, above all, Alexei —Olga, do you really understand how the townsfolk feel, do you *know* how close the Czechs are? There are two choices before you— say that Alexei is unfit to travel—maintain it until the end of the month, and either the people here will rise in revolt or the Czechs and Cossacks will take Tobolsk, or be ready for an escape to the north—the White Sea—'

'No,' she said strongly. 'We can't do that. *We* can't desert him.

Andrei, if you had seen him in those first days after he came back to Czarskoe! He wept in Mamma's arms. Do you know what he wrote in his diary: *All around me I see treason, cowardice and deceit.* Since we have been at Tobolsk he and I have breakfasted together each morning. Just before Christmas he told me that the only reason he had been able —as he put it—to 'emerge' from his despair was because he was with us, and was surrounded by our love and loyalty. Andrei, if we deserted him now '

I began desperately, 'Alexei—'

'Someone is coming—Rodionov, I think. Andrei, there is something else I—want to let you know.'

Round the corner a voice shouted harshly, but, closer, I heard a sudden movement above me. She was out on the balcony, bending over. I could see her hand on the railing. The sentry who could see me had run round the corner to answer Rodionov, but even if he had been there, still I should have sprung up to climb so that I could reach up my hand to touch hers. And I felt her tears wet on my hand—I knew it was tears, not rain, for rain isn't warm, and she bent to put her wet cheek, then her lips, to my hand.

'Thank you for the dear past,' she whispered, and was gone.

On May 17 the Red Guards from Ekaterinburg arrived.

May 19, a Sunday, was the Czar's fiftieth birthday, the feast of Job. Rodionov told the girls that they would leave for Ekaterinburg next day. Alexei had not recovered, but they made no demur.

22

An Important Railway Centre

So on May 20 they came out into the open and one saw them clearly again. Alexei looked ghastly. He was terribly thin, unable to walk, pallid. His large dark eyes seemed enormous in that small narrow face. It did not do to remember the energetic little figure that had romped with us at Stavka.

I was prepared for the change in Olga, the fading of her brightness, the ageing.

The two other girls seemed oddly untouched.

They travelled on the boat which had brought them to Tobolsk, but conditions were far different now. The girls were to leave their cabin doors unlocked at night. Only Alexei, the sick child, was locked in his cabin. As if *he* could escape!

Olga wept on the boat, but not because of the hardships. Soldiers not on guard spent their time on deck singing and playing the accordion. Some had good voices. They sang *Stenka Razin* and *The Song of the Volga Boatmen*. She wept because the singing carried her back to the happier days when there had been concerts for wounded soldiers in hospitals. I remembered it, too.

After a long day and night we arrived at Tyumen. The girls, each escorted by two soldiers, were marched across the landing-stage. A sailor attendant, Nagorny, carried Alexei. The waiting train was indescribably filthy—worse than anything I had encountered in all my journeying. No food was provided.

The girls—even Anastasia—were very quiet now. Olga seemed scarcely conscious of her surroundings. It was as if mentally she were drifting further and further away from us. The only violent emotion she showed was when one of the Commissars hurt his foot disembarking. 'Let me bandage it up,' she said. 'I was a nurse—I helped with many wounded.' He refused violently; she flushed and said, 'I beg your pardon—I was only trying to ease the pain.'

After that, silence. The last part of the journey seemed interminable. The children travelled with the ladies-in-waiting; I was told to stay with Gilliard. The train jolted onwards, stopping frequently. The heat seemed to press down on us. Then there was a thunderstorm, and rain.

Just before midnight we realised that the train had been at a standstill for a long time. Being only May, it was dark outside; there was one feeble lamp, but it was too distant to help us see anything. But we could hear voices, there were soldiers passing the windows, and then the Commissars were coming into the compartments, shouting, 'Well, we're here!' Ekaterinburg—not the main station, but the goods station. No one could leave the train until the morning. There was nothing for it but to lie down, fully clothed, to see what that morning might bring.

At dawn I was peering through the windows at greyness, drizzle, open platforms, pine forests in the distance. Everywhere broken-down railway coaches, the burned-out wrecks of first- and second-class carriages destroyed by the soldiers because they were 'undemocratic'.

Then we heard Red Guards coming.

They brought with them Baroness Buxhoeveden, white-faced, bewildered, trembling.

'They're taking away the children,' she said. 'Four men came in— they said the carriages were coming—'

'Look,' said Gilliard.

Some wretched-looking cabs were assembling beyond the open platforms.

'Tatiana kissed us goodbye,' said Baroness Buxhoeveden, 'and said, "What's the use of all these leave-takings? We'll all be together in half an hour's time!" One of the guards laughed and said, "Better make it goodbye!" Olga looked at me and—'

'They are taking them away,' someone said. I don't know who. It may have been myself.

Alexei, carried by his attendant Nagorny. The girls staggering under the load of heavy suitcases, their feet sinking and slipping in the greasy mud.

'I am feeling old,' said Gilliard.

The Baroness gave a sudden sob. '*Ne criez pas*,' said Gilliard with sudden harshness.

I wished he had not said that.

The carriages drove off.

The rain began to fall in a steady deluge. Against the noise of the downpour, a voice shouted: 'Kharitonov, Trupp, Sednev to join the Romanovs,' and the cook, footman and kitchen boy were hustled out. A ramshackle cab drawn by a wretched horse appeared and took them away.

'The prisoners Tatischev, Hendrikova, Schneider—'

It was our last sight of them.

They passed our window—Tatischev, very upright, Countess Hendrikova pale, but calm, old Mademoiselle Schneider with her usual look of fussy disapproval. Tatischev saw us at the window. He asked loudly, 'Where are we being taken?'

'To the prison,' replied a guard.

The General said to Mademoiselle Schneider, still in the same loud voice, 'Don't worry, there are British and French consuls here.'

We remained at the window. It seemed extraordinary that we had been left in limbo. I peered through the rain to see if any more cabs were arriving, but all was empty desolation now. There was not a soul to be seen on the empty platforms. The buildings and offices looked as if they had been ransacked weeks before. There was, I remember, a letter box filled to overflowing, it probably hadn't been cleared for months. The sight of it got on my nerves.

Feet clumped again through the mud.

A voice shouted, 'You can go.'

'Go?' If he had said we could fly we should not have been more incredulous.

'Yes. You're free.'

'Can we go to join *them*? As we did at Tobolsk?'

Laughter. 'Don't worry—they'll be getting taught lessons enough—As for you—you don't join them, that's all we know.'

I moved to the window. Gilliard dragged me back. 'They're letting you go free because you're not Russian, but how can I masquerade—'

'For God's sake be quiet! You're more use to them free! You must start making plans again—'

Such was the extraordinary secrecy preserved in this town in the grip of Red martial law that it was two days before those left behind found the exact house where the Imperial Family had been taken—and many of the inhabitants of Ekaterinburg never knew that they were there at all. Somewhere in a house that had belonged to a merchant, Ipatiev, they were imprisoned, but there was no evidence whatsoever of their presence.

It was decided I must go back to Tyumen to pass back news of what had happened; Gilliard and the rest would try to get more definite information and contact the English and French consuls.

We spent the night in the coach. No one came near us. I sat up staring out into the darkness, at the flames of the blast-furnaces in the distance, thinking useless thoughts.

I made an early start next morning, but before I left I saw the unloading of the luggage brought from Tobolsk.

The Commissars had laid haphazard hands on the Family's possessions. Little of real value had been brought—much had vanished at Tobolsk, and of that which came to Ekaterinburg, a great deal disappeared from the station on its way to its former owners. But a large crowd had assembled here—not by chance, I would say, for though the faces differed widely in looks and age, all had one thing in common—the expression of intense hatred. They jeered as the pathetic flotsam of luggage was thrown on the ground, some so violently that boxes broke open. Some old pairs of boots belonging to the Czar fell out, which did not prevent the crowd from shouting that the other boxes were 'full of the gold dresses of those filthy wantons,' from yelling, 'Death to the tyrant! Death to the *bourgoui*!'

There was a music box that I recognised, which tinkled out music by Strauss until the mob finally smashed it.

Any new plans would take time, for definite information about the White armies was almost impossible to obtain. One heard rumours enough—whispered hysterically. Placards full of great Bolshevik victories were posted up at all street corners, but every place outside the immediate neighbourhood of any town might have been on another planet.

And then came the evening a week after I had come to Tyumen when an easterly wind sent great clouds of dust whipping through the streets, and an immense black cloud presaged thunder. One of my contacts was a friendly neutral, a Dane. We met by chance in the street when the dust storm was at its height; he choked, and took refuge in a doorway, and I, blinded, did likewise. He stood coughing beside me for a few moments, then plunged out resolutely into the gale, leaving in my hand a slip of paper. In due course I went off in the opposite direction.

I went back to the room in the back street, in the old wooden house, full of small, distant noises, creaking and groaning now in the high wind. The black clouds darkened the sky so much that although this was a Siberian June evening, I had to light the oil lamp, and draughts of hot air crept into the little room from a dozen cracks and crannies and the feeble flame flickered wildly so that it was difficult to read the scribbled message of two sentences.

'Tobolsk has turned against the Bolsheviks and declared its allegiance to the East Siberian Government. The Commissars have fled.'

The date was ten days after the transfer of the girls and Alexei.

I think that night brought me as close to insanity as I have ever been. I kept remembering the wet darkness as I argued feverishly against the move to Ekaterinburg, kept hearing her voice, 'But of course we must go. We owe it to them.'

Would it have made any difference if I had said, 'You must do what your parents have never done, make a distinction between your family and Russia,' argued about the importance of Alexei?

There is something else I want to let you know—

Ten days—

The storm broke, but didn't clear the air. After the rain and the thunder had stopped, the heat was still there. I didn't go to bed. I sat at the table, my head propped in my hands.

There was a clock in the room, the kind where the hand doesn't move until the minute is up, and then the hand jumps. I sat watching it in the lamplight, but it always tricked me, I thought the hand would never move, and then when it did I was startled. And then the lamp flickered out, and I went on sitting there waiting for the tick, I'd count up to sixty, but I never timed it properly, the click always startled me.

I kept sane, but the shock left me stupid, so stupid I didn't take precautions. I went out walking aimlessly about the streets, forgetting the eight o'clock curfew that had been imposed. And so I was arrested by four soldiers flourishing bracelets and women's rings on their little fingers and was dragged off to the gaol.

The prison to which I was taken, like all the prisons, was filled to overflowing. Each cell held twelve to fifteen people, men and women being huddled in together.

Every day people were taken out to be shot. The selection seemed to be haphazard. Women on the whole were braver than men; one woman

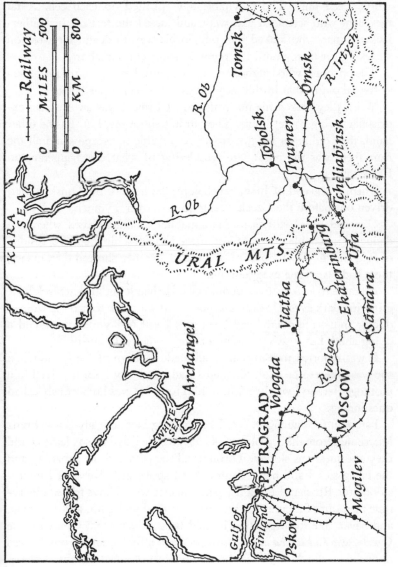

RUSSIAN RAILWAY 1917–18

doctor was magnificent. Children, thank God, often didn't fully comprehend what was happening.

One retains confused memories. The smell of dirt and fear and women who'd been hurt. The inevitable spy 'planted' in each cell. A fat merchant who screamed and wept and kissed the feet of the leather-jacketed man who kicked him out on his way to death. He went on shrieking for mercy until the revolver shots cut him short.

The prisoners who laughed when the guards beat up one of the others —they thought that in this way they'd save their own skins.

When they picked me up in the street I said I was an Austrian ex-prisoner trying to get home. They didn't shoot me, but, on the other hand, they didn't let me go. It was impossible to escape—and all the time there was the nightmare wondering of what was happening in Ekaterinburg.

Then, at the end of June, Schebaldin, the head of the Omsk Soviet, driven out before the Czechs, came to take over Tyumen.

One had heard stories of his appalling cruelties. Even when one deducted inevitable exaggeration, there was left a bloodchilling residue of fact, and his first actions on arriving in Tyumen showed that, in fact, there had been little exaggeration.

He came to look us over in our cells. He had long, greasy black hair, glittering dark eyes. He didn't look sane. It was he who had the woman doctor shot—the doctor had been going out of Tyumen to attend a dying child, but it was an offence to try to leave Tyumen.

It was reported to him that I had made the sign of the Cross when she was taken to be shot. She and I had obviously been involved in a plot together. So I was brought to him for what was humorously called questioning.

I stood it for one night. No, I kept saying mechanically, I was Franz Mayrhofen from the Tyrol. I spoke only a little Russian, so please would they ask questions slowly. Through all the pain and the groaning and the being sick I still never forgot that I spoke little Russian, I understood little Russian. I think my performance would have fooled ninety-nine men out of a hundred, but this was the hundredth, a little insane, and never able to forget that he had been driven from Omsk by the Czechs *who had served in the Austrian armies*. By supreme irony he was obsessed by the thought that I was one of the loathed Czechs. Tomorrow, he shouted, he'd break down my resistance. What I'd had tonight was a mother's kiss in comparison. They dragged me off and threw me in a cell of my own. One guard stamped on my hand as he went out and I fainted.

When I came round, it was about four o'clock in the morning—not dark, of course, because this was Siberia in mid-summer. I decided I must not see another morning. If they came for me again tonight I might start babbling fluent Russian, I might even be reduced to the state of the shrieking merchant, I might start yelling out wholesale confessions.

Perhaps I could kill myself by banging my head on the wall.

I put out my good hand to touch the wall—and instead touched something soft. One of the guards had dumped my filthy sheepskin jacket down beside me. Before I'd left Petersburg for the last time I'd sewn into the lining two of the cyanide tablets given me by the French doctor.

With teeth and five good fingers I tore away at the lining. There they were.

I dragged myself up into a sitting position.

'Oh, God,' I muttered, like an apologetic child, 'if I offend You, I don't mean to, but one can over-estimate endurance, and I might betray others.'

I crossed myself and swallowed both tablets.

After a minute or so there was the most appalling pain in my injured hand; in both hands the blood vessels seemed to be swelling. I gritted my teeth and fell back. I seemed to feel a contraction of the heart; this, then, was the beginning of death. And after that nothing.

I have not been trying to work up any cheap dramatics. Obviously I didn't die. And there is nothing dramatic in my escape from death. Merely bicarbonate of soda.

Most of the time they had starved us. When they brought in the doctor I was suffering agonies of stomach cramps. They'd searched her, but let her keep a packet of bicarbonate of soda she had in her pocket. She'd given it to me. Long afterwards a chemist told me that soda, taken before cyanide, neutralises the effects of the poison. Also, I had had the cyanide for a long time.

So bicarbonate of soda saved my life—just. I lay there senseless on the floor for hours. When the guards came to collect me, I learned later, and kicks and punches failed to rouse me, on Schebaldin's orders they left me alone; no point in torturing me because I couldn't feel anything, no point even in shooting me because I wouldn't realise what was going to happen. So wait until I could feel pain and fear—there were plenty of other matters to keep Schebaldin occupied. They dragged me off to another cell filled almost to overflowing.

Faces came and went, like the faces of hobgoblins seen in a child's nightmare. There was laughter. And then other faces, other voices. Someone pulled me into a corner. Someone else tried to bandage my hand. People were talking, but I couldn't distinguish words. Someone gave me water—obtained God knows where. I opened my eyes for a moment. A priest was bending over me. I don't know how long it was afterwards that he was taken. This was when I began to distinguish sounds clearly. Heavy feet coming along the corridor. A voice beside me whispering, *'My soul, my soul, arise! Why are you sleeping? The end is drawing near, and you will be confounded—'*

The door slammed open. A voice, 'You! Here!'

'Awake, then, and be watchful, that Christ our God may spare you—'

'Quick!'

*'—Who is everywhere present and fills all things—*I am coming.'

The door slamming shut. Footsteps retreating. Absolute silence, though by this time the cell housed enough people. Then the crash of two shots.

'At least,' said a man's voice, 'it was quick. Not like what they did to the Archbishop.'

Next time I was fully aware of what was happening, I must have been roused by the door of the cell crashing back again. Another prisoner. A prisoner who, asked his offence, said, 'They caught me saying I'd heard the Czechs are only thirty miles away.'

There was a hush, a hush of ecstasy. Then a woman whispered with a sob, 'Oh, God! So close!'

In the next days only the poor devils in Paris gaols at the time of Robespierre's fall could have appreciated our feelings. I still kept drifting off, but besought people to rouse me every time fresh news came in. And so I would feel hands—trembling hands—shaking me, and trembling voices whispering, 'The Commissars are leaving—they *must* be close—Oh God, dear God, the Cossacks have actually been reconnoitring into the town at night—they've stuck up posters—'

And then one day, July 15, as I sat propped up against the wall, still more dead than alive, there came a noise I had first heard on another day blanketed with heat, nearly four years before, in East Prussia. Heavy guns.

Orders were given that all prisoners were to be shot before the Reds left on the evening of the 17th. We survived because the prison guards headed the rush to leave town.

By midnight, Tyumen might have been a city of the dead. Not the faintest sound could be heard. The guns had not fired for hours.

At dawn on the 18th a boy went tearing up the street outside. His voice soared, cracked ecstatically, 'They've gone! They've gone!'

We shouted, and people ran to let us out. The streets were full of strangers embracing as they do at Easter.

At eight o'clock on the evening of the 18th of July, the Cossacks entered Tyumen.

Next day I left with them. Old fears choked me. Would the Czechs agree to Ekaterinburg being the next objective? 'They don't listen to us,' had been the constant refrain, so I took Uncle Raoul's uniform from the cupboard in that back-street house, had it cleaned and pressed, and a fairly spruce French colonel made a strong plea to an impassive Czech general.

But Ekaterinburg *must* be the next goal—such an important railway centre!

23

Joy

So it was grudgingly agreed by the Czechs that the next place to be liberated should be Ekaterinburg—'Because, as you say, it is an important railway centre, and we must secure it before the Volga front can be established safely.'

At first this reason nearly drove me mad; later I clung to it as the only reason keeping me from insanity. I was a French officer, taking part in the drive to seize an important railway centre—no more than that. I must keep to that thought alone as we came in through the forests, past clearings and mineshafts; I must keep to it all the more strongly after I was hit—a grazed head—storming an armoured train the day before Ekaterinburg fell, and could not move for a week. Only an important railway centre.

When a Czech officer said to me as an unimportant postscript that they had found no living human person at the Ipatiev House, I replied, 'It wasn't to be expected, of course'—offhandedly, because he had given me the information solely as an afterthought to the real news that the railway system remained intact.

I managed to get a message through to our own people; could a loyal Russian come to the station to meet a French colonel, hatless, head bandaged?

And there I stood in that ugly red brick building, that important railway centre, that goal achieved intact, and someone was talking hesitantly to me, had been talking for some time, a boy introducing himself as a student of the Military Academy, transferred to Ekaterinburg by the Reds, and somehow left alive when the Bolsheviks left the town.

'We were the first to enter the Ipatiev House, sir,' he began, and then broke off.

'Go on,' I said.

'I think you knew the Family, sir,' he stammered.

'You mustn't hesitate,' I said. 'I'm not hoping now; I must get at the truth—whatever it is.'

I don't think I was consciously lying, though looking back, I know now that there was still one hope left to me—I was hoping that whatever had been done had been done quickly.

'Tell me as we go,' I said.

This station was of course the main station, not the one to which they had been brought, where the guards had told them to make a good job of it when they said goodbye, where the mob had ransacked their possessions, and the music box had played for the last time. If I talk like a page from Baedeker, bear with me, for it's the easiest way for me —the main station lies to the north of the town. From it the Arsenyev-sky Prospekt runs south to the Vosnesensky Prospekt, so called because on its left side, set a little back from the street, is the Church of the Ascension.* Also in the Vosnesensky Prospekt is the Ipatiev House, the House of Special Purpose.

When the Reds had left Ekaterinburg, the cadets, knowing nothing of what had happened at the house, had rushed there in desperate anxiety.

They found it empty—quite deserted. All the doors stood open. The rooms were in a state of indescribable confusion. There were heaps of ashes and cinders on the floors, stoves choked with half-burnt clothing, charred bits of hairbrushes, toothbrushes, buttons, safety-pins. Ordinary things. Or, from another viewpoint, terrible.

'I think we exclaimed—remarked about things and so on—in the first room, but after this we said nothing, nothing at all. Each knew what the others thought. It could mean only one thing, couldn't it? Then there was just the basement left.

'We couldn't face it for a time, and stood outside in the courtyard (you have to go out into the courtyard to get into the basement). One of us said, "Let's look through the window first," and he squatted down and looked through the little barred window. At first, looking in, after the bright sun outside, he couldn't see much, then he began to say, trying to be cheerful, "Plaster peeling off," and then he got up, very suddenly, and made the sign of the Cross. He said, "We must go in at once. The walls are riddled with bullets, and there are—marks on the floor."

'But we hadn't really needed to know that. There's a white outside

* *Vosnesenia* in Russian.

203

wall, directly by the basement window. It was all splashed with a mixture of dirt and blood and water. Someone had scrubbed the floor in that basement, and then emptied the bucket out of the window. And on the white-washed wall of the house, near the steps leading down from the verandah, there were thirteen splashes of blood, all in a line, as though someone had shaken blood from his hand—it must have been one of the murderers, not simply one of those called in to scrub the floor. By that time the blood would have congealed—and congealed blood doesn't splash. It must have been one of the murderers, his hands wet with blood that was still warm, because he'd been—touching the bodies.'

I remembered the first time I had seen a man hit by a bullet, my trooper in East Prussia. It had flung him backward, kicking his legs high. He could not have felt any pain at first, only numbness, for he made no sound, but then the pain must have come, because he screamed, and the blood gushed out.

'But even so,' I said after a moment, 'we've no definite knowledge of what happened.'

'No proof, but from the day the Reds left the town was alive with rumours that the Family had been murdered. A few peasants are supposed to have said they'd seen them taken off to a place of safety, but we think those "peasants"—we couldn't find them ourselves—were agents left by the Reds.'

I said, 'Perhaps when we're in the Ipatiev House—'

After a moment's silence: 'You probably won't be allowed in, sir.'

After another moment.

'Will you explain why?'

'Because the Czechs have taken it over, sir. Directly they occupied the city their general, Gaida—you may know him—'

'He was a pharmacist,' I said. 'Now it seems he acts like a Czar.'

'—forcibly took over the premises, although we protested. Believe me, sir, we protested, knowing how clues might be lost! But their engineer's department's taken over the upper storey, and they're going to start altering the rooms any day now—'

'Then I had better flourish my French credentials.'

The Ipatiev House—the House of Special Purpose—stands dull and isolated at the top of the street, an ugly white ramshackle building.

I stood inside the barricade, and looked up at the house, while a Czech sergeant went to get a superior officer.

'Those four windows,' said the cadet, 'in pairs, at the angle of the upper floor, are those of the rooms occupied by Their Majesties and the Heir, in the angle formed by the square and Vosnesensky Lane.'

'And that window?' I asked pointing.

'The Grand Duchesses' room.'

It is a difficult building to describe. For example, the greater part of the ground floor was in fact below ground. On this floor, directly below the Grand Duchesses' room, was a window between two trees. The top came about level with the head of a man of medium height—I should have had to stoop to look in. There was a rather elaborate grille covering it, and, to one side, a dirty smear.

There is, I thought, something about that substance which makes it quite unmistakable, distinguishable from any other, even if you have never seen it before. Something more than your eye tells you, *This is blood.*

Flies still circled endlessly. I had forgotten that, in this heat, there would be flies.

'Why did the man who looked in have to squat down?' I asked after a moment.

'He was trying to see the floor, you see, and—and most of the marks on the walls are low down as if people were—kneeling.'

'There's no other window?'

'No.'

'And—only one door?'

He said in a low voice, 'Yes, there's another door, but it leads only to a second basement room where their belongings had been stored. And it was locked.'

So there was no way of escape.

A Czech officer approached; my French papers were produced. The Czechs would need Allied help now, and later, so they gave me as guide a *pince-nezed* major who spoke French and an invitation. Would I join some of the officers for coffee afterwards?

No, they hadn't cleared up properly. The disorder had been so incredible—these Russians were such dirty pigs. The worst mess they hadn't tried to cope with yet.

Heaps of ashes had been raked out of stoves—they contained small articles, half burnt, such as toothbrushes, hairpins, buttons. I picked up part of a hairbrush, on the brown ivory of which you could still see the initials. 'A.F.' I said. 'The Czarina Alexandra Feodorovna.'

We stood in the four-windowed room in the angle of the upper floor. On the walls were pinned photographs of Alexei, Olga at eighteen in traditional Russian dress. In the embrasure of one of the windows, there was drawn in pencil—

'Ah,' I said, 'a swastika, an Indian religious symbol, I think. I believe it was the Czarina's favourite charm; she put it up everywhere to avert bad luck.'

She had added, underneath, the Russian and Western dating, 17/30 April—the day their imprisonment in the House of Special Purpose began.

And she had drawn the same symbol, but without a date, on the wall-paper—on the level of Alexei's bed.

There were tresses of women's hair, different lengths and colours. I touched the golden, and said, 'The Grand Duchesses had their hair cut when they were so ill at Czarskoe. Their mother must have brought this with her—mothers always treasure such things.'

The heat was sweltering, the rooms, although the windows were open now, were like steam-baths. They had found some books, said the major, but they would show me those over coffee. He had given orders that the door to the basement should be unsealed, so if I would follow him to the most interesting exhibit—

From the bedrooms you came down by a flight of back stairs leading from the upper to the ground floor. There was a door from the lower landing (by the kitchen) to the rooms of the ground floor, but this had been boarded up, so we had to go out into the yard and enter the lower floor by a separate doorway.

'The door was boarded up when you came?'

'Oh, yes. It had been boarded up when *they* arrived.'

You then crossed all the rooms of the lower floor, and came at last to a small lobby, adjoining the front entrance on the lane side. This lobby was lighted by a small window heavily grated, looking on to the garden. (A courtesy title for the dusty, flyridden prison courtyard.) Opposite this window was a door, leading into a small semi-basement room, vaulted, about eighteen foot by sixteen foot, with a heavily grilled double window facing the lane.

Forgive my dry account of all this. Forgive the lack of description of the rooms through which we had passed to reach this vaulted semi-basement. Forget that I was conscious of every footfall, every heartbeat, each remorselessly leading one closer to *that*—

A click of a switch, and the room was brightly illuminated, as it must have been *then*. I looked about me.

Until I saw that room I had let myself hope—a little. I had believed that possibly the Czar had been shot, and I thought that the Czarina had died with him—yes, they would have died together. But to kill the children? My whole being had cried out against the idea. Yet here all showed pitilessly that there had been several victims.

You could still see the trace of bullets, the direction of bayonet thrusts. In one part of the wooden floor were eighteen bayonet holes, close together, where a victim had struggled. I counted them three times to make sure. And there were still splashes of blood everywhere, on the walls, on the floor. All the washing and scouring done by the murderers could not remove those signs that, mute as they were, cried out that more than one or two persons had been done to death here, that the place had been a shambles, that some victims had been sitting, others standing, others kneeling when they were butchered.

The peeling walls had been scrawled with obscene drawings and inscriptions. Were those vilenesses the last things on earth dying eyes rested on?

Beside me the Czech major was saying something. That the cadets who first entered the cellar had scrubbed off most of the obscenities, 'shouting and cursing—and now reproach *us* with destroying useful evidence. But we managed to save two inscriptions, which we thought interesting.'

His stubby forefinger pointed to the first.

> *'Belsatҳar ward in selbiger Nacht*
> *Von seinen Knechten umgebracht.'*

Somewhere in another world I had read those lines. My great-grandfather's library in Vienna, the sun streaming in through the windows.

'It's Heine,' I said. 'His poem on Belshazzar.'

'Verse 21,' he said with pedantic precision. 'There is, of course, a textual change—what we see is an adaptation; *"Aber"* is omitted after *"ward"*, and *"selbigen"* has been changed to *"seinen"*. Heine also wrote *Belsaҳar.'*

Eighteen holes made by bayonets in a part of the wooden floor where someone had lain. So much blood.

'The Book of Daniel merely says, in Chapter 6, verse 30, *"In that night was Belsha₂₂ar the King of the Chaldeans slain."* Obviously, whoever scribbled on that wall wanted to stress the fact that "Belsatzar" was slain by *his own people.'*

Through his rimless *pince-ne₂* he peered more closely at the writing.

'Not many men,' I said, 'would be able to produce such information.'

'Ah,' he said, 'I studied theology at Prague University. And so I was able to read the second interesting inscription—here.'

Again the pointing finger. It did not shake. 'Written in Hebrew— would you like me to translate? *"Here was slain the Head of the Church and of the State. The order has been obeyed."* '

'You cannot place that quotation?'

'Oh, no. It must have been written by a Hebrew-speaking guard. And now, I think, the coffee will be ready.'

As we came away, he said, 'My apologies for the flies. We cannot get rid of them.'

I drank coffee in one of the rooms they had cleared, and they gave me the books for entertainment, and then, thank God, excused themselves, and left me for a time. A Bible, dried flowers and leaves pressed between the pages. The Czarina's. A bottle of verbena water. A little ikon on wood, with the inscription on the back, 'From the old woman Maria Mikhailovna. Novgorod. December 11, 1916.' The last visit to Novgorod, when the old voice had muttered, 'Here comes the sainted martyr, Alexandra Feodorovna.'

A wooden figure of Christ, with the writing of Vyroubova and Rasputin on the back. I did not read what was written.

An English book belonging to Marie—Thackeray's *The Rose and the Ring.*

A French exercise book belonging to Alexei, and his instruction book, *How to play the Balalaika.* His toy soldiers. His medicines.

Books belonging to Tatiana—including an English one whose author I can't recollect, but I can't forget the title—*The Wider Life.*

And Olga? *The Princess and the Goblin* ('But you must go on to read *The Princess and Curdie,'* Alix had said. 'I'll lend you my copy, if you like.' 'How dreadful,' Olga said later, 'that people should believe such things of their king.')

There was another English book, too, in a paper cover, *And Mary sings Magnificat.* I do not remember the author's name, for when I took it, my hands being unsteady, I dropped it, and three little pieces of paper fell out.

One was yellower, more crumpled than the others. *Le Vase brisé* ('My uncle told me to bring you this book of poetry, with his humble duty.' The quick decisive voice. 'I think your mother would like your uncle's book—until she meets him again. So I'll just copy out the poem I like best.')

The other two pieces of paper were covered with a prayer—also in her handwriting.

> 'Give patience, Lord, to us Thy children,
> In these dark stormy days to bear
> The persecution of our people,
> The tortures falling to our share.
> Give strength, Just God, to us who need it,
> The persecutors to forgive,
> Our heavy, painful cross to carry
> And Thy great meekness to achieve.
> When we are plundered and insulted,
> In days of mutinous unrest,
> We turn for help to Thee, Christ-Saviour,
> That we may stand the bitter test.
> Lord of the World, God of Creation,
> Give us Thy blessing through our prayer.
> Give peace of heart to us, O Master,
> This hour of utmost dread to bear.
> And in the threshold of the grave
> Breathe power divine into our day
> That we, Thy children, may find strength
> In meekness for our foes to pray.'

'This hour of utmost dread,' I said to myself. Then I replaced the paper in the book in a kind of groping horror, managed to set it down, sat dumb, cold in the sweltering Siberian summer heat, trembling, incapable of speech or thought or action until a sound roused me as few sounds would have done.

In the deathly stillness of the room, I could hear a dog whining faintly.

The noise came from beyond the door, the door leading to these rooms, once used by the Family—silent now, as they had been since that morning.

It must be Joy, of course, the little ill-named spaniel. Alexei had been ill again. When he was ill, Joy was never allowed to sleep in his master's bedroom, because he moved about restlessly in the heat, raised his big eyes, whined in his throat, scratched at the door, and the signs of his distress fretted the sick boy.

So Joy, excluded, had survived, and lay whining outside the Family's rooms as he did day after day, when the Czechs did not drive him away.

They were driving him away now—I could hear them. I ran to the door, flung it open. There he was, bewildered, dejected—half-famished, by the look of him, hardly recognisable as the gay companion always frisking about Alexei at Czarskoe and Stavka, or even as the temporary enemy who had recognised me at the gate of the house in Tobolsk, and slipped out to greet me with noisy delight.

I called to him, and a miracle happened. He made one great bound past the Czech trying to drive him out, and tore across the room towards me, jumping in the air in ecstasy, running about me in wide circles, putting up his forepaws and begging, then walking about me like a circus dog, whimpering all the time with joy.

He recognised me—and thought that because I had come Alexei would soon follow. As had happened before.

His joy continued a little longer. Then he began looking for his master again, scratching at doors that would not open, whimpering, crawling on his belly like a dog in disgrace for no reason he can guess. He had been looking for Alexei since the morning after the murder; the Czechs kept driving him from the house because his crying got on their nerves. His half-famished look did not mean he was uncared for; the cadets looked after him with all the love in the world, but he would rarely touch any food. His only thought was the frantic need to go back to the house and search again through the empty rooms.

24

Cherubim Hymn

HE FOLLOWED me as I went from the house, docilely at heel for most of the time, but once in a while he would run ahead and get up on his hind legs and beg imploringly. He did not know what to do— to come with me, the first familiar figure from the old life since the silence had settled in their rooms, or to go back to wait again outside the closed door.

The cadet had rejoined me, and talked about the dog as we went to his lodgings, where Joy could be left.

'There was another dog, too,' I said. 'A tiny thing—Jimmy.'

But no trace of Jimmy.

After a moment I said, 'There's a church not far from the house, isn't there?'

'Yes, sir, the Church of the Ascension—it stands in the big square, quite a landmark.'

'Was it true that they were allowed to have services in the house?'

The boy said, 'Father Storozhev celebrated Mass there on July 14, a Sunday.'

The Father was not what I had expected, being far more logical and better educated than the majority of priests. How unusual he was I learned five minutes after meeting him; he told me he had been an Assistant Public Prosecutor before renouncing the Law for the Church. 'Therefore,' he said, 'I hope you will accept that I've considered what evidence is available and haven't gone merely by priestly intuition.' But then, after a moment, he added, 'Yet, God knows, intuition cried out to me on that last Sunday.'

'Tell me of it,' I said.

'If you have the time and patience to spare, I'll first describe the other time I celebrated Mass at the house; the change in expressions, attitudes, was quite—frightful.'

This hour of utmost dread—

His first summons had been ten days after the three girls anc Alexei had rejoined their parents. 'I think that on that Sunday they were still very happy because of the reunion. The Family were all there, and the household—it was before they took away the Czar's valet, and the sailor attendant—'

'Nagorny was shot, wasn't he?'

'Yes. His crime was his inability to hide his indignation when the Bolshevik Commissars seized the little gold chain from which the holy images hung over the bed of the sick boy—the effect on the child! But he was happy enough when I saw him on this first occasion; he was ill, lying in a camp bed, but when I came up to him with the crucifix, he looked at me with eyes that were so bright and alive. He wanted to say something, I think, but I'd been strictly forbidden to speak to them, and dare not for fear of making things worse for them.

'Mass was celebrated in their living-room—there was a little table they'd turned into an altar, putting their ikons on it. The Czar and the Grand Duchesses joined in the singing. Avdeiev, the Commandant, of course, was there, though not so drunk as usual. He didn't interrupt, just sat smoking and grinning.'

'And the last Mass?'

'God forgive my stupidity, but I expected to find them trying to hide their excitement, their eyes shining with hope—we could hear the Czech artillery in the distance, you see. As if the Reds couldn't hear it, too, and react to it! The pathetic little converted altar had been erected again, but now there was all the difference in the world in the congregation. In those few weeks the Czar's hair had gone quite white, his eyes were hopeless, haunted. The Grand Duchesses were pale, drawn, their eyes filled with tears when they kissed the Cross. The child was grey-faced, suffering. He rested on his mother's knee—she sat in a chair, more cold and stiff than ever, one would say. When I passed the Grand Duchesses as I came away, one whispered, "Thank you—thank you—" I cannot convey to you the utter anguish I felt at being unable to utter a single word of comfort! If Avdeiev had been there, I would have taken the risk; he was a filthy, uncouth scoundrel, but not absolutely inhuman. But now there was Yurovsky.'

'I must find out more about Yurovsky.'

'When he dies, Hell will be the viler for it. To celebrate Mass in the presence of that jeering devil—a Mass in which, when the deacon made

a frightful mistake, and *chanted* "Rest in peace with the Saints",*
instead of merely saying it, standing, *the whole Imperial Family knelt,
and one of the Grand Duchesses sobbed.* Now you will understand why my
deacon whispered to me afterwards, "Something must have happened
there, Father Archpresbyter," and why I could make no answer.'

'Tell me more of Yurovsky.'

'He is about thirty years old, Jewish by race. He was born in Tomsk;
his father'd been sent to Siberia for armed robbery. He's lived in Berlin
for a year. He talked German to the last sentries posted in the house,
the Letts.'

'They weren't Russians?'

'In the last days only one Russian was allowed inside the house—
Medvediev. The Russians stood guard outside the building, were
quartered in the house opposite.'

He could tell me little more. 'The house was so guarded that there are
still people in Ekaterinburg who don't believe the Family were there at
all, but, then, with everybody in fear of death, no one had any curiosity
left. But have you been to the Convent? They might be able to tell you
something, they took food.'

Outside the sun beat down like a furnace, and everywhere there were
dust and flies. I passed the Hotel America, where Mother had stayed
three years before. Now the Cheka headquarters.

With a sudden shock I realised I had sent no word to Mother since
my release from prison.

Where the Vosnesensky and Glavny Prospekts intersected I found
the Post Office, but there was no chance of contact with the outside
world.

Well, I must make my way to the Convent—but first I must try to
eat something. And here before me was a 'Soviet dining-room'; possibly
it was no better than the others I'd known, but usually once a town was
liberated, peasants began to bring in food quickly enough.

I managed to get pale sausage, greyish bread, but quite good hot
soup, and a little butter. I don't know who was running the place now
the Soviet had disappeared, but the waitresses looked cheerful and the
service was quick.

My particular waitress eyed my uniform with interest and said in the
slow, patient way one addresses a foreigner, 'That's not a Czech
uniform, is it?'

* Usually this was said; it was only chanted at funerals.

213

'No; French.'

'You talk lovely Russian,' she said.

'I'm half-Russian,' I said.

'If I were you, I'd forget that,' she said frankly. 'There's more future in being French these days. In fact, you ought to go about thanking God you're French as well as Russian.'

'Sorry,' I said, 'I find it difficult to thank God at present. I used to know the Imperial Family.'

Her expression changed. 'They're dead,' she said. 'Everybody knows they're dead. Don't believe the stories that they were taken away—the Reds started all that. And, if you knew them, be glad they're out of it all. Better dead than alive as *they* were—'

'How do you know?'

'Because one of the women who washes the floor here—Maria Starodumova—was at the house cleaning on July 15, and she reckons she was one of the last to see them alive.'

Someone called her, and she had gone before I could reply to this. I pushed my plate away; the food was disgusting to me. The waitress was back, with a glass of tea. 'Here,' she said. 'Drink this at any rate.'

'I'd like to speak to Maria Starodumova.'

'I guessed you would. Here she is, coming across.'

Maria Starodumova, broad-faced, stockily built, honest-eyed, sat down at the table, agreed to drink tea, said, 'Don't worry; I shan't let on.'

'Let on what?'

'She said you're French, but you were in the Imperial Guard, weren't you? There was a photograph of you in the Grand Duchesses' room. I can't tell you much. I'm a charwoman, you know; since the Revolution they've given me a fancy name—trade union woman-worker—but it doesn't alter my job, I still scrub floors. I went to the house on the 15th, but I couldn't speak a word to any of the Family, because Yurovsky was there all the time. Listen, sir, they said Rasputin was a devil straight from Hell, didn't they? Well, I tell you he was a saint from Heaven compared with Yurovsky.'

'Why do you say that?'

She gave a sudden shiver. 'There,' she said, 'and God knows I don't scare easy, and it's sweltering hot. But if you'd seen him sitting down there by the boy's camp bed in the dining-room that day, asking the little one how he was—God, it gave me the horrors.'

'Why?'

'I don't know—I was cold all over, that's all I can tell you, and to be cold in that house—suffocating it was, and the air so bad with no windows open, they wouldn't allow it, even painted the panes a dirty white so that no one could look out. That air stank, all the Family suffered, but the boy was wasting away, and that devil sat down at his bedside and asked him how he was.'

After a moment she resumed. 'They didn't complain, though once I heard the Grand Duchess Olga say, "Tobolsk seems like Paradise now." She'd just brought her brother in from the yard—five minutes' fresh air a day, that's all they were allowed, and she used to carry him out. I think the girls would have liked to talk to us when they were making the beds and we were cleaning, but Yurovsky or some of the guards were always there.'

'In their bedroom!'

'My God, sir, you don't know the half of it. They'd hang over them at their meals, spitting, dropping cigarette ash in their food, putting their dirty fingers in the gravy, sucking 'em, dipping 'em in again, they'd retch on the floor in front of them, talk filth, write filth on the walls, they'd follow those girls to the lavatory, and wouldn't let them shut the door—My God, sir, if they thought Tobolsk was Heaven, they knew Ekaterinburg was Hell. There was one devil who used to bawl filthy songs—'

'What did the girls do?'

'They started singing the Cherubim Hymn—they often sang that. One of them had a lovely voice.'

'Olga.'

'Let us who mystically represent the Cherubim and sing the Thrice-Holy Hymn to the life-giving Trinity, put away all worldly care—'

Later I went to the Novotykhvin Convent and talked to the Superior, Mother Augustine, in her bare room.

She said they had heard of the arrival of the Imperial Family—'And of how they were fed, or, rather, not fed, because when the food arrived it was hours late, and cold, and sometimes it did not arrive at all. We asked the Bishop of Ekaterinburg if we might send the Czar milk and vegetables from our kitchen garden—nothing luxurious, because we simply don't produce luxuries, of course, but things that might be particularly useful for a sick boy and an ailing woman.'

'And also,' I said, under my breath, 'they would realise they were not entirely forgotten.'

She gave me a quick shy smile, and suddenly I found her heavy black habit and tall *klobuk** less intimidating.

'Yes,' she said softly. 'That also.

'We got in touch with Avdeiev. We expected a refusal, but we were surprised. He said it was allowed—if done unobtrusively.'

Avdeiev would have taken the food for himself, of course, would have grinned as he informed the prisoners. But their sudden radiant looks would amaze him; he would not understand how the news that the nuns had remembered them in their charity would be infinitely more cheering than the actual comforts.

'Two lay sisters volunteered to go to the house; I told them to put on town clothes to lessen the fear of insult. I will send for them, and they shall give you their own accounts of what happened. They went more than once, and the last time—something happened then that I think important, but you, of course, must judge for yourself.'

Sisters Antonina Trinkina and Maria Krokhaleva, lambs with the hearts of lions who had volunteered to dare bestial danger in the name of charity.

Of course, they said, looking surprised, they had been willing to go, even though the Reverend Mother had told them it might be danger-ous. 'We never told her,' said Sister Maria breathlessly, '*quite* how bad it all was—the guards were drinking *denaturat*,† you see; I don't think she'd even know what it is. I do because I renounced the world only two years ago, and, of course, it's since they banned vodka at the beginning of the war that so many men started drinking this awful stuff.'

So they had taken milk, cream, butter, cucumbers, some pastries. The first visit had been on June 18, and others had followed. Always, Avdeiev took the stuff himself. Once in the town they had daringly bartered some ham and a little meat for tobacco for the Czar; that, too, had been taken.

So it had gone on for a month, and then, on July 10, there was a change. In the first place, Avdeiev was not there, and the guards—yes, Russian guards—were confused, would not take the gifts at first. The nuns begged them to have the food, and eventually they did. The sisters walked away. 'And then the soldiers came running after us.'

* Head-dress.
† Methylated spirits.

'Were you not frightened?' I asked.

'Oh, no, although they were holding their rifles; we had, after all, only been doing our duty—Our Lord said we must visit captives, didn't He? And when they caught up with us, they were quite polite. "Please come back," they said. So we went back, and there was this stranger, Yurovsky. He asked us very harshly who had authorised us to bring the gifts. We said Avdeiev. "Oh, he was in it, was he?" he shouted.

'He asked us then where the stuff came from. We told him from the convent farm. He took our names and after a pause said we could come again, but we must bring milk, and nothing else.'

'We were afraid when we spoke to *him*, though we knew we were doing Our Lord's work,' said Sister Antonina abruptly. 'No—not when he shouted at us at the beginning. Later. There was a an assured, a sneering grossness about him.'

Afraid or not, they continued to visit the house, and on Monday, July 15, Yurovsky took the milk and said, 'Bring fifty eggs tomorrow.' They had done so gladly, thinking the prisoners would have a good meal. 'We heard him shouting to Medvediev that Kharitonov—the Family's cook, we believe—was to boil them, hard,' said Sister Maria. 'Since then, despite all the rumours, we have hoped. If they were going on a journey—?'

Her soft voice broke off; her blue eyes watched me hopefully.

Sister Antonina said, 'I cannot think of that man—and hope. We went back on Wednesday morning with milk. We waited for a long time, but no one would take it. We asked where Yurovsky was; they said he was eating. They told us to go away, and not to bring anything more.'

I stood in the forest, listening to the sound of birdsong, the cooing of pigeons, the bleating of a goat in some distant clearing. I waited for the creak of boughs, the rustling of pine-needles to tell me that Father Storozhev was returning. A late cuckoo called; an oriole sounded like a flute, there were mushrooms and wild strawberries beneath the white birch stems, from the distance came the fragrance of new-mown hay, and I thought of murder.

Since leaving the Convent I had been told that there had been an official Red bulletin—Nicholas the Bloody had been shot, and his family moved to a place of safety.

But murder of many people had been done in that basement.

Father Storozhev said he wanted me to talk to certain people.

A young mining prospector, Fessenko, who on July 16 had met Yurovsky near some disused mines in the middle of the forest five to six miles to the north-west of Ekaterinburg. Yurovsky had demanded what Fessenko was doing; Fessenko replied he was an engineer trained in the Mines School of the Urals. Yurovsky had shown sudden interest. 'Here,' he said. 'Could we get a lorry with a load of 800 puds*—a load of grain—along to Koptiaki without it sinking through the surface?'

An elderly woman from the village of Koptiaki, raising her voice above the honking of her geese:

She and her son and daughter-in-law had set out in their wagon well before morning on the 17th to sell fish in the town. They had been stopped by a horseman who had told them to turn back, and to make sure, he'd galloped along beside them. 'He told us that if we turned round or even looked back, we'd be shot, and so we didn't, but we'd seen before he came up to us† that he wasn't alone, he was riding ahead of something big and dark coming up behind him.'

They had told the other villagers who, after several hours, had gone out to reconnoitre, but they had run into a cordon of guards who had turned them back.

There had been a curfew in the Ekaterinburg district since eight o'clock on the evening of the 16th. Anyone found in the streets was shot. The peasants thought themselves lucky to be alive.

'What do you think the Reds were doing?' I asked.

The woman's son said, 'Some men came to our village four or five days later and told us they had been burying rifles in the mine-shafts—hundreds. We knew better. There were fires in the forest, and you don't burn rifles. They were getting rid of the Czar and his family.'

A grave in a mineshaft, but there were many mineshafts in the area, the open workings had filled up with water so that they were like little lakes, and so overgrown with grass and bushes that it was difficult to find them even when you were a few yards from them. They could be reached only by footpaths almost completely overgrown with shrubs, saplings and weeds.

I read and re-read the tattered copy of the newspaper *The Ural*

* 1 pud=36 lbs.

† At 'night-time' in July at Ekaterinburg it was light enough to read—even to take photographs.

Worker. On the evening of July 21, just before the last Red troops moved out of Ekaterinburg, it had printed the *communiqué* of the 20th, that 'the crowned butcher' had been shot on the night of July 16/17 in order to forestall a plot to abduct him. 'The Romanov family has been transferred from Ekaterinburg to another and safer place.'

I did not believe it. The 'other and safer place' was in the forest near Koptiaki.

Days and nights of pitiless heat, more pitiless thought, and then, at the end of August, news that gave hideous confirmation to my belief.

The Grand Duchess Elizabeth, the Czarina's sister, saint of the Imperial Family, was dead. She had been brought from Moscow so secretly that no one knew it, imprisoned with lesser Romanovs at Alapaievsk, to the north of Ekaterinburg, and finally, on July 17, was taken with her companions into the forest to be hurled, living, into a mineshaft. Hand-grenades were thrown in after them.

The Reds had announced that the Romanovs had been carried off by White 'bandits', but a horrified peasant, hiding among the trees, had seen all that happened, and, with other companions had listened helplessly as for two days the sound of the Cherubim Hymn came up from that dreadful opening, still surrounded by guards. Silence came only with the third day.

He had heard the Grand Duchess, kneeling at the brink of her grave, say, quite clearly, 'Dear God, forgive them. They don't know what they are doing.'

Dear God, I cannot forgive.

Dear God, I thank You I was there when we found her. The three fingers of her right hand were folded as if in the moment of dying she had made the sign of the Cross. Except that she did not look dead. She had died a lingering death of exposure, starvation and injury, and she merely seemed to sleep.

I kissed her hand for the last time and came back to Ekaterinburg.

25

My kingdom for a grave

'And my large kingdom for a little grave,
A little, little grave, an obscure grave.'
Shakespeare, *King Richard II*, III.3

THE CONCEPTION of the two plans had been the same—the victims were to be reported as having 'escaped' or being 'transferred to a place of safety'. The execution—no, one must avoid the word—the carrying out of the plans was different largely, I suppose, because the Cheka organisation in a place like Alapaievsk would be nothing like so large or professional as in Ekaterinburg.

And the use of mineshafts—

Mineshafts had been used in Ekaterinburg, too, the peasants were convinced.

And then the autumn and the snow set in. Nothing more in the way of investigation could be done. But in mid-November Admiral Kolchak became ruler of a free Siberia with his headquarters at Omsk. I might write much about the thin-faced, reserved man whose valorous, honourable life ended with Red bullets and a hole in the dirty ice because he was betrayed by the Czechs and the French general Janin, but I am sick of treachery, cowardice, greed, panic, selfishness, and the humiliations heaped upon the helpless. All I need say here is that he appointed an Official Investigator into the fate of the Imperial Family, and sent me to him.

Omsk railway goods yard—third class carriage No. 1880 was extremely difficult to find among all the congestion. Eventually I located it, and entered.

'M. Sokolov? The Admiral saw me yesterday—'

A man of middling height, aged about forty, tired-faced, soft-voiced, nervous-looking. I must have shown my astonishment, for he smiled. 'I assure you I *am* Sokolov.'

'I am sorry,' I said. 'The Supreme Ruler told me a little of your journey here—'

At the outbreak of the Revolution Nicholas Sokolov had been an examining magistrate at Penza, in Central Russia. He was a convinced monarchist. After the Bolshevik seizure of power he had taken refuge in a neighbouring village, where he had many friends among the peasants. He had crossed the Urals on foot in winter and made his way through the fighting to join the Admiral, who had described the journey with admiration.

'What can *I* do to help?' I asked him.

Sokolov said, 'You can help in two ways. Military rank—a civilian has little standing in Siberia these days—and knowledge of the Imperial Family.'

'My chief role, then, would be the identification of bodies?'

He reached out and gripped my arm. 'We *must* establish the truth, however hideous it is.'

'Do you think we can? We can't do much until the snow melts—by that time it'll be eight, nine months too late.'

I didn't realise that before the end of February we should have captured Medvediev.

Yurovsky had been in charge of the House of Special Purpose in the last weeks, after the fate of the Family had been decided in Moscow. Medvediev had been there longer; he had been in command of the outer guard of Red workmen, and had been the only one of these Yurovsky allowed into the house. He had got away from Ekaterinburg before its capture; now our troops had taken Perm, and found him there.

There was a good inspector on the spot, who would carry out the preliminary questioning. Sokolov had more than enough to do; he asked me to go to Perm and bring back Medvediev's deposition, if possible Medvediev himself.

I journeyed to Perm.

They were dead, of course. I'd known that, I think, from the moment I came out of prison at Tobolsk and talked glibly to the Czechs of the *need to capture the important railway centre of Ekaterinburg if the Volga front is to be established.* Even then I had not really hoped.

I had known my last sight of them was that laborious trudging through the rain and mud of the railway siding.

I had seen the blood, and the bullet and bayonet marks. I knew exactly when it had happened. Two men had at last dared tell their story to Sokolov. One was a night watchman. In the middle of the night of July 16 there had been a lorry outside the house. Its engine had been kept running, but it didn't drown the noise of gunfire. Soon afterwards the lorry drove away. 'I guessed what had happened, but I was afraid to tell anyone. The Cheka—Yurovsky—would have shot us—'

And one of the Red Guards, the outer guard, never allowed into the house, had drunk too much, and had gone out into the garden of the house opposite to be sick. Suddenly he too heard the gunfire—and afterwards the sound of a woman screaming, screaming. Scared into sobriety he crept back to his bed. The other man in the room was awake.

'Did you hear?'

'Yes, I heard.'

'Did you—guess?'

'Yes, I guessed.'

They spoke in quick, stealthy whispers. Their voices shook so much with terror the words were scarcely distinguishable.

I had guessed, and soon I would know, not only where, not only when, but how.

It was February, and the snow was deep, and it had been in the snow of another February fourteen years before that my personal world had first been torn apart by violence.

The old Scottish ballad loved by my father's mother—

> *'None but my foe to be my guide—*
> *None but my foe to be my guide—'*

I went to Perm by night; the moon and the stars shone brilliantly above, once to the north the bluish-green aurora of the northern lights flashed out.

'The *spaciousness* of Siberia,' I had said to Olga once.

My large kingdom for a little grave—a little, little grave—

Two years before he had ruled over the greatest empire in the world. By July, 1918, his only concern was a stifling provincial house—and sounds in the night that might lead to rescue.

I had a sudden image in my mind of them all together at night, waiting for the face of a friend to look at them against the light of a single lamp in a dark room. And the friend never came.

'I would I were where Helen lies
Night and day to me she cries—'

But we didn't know the burial place, we might never know the burial place. It was like the description in *The Rose and the Ring* that I'd seen in the House of Special Purpose:

'—and she went into the court, and into the garden, and thence into the wilderness, and thence into the forest where the wild beasts live, and was never heard of any more—'

I saw the police inspector first. He said, 'Do you want to see his statement, sir?'

'Is it worth reading?'

'He gives the classic stupid defence of most criminals when they're brought to book—he saw the crime committed, but didn't take part in it.'

So here was the last horror, the clear explanation of what had happened.

I took the statement.

'On the evening of July 16th, between 7 and 8 p.m., when the time for my duty had begun, Commandant Yurovsky ordered me to take all the Nagan revolvers from the guards, and to bring them to him. I took twelve revolvers from the sentries as well as from some other of the guards, and brought them to the Commandant's room. Yurovsky said to me: "We must shoot them all tonight, so notify the guards not to be alarmed if they hear shots . . ." '

Some days later, Sokolov finished reading the new statement.

'You've brought him here?'

'No.'

'You mean they've shot him in Perm? Well, he was obviously guilty —for all he says Yurovsky ordered him out to the street—"See if it's clear—wait to make sure if the shots have been heard—" He says himself that Yurovsky gave him one of the revolvers. But they shouldn't have shot him, there was so much more to be learned.'

'They didn't shoot him, but he's dead.'

'How?'

'Typhus.'

After a moment I said, 'I have never seen anyone so afraid to die. It was because of Alexei, I think.'

He had fallen sick on reaching Ekaterinburg. After making his first statement at Perm, he had refused to say anything else. When the doctor had said, 'It's typhus—exanthematic,' I had gone in to him and said, 'Medvediev, you're dying—did you know that?'

He grinned. 'You're lying. You're saying that to scare a confession out of me. I've got a headache and there are these lice-bites, but—'

'You'll be dead within a week. It's typhus. The doctor will confirm it.'

Beside me the doctor nodded.

His mouth and jaw went slack. Sweat poured from him. He began to scream in a high voice, inarticulately, like an animal.

I looked at the doctor. 'Symptoms of typhus?' I asked.

'No,' he said. 'I've seen coma, low muttering, never this. These are the symptoms of fear. Anyhow, you must leave him.'

'No, he has to answer more questions.'

'I say leave him.'

'No. It may appear sadistic to you, but—'

'I don't give a damn for that. I've heard too much about his activities to have any sympathy to waste on him, but it's your own risk, you fool, he has *typhus*, don't you understand?'

'I'll take the risk.'

So I was with Medvediev for most of the week before he died. I think he was—if anything—glad of my company. He always screamed most loudly when he was alone. I myself was soon able to ignore the sounds he made. There are times when all noises, from the loudest to the faintest, seem diminished, even frozen, and I cannot recall which part of his account was shrieked at me, and which part came in a vile whisper.

In the House of Special Purpose, smothered under the heat, the Family could hear the artillery fire which meant the White forces were coming in from the east. But if the sound gave them hope, their captors could hear it, too.

There were meetings, in the Hotel America, and telegrams to Moscow, to Lenin and to Jacob Sverdlov. And then:

'On the evening of July 16th—'*

It had been exceptionally hot, and it was difficult to tell what was the sound of distant gunfire and what the sound of approaching thunder.

* I have strung together his answers to my questions to have narrative form. I have tried to avoid personal comments, but not always successfully.

The Family ate their supper—the cold remains of what they had been able to save from dinner. Alexei lay in bed, playing with a model ship. The rest of the family read or sewed. The atmosphere in the House grew more stifling and stinking every day. When they went to bed, after the customary evening prayers, at 10.30, it was unlikely that they would sleep.

I cannot escape the thought of that last night. I think of that member of the family most changed by the Revolution, finding sleep impossible, sitting there amid the regular breathing of her sisters, writing the prayer—

> *'Give peace of heart to us, O Master,*
> *This hour of utmost dread to bear.'*

And I think, in this nightmare sequence, that as she heard the heavy footfalls outside she finished writing the final verse.

> *'And on the threshold of the grave*
> *Breathe power divine into our clay*
> *That we, Thy children, may find strength*
> *In meekness for our foes to pray.'*

The door flung open.

Yurovsky, ordering everyone to get up, there were disturbances in the town, the prisoners must leave at once. They must dress and assemble below to wait for the motor-cars that were to take them away.

Did she guess?

If she did, she would still have been the calmest of them all. She had been prepared for this before she left Tobolsk.

'None of the Family asked any questions. They did not weep or cry.'

In silence they came down, past the walls scrawled with obscenities, the last little procession of Imperial Russia—automatically they would cling to protocol still. The Czar, carrying his sick son in his arms, both in soldier's dress, Alexei, worn out with pain, clinging tightly to his father. The Czarina in a violet costume, her daughters in grey, bare-headed. Dr Botkin, the maid, Demidova. The cook and footman.

Anastasia carried fat little Jimmy. He couldn't get downstairs, in any case, but even if he had been able to manage it I think she, at sixteen, would have carried him for the reassurance of the warm, lively little body, the comfort of his affection in this new bleak world of hatred and cruelty.

To reach the basement room they would have to cross the courtyard. Just outside stood the lorry, with its engine running. It is never dark in Siberia in the summer; they would have seen the outline, and I think they would have found it reassuring. This was to take their luggage, they would imagine. I do not believe they would have suspected at that point that it was to carry their corpses.

They went into the basement. Beyond them the locked door. The Czar asked if they might sit, and Yurovsky had three chairs brought in. The Czar sat on one, Alexei, half lying against him, was in the second, the Czarina took the third. The three elder girls stood behind their mother; they had brought down pillows, which they arranged behind the Czarina and Alexei. After this they stood upright, their eyes staring patiently ahead, waiting. Anastasia, holding Jimmy, and Demidova stood to the left of the locked door. Demidova carried a pillow which she kept clasped to her.

Armed men came into the room until, including Yurovsky, there were eleven of them.

'It seemed as if all of them (the Family) guessed their fate, but not one of them uttered a single sound.'

There is a certain unique terror, the knowledge of imminent violent death. Did they really know?

Yurovsky said, 'Your friends have tried to save you. They have failed, and we are going to shoot you.'

The Czar cried, 'What?' He tried to get up, but his arm and shoulder were supporting Alexei. Yurovsky shot him in the head. This was the signal for massacre. The Czarina had only time to raise her hand in the sign of the Cross before the bullets hit her. Olga, Tatiana and Marie fell on their knees, crossed themselves as the shots were pumped into them. Anastasia, Botkin, the two men-servants fell to the ground. But Demidova remained on her feet. Sewn in the pillow she clasped to her were what remained of the Imperial jewels, and these had shielded her.

'Don't bother to reload,' said Yurovsky, grinning. 'Get the bayonets.'

So in the gunsmoke they hunted Demidova as she stumbled along the far wall, slipping in the streams of blood, screaming continuously, despairingly like a hare being torn apart by hounds. When they got her down she went on screaming, rolling over and over as if she would never stop, but at last with thirty bayonet wounds even Demidova had to die.

For a moment there was stillness, while they breathed hard. The smoke made some of them cough. Then they heard an odd little sound, a mewing like an animal.

'The dog,' somebody said. 'One of the girls had a dog in her arms.'

'I smashed his head in with my rifle,' said another. 'Two minutes ago.'

They saw a faint movement. Alexei, still lying in his dead father's arms, made that little wailing noise again, put out his thin hand to touch his father's jacket, opened his eyes. One of the men kicked his head; I think this man was Medvediev, from what he muttered in delirium about the look in the eyes of the dying boy in the dead father's arms. And then Yurovsky bent over and fired two more shots—between the eyes.

There was one last hitch before they could proceed with their plan. Anastasia had only fainted; she regained consciousness now and screamed. They turned on her and that is how there were eighteen bayonet marks on the floor.

This was the story I took back to Sokolov. He sat with his face in his hands, weeping. I said, grinning like an ape, 'So Alexei *did* survive his father after all—Czar of All the Russias for five minutes—the reign of Alexei—before one of his subjects kicked his head in—the strong autocracy that was to be handed over intact—'

Sokolov's hand might be wet with tears, but it still hurt as it cracked against my cheek. 'Shut up,' he said.

A further task had been assigned to Medvediev; he had been told to organise a squad to wash away the blood.

In his delirium he had muttered endlessly about those streams of blood. He said they worked ankle-deep in blood, it seemed to well up from the floor as if coming from a spring. I said to Sokolov, harshly, 'Of course, Alexei's body wouldn't stop bleeding, would it? The blood would never clot— Do you think he's—bleeding still somewhere?' I had a sudden monstrous vision of blood seeping up from under the soil.

Sokolov said sharply, 'Medvediev wouldn't give any information about the disposal of the bodies?'

I shook my head. 'He would only describe how they were carried out of the house rolled up in pieces of khaki cloth on stretchers made of sledge-shafts and bed sheets. They were put in the waiting lorry and covered with old mats—it was all done hastily, they wanted to get out of town as soon as possible. But all he would say after that was "*I don't know where the bodies were taken; I don't even know the direction the lorry went.*" I think he was speaking the truth there. Yurovsky wanted it kept as secret as possible. When he was delirious Medvediev repeated twice

"If you know too much, you'll soon grow old, Pavel Spiridonovitch"; I think Yurovsky had said this to him, he was scared of Yurovsky. And he didn't go into the forest at all because we know he was ordered to go on keeping guard round the house as if nothing had happened—as if there were still people to guard.'

Sokolov said, 'When the snow melts, then we'll find the truth. In the meantime, I want you to try to break the code of these telegrams.'

At least it took my mind off what the dead damned wretch had said. Sometimes. Not often.

We broke the code of the telegrams sent in those July days. The most important, sent to Moscow, was a series of numbers—'39/34/35/42/29/35/36/49/26'—and so on.

Finally we worked it out:

39	34	35	42	29	35	36	49	26
P	E	R	E	D	A	I	T	E

Et cetera.

In English the whole of the telegram ran as follows: 'Tell Sverdlov that the whole family suffered the fate of its head. Officially, it will perish during the evacuation.'

And then one could only wait for the snow to melt.

As soon as the snow was a mere light, melting carpet, we began our task. 'It is quite simple,' said Sokolov. 'All we have to do is to *walk* all the way from the Ipatiev House, along the route the lorry must have taken. Eight months and the winter's snow can't have obliterated every mark.'

So, one bright morning, we walked out of Ekaterinburg, following the road the lorry had used, westwards first, passing the Verkh-Issetsk factories with their cracked brick walls, and then veering northwards. There were two level crossings to be passed, the Perm line, then the Ural railway, and at last we were in the forest.

Ten miles to walk. A sandy road leading through beautiful pine trees. There were new ferns, and green shoots, the air was exquisite with the scents of young growing things, teeming with new life, birds were singing, building their nests. The sun came down through the pines in shafts of pale gold.

Quite suddenly—and unbearably—I was reminded of another long walk years before—at least it had seemed a long walk to me at the time; Alix's funeral, and Olga beside me, white roses everywhere, and Olga at twelve half-envious of Alix, because it was such a beautiful funeral—

'Look,' said Sokolov. 'The tracks of a heavy lorry.'

We followed the tracks of the heavy lorry.

I remembered Olga crying over the fate of Mary Queen of Scots, 'The poor body, despoiled by her executioners!'

A feather, still warm from the mother bird's breast, fluttered down before me. I picked it up and stroked it.

A sandy track. Samsonov's men moving along sandy tracks to destruction. Colonel Revashov praying to Christ, Who had known the way to Calvary.

But they had been dead when they came this way. My God, they were dead! Doubly dead, Alexei and Demidova and Anastasia.

Idiotic memories of Alexei's christening. The splendour with which the little creature had been carried to the Cathedral.

A lorry crashing along a forest path for the last journey.

His godfathers the King of England, the Kaiser, the Russian Army—

Had he gone on dripping blood along the track? That at least the snow would have erased.

The sun was high now.

'Look!' said Sokolov. 'There to the left!'

Several paths, grass-grown, turned off to the left.

'Look at the tracks. They forced the lorry through the undergrowth—'

'My God!' I said, staring. 'They nearly went into a ditch there—see the wheel marks!'

'Yes, and see here—a beam they used to jack up the lorry!'

I said, my skin crawling, 'We're close to a mineshaft now. The Koptiaki peasants call the clearing the Four Brothers.'

Pinetrees gave way to exquisite birches. It was very fragrant there, I remember that very clearly. I remember too that peasants from Koptiaki came to join us later, and said, 'The Reds, were working here for three days and nights. Then they went away because they'd finished what they had to do.'

I counted carefully. 17, 18, 19, 20. They had finished on July 20. On July 20 I had been arguing with the Czechs about an attack on an all-important railway junction. Perhaps the poison had worked after all, and I'd been in Hell ever since.

There were three great patches of black ash. 'They must have been the funeral pyres,' said Sokolov steadily. 'Remember what the peasants

229

said to you from the start—there were fires in the forest, and you don't burn rifles. The Reds were getting rid of the bodies.'

The ash had to be sifted through. I turned away for a moment. There was a sapling fir-tree quite close to the biggest of the black patches. It had deep cuts in it.

'Look!' I said to Sokolov. 'What does that mean?'

'Axe marks,' he said, still very steadily. 'Testing out the keenness of the axe. Oh, my dear fellow, don't you see, they *had* to dismember the bodies first.'

Like a rather stupid child trying to learn a difficult lesson, I said, 'They dismembered the bodies—then burned them.'

I walked away, about a hundred paces, to a point in that fragrant little clearing where a treestump offered a comfortable seat. But I did not sit there long.

'Nicholas Alexeievitch! Come here, please!'

'What is it?'

I pointed. 'On July 15 Yurovsky told the nuns to bring fifty eggs next day—do you remember? Some people have argued that this was because the Family was going on a long journey. The journey ended here.'

We found not merely eggshells; there were cracked chicken-bones too. The appetite of whoever sat there had not been affected by what he was watching.

Still sitting on that comfortable tree-stump, I went on mechanically groping in the grass. My blind fingers touched pages torn from a book —still readable. A German book.

I believe I made an honest attempt to think out things for myself, but my heart, I suppose, fought against my mind. Eventually—and mutely —I held out the damp crumpled sheets to Sokolov.

'Whoever sat here—Yurovsky himself, no doubt, he'd lived in Berlin—ate his chicken and eggs as he watched, and read . . .' he began.

I found my tongue. 'In Christ's name what would a man read while watching—that?'

He looked up, his pallor very marked. 'A manual of anatomy,' he said.

In the long grass closer to the remains of the fires we found broken diamonds.

'But why broken diamonds? They wouldn't try to crack precious stones with axes, would they?'

'No, don't you see, the stones were cracked unwittingly. *Think.*'

'The Grand Duchesses,' I said, my voice lagging, 'hid most of their jewellery in their clothing before leaving Tobolsk.'

After a moment's pause Sokolov said abruptly that he had worked out that the first pyre was for the Imperial Family, the second for their attendants, the third for clothes.

'How can you tell?'

'There are splashes of acid around the first two pyres. Clothes aren't as indestructible as human bones. I want you to come to the third pyre —we've found the remains of shoes there.'

A fragment with a few letters still discernible. 'Yes, that's *Weiss*— Weiss made shoes for the Family. And this buckle—I've seen it. Olga had shoes with buckles like it.'

In the long grass, three small ikons. I knew them—the girls had worn them. In each case the face was smashed as if blows had been deliberately aimed at it.

A pearl ear-ring I had seen the Czarina wearing.

A metal pocket case. 'Yes, I know that. The Czar always carried it with him; it held his wife's portrait.'

It may seem strange that so much was left to us to find in the grass, but two facts should be borne in mind. First, the grass had been long in July, long enough for the peasants to have commenced hay-making. Secondly, butchering is a tiring and difficult job, even if one is given advice by a man translating from a page of an anatomy manual held in one hand while in the other he holds a chicken leg, and punctuates his instructions with hungry bites. They were hot, those July days and nights, and butchering is physically very demanding.

All the discoveries were not made on the first day, of course. The investigation stretched on into the summer. The charred remains of bones, partly destroyed by acid, but still bearing saw and axe marks, came to light soon enough, in the black ashes. So did the pieces of lead —bullets from inside the victims' bodies that had remained as molten lumps when the retaining flesh was burned away. But it was much later, on a day when tall foxgloves were making great splashes of colour in the clearing, that we found, near the clothes pyre, three objects seemingly so insignificant that even the butchers would not have thought them worth destroying. A small, rusty lock, a bent hairpin, and some blobs of red wax. But they were significant enough to M. Gilliard, who had come to join the investigation. They had all belonged to Alexei.

'Little boys,' he began to say, 'always carry—curious oddments about in their pockets, don't they?' and then his voice had broken off. After a moment he tried again.

'He just—took a fancy to the lock. You know how he rather went in for collecting things—he always used to say—gravely—"You never know when it will come in useful." The bent hair-pin—he used that as a fishing-hook. He begged it from his mother when they were at Tobolsk, and got hold of a piece of stick and some string and sat fishing over a rainwater butt. The wax—the monks at Tobolsk sent in some red candles. He asked for one so that he could model toy soldiers.'

He put his hand up to his eyes. 'You may very well find little pieces of wire, too. In the evenings, when he was well enough, he used to make little chains for his toy ships.'

Alexei had been right. 'You never know when it will come in useful.' As when it told us that the ghouls had examined the murdered child's pockets before throwing his clothes on the fire.

But the ashes that remained were not enough. Somewhere the remains had been disposed of. Engineers and miners drained the pit, and nothing was found.

'But they must be there!' said Sokolov. 'Where else would they be?'

We talked to the villagers again.

The area had been cordoned off—they hadn't been able to get on with their haymaking—the fires had burned for days—and there had been the explosions—

'Explosions? What kind of explosions?'

They tried to explain, and suddenly I remembered another peasant who had heard explosions. 'When the Grand Duchess Elizabeth and her companions were thrown into the mineshaft, hand-grenades were thrown in on them,' I said, and questioned the peasant more closely. From his description the explosions sounded very much like hand-grenades. 'But why?' said Sokolov. 'The Grand Duchess and her companions were thrown in *alive*. *Here*—oh, my dear fellow, fires for three days, burning all the more fiercely because of the benzine poured on them, and then sulphuric acid for what resisted the flames!* What was there left to destroy?'

'I don't know.'

It was a glorious day. In the forest the clearings were carpeted with

* We had established that the murderers had ordered 175 kilogrammes of sulphuric acid and more than 300 litres of benzine.

wild strawberries and mushrooms and the grass and flowers were almost man high. So few people ever thought of high summer in Siberia; Siberia always symbolised snow and—

'Ice!' I said. 'They used the grenades to break up the ice. In the deep workings the ice is there even in the summer.'

'But why break *ice*?'

'To let the cinders and ashes sink through to the bottom of the water. And then—or is this too wild an idea?—over it anchor a false flooring?'

Sokolov's eyes blazed. 'Wild or not, it's the only possible explanation! How did you hit on it?'

'I don't know. I can only think that for the last few weeks I've been trying to reason as—as Yurovsky did.'

None but my foe to be my guide.

The engineers and miners resumed their task. The water was pumped out. The fake wooden floor was removed on June 25, and we found directly under it, battered but quite recognisable, for the ice had preserved it, the black and tan corpse, quite entire, of little Jimmy.

Below the little dog, a heap of cinders, all that remained of the Family. With the addition of the thirteen drops of blood, now preserved in arsenic capsules, which were shaken from the hand of one of the men who shot and bayoneted them down.

And so I end the story of how the members of the Imperial Family came to the House of Special Purpose—and how they left it for the Four Brothers near Koptiaki.

I had a dream that night. It has since returned. I am back in the forest near Koptiaki, and it is summer, with the smell of mushrooms and strawberries and new-mown hay and the ferns and moss I crush under-foot as I make my way to the meeting-place. Olga stands there among the purple foxgloves and the birch-barks silver in the sunshine, and she is smiling, and no longer looks as she did at Tobolsk. And she says, very gently, 'You mustn't reproach yourself because we didn't escape, Andrei. You're wrong—we did escape. *We are the survivors now.*'

But when I wake I cannot believe it.

Epilogue

THE TIDE of war turned against us. The long retreat which for me had begun at Tannenberg continued.

Frequently a personal experience of disaster and tragedy outruns what poor means of expression one possesses. We cannot all be Dantes; most of us are hopelessly ill-equipped for describing Hell.

So I cannot give an adequate account of the retreat through Siberia by Kolchak's White army and the millions fleeing the Revolution. Forced marches were things of horror, endless stumbling forward on frost-bitten feet. Against the Siberian winter we padded our ragged tunics with straw and moss. There was always the knowledge that Red bullets might be avoided, but typhus and starvation were less escapable. Or madness. I have often wondered why more of us did not lose our reason.

We retreated across the Trans-Siberian Railway, once the pride of Russia, now a trickle of filthy trucks running on rusting lines bordered with corpses flung from the trains to lie alongside the tracks to rot and infect the district.

There was little noise or excitement on that retreat. Russia was becoming a very quiet place. Starvation has that effect.

Sometimes people who had escaped whispered in despair that they would have been better off if they'd stayed in Russia, but they didn't really mean it. Better destitution in a foreign town than remaining in Russia, that greatest charnel-house in history, Russia that was ruled by a bloody froth of cruelty that had risen to the surface. It happens in every revolution, of course; the creatures from the lower depths, the sick, mad Marats, will always crawl up out of the sewers and preside over such anarchy and inhumanity that the Mongol hordes themselves might pity our Russia today.

At last I reached England. I had managed to lose all my lice, and had become reasonably clean. I didn't embarrass those people who knew I was the heir to a grandfather with a *château* in Brittany and a 'divine' house in the Parc au Prince. (And they, well-fed, spiritually unburned, didn't embarrass me—they were merely unreal.) A fashionable hostess rang me up, and asked me to luncheon next day. Rather, she commanded me, for English royalty would be there, a grand-daughter of Victoria— and, therefore, a first cousin to the Czarina.

'She is very worried about the Imperial Family,' quacked the voice from the receiver, 'although, as she herself puts it, your Empress was *very naughty*, encouraging that dreadful man, Rasputin, and meddling with appointments. You mustn't be afraid to speak frankly to her, she says, she quite accepts the Emperor and Empress brought all this upon themselves, working for a separate peace as they did, but—Did you say something?'

'No.'

'—but, of course, she hopes they've come to no harm— Are you there?'

'Yes. Before the Czar was taken from Tobolsk he said he would cut off his right hand rather than sign the Brest-Litovsk treaty.'

She purred with pleasure. 'How marvellous, then it *is* true, you *were* in touch with them in Siberia. You're *just* the person we want to set us all right on—'

'On the fate of the Imperial Family? That's soon done. Their ashes are at Harbin.'

'Harbin,' she said uncertainly. 'What a horrid-sounding place, I've never heard of it! Where is it?'

'The location doesn't matter; everywhere the situation will remain basically the same. A lawyer, Sokolov, completed the official enquiry into the fate of the Family, and was trying to bring the ashes to Europe. He doubted whether he himself would ever complete the journey, and appealed to the British High Commissioner, who was leaving for Pekin, to take the ashes with him. Your countryman said he must await instructions from his government, and that government forbade him to help.'

'I can quite see,' she said, after a moment, 'why you feel upset, but—'

'I have been more upset, and at least your government is consistent. It refused the Imperial Family a refuge in life; one couldn't really expect it to grant a belated sanctuary after death.'

She did not renew the invitation.

The news of the murders had been greeted with general indifference in the Allied countries. Newspapers printed the shortest of obituaries, all the while giving the impression that this was a virtue, and that only their delicacy of feeling prevented a most overwhelming condemnation of the Czar's life and actions.

But surely there might have been some feeling for the fate of the innocent?

One day, perhaps, the West will look at Lenin's Russia and remember uneasily the parable of how the casting out of one devil may only make room for seven devils each worse than the first.

And the general indifference to the fate of the Imperial Family extended to the fate of all Russia—rather, Britain and France acted as if their Russian ally had never existed.

I have been told of the Victory Parades held in hysterical Paris and London. There were the flags of the Allies, swinging past to rapturous cheers—Belgium, Britain, France—the later Allies, Roumania and Italy—the most recent Ally of all, the United States. But no flag of the first Ally in the struggle, the Ally who sustained the heaviest losses, *who had deliberately risked those losses in order to save the capital of a comrade.* It was as if that Ally had never been.

Mother, hearing the account, had wept. She heard a whisper—*'Les morts de Verdun.'* *'Non,'* she contradicted fiercely. *'Les morts de Tannenberg.'*

I have already described a dream that sometimes comes to me. More often, there are nightmares. I am back in the sweltering heat of a Siberian summer, trying to escape from a confinement in which dust is everywhere, creeping through every crack and cranny. I know that outside there are shady woods where purple foxgloves make patches of colour, but I can't get out, can't escape the flies that settle on clothes, food, hands, face, can't escape eyes that stare with bestial hatred, can't escape the voices shouting an increasing torrent of filth, I am in a torture chamber that is both physical and moral, there is no escape, my soul is drowning in foulness.

Or there is the dream of Petersburg; at first I walk through my beloved city of the wide, shining waterways and spaciousness and pure clean colour, and at first the sky is pale and clear, but within minutes, so it seems, all is dark, and I grope blindly through narrow winding alleys, and the stench of Revolution is always about me, sweat and dirt and fear, and the smell of starvation. Starvation has a smell, you know. And then I am stumbling downwards in darkness to a basement room, and there is a new smell, the smell of blood, growing stronger, stronger.

I tell myself, retching, that I should be used to the smell of blood, being a soldier, but blood always seems to smell worse in a great city—or in a town in the Urals—especially when it's women's blood.

The day after I reached Paris, Mother brought a doctor to see me. He had just come from Vienna to try to get foreign help (for there was starvation in Austria, too) and had approached Mother because he knew her by name; in another age and world he had written to us about Franz von Mayrhofen, wounded at Sarajevo. And he said to me now as he had said to Franz then, 'Write down your thoughts, they must have utterance.'

Franz himself is staying with us now, and I have shown him what I have written. After he had read it, he said very gently, 'Don't you think you've written too much about the Imperial Family? At the end, I mean—you had to give plenty of space to them at the beginning, before the Revolution, when they *were* Russia, but, except for people like you, my dear fellow, they didn't matter so much afterwards, did they, when they were reduced to their essential unimportance, ordinariness?'

But it is precisely because they had no more importance, because they were now so ordinary a group of human beings that what happened to them was important. Firstly because of the shockingness of their fate. Just as the smell of blood was strong and rank in the nostrils of the butchers in that basement room (for they were not madmen, or marionettes, but dreadful flesh and blood), so the smell of blood was to be strong in the nostrils of the Russian people for years to come.

And what happened in that basement room in Ekaterinburg is significant for another reason; in a way it symbolises the fate of all Russia.

In that group of eleven victims there were only two who might be adjudged to have sown the wind and who therefore must now reap the whirlwind. And yet with them died gentleness, youth, innocence, devotion, and that simplicity whose chief offence is loyalty.

And there is Alexei. Alexei, who, by the most terrible of ironies, did indeed survive his parents—a little.

To have killed a defenceless sick child, whose lifetime of sufferings should have protected him—surely this is a crime amounting to blasphemy?

Not that blasphemy is a sin in Red eyes, but even in Moscow they must have felt that full details of the massacre were too atrocious to be published. Remember that the only announcement ever made was that sentence of death had been carried out on the Czar, but the Czarina and children had been removed to a place of safety. The conspiracy of silence continues. Recently the Imperial correspondence has been published in Moscow; in the index of personal names you read:

Alexandra Feodorovna, wife of Nicholas Romanov, born 1872.
Olga Nicholaevna, eldest daughter of Nicholas Romanov, born 1895.
Alexei Nicholaevitch, only son of Nicholas Romanov, born 1904.

In no case is the date of death given. The Reds, with grisly humour, seek to reanimate dismembered corpses.

Outside Russia, because of Sokolov's findings, the truth is known, but inside Russia it is different, rumour follows rumour; the Czar is in Rome, where the Pope hides him in the Vatican, the Czarina in a sanatorium insane, Alexei is dead, one daughter is married to an Englishman, two to Italians, the fourth remains with her father.

And in Western Europe there are rumours concerning one daughter, Anastasia, Anastasia to whom once could be applied the description Marie Antoinette gave to the Dauphin—'He was born gay.' Yes, goes the story, it is true that she was bayoneted when, recovering consciousness, she screamed, but she was still not dead when the corpses were removed, and she was saved by a Red soldier. At seventeen, she had a child by him. Later, in Berlin, she attempted suicide.

I pray to a merciful God that Anastasia died with the rest, ghastly though this death might be, with brother and sisters, father—and mother, that unhappy woman who wished only for righteousness and the greatness and prosperity of Russia, and who was fated to bring destruction on all she cared for, the monarchy, the church, her husband and children.

I do not pretend that there is any tremendous value in what I have written. Soon the academic historians, the professional dissectors and embalmers of history will begin to describe what happened in Russia. They will lay unerring fingers on those causes to which we, living in Russia at the time, were so wilfully blind, they will burrow endlessly through acres of documentation, and their dicta will be generally accepted, *This is why it happened*—

And we—the Russians—will all be abstract things, for all that they will diligently read our letters and diaries, may even scrutinise our photographs and portraits, but to me, no intellectual, there recurs the obstinate thought that there will always remain room for personal knowledge, physical, if you like—the remembrance of a perplexed tone of voice, the glance of imploring eyes, the brush of unseen lips on a hand wet with tears.

Completed in Brittany, on the night of July 16/17. The year doesn't matter.

Author's Note

This book, together with its predecessor, *Three Lives for the Czar*, owes its origin to a description by Baroness Buxhoeveden, in attendance on the Czarina, of a scene in the falling snow at Czarskoe—'A small, bedraggled group of horsemen, parleying in front of the great closed gates,' a reserve squadron of the Chevaliers Gardes, who had ridden from Novgorod through two days of bitter cold and deep snow. 'At the gates of the Palace, they were told that they had come too late. There was no longer an Emperor.'

The name of the young officer commanding the squadron was not given; in ascribing to Andrei Hamilton an act of similar useless loyalty I have intended to imply only admiration.